IVAN FRANKO

DOWN AND OUT IN DROHOBYCH

UKRAINIAN
//IIIBOOK
INSTITUTE

This book has been published with the support
of the Translate Ukraine Translation Program

DOWN AND OUT IN DROHOBYCH

by Ivan Franko

Translated from the Ukrainian by Yuri Tkacz

**This book has been published with the support
of the Translate Ukraine Translation Program**

Proofreading by Stephen Dalziel

Cover image © Max Mendor 2024

Book cover and interior book design by Max Mendor

www.glagoslav.com

ISBN: 978-1-80484-180-8
ISBN: 978-1-80484-181-5

Published in English by Glagoslav Publications in November 2024

A catalogue record for this book is available from the British Library.

IVAN FRANKO

DOWN AND OUT IN DROHOBYCH

TRANSLATED FROM THE UKRAINIAN BY YURI TKACZ

GLAGOSLAV PUBLICATIONS

IVAN FRANKO

(1856 – 1916)

CONTENTS

LITTLE MYRON

I

Little Myron was a peculiar child. His father took great delight in him, often proclaiming him to be exceptionally intelligent. But then a father can be partial, especially one such as Myron's. He was an older man who had eagerly awaited the birth of his child, and any child would have been considered precious to him, regardless of their actual abilities. The neighbours quietly whispered among themselves that Myron was 'not quite like other children'. He would walk around gesturing wildly, muttering to himself, picking up a stick and swishing it through the air, deadheading weeds. With other children, he was shy and unassertive. And when he did speak up, his words were so peculiar that older folks merely shrugged their shoulders in response.

"Vasyl," little Myron said to little Vasyl, "what's the biggest number you can count to?"

"Me? And what number am I supposed to count to? Five, seven, parkateen."

"Parkateen! Ha-ha-ha! And how much is parkateen?"

"How much is it meant to be? I have no idea!"

"Well, it means nothing at all. Sit down with me and we'll count together!"

Vasyl sat down, and Myron began to count, tapping a stick on the ground as he uttered each number: "One, two, three, four..."

Vasyl listened for a while, then got up and ran off. Myron didn't even notice: he sat there, tapping away and counting on and on. Along came old man Riabyna, coughing, clearing his throat, and sighing. But Myron was oblivious to him, he was in his own world. The old man stopped nearby and listened… Myron had already reached four hundred.

"Ah, you little imp, you!" the old man uttered in his usual slightly nasal voice. "What are you up to here?"

Startled, little Myron looked up at Riabyna with frightened eyes.

"You're beating the holy earth there, eh? Don't you know that the earth is our mother? Give me that stick!"

Myron handed him the stick, not quite understanding what the old man wanted from him. Riabyna flung the stick into the nettles. Myron almost cried, not so much because of the stick, but because the old man had interrupted his counting.

"Run off home and say the Lord's Prayer before you start causing any more trouble!" said the old man sternly and he shuffled off. Myron watched him go for a long time, unable to understand why the old man was angry or what he had wanted of him.

II

Little Myron loved nothing more than running alone through the green meadows festooned with flowers, among the broad leaves of burdock and the fragrant wild chamomile. He delighted in the sweet scent of dew-covered clover and revelled in being covered from head to toe in sticky burdock burrs. And then there was the stream, which one had to cross to reach the pasture. Nestled in the hills, it was small and tranquil, with steep rugged banks, a clay bottom, and gurgling shallows paved with small stone blocks overgrown with soft weed, its long silky strands resembling green hair. The river was magical and Myron was drawn to it. He loved to sit there for hours on end, nestled in the tall green grass or among the dense leafy undergrowth of the riverbank. He would sit and gaze into the rippling water, at the flickering grass swaying in the current, at the small fish that occasionally darted out of their hollows or emerged from deeper pools, scooting along the bottom, chasing water insects, then poking their blunt, whiskered heads out of the water, grabbing a mouthful of air, before disappearing into their hiding places, as if they had just tasted some rare tidbit. Meanwhile, the sun beat down from the cloudless blue sky, warming Myron's shoulders and his entire body, but the leafy cover shielded him from its harsh rays. He enjoyed this. His small grey eyes darted about, his childish forehead became wrinkled as thoughts began to stir in his mind.

'Now look at the sun above,' he thought, 'why is it so small, when daddy claims it's very big? There's probably just a little hole cut out in the sky for it, so you can't see all of it!'

But then another thought began to stir in his head:

'But how can that be? There's a small hole where it rises, and another one where it sets. So does the hole travel along with the sun across the sky?'

This became too much for him to comprehend, and he promised himself that as soon as he got home, he would ask his dad what kind of hole had been cut out in the sky for the sun?

"Myron! Myron!" he heard someone calling from afar. It was his mother. Myron jumped up and dashed along the riverbank to the shallow crossing, but then suddenly stopped. He had crossed the river many times before, and nothing had happened, but now he noticed something different. He was standing facing the sun, staring into the water, and instead of the usual shallow water, pebbles, and soft green strands of weed, he saw an extremely deep blue stretch of water. He didn't understand that the sky was being reflected from the water, and he stopped. How could he venture into such deep water? And where had it appeared from all of a sudden? He stood and carefully examined the depths. Everything was the same. He squatted. Yes, everything was the same, except that near the bank he could see the familiar pebbles, and hear the usual murmur of the water in the shallows. He turned away from the sun: the deep water disappeared and the crossing was shallow once more. This discovery both reassured and surprised him. He began to turn in all directions, trying to understand, and marvelled at this strange phenomenon. And he completely forgot that his mother had called him!

Little Myron stood there for a long time, sometimes bending down, sometimes turning around, but still unable to bring himself to venture into the water. It seemed to him that at any moment, amid the shallow pebbly crossing, the earth would open up and a bottomless blue pit would appear in the stream, and he would fly headlong into the depths, disappearing like a twig thrown into a deep dark well. Who knows how long he would have stood there at the crossing, had the neighbour Martyn not appeared, on his way with his forks and rakes to the hayfield.

"Why are you standing here? Your mum's been calling you. Why aren't you heading home?"

"I want to, but I'm scared."

"Of what?"

"Look there!" and he pointed to the bottomless deep blue water. Martyn did not understand.

"What's there to be scared of? It's shallow water."

"Shallow?" Myron asked sceptically. "But look how deep it is!"

"Deep? It's not deep at all," retorted Martyn and, without removing his moccasins, made his way across the river, barely getting his feet wet. This emboldened Myron, and he crossed to the other side and ran home uphill through the garden.

"What a foolish boy! Five years old and still afraid of crossing the river," muttered the neighbour as he set off to deal with his mown hay.

<h1 style="text-align:center">III</h1>

When all the adults had left the house in summer to work in the fields, Myron stayed behind, but not inside the house. He was afraid of being indoors. Afraid of the 'old men in the corners', meaning the shadows, afraid of the bulging chimney, black inside from soot, afraid of the rough wooden hook embedded in the trapdoor in the ceiling, so that it could be propped open to allow smoke to escape from the burning kindling used to provide light in the house in winter. Myron remained outside. There he could play, pick plants and divide them up, build little houses with twigs and sticks from the woodpile, or just lie on his back and bask in the sun, gazing into the blue yonder and listening to the chirping of sparrows in the young apple trees. He enjoyed this, until a cloud seemed to pass across his childish forehead as another thought crossed his mind.

'What allows people to see things? The sky, the plants, mummy and daddy?' The question popped into his head out of nowhere. 'And what allows people to hear things? The screech of a hawk, the clucking of hens... What allows me to hear these sounds?'

It seemed to him that people used their mouths to see and hear. He opened his mouth and there it was: he could see and hear everything...

'Maybe not! Maybe people use their eyes?'

He closed his eyes tightly. There, he couldn't see a thing. He opened them – he could see and hear. He closed them again – he couldn't see, but he could hear this time.

Aha, so that's how it worked! You could see with your eyes, but how did you hear? Once more he opened and closed his mouth – he could hear. Then he closed and opened his eyes – he could hear everything. Suddenly he had a thought – what if he tried poking his fingers into his ears. There was a rustling sound. What was that? He could hear the rustling, but not the clucking of the hens or the screech of the hawk. He pulled his fingers out – he could hear the clucking, but not the rustling sound. He repeated this with the same result.

'What can this be?' Myron thought to himself. 'Aha, I know now! With my ears I hear the clucking, and with my fingers – the rustling sound! Of course!'

He tried it again and again – yes, that was exactly the way it was!

And when the reapers came back to have lunch, he raced up to his father, skipping with excitement.

"Daddy, Daddy! I know something!"

"What is it, my child?"

"I know that people see with their eyes."

A smile played on his father's face.

"And they hear clucking with their ears, and rustling sounds with their fingers."

"What, what?"

"Yes, just like that! If you don't poke your fingers into your ears, you can hear the hens clucking, but if you do, you only hear a rustling noise."

His father burst out laughing, while his mother glared sternly at Myron and, waving a wooden spoon at him, de-clared:

"Go, you little troublemaker! You're big enough to have been married off already, and yet you talk such nonsense? Why don't you ever think before you blurt something out…? Of course, people hear everything with their ears! Both the noise and the clucking."

"But why can't you hear both at the same time? Why can you hear the clucking only when you don't cover your ears, and when you do, you hear the rustling noise?" the boy asked.

"Here, try it!" And to convince her, he poked his fingers into his ears.

His mother mumbled something, but she was unable to find an answer to the question.

<h1 style="text-align:center">IV</h1>

Myron's biggest problem was with thinking! He just couldn't think properly, and that was that. Whatever he said was always somehow not right, not as it should be, and his mother or other people would say to him:

"Dingbat, why don't you think before you speak, instead of flailing about like a fisherman striking the water with his oars!"

But no matter how hard poor Myron struggled to gather his thoughts and come up with something smart to say, he just couldn't manage it. Eventually Myron came to the conclusion that he simply was unable to think!

Once, the whole family was sitting down to a meal around a large table in the middle of the room. His mother was serving cabbage. It was a delicious cabbage dish, with bacon and it even had cooked grain mixed in. Everyone was eating in silence. Little Myron took a couple of bites, then noticed how quiet it had become in the house, not a peep from anyone. Out of the blue, he felt that it was up to him to say something. But what? He needed to think things through first, or else everyone would laugh, and his mother might even scold him. What should he say? And little Myron began to think hard. His spoon, as he moved it from the bowl to his mouth, suddenly froze in mid-air along with his hand. His eyes stared into empty space, then became inadvertently fixed on the Mother of God icon hanging on the wall. His lips began to move, as if he was whispering something.

The servants noticed this. They glanced at one another, nudged each other with their elbows, and the maid even whispered to old Ivan:

"Watch out, he's about to blurt out some nonsense."

"Heaven only knows," Myron began slowly, "why the Holy Mother keeps looking and looking, but never eats any of this cabbage...?"

Poor Myron, despite his struggle, couldn't come up with anything better, perhaps because he was trying so hard to think 'like people'.

There was laughter, he was ridiculed, and the usual reprimand from his mother left poor Myron in tears.

"I'm sorry, I just can't think like other people!" he said, as he wiped away his tears.

V

What will become of this boy? What kind of flower will bloom from this little bud? It is not hard to foresee. One can come across quite a few such unique people in our villages. From a young age they are quite different to other people in the way they walk, their looks and the cut of their hair, together with their speech and actions. If such a child spends their life in the confines of a thatched village house, without being exposed to wider experiences, without obtaining a clearer knowledge, and if from a young age their narrow-minded relatives begin to inculcate in them a need to act 'as other people do', the child's innate inclination toward being unique will simply be suppressed. All the unused and thwarted abilities of the child will wither and die in the bud, and those like little Myron will grow into poor farmers, or worse still, their unfulfilled vivacity and energetic character will push them toward the dark side – they will become bullies, sorcerers who believe in their own phantoms, and they will confuse others with their sincere heart.

But if such a child encounters a loving and broad-minded father who wants to provide his child a window into the world and is prepared to go the extra mile, then what?

Do you think the child's fate will be better, as most people would understand this? Hardly! In school, the child will grasp at knowledge at an astonishing rate, imbibing it like a sick person would fresh air, and end up enthralled by the truths of science and a burning desire to apply them to life. Little Myron will then become a fervent preacher of such truths, bringing them like a candle among the dark and the oppressed, into village homes… In any case, an enviable fate would not await him! He would curse both prison walls and dungeons, denouncing the violence men perpetrate against men, and would end up either perishing somewhere in poverty, solitude, and degradation in some attic, or behind bars. He would carry the seeds of some deadly disease that would prematurely drive him into the grave or, having lost faith in lofty truths, he would start to drown his despair in liquor. Poor little Myron…!

1879

THE PENCIL

Please don't think for a moment that I am spinning a yarn or that the title of this narrative is some kind of metaphor. No, indeed, it really is about a pencil. Not a whole one, but a piece of it, let's say, three inches long. And yet, if someone were to argue that it was three and a half inches long, I wouldn't go to court over it. But I know full well that it wasn't four inches long. I could, as lawyers say, 'affirm under penalty of perjury', or as our people from Yasenytsia-Silna say, "swear and swear again, as sure as the world stands." Three and a half inches, no more, that was the length of the hero of this tale. Although it's been quite a few years since I met with our hero, or rather, since I last saw the pencil, because could it really see me with its sharpened nose? And even then, it lay in the darkest corner of my school bag for a whole day and a half, buried under books! In fact, it must have been at least sixteen years ago, plenty enough time to forget even a close friend. But I haven't forgotten about our hero, about those three and a half inches of pencil, encased in dark-red wood, hexagonal and polished to a golden sheen, with the inscription 'Mittel'[1] embossed in silver on its blunt end; at the other end it was sharpened – not too sharp, but not too blunt either, just right for a rural schoolboy.

One winter's morning, looking just like this, it lay on the snow in the Yasenytsia schoolyard, beside the path the

....

[1] German: Medium.

pupils had trodden that morning. It was a fine, wonderful morning. There was a gripping frost and the tiny flakes of snow floating in the air were completely transparent, visible only when the sunlight caught them and made them sparkle like diamonds. The pencil wasn't embedded in the frozen, glistening snow, but lay on the surface. Its polished wood gleamed in the sun, and the embossed silver letters were visible from afar. Surely, some pupil, rushing to school, had dropped it. It lay there, its black, sharpened nose pointing toward the school building, as if trying to indicate to every passerby that its rightful place was there; as if pleading with its silver gaze to be taken away from its albeit nice, but very cold bed and brought into the school, from where the noise of boys waiting for their teacher spread far and wide across the village.

Now, be honest, what would you do if you happened across such a 'Mittel' lying in such an inappropriate place? I think that 90 percent of you, not suspecting it to be the hero of a narrative, let alone of a newspaper article or a brief mention in the press, would simply pick it up and put it in your pocket. The other 10 percent, undoubtedly, wouldn't even bother bending down to grab it.

I must confess, I belonged to those 90 percent, which means, suspecting nothing bad, I stooped to pick it up and, not having an accessible pocket, slipped it into my leather school bag with my books. But what was not so ordinary was that I was very pleased with my find. I was a poor village boy and at my age had never owned a pencil, always having to write with a cursed goose quill, which dripped ink, splattering and scattering it so terribly under the pressure of my hand. And now suddenly I had found a pencil! And such a nice one too! True, I had only caught a glimpse of it lying in the snow, because as soon as I grabbed it, I quickly slipped it into my bag, as if afraid that the sun, shining so brightly, would steal it from my hand. Another interesting thing about this operation was that it never occurred to me that another pupil might have lost it – this never even crossed my mind.

I mean, really! Which schoolboy here loses pencils! It must have been some unknown gentleman who had come to see the teacher. He must have somehow lost that pencil in some strange way. Maybe it was a peddler to whom the teacher had sold a cow the year before; maybe this pencil had been lying here since then and no one had noticed it, poor thing. Maybe it had fallen from the sky during the night along with the snow? After all, grandma said that frogs occasionally fell from the sky. So why couldn't pencils fall as well? This was what I was thinking as I made my way through the schoolyard. Well, can't a six-year-old schoolboy think such things? But no! I really liked that pencil. I kept my hand inside my bag, holding onto the pencil. I turned it this way and that, trying to guess its shape, to restore its form before my eyes. In short, my imagination was constantly spinning and fluttering around the pencil, like a butterfly around a flower. It kept at bay any thought that the pencil might belong to one of the schoolboys, and that I would need to return it to its rightful owner.

The classroom was already full of pupils. Some were sitting at their desks and mumbling through their homework, anxiously glancing at the door, wondering if the teacher was coming. Others, the braver ones, were walking around the classroom, picking fights, bumping into desks, doodling various things with chalk on the blackboard, and quickly erasing them with a wet cloth that served as an eraser. No one asked about the pencil. This pleased me greatly, and I quickly slid across another desk and sat in my usual spot. As I took out a textbook for the lesson, I heard the pencil rattle against the leather of my bag, and I trembled all over – unsure if it was out of joy or some vague anxiety.

Finally, the teacher arrived and the lesson began. Nothing! The lesson finished, the teacher left, and the noise and chatter started as usual. No one mentioned the pencil. I sat looking around and trembling, like a thief with stolen goods, afraid that someone might come and demand the pencil from me. But no one wanted the pencil. The pupils either walked about or studied, or misbehaved and jostled one another. Stepan Leskiv, my good friend, came up to me.

"Hey, it looks to me like you haven't learnt your sums today. You'll be in big trouble! And if the teacher tells me to beat you up, well, expect the worst!"

What a rascal that Stepan was! He knew that arithmetic was my weak point and loved to tease me about it. But I knew that he was just joking. Besides, I was not afraid of the teacher because I had learnt how to count (writing numbers up to 100). I sure did! Who was it, that had spent all day yesterday writing numbers with their finger on misted windowpanes?

"You shouldn't worry so much about me," I answered. "Careful you don't end up in hot water yourself!"

Wonder of wonders! I had wanted to respond to Stepan in jest, with a smile, kindly – but for some reason I answered very bitterly, angrily, with such a sullen voice that it made me feel bad inside! Indeed, I even felt my whole face flush with embarrassment. Stepan stood before me for a moment, not saying a word, looking at me in bewilderment, and then walked away, as if saddened that he had upset me with his joke. He liked me a lot, that gentle, quiet, courteous, and kind boy! Why had I responded so harshly? Why had I upset him? After all, he was only joking, and there was no reason to react like that!

Such thoughts crossed my mind as Stepan walked away and quietly sat at his desk. He was a small, sandy-haired eight-year-old boy. His father was a poor peasant, and lived next door to my uncle, with whom I was staying. So, both of us boys often spent time together. Stepan's father had once been a wealthy man, they say, but a great fire and various other misfortunes had ruined his farm. He was a tall, strong man, with a stern face, getting about with his head hung low, and he spoke with a rough, sharp voice. For some unknown reason I was scared of him and considered him to be a harsh man. In contrast, Stepan took after his mother, a quiet, gentle woman with a serene smile, kind face, and bright greyish eyes. Which is why more than once, while hiding behind the fence in the pasture, I waited for old man Leskiv to leave the house, so that I could run over to play with Stepan for a while. True, we often argued, as children are wont to do, but never for long. Being hot-headed and quick to start a fight, I was usually also the first to make up, and Stepan would inevitably smile sweetly, as if to say: 'See, I knew all along that you couldn't do without me!'

Why had I been so angry with Stepan right now? Although no, I clearly felt that I was not angry with him at all! On the contrary, his sad, miserable look made me feel sorry for him. I felt ashamed of something, not yet realising what it was, and forgot all about the pencil. After these impressions had faded, I again noticed the bag before me, and my attention once more was drawn to the pencil; I began to imagine what it would be like to the touch and, for a while, completely forgot about Stepan and his abject look.

The teacher entered the classroom, the lesson began and slowly finished; and still there was not a word from anyone about the pencil.

The third lesson was Arithmetic. That lofty and terrifying science was conducted in a way where the teacher would call a pupil to the blackboard, tell him to write numbers with chalk, and all the other boys had to write the same numbers in their notebooks. The teacher constantly walked among the desks, checking here and there to see if everyone was writing, and writing correctly.

Before the lesson had begun, I heard a commotion in the back row where Stepan was sitting. There were some anxious, fragmented questions and answers, but because of the overall noise in the room, I couldn't follow what the talk was about. Still, something stirred inside me, an unease arose within me. I thought to myself: 'I won't take out my pencil now; I'll write as usual with my pen, even though I'm sick of it.'

The teacher entered. After taking a moment to catch his breath, he stood up from his desk and called me to the blackboard. I came out, frightened and trembling, because writing, whether it was numbers or letters, was always a tough nut for me to crack: various symbols always came out crooked, hook-like, or sprawling, so that they usually resembled an old fence where every post stuck out in different directions, and the crossbars pointed into thin air, unable to connect with the posts. But what could I do? The teacher had called my name, so I had no choice but to go. I stood at the blackboard, taking the cleaning rag in my right hand and the chalk in my left.

"Thirty-five!" the teacher called out and turned around to face me. "Ah, you dunce, how are you holding that chalk? Going to write with your left hand, eh?"

I switched the unfortunate tools of wisdom in my hands, then raised my right hand as high as I could and barely reached halfway up the blackboard. The task of writing the number '35' on the blackboard was very difficult because it involved writing some particularly tricky numbers. Yesterday, while practicing with my finger on the windowpane, I spent a long time thinking about how to write that cursed three, to make it look nice and round with a little notch in the middle. There was no one to ask for help, so I decided to write it starting from the middle notch, first drawing the upper curve, and then the lower curve. That's how I learned to write it at home, and now, with a trembling hand, I tried to replicate this on the blackboard. But unfortunately, my hand was shaking, and I had barely any strength, so no matter how hard I pressed the chalk to the board, the wretched strokes kept coming out very thin and wispy, so that they were barely visible. With great effort, I drew the number three.

"Finished already?" the teacher shouted and spun around to face me.

"No… not yet," I replied and, covered in cold sweat, set about writing the number five, obviously according to my own method, that is starting from the bottom.

"What's this?" exclaimed the teacher and rushed up to me. "How are you writing it? Eh?"

I said nothing as my trembling hand finished drawing the number on the blackboard. My number 'five' looked more like an upside-down letter 'L' than a round-bellied, crested 'five'.

"You lump of pork belly (the teacher's usual way of addressing pupils), don't you know how to write a 'five'?"

Without waiting for an answer, the teacher took a wide ruler from his table and grabbed hold of my hand. The chalk went flying to the ground and a loud slap echoed across the classroom. My palm reddened and seemed to puff up, and I felt as if ants were running under my skin. Because I have been good at withstanding pain since childhood, I only winced.

"So, you don't know how to write a 'five'? Haven't you seen me writing it? Then look how it's done. Like this!" The teacher grabbed the chalk and with a flourish first wrote a large five on the blackboard, and then an exact copy of it on my forehead (alright, maybe it wasn't as flowing and distinct).

"Continue writing," he yelled at me. "Forty-eight!" I took the chalk and began writing. The teacher watched me for a moment longer. The 'four' satisfied him, and he continued walking among the desks.

"Why aren't you writing?" he shouted menacingly at the boys, who watched half-smiling, half-terrified at what was happening at the blackboard. After the teacher's exclamation, all heads bowed like heavy ripening ears of wheat being pressed down by the wind.

"And you, class captain, how have you written your 'three'?" the teacher asked one fellow.

Instead of an answer, instead of an explanation, there came the sound of a ruler striking his hand.

"And what's that above the 'five'?" he asked another fellow.

"The ink dripped from my pen, sir."

Another slap across the knuckles.

"And you, reverend, why aren't you writing?" he asked a third fellow.

"I've… lo… please, sir," I heard Stepan Leskiv's voice almost in tears.

"What?" the teacher shouted angrily.

"I've lost my pencil somewhere, sir."

At that moment, the chalk fell out of my hand for some reason. I repeat: I had no clue as to why, because I was certain that the pencil lying peacefully in my bag was not Stepan's. No way in the world! Yet, still, at his words I became so frightened and my hand began to tremble so much, that the chalk slipped out of my hand like a slippery eel. Luckily the number was already written, because I wouldn't have been able to write it otherwise.

"Right," exclaimed the teacher, "you've lost it? Just you wait, I'll teach you!"

What the teacher actually wanted to teach Stepan, only the good Lord knew. All we pupils knew was that two days earlier the teacher had had a big argument with Stepan's father and, evidently, was only looking for an excuse to take revenge on the boy; moreover, we saw that today the teacher was tipsy, which meant that a beating was inevitable.

"Quick march to the middle of the room!" he yelled at Stepan. The poor boy must have known what was awaiting him and moved slowly; the teacher grabbed him by his long blond hair and dragged him into the middle of the room.

"Stand here! And you," he swung around to face me, "have you finished writing there?"

"Yes, sir."

"Sit down! And you, boy, to the blackboard!"

After uttering these words, the teacher gave Stepan a push. I breathed a little easier, partly because I was sitting in a safe place, and partly because I thought Stepan might not be punished for losing his pencil since the teacher had sent him to the blackboard, and I knew Stepan was good at writing. But hearing the teacher's annoyed voice as he dictated numbers to Stepan, and seeing him become steadily more angry as Stepan wrote everything correctly, I felt a sense of dread. It weighed on me, and a voice seemed to whisper inside me that if Stepan got into trouble over the pencil, I would partly be to blame. How such strange thoughts had surfaced in my head, I had no idea, but the only certain thing was that I was shaking like an aspen leaf.

Stepan kept writing numbers, filling the entire blackboard. The teacher constantly watched him, hoping to catch him at some mistake, but to no avail.

"That's enough!" the teacher shouted. "And now lie down!"

"But why, sir?" Stepan asked.

"Why? You want to know why? Lie down immediately!"

When I heard these words, I felt as if I was being choked. The teacher searched for a cane in the last row, while poor Stepan, pale and trembling, stood by the blackboard, clutching a rag in his hands.

"Why am I being punished, sir?" Stepan asked once more through his tears, as the teacher approached him with a cane in his hand.

"Lie down!" yelled the teacher and, without waiting, grabbed Stepan by the hair, flipped him over onto the chair, and began beating him with the cane as hard as he could. Stepan cried out in pain, but his cries only seemed to irritate the tipsy teacher even more.

"So that you'll know next time not to go losing pencils!" he shouted in a breathless, cracked voice, and the cane whistled through the air even louder as it struck the poor boy's body.

The things that were going through my head during that long, terribly difficult moment? The first thought that occurred to me was to stand up and say that I was to blame for everything, that I had Stepan's pencil, that I had found it and hadn't returned it to him. But my fear of the cane's whistle seemed to pin me to my seat, tying my tongue, and gripped my throat with iron pincers. Stepan's cries pierced my chest. I became drenched in cold sweat; I distinctly felt the sharp pain of the cane, felt it all over my body so acutely, that all my muscles involuntarily convulsed and trembled, and loud sobs emanated from my throat, loud enough for the whole class to hear. Yet fear cast such a pall over everyone that, despite the grave-like silence, no one heard my sobbing.

And still the teacher did not stop his beating! Poor Stepan was already hoarse, his face had turned blue, his fingers gripped the teacher's knees convulsively, his legs flailed in the air, but the cane continued to whistle through the air. With every whistle, with every slap on Stepan's thick linen shirt, thirty children's hearts in the classroom trembled and contracted, as Stepan uttered fresh cries of pain and despair. I no longer remember – and have no wish to remember! – what was happening to me during those dreadful moments, what feelings coursed through my body, what pain penetrated my joints, what thoughts flashed through my mind. But no, there were no thoughts at all! I sat cold and rigid, like a stone! Even now, sixteen years later, when I recall that moment, it seems to me that it had left me overwhelmed for a long time, it was like receiving a blow to the head with a rock. I felt that if there had been many such moments in my childhood, I would have turned out like one of those dim-witted children which we see by the hundreds in every primary school in our region, those unfortunate children, physically and spiritually abused, whose nerves have been dulled from a young age by being exposed to such terrible, repulsive scenes, and whose brains have been stunted from the age of six by the actions of such teachers.

At last, the whistle of the cane stopped. The teacher let go of Stepan. Powerless, exhausted, and breathless, he rolled onto the dais. Red as a beet, the teacher dropped his cane and settled into the chair from which Stepan had just fallen. He caught his breath for a while without uttering a word. The whole class was deathly silent. Only the sound of the poor Stepan's laboured breathing and convulsive sobbing could be heard.

"Can you get up?" the teacher whispered, kicking him in the side.

After a moment Stepan barely got to his feet, holding onto the table.

"Back to your desk! And know better than to lose your pencil next time!"

Stepan returned to his desk. The class was silent once more. The teacher had obviously sobered up somewhat and realized that he had done wrong by beating the boy so severely. He knew that it was not wise to provoke old man Leskiv and the thought irritated him even more. He jumped up and began to pace about the classroom silently, breathing heavily.

"Ah, the ragamuffins, the scoundrels!" he exclaimed while pacing about, and it was hard to tell if he was referring to us children or the absent residents of Yasenytsia.

For a long time, he continued to pace about the room, snorting and grumbling something under his breath, and then he turned to face us and screamed:

"Home time!"

But even this usually very magical phrase, which promised us at least a day of freedom from the burden of school wisdom, now seemed to fall on deaf ears. Anxiety and uncertainty had stunned all the pupils and robbed them of their acuity. It took a second, louder shout from the teacher for everyone to stand up for prayers.

After saying prayers, the pupils moved from their desks and began to leave the classroom without the usual noise and commotion; everyone walked slowly, casting cautious glances at the teacher, who stood by his table until all the boys had left. Each one felt crushed. Stepan was sobbing as he walked, and when he glanced at the teacher as he was leaving the classroom, the teacher threatened him with his fist. I was practically the last pupil to leave and could barely lift my feet. I was so terribly afraid and ashamed, that I wished I could have sunk into the ground at that moment. I don't know, maybe a criminal feels the same weight on his shoulders after killing someone, as I felt then. Nothing in the world would have compelled me then to look at Stepan. I imagined his pain so acutely, that I felt I was suffering no less than he was, and meanwhile that accursed inner voice kept whispering inside me that his suffering was all my doing, because of that pencil! Yes, now something clearly told me that it was his pencil which I had found! And what would seem more natural than to go up to him now and return his lost pencil! But no! Though it seemed natural, it was completely impossible for me to do, crushed as I was by fear, sorrow, and shame. It wasn't as if I still wanted to keep the pencil for myself anymore – no way! It now weighed like a heavy rock in my bag, burning my hand from a distance. Nothing in the world would have made me touch it now, or even look at it! If only someone could have grabbed my bag and emptied it so that the pencil would fall out and Stepan could take it – oh, how happy I would have been then! But nothing of the sort happened, and it was not something on the minds of the other pupils.

As soon as we were out of the classroom and had left the teacher's yard, everyone surrounded Stepan, who was still sobbing, and began to ask him how and where he had lost his pencil, and what kind of pencil it was. Some loudly criticized the teacher, others felt sorry for Stepan and told him that he needed to complain to his dad.

"How do I know where I lost it?" sobbed Stepan. "But what will my dad say now! He bought me the pencil only the day before yesterday in town, and I've gone and lost it! Oh, oh, oh!" the poor boy began to cry, fearing his father no less than the teacher.

"Don't cry, silly, don't be afraid," the boys tried to comfort him, although none were keen to be in Stepan's shoes.

"Yeah, don't cry!" Stepan replied sadly. "He'll kill me because of that pencil! Six kreutzers, he said he paid for it in town... And he said if I lost it, he'd take the hide off my back! Oh, oh, oh!"

I couldn't listen to Stepan. Each of his words were like a pin being driven into me. I ran quickly home, shaking all over, pale and breathless.

"Oh, fighting with the boys again!" my aunt yelled as soon as I entered. "Why are you out of breath, like some retriever! Ah, you scoundrel, you good-for-nothing, incompetent, worthless wretch!"

My aunt was still a girl in her twenties. She was 'very good' – at least that much could be said about her tongue, which liked to 'earn its keep' – and was never short of a word.

I hung my schoolbag on a hook and sat down to eat without saying a word. After eating, I sat at the table and grabbed a book, not to study what we had been assigned for the following day – homework was the last thing on my mind! I sat over the book like a log, reading the same words over and over a hundred times, not comprehending a thing of what I was reading. I tried not to think about Stepan, the teacher, or old man Leskiv, but their faces kept appearing before me, giving me the chills, gnawing at me, and tormenting me like a sinner's memories of past misdeeds. I so wished for evening to come sooner, but it seemed to never come. I was afraid to look at my schoolbag with the pencil, as if it were some terrible burrow, and the pencil inside it – a snake.

I won't recount how I tormented myself until evening finally came. The nightmares I had that night, how I screamed as I ran and hid in my dreams from flying lizards with sharp snouts and the word 'Mittel' inscribed in large letters on their backs, and how a stick with six equal sides and covered in shiny yellow bark, sharpened at both ends, kept pricking me – let all that pass into oblivion. Suffice to say that when I got up in the morning, I felt like I had been beaten or boiled alive in a pot. To top it off, my aunt scolded me for tossing about and screaming all night, keeping her from sleeping.

Early that morning, before I had set off for school, uncle came home from the village and, after removing his course woollen gloves, began to recount various news he had picked up in the village.

"Tell me, why did the teacher give Leskiv's Stepan such a hiding yesterday?" uncle suddenly asked me. The question frightened the daylights out of me, I felt as if someone had doused me with boiling water.

"Ah… ah… ah… that… he lo… lo… lo…"

"What's the matter, have you forgotten how to speak?" auntie exclaimed. "So, what happened to Stepan there?" she asked uncle.

"The teacher beat him so badly yesterday because of some pencil, that the poor lad barely made it home."

"What pencil?"

"Well, it turns out his dad bought him a pencil on Monday, and he lost it yesterday. The teacher was drunk and began to beat the lad black and blue, as if he was to blame. Listen, the poor lad barely made it home. And when he got home, he told them what had happened and that bear of a father of his lost it and began to beat the child! Grabbed him by the hair and began to kick him with his boots! Good Lord! The old woman burst into tears and began to scream, the boy fainted, they barely managed to revive him with cold water. They say that he's in bed now, unable to move! How can you torture a child like that…!"

Before uncle had finished talking, I burst loudly into tears and interrupted his conversation.

"And what's with you?" uncle asked in bewilderment.

"Have you gone crazy, lad, or what?" auntie exclaimed.

"I… I… I…" I babbled, sobbing, unable to finish the sentence.

"Well, come on, out with it!" uncle said in a gentle voice.

"I… found… Stepan's pencil!"

"You found it? Where? When?"

"Yesterday, in the schoolyard in the snow," I said a little more boldly now.

"Well, and why didn't you give it back to Stepan?"

"I didn't know it was his, and he never asked if anyone had found it."

"And later, after school?"

"I… I was afraid."

"Afraid? What the club-footed devil were you afraid of?" auntie asked, but I said nothing in reply.

"Well, and where's that pencil now?"

"It's in my schoolbag."

Uncle went up to my schoolbag and removed the unfortunate pencil. I dared not even look at it.

"Well, good people, will you take a look here, over such a silly little thing that poor lad was beaten black and blue! May hell swallow the two of them!"

Uncle spat on the ground and left the house, taking the pencil with him. Auntie pushed me out of the house and off to school. I sobbed along the way, and tears rolled involuntarily down my face, but at least I felt much better.

That day and the whole of the following week, Stepan did not come to school, remaining in bed. Besides, that week the teacher suddenly took poorly as well: my uncle guessed that old man Leskiv must have 'worked him over' well. Whether that was the case or not, I never did find out for sure – suffice to say that I didn't see Stepan for two whole weeks. Oh, how much I dreaded meeting him now! In my restless dreams I often saw his kind, peaceful face, still blue from the beatings, pained and thin, and his gentle grey eyes looked at me with reproach! But when I finally did see him, when I heard his voice, all the torment and unrest of the past few days seemed to come alive all at once in my soul, but only for a brief instant. Stepan was once more his usual healthy and cheerful self. He spoke to me kindly, as if nothing had happened between us; there was no mention of the pencil. Did he know that I had his pencil and was the cause of his pain? I have no idea. It was enough that we never mentioned that pencil again.

1879

SCHÖN SCHREIBEN[2]

In the spacious second-grade classroom of the Basilian Fathers' elementary school in Drohobych it was so quiet you could hear a pin drop. The calligraphy class would be starting soon, dreaded not so much because of the subject itself, as because of the person teaching it. In the Basilian school, the fathers themselves taught all the subjects, except for the art of handwriting, for which they hired a layman, a former steward or tutor, Mr Valko. Mr Valko still seemed to think that he was a steward, even though he no longer carried a whip. But he saw no reason to abstain from using a cane and never neglected to make appropriate use of it. Naturally, the children, subjected to the authority of such a teacher for a mere hour, sat trembling in anticipation, and calligraphy became their greatest torment.

Little Myron was the only pupil sitting calmly, almost cheerfully at his desk. He wondered why it had suddenly become so quiet in the classroom as soon as some brave soul, sent into the corridor as a look-out, rushed into the classroom and announced: "Valko's coming!" At that moment, silence fell over the class. Little Myron had not yet encountered Mr Valko. He had just arrived from a village school, his father had enrolled him in the second grade of the Basilian Fathers' elementary school, and today was his first class in calligraphy. Although he was quite weak in handwriting back

....

[2] German: Calligraphy.

in the village school, not knowing how to properly hold a pen or draw a smooth straight line, he was still only a child, not preoccupied with worries about what he did not yet know. He was surprised by the sudden silence but didn't dare ask any of his neighbours, with whom he was still barely acquainted, about the reason. And, after all, it didn't concern him much. Amid the silence, dreadful and anxious for the others, he indulged more comfortably in his favourite pastime, musing about his native village. It wasn't that he longed to be there, for he knew that he would see his parents every Monday. He simply imagined how wonderful it would be to return home in the summer, to dash through the pastures, sit by the river, or wander in search of minnows; these were thoughts brimming with joy, clarity, and brilliance, rather than sadness or longing. Little Myron luxuriously dived into the beauty of the natural world that blossomed in his imagination amid the grey, cold walls of the Basilian school, oblivious to the looming threat hanging over the class.

"Hey, why haven't you prepared your notebook for writing?" whispered one of Myron's neighbours, nudging him in the side.

"Huh?" Myron responded, unpleasantly awakened from his golden daydream.

"Get your notebook ready for writing!" the fellow repeated, showing Myron how to arrange his notebook, inkwell, and pen according to Mr Valko's instructions.

"He's coming, he's coming!" a whisper spread through the class, as if some fearsome king was approaching, as the footsteps of the calligraphy teacher echoed in the corridor. The classroom door opened and Valko entered. Myron glanced at him. The teacher bore no resemblance to any king. He was a man of average height, with closely cropped hair on a round, sheep-like head, with a reddish short-clipped moustache and a small Spanish beard. His broad face and wide, strongly developed cheekbones, along with his large, protruding ears, gave him an appearance of someone who was obtusely stubborn and carnivorous. His small frog-like eyes were set deeply in their sockets, gleaming somewhat malevolently and unpleasantly.

"Very well!" he exclaimed menacingly, closing the door behind him and waving his slender cane about. At these words, it was as if some breeze on a cloudy summer's day had lowered all the wheat ears in the field – so did all eighty-five of the pupil's heads in class bow down over their blue and red lined notebooks. Every pupil's pen trembled in their hand. Only little Myron, still unfamiliar with Valko's temperament, sat facing the front of the class, staring at the new teacher.

"And what about you?" shouted Valko, glaring at him, and took several steps toward him.

Little Myron was seized with sudden dread. By some unconscious impulse, he curled his body into the same posture that his classmates had already assumed a minute earlier.

Valko took the chalk in his hands, approached the blackboard and, with a flourish of his hand, began to write. At first, he wrote only letters, in lowercase and uppercase, then vowels and consonants, without any particular meaning. But then he progressed to words, and finally to whole sentences, such as: 'God created the world', 'Man has two hands', 'Earth is our mother'. Having thus exhausted his wisdom and demonstrated his rich knowledge of calligraphy with numerous flourishes and long, sausage-like tails, Valko laid down the chalk, stepped back, glanced once more with satisfaction at the writing on the blackboard, and then, turning around to face the trembling class, shouted menacingly:

"Write!"

His scholarly activity had happily ended at that moment, and now his activity as a steward began. To demonstrate this clearly, he shook his fingers vigorously to be rid of the scholarly chalk dust and took his cane in his hands. Like an eagle watching prey from above, he surveyed the classroom, then descended from the dais and began his inspection.

The first pupil unfortunate enough to attract his attention was a small, weak, and very frightened little schoolboy. Sweating all over, he bent over his writing, trying with all his might to keep his pen steady in his trembling fingers, constantly glancing at the board in an attempt to reproduce on paper the same hooks, loops, and sausage-like curves that the skilled teacher's hand had drawn on the blackboard. But alas, his hand trembled, the hooks, loops, and sausages came out jagged and uneven – even his disobedient pen kept twisting about in his fingers, squeaking and splattering ink, as if it was angry about something and wanted to escape from his grip as quickly as possible.

Valko towered over him like an executioner beside his victim and, smiling maliciously, without saying a word, began to observe the boy's work. The poor lad sensed trouble and completely lost control of his hand and the disobedient pen.

"Is this how you write?" Valko slowly hissed, but his cane whistled through the air lightning-fast and struck the poor boy's shoulders like a snake.

"Ooh-oh-oh!" the boy screamed, but immediately grew silent as he caught the teacher's menacing serpent-like gaze.

"Can't you write any better than that?" Valko asked.

"I can, I can!" the boy stammered, not even knowing what he was saying.

The steward-teacher might have truly believed that the boy was able to write better and that he was only pretending to write badly just to annoy him, or perhaps because he enjoyed being caned.

"Well, take care then!" And Valko moved on without verifying what beneficial results his thorough teaching method had produced. In any case, he couldn't care less about these results – he was only a steward now and nothing more. His eyes had already turned to the other side of the room, searching for a fresh victim. There sat a little Jewish boy, who, according to the old habit of his people, wrote backwards, trying to reproduce Valko's flourishes from right to left, from the end of the line to the beginning. He had already completed one line this way and was starting another with the words 'sot god a z k sir'. The finished line looked more or less acceptable, but the new, unfinished one, which started from the end, caught Valko's eye.

"What are you writing there, Moishe?" he shouted, rushing up to the lad.

Valko called all the Jews in class Moishe – unless they were the sons of wealthy city bigwigs, whom he held in great respect. The Jewish boy, whose name was Jonah Turteltaub, hearing the shout and seeing the approaching enemy, shrank back and curled up like a snail in its shell, stopping his writing.

"Ha, ha, ha!" chortled Valko, looking at the writing.

"Sir…" began the boy, but then grew quiet.

"Come here!"

And without waiting for Jonah to get out of his desk, he grabbed him by the ear and dragged him to the middle of the room.

Seeing the poor, trembling, and slobbering Jonah, the whole class burst into loud laughter, even though everyone was trembling and cowering in their seats. But such is the power of tyrannical oppression, that as soon as the tyrant smiles, everyone under his yoke will laugh, regardless of the fact that they are actually laughing at their own misfortune.

"Come to the board! Now, write!"

Valko erased part of his own writing with his hand and shoved the stick of chalk into the boy's hand. The boy began to write in his usual way, from right to left. The class burst into laughter again, Valko smiled, but then his face suddenly darkened, and he turned to address the back row, where the biggest and strongest boys were sitting, and shouted:

"Come here, and give him a helping hand!"

The boy trembled all over and mumbled something, but his two classmates quickly rushed to him and dragged him onto the dais. Silence descended on the classroom. Instead of laughter, pale faces watched from every corner of the room – only Jonah's painful screams echoed from the brick walls of the Basilian monastery.

"That's enough!" said Valko and Jonah returned to his desk, sobbing.

Having accomplished this highly pedagogical act, Valko resumed his inspection of the classroom, and once again, the blows of his cane landed upon the shoulders and hands of the unfortunate boys.

It was hard to say what impression this lesson had made on Myron. He trembled from time to time, as if with a fever; there was ringing in his ears and everything spun before his eyes as if in a storm. It seemed to him that this storm would not pass him by either, and every blow from the terrifying teacher seemed to fall on him. The written words and lines danced before his eyes, swelled and became entangled, looking worse than they actually were. He didn't even realize that he had stopped writing – a grey haze appeared before his eyes.

"Is this how you write?" Valko hollered above his head.

Myron flinched, grabbed hold of the pen, dipped it in ink, and dragged it across the paper like an ox pulling a plough.

"Don't you know how to hold the pen?"

"No, I don't, sir!" whispered Myron.

"What?" Valko roared. "Haven't I shown you a dozen times already?"

Myron stared in bewilderment at Valko's angry face. But instead of answering, Valko struck the boy in the face with his clenched fist. Little Myron fell onto the desk like a mown-down stalk of wheat, then slid from the desk onto the floor. Blood covered his face.

"Pick him up!" Valko commanded. Two boys, the same ones who had just beaten up Jonah, raced from the back of the classroom and lifted the unconscious Myron.

His head lolled about on his neck and hung down lifelessly.

"Hurry and fetch some water!" Valko commanded and looked at Myron again.

"Who is this boy?" he asked.

"Myron," replied the class 'captain', the oldest and strongest boy in the class, whom the reverend fathers had appointed as a supervisor over his classmates.

"Who is he?" Valko persisted.

"The son of some peasant from N…"

"A peasant's son! Really, why do these peasants bother to push their way in here?" Valko muttered. He felt somewhat relieved. For he had begun to worry about his actions, but if this was a peasant's son – he could beat and humiliate him as much as he liked and no one would stand up for the boy.

Valko was not mistaken in his reckoning. No one would bother defending a peasant's son. This inhumane act went unpunished, just like many of the teacher's other inhumane acts. But in the heart of the peasant's son, it became the first seed of indignation, contempt, and lasting enmity toward all forms of oppression and tyranny.

1879

THE MYKYTYCH OAK TREE

This took place a long time ago. Not only those times, but even the memories of them have dimmed in my mind. Occasionally, like lightning piercing darkness, moments from the past appear in a flash and evoke an indescribable melancholy. They shimmer and flicker, and joy, fear, laughter and tears become intertwined in them, and one's memory is barely able to compose a vivid, true picture from such fragmented, chaotic recollections.

I see myself as a small five-year-old boy in a crowd of similar raucous and animated village lads. It is summer. The sun burns hot from a clear sky. It is warm outside but we are busy having fun in the shade of the storehouse and don't feel the heat. Then we all rush off toward the cattle pen, crawl over the stile (some even squeeze through holes in the paling fence, like mice) to the Mykytych yard next door. There are lots of trees here, it is cool, and there is lots of grass, just like in a meadow, and we have somewhere to run.

How we loved to dash around that yard and play there! But there was one thing in the yard that appealed to us more than anything – an enormous oak tree, more than two yards in diameter, tall, and with lots of branches. Its crown was like a rounded green dome and could be seen from afar, towering over our small village. It grew near the road, close to the fence, and there in the corner, like children clinging to their father, broad-leaved burdock, nettles, and plantain grew around its enormous base. But in front of it, to one side of the path leading up to it, there was a well-trodden patch; this was where we loved to hide from the rain, as if under a secure thatched roof. We felt at ease here because the place was in the middle of the yard, far from anyone's house, so that no one could scold us for shouting too much or dashing about too energetically.

There were lots of things to play with here and there was lots of room to run.

"Come on, boys, let's make some chains!" someone would call out, and immediately the whole group would scatter through the garden, plucking plantain leaves, picking flowers, and from the soft, tube-like shoots we'd make very long chains, constantly adding more and more links until the bottom ones would tear from the sheer weight of the chains. We'd drape ourselves from head to toe with these chains, stand together in a large circle and then race off single file to the bottom of the yard, until the tall heads of weeds and the broad leaves of burdock were rustling behind us.

"Hey, let's grab some buttons here! Are we not brave soldiers?" another fellow called out, and everyone left the torn chains behind and pushed their way in among the coarse burdock, pressing down the stems and picking off the barbed whitish, pewter-coloured flower heads, which clung to clothes so easily. Finally, with gleeful shouts, we carried whole piles of those flower heads in our hats, sat down on the ground side by side under the oak tree, and someone pinned several 'buttons' to each person's chest in turn, reminding them: "You'd better behave yourself! You're in the army now."

Finally, the buttons were all attached. "Atten-shun!" yelled the commander, and everyone jumped to their feet. "Double march!" he ordered and ran off in front of everyone. Screaming, we all chased after him to the far end of the yard, holding onto our hats…

At last, after lots of running about, we were exhausted.

"Let's sit down!" said one of the weaker boys, short of breath and red from the heat and physical exertion.

"Wait a minute, I'll join you too!" yelled Mytro.

"Where are you off to?!" we called after him.

"Go, go and sit down, I'll bring something, something really nice!"

We sat down and caught our breath, waiting for Mytro. He was the son of Anna Melnyk, who boarded at Mykytych's with her younger sister, whom we children called Scarecrow, because she usually went about downcast and grizzly, all dishevelled, hair uncombed and unwashed.

Mytro's mother and Scarecrow were strangers in our village: we had no idea where they had come from. They had worked as domestics in nearby villages, until the older sister gave birth to a boy. Then she went off to Drohobych and found work as a wet-nurse in some Jewish household. Meanwhile Mytro was left to be raised in a village on the outskirts of town until he was five. Then his mother left domestic work and came to our village, together with her younger sister, and convinced Mykytych to let them board with him in return for various work. We boys had often heard talk at home about Mytro's mother, Anna Melnyk, and we even felt concealed resentment toward Mytro because he was illegitimate, and because his mother had worked in the employ of Jews; which is why we regarded him as being semi-Jewish.

At the same time, Mytro's very posture, disposition, and facial features endowed him with a peculiar character, quite different from the other village children. Small, stocky, and dark-faced, with large bulging eyes that lacked any shine or vibrancy, he was usually the meekest among us. He ran with the others as if he were compelled to, and during races he always came in a distant last. In all situations, he seemed to keep to himself, as if he could sense that he was not warmly welcomed by us. Yet, he never lagged behind, always tagging along wherever we went, although it was obvious that our games were not really to his liking. In his demeanour and speech there was always something slow, lethargic, and forgetful; he always looked dejected and sleepy, which further distanced us from him. However, we never showed any hostility toward him and never quarrelled. He never resisted, doing what the others did, and none of us had the heart to provoke or hurt him. He shuffled along with us, and most of the time during our noisy childish games, we forgot about Mytro, even though he was right there with us, wheezing and watching us with his black, glassy eyes.

But at times, when we were all tired and sat quietly, catching our breath in some shady cool spot, Mytro suddenly seemed to come alive and began to recount stories, all so frightening and gloomy that more than once, more than one listener would suddenly burst into tears. At such times, when everyone sat quietly, anxiously listening to one of his tales, where cursed kings, unfortunate children, fairy-tale animals, and palaces seemed to come alive before our childish eyes, Mytro remained unmoved and spoke in an even and cold tone of voice, which made the story sound even more horrifying. Even in broad daylight, we involuntarily pressed closer together. We didn't dare interrupt Mytro's narrative. Most interestingly, Mytro spoke in a solemn voice, describing everything in minute detail, and dwelt on every minutia, as if he had seen everything with his own eyes. Sometimes he would sing us songs, but these were usually very short, monotonous excerpts, and they froze the blood in our veins. We turned pale, trembled, and dared not make a move as we listened to his dull, not entirely pleasant voice.

"Where d'you get these songs and tales from?" we often asked him.

"Auntie taught me," Mytro would reply briefly.

He was referring to Scarecrow.

We sat quietly, waiting for Mytro to return. Finally, he appeared, slowly dragging his feet, carrying a few stems of 'dog's milk',[3] for which, apparently, he had run all the way down to the stream at the bottom of the yard, where whole clumps of it grew on the sandy banks.

"Why have you picked that?" called out one of the boys. "Throw it away, it's an impure plant. My daddy says you shouldn't pick it."

"Shoosh!" Mytro replied coldly. "Sit around in a circle and I'll show you something."

We sat around Mytro.

"Do you know what's inside this weed?"

"Dog's milk," we replied. "Just break off a stem and it will come oozing out."

"No, it's not dog's milk at all," Mytro replied authoritatively, "it's blood."

"Whose blood?"

"There was once this rabbit and it had three sons. The rabbit went off to war, and its sons were still babies, and an evil stepmother was left to look after them. Before leaving, the rabbit warned her: 'Remember to look after my sons, give them milk and wheaten bread with honey, because if I return and find they have gone, you will pay dearly.' Well, that rabbit went off to war, and he was there for three years, and when he was returning home, his horse tripped and broke its leg as he was riding across a bridge. The rabbit dismounted and said: 'Oh, this is a bad omen, my sons are probably no longer among the living.' And then he heard singing coming from under the bridge:

> *Ride out, ride out, oh rabbit,*
> *On your steed of fiery light,*
> *Your sons were cut down, slain,*
> *Buried 'neath the bridge's strain.*

....

[3] Cypress spurge or graveyard weed (Euphorbia cyparissias) – an invasive noxious weed, its milky sap is a skin irritant.

"The rabbit looked under the bridge, but there was nothing there, just a lot of weeds, like these ones here, growing from the sand. The rabbit began to pull out the weeds and blood dripped from them. The rabbit realized that it was the blood of his sons, and cast a spell on the weeds. 'Weed, oh, weed,' he said, 'don't show people that you have blood inside you, let them see it as milk.' And since that day, whenever someone pulls out this weed, it appears to them that it contains milk, but in fact it is blood. Let me prove this to you."

We were all trembling and watching Mytro. He grabbed a thin dry stalk of grass and bent it into a small oblong ring, smearing saliva across it, so that it created a thin film across the ring; then he let some milky sap drip onto the film, and we immediately saw multi-coloured circles spread across the film of saliva, which steadily began to turn a blood-red colour. Our hearts were penetrated by an icy chill, while Mytro began to sing calmly in his monotonous voice, as if oblivious to everything around him:

> *Ride out, ride out, oh rabbit,*
> *On your steed of fiery light,*
> *Your sons were cut down, slain,*
> *Buried 'neath the bridge's strain.*

"Mytro, Mytro!" a hoarse, sepulchral voice called out from behind our shoulders. We all nearly screamed in fright, and turned around to where the voice had come from. Scarecrow was standing on the far side of the fence.

Scarecrow was a girl of not yet seventeen years of age, short, also with a dark face, with a flat nose, a low forehead and large murky eyes like Mytro's. I never saw her being cheerful, talkative, never heard her joke, or sing, never saw her nicely dressed, like other village girls. She was always gloomy and silent, and went about looking as if she were half-asleep. Lately she seemed to have become even more downcast. We children were even a little scared of her and if we came across her in the street, we always walked past in silence, as if expecting she might do something bad. But the reason for our fear was not her actions, for she never said a bad word to anyone. It was her gloominess, imbecility and silence, which were clearly imprinted on her plain, flabby and slightly spotty face, in her eyes and her lethargic movements. For this reason, not only us children but older people too kept their distance from her, being squeamish about the slightest thing.

No one ever spoke a word about her without a note of disdain or contempt, although no one could say anything bad about her. True, no one knew how she had been brought up, how she was managing now, where that shyness and timidity of hers had come from, and once the nickname Scarecrow stuck, everyone used that scornful name without looking deeper to see if under that repulsive exterior there beat and suffered a living human heart that desired happiness and a good life no less than anyone else.

I mean, do our peasants have the time and skill to sort these things out, especially where a person, downtrodden by long years of misfortune and humiliation, despised, bullied and ridiculed from childhood, withdraws into themself, squirming about like an impaled slug, anxiously hiding any sign of a living human being inside them. And I learned, although many years later, that Scarecrow was one such a person.

"Mytro, are you there?" she yelled from the other side of the paling fence. "Come here."

Mytro scrambled to his feet somehow faster and livelier than usual, and went over to the stile, which led into the street. Climbing over the fence, he ran up to Scarecrow. She was dressed in her usual garb – in a baggy, coarse, dirty shirt and a gaudy dress, without a kerchief on her head. The wind played with her long-unbraided black plaits, from which protruded stalks of straw here and there. She grabbed Mytro by the hand and, without saying a word, walked down the road and into the field.

We remained sitting under the oak tree, and before us lay the pile of 'dog's milk', which Mytro had brought. After a while, we sobered up, so to speak, and resumed our games.

"Does anyone know where they might have gone?" one of the boys asked.

"Let's run after them and see."

"Run after Scarecrow?" one of the boys said, with a hint of fear in his voice. "Don't you know she's a witch?"

"That's alright, we'll keep our distance," said another fellow. "Let's head to the village common."

We made our way up to the village common, then ran down and turned into the field in the direction Scarecrow and Mytro had headed. But we couldn't find anyone in the field, and after running our fill up and down the road, we returned home toward evening.

In the afternoon the following day I was busy near the cattle shed, fashioning runners for my sled, when I suddenly noticed Mytro's face staring at me from a hole in the fence surrounding Mykytych's yard. He was breathing heavily and barely managed to whisper:

"Ivas!"

"Yeah? Is that you, Mytro?"

"It's me. Know what? Go inside your house and bring me out a large slice of bread. Mum's run out today."

This wasn't the first time that Mytro had asked me for bread. I didn't ask questions and ran inside our house. Luckily mum had gone into the garden, otherwise she would have scolded me for taking such a large piece of bread. But as I was walking past the table, I noticed that mum had baked some potato pies, and without a second thought, I broke off half of one. ('I'll say that I ate it. And why not?' a thought flashed through my mind.) and I ran off with all this to Mytro.

He gave me a strange, indescribable look, as he slipped the bread and the pie down his shirtfront! For some reason it made me feel good, but I also felt a stab of fear…

"I need to run!" he whispered and disappeared.

"Where you off to, Mytro?" I asked, but he was already too far away to have heard my question.

Over lunch, our hired hand Mykola, always angry at everyone and everything, said among other things:

"How about this! Anna, the one who boards with Mykytych, meets me in the street and asks if I've seen her girl, by any chance. To hell with you, you devil, do I, an old man, need to keep track of your girls?"

"So where has her girl disappeared?" asked Maryna, the servant-girl.

"The devil – forgive me for mentioning his name while eating – knows. She disappeared yesterday, and never returned home for the night. No one's been able to find her or learn where she went."

"Hm! She's probably… ready to…" muttered Maryna, as she served borshch from a large pot. I couldn't understand what Scarecrow was 'ready' to do and there was no more talk on the subject, so I didn't find out what happened to her. That evening, when the cattle had already returned from pasture, I heard screams coming from the common, crying and quarrelling. All of us who were in the house ran outside to see what had happened. People had assembled on the village common, sighing, shushing, and trying to placate someone.

"What's happened here? What's wrong?" people asked, as they came running from everywhere.

"Anna here almost crippled her boy."

"The woman's gone mad. She whipped her boy with thistles – the poor kid's shoulders are soaked with blood."

I pushed my way to the front, to get a better look at everything.

"I'll beat the scoundrel to death," Anna shouted, brandishing a whole bundle of thistles. "I'll hang him upside down in the smoke! Until he tells me where that wretched girl has gone!"

"But how can he tell you, if he doesn't know himself?" the women tried to calm Anna down.

"Like hell he doesn't know! Don't you worry, the little thief knows only too well! He's been running around all day, who knows where! You hear me, you rascal?" she threatened Mytro. The poor fellow was huddled up against one of the women and stood there, neither alive nor dead, seeming to see nothing, hear nothing, and only sobbed from time to time.

"Come on, Anna, come on!" Old Prokip, the oldest grandpa in our village, piped up. "Have you gone mad, or has your sound mind left you, if ever it was present? To beat a child so badly, come on!"

Mykytych was standing behind Anna, silently watching everything.

"You need to stop her, Mykytych!" the women lamented.

"What does Mykytych have to do with me and my boy!" Anna yelled. "It's not as if it's his child. He has no right to intervene! I'll do whatever I please with him!"

Mykytych grimaced as if he had bitten into a hot pepper.

"I'm not in much of a hurry," he said, forcing a smile and looking somewhat annoyed. "I'm in no hurry to interfere with your rights! Do whatever you want with him, as far as I'm concerned!"

He left. There was a minute's silence.

"Come along home, you little wretch!" exclaimed Anna and grabbed Mytro by the hand.

"I won't go, you'll kill me!" Mytro said in such a resolute and level voice, as if he was convinced of this.

"Anna," the women chattered away, "have some sense! What is the child guilty of? Why are you punishing him? Shame on you."

"You should be ashamed yourself, you bedraggled fool!" Anna yelled. "And why should I be ashamed? Aren't I my child's mother? I'll give him a beating, and I'll console him!"

And Anna took Mytro by the hand and led him off. He wasn't crying, or screaming, or trying to resist – he turned around only once and looked at the people, but with a look that filled my heart with so much dread, more than I ever felt after those stories of his.

"Why has she gotten struck into the lad, what does she want from him?" some people asked.

"Her girl's disappeared somewhere, and evidently he knows where she is."

"Why did the girl go and run away?"

"Oh, come on! You know, it's because her time had come! She was probably afraid of her sister and that upright Mykytych."

"There's no need to call her a fool!" said one fellow. "She had her wits about her, but they beat them out of her, crushed her. My God, the things that girl had to suffer in her lifetime. It would make the wisest among us go insane! If I started telling you her story, we'd be here till morning."

"Now, now, my storyteller, you're getting carried away again," his wife berated him. "Come on, time to head home! Can't you see those clouds coming in? It's going to rain!"

Everyone reluctantly turned to look toward the west. A terrible dark cloud hung over the ridge, bubbling away like water in a cauldron and emitting flashes every few moments. A wind blew from the ridge, so cold that it felt like it had come off an ice field.

"Oh, it doesn't look too good! God forbid lest it hails."

"Christ Almighty, that would ruin all our work."

"But really, where has that girl disappeared?" someone piped up. "Could she have lost her marbles and gone off into the forest to give birth? In this weather, she'd freeze to death overnight. We should go and look for her."

The people stood talking in the clearing and didn't disperse. Suddenly, Mytro's terrifying screech sounded from Mykytych's house, frightening everyone to the core.

"God, the woman really has gone insane, she'll torture the poor boy to death!"

"Why are you standing here like sheep? Why don't you go to the house and pull that crazy woman away from the child?" Old Prokip said sternly. "If she gave birth to the boy, then she needs to take care of him! She can't just torture and abuse him now."

"Ah, she'd rather get rid of the burden!" someone said.

Chattering among themselves, the people made their way to Mykytych's yard, but they had barely entered it, when Anna, dishevelled and out of breath, ran out to meet them and cried in an anxious voice:

"Good people, please hurry into the forest to look for her. She's somewhere there above Deep Ravine among the spruces. I barely got that little bastard to confess. Run, please, run, see the stormcloud that's approaching. The poor unfortunate will die and they'll blame me, they'll say I drove her out of the house!"

The old women crowded around Anna and began to exchange whispers with her, while the men raced off into the forest to look for Scarecrow. My mother dragged me home.

Not even a moment had passed since sunset, and already it was so dark that when I looked out of the window, it was as if the glass had been tarred over from the outside. Only the wild wind howled between the outbuildings and tore at the gables of the houses. From time to time, large drops of rain pelted the windowpane. Blood-red flashes of lightning tore through the darkness, and thunder shook the house, the air, and the ground.

"My Lord, what a frightening storm," mother said, as she stepped inside. "Something bad will happen. I distinctly heard something groaning under Mykytych's oak tree. The sound was so pitiful and terrible, that it made my hair stand on end."

At that moment lightning lit up the sky, there was a loud rumble of thunder, and the maid dashed into the house with a loud crash of the door.

"Mother of Christ," she exclaimed, barely able to catch her breath, "someone must be atoning for their sins under Mykytych's oak tree, they're groaning so loudly! Lord, when I heard it, my heart froze, and the voice kept repeating: 'Oh, my poor misfortune! Oh, my dear child! Oh, my wretched life!' Just like someone mourning the dead."

Everyone who was in the house rushed outside, despite the wind, thunder and lightning. We ran up to Mykytych's fence, but aside from the noise of the storm, which shook the mighty branches of the oak, nothing else could be heard. We came back inside.

A good time later my dad and our servant returned home: both had dashed off into the forest, clambering among the fir trees and fallen branches, but they couldn't find any trace of Scarecrow. We went to sleep overcome with gloom and dread. We spoke about Scarecrow only in whispers. Meanwhile, the rain bucketed down, and the lightning pierced the darkness from time to time like fiery snakes, followed by the grumble of distant thunder.

The following day the sun rose joyously onto a clear blue sky. The storm had passed, without doing too much damage, leaving everything refreshed after a long spell of heat. Everything was green, stood straighter and gleamed with blessed drops of rain, boldly and joyfully embracing life.

It was still cold in the morning, but soon the sun warmed the air a little and evaporated the dew, and we children gathered to play games. A small crowd of children, both boys and girls from all the surrounding houses, gathered in our yard. Only Mytro was missing.

"Well, Mytro would have received a good hiding from his mother yesterday. Probably can't walk today," said one of the girls.

"Did you hear something crying out under the oak tree last night?" I asked.

"No. Why, did you hear something?"

"My mum heard it," I replied, "and Maryna as well. It was just when the thunder started and the men still hadn't returned from the forest."

"Let's go and see what happened there?"

"No, we shouldn't go," said a girl timidly. "Dad said that if you hear moaning at night, it means it's an unclean place. If someone steps there, their leg will wither."

But even though we were afraid of such tales, with which adults had scared us since we were tiny-tots, our curiosity got the better of us.

Besides, it was a bright day, and dad was chopping wood right there in the yard, and it was so nice under the oak tree, not scary at all. We summoned our courage and headed off there.

"What are you afraid of! Look, there's nothing here, come on," yelled one of the boys, running ahead of everyone. But suddenly he slipped and almost fell over, and glancing down at his feet, he stopped, as if petrified.

We didn't notice the changed expression on his face at first, but as we approached, our eyes involuntarily turned to the spot where Mykhailo had slipped. And for a moment, we all stood stock-still, petrified with fright. It was the very same spot where Mytro had shown us the blood of the rabbit's sons the day before. We now saw a puddle of real human blood there.

"Oh no, blood, my gosh, it's blood!" we suddenly screamed and raced off in single file away from the oak tree.

"What's the matter? Lord Almighty! What's wrong?" my dad yelled, as he ran up to the stile.

"Blood, blood, there's a whole puddle of it!" we yelled, horrified.

"Where's the blood, where?" my dad asked as he negotiated the stile into the yard next door.

"Over there, under the oak tree!"

Dad walked over to take a look and muttered:

"Some misfortune must have happened here!"

And then he addressed us:

"Kids, go and tell Mykytych to come here, and fetch Old Prokip and all your dads, those who are at home."

The children raced off.

"Here we go again, more trouble is about to happen! God forbid lest they send a commission, and start writing protocols! And it's all because of that upright fellow!"

People gathered, asking what had happened. Dad showed them the puddle of blood.

"What's all this hullabaloo about?" some of the men piped up. "Some ferret has probably eaten a chicken here during the night, and you're summoning people here."

"Really?" exclaimed Old Prokip. "Oh, a chicken has definitely been eaten here, but what kind of chicken. Come, look here!"

Prokip was standing to one side, and people turned around to face him. With his ironclad walking stick he began to poke about the earth, pushing aside one clod, then another, then moved some clay to one side. The men looked and gasped, some began to cross themselves.

"Lord, have mercy on the sinful little soul. My, oh my!" they murmured.

The blue, puffy face of a baby stared up at them through the clay. Seeing it, Mykytych bit his lip and went terribly pale.

"And where's that… Scarecrow?" one of the men called out. "We need to find her! Where could she be?"

At that moment one of the boys yelled from further along the path.

"What now?" the men muttered.

"A trail, dad, there's a trail of blood on the path!"

"Follow the trail!" said Prokip. "Perhaps you'll find her, if she's still alive after spending the night out in the open."

The men hastily followed the bloody trail, down through Mykytych's orchard. On and on they ran to the bottom of the yard, to the riverbank, where the trail disappeared. The men stopped.

"Well, and now where?" one fellow asked.

"Shoosh, can you hear that?" whispered another.

Everyone froze. Quietly, as if from somewhere underground, a heavy, painful groaning could be heard.

"Good Lord, it must be her! Right here in the gully! Come, we might still be able to rescue her!"

I'll never forget Scarecrow's frightening face, marred by pain, horror, and torment, after they led her out of that overgrown gully. Her hair was caked with mud, there were traces of blood on her hands, her clothes were wet and filthy.

"Spare my life! Spare my life!" she pleaded with those who were accompanying her.

"Come on, you fool, no one's going to do anything to you. Go back home."

"No, I can't go there! He'll kill me! Lord Almighty, he'll kill me!"

"Who are you talking about?"

"I know that he will. No, I won't go! I'd rather go to the grave."

"Why did you strangle the child?"

Scarecrow grew silent. They brought her into the village, but from fright and pain, she couldn't stand on her feet and collapsed onto the ground. The people didn't have the heart to keep questioning her. They sent for a commission from town, and Scarecrow was taken to Mykytych's house. A commission arrived shortly after, consisting of a judge and a gendarme. Scarecrow was put in irons; they took the dead child and went on their way.

Our people talked about her for a long time afterwards. She admitted in court that she had strangled the child, but adamantly refused to say who the father of the child was or why she had killed it. She had wanted to jump into the water herself after that, but was so afraid of water that she couldn't bring herself to do it. She was tried in Sambir. Mykytych, Anna, my dad and a few other people turned up as witnesses. She was given five years, but those who saw her at the trial, said that she was a mere shadow of herself and that she probably hadn't long to live. Little Mytro never came out to play with us again. Ever since the commission had taken away his aunt, who had probably been the only person who truly loved him, he became even more sullen, indolent and reclusive. He rarely left the house, and I hardly ever saw him. Sometimes, and only when the weather was fine, I would see Mytro through a hole in the fence – he would be sitting under the oak tree in Mykytych's yard. Spitting onto a stem, he would let a drop of dog's milk fall onto a mirror of water and, gazing transfixed at the iridescent sheen, he sang in a gloomy voice:

Ride out, ride out, oh rabbit,
On your steed of fiery light,
Your sons were cut down, slain,
Buried 'neath the bridge's strain.

In autumn I was sent off to school, and when I returned home for the Christmas festivities, Mytro was no longer among the living. He had died on the Feast of the Intercession.[4] After he was buried, Mykytych kicked his mother out of the house and she disappeared from our village: no one knew where she went, just as they hadn't known where she had come from. The ebb and flow of life and new impressions quickly erased from my memory those two strange mournful faces, the gloomy inhuman figures of two young people disfigured by fate and seemingly cursed by God.

. . . .

4   October 1.

But many years later, when fate threw me into the cesspit of society, and forced me to experience moments when a man involuntarily asks himself: 'What's the point of living? Is it just to keep suffering like this?' – only then did their martyred, long-forgotten faces resurface in my memory. Here they were, these pariahs of human society, the blameless guilty ones! They suffered their entire lives, without any rosy memories or inspiring hopes, reminiscent of those travellers who set out on a journey in heavy fog and made their way through the fog the whole way. And although they trudged past green meadows, flowering floodplains, fruitful orchards and bustling villages, passing myriads of beautiful and joyous things, yet they saw nothing apart from the grey fog and drizzle, the grey trunks of trees, and grey unfriendly faces. And if one could speak of any good fortune that they may have enjoyed, it might perhaps be the fact that they had never experienced anything better in their lives.

And as I recalled them, I felt a reproach in my heart for daring to compare my fate to theirs, and that bitter reproach was like the quinine powder given to malaria sufferers: it was bitter, but it averted any paroxysm.

1880

HRYTS AT SCHOOL

> Hryts, a wise lad in Kolomyja born,
> Studied rather well philosophy's form.
> *An old ditty*

I

The geese knew nothing about this. That same morning, when his father had decided to enrol Hryts in school, the geese were still unaware of his plans. And Hryts himself knew even less. He got up early as usual, had breakfast, shed some tears, scratched himself, grabbed a switch, and with a skip drove the geese out of the barn to pasture. The old white gander, as usual, hissed sharply at Hryts, stretching its small head with red eyes and a broad red beak toward him, and then, cackling something uninteresting to the geese, led them off. As usual the old grey goose refused to stay in line, and lumbered behind the small bridge and into a ditch, for which Hryts struck her with the switch and called her a 'scoundrel', as he was accustomed to calling anything that did not submit to his supreme authority on the common. It was obvious that neither the white gander nor the grey goose, nor any of the flock – there were twenty-five of them – knew anything about the imminent transfer of their lord and master to another, far less honourable station in life.

The news came suddenly and unexpectedly – his father, on his way home from the fields, told Hryts to come home with him and there handed him over to his mother to be washed, combed, and dressed, just as God commanded. And then, without uttering a word, his father took him by the hand and led the anxious lad back across the pasture. When the geese saw their master completely transformed, dressed in new boots, a new felt hat, and girded with a red belt, they let out a sudden and very loud cry of astonishment. With neck outstretched, the white gander ran up to Hryts, as if wanting to get a better look at him; the grey goose also stretched out her neck and was so impressed that for a long time she was unable to utter a sound, until finally she quickly blurted out: "Where-where-where-where?"

"Dumb goose," Hryts replied with scorn and turned away, as if to say: 'See, I'm in such high company now that I have no need respond to your goofy questions.' But maybe he did not answer because he himself did not know where he was headed.

They walked up through the village. His father said nothing, neither did Hryts. Until they reached a rambling old house with a thatched roof and a chimney. Many boys of Hryts' age or older, were making their way toward this house. A gentleman dressed in a waistcoat was walking about the garden behind the house.

"Hryts!" said his father.

"Hah?" replied Hryts.

"See this house?"

"Yeah."

"Remember, that's the school."

"Aha," said Hryts.

"You'll be coming here to learn."

"Aha," said Hryts.

"Behave, don't fool around, and listen to the teacher. I'm off to enrol you."

"Aha," said Hryts, hardly understanding what his father was saying.

"Go with these boys. Lads, take him with you!"

"Come along!" said the boys and took Hryts with them. Meanwhile his father ventured into the garden to speak to the teacher.

II

They entered the porch, where it was pitch dark and stank of last year's rotten cabbage.

"See, there?" said one of the boys to Hryts, pointing to a dark corner.

"Yeah," said Hryts, trembling, though he saw nothing at all.

"There's a pit there," said the boy.

"A pit!" repeated Hryts.

"If you misbehave, the teacher will place you in that pit and you'll have to stay there all night long."

"I don't wanna!" exclaimed Hryts.

Meanwhile, one of the boys whispered something to another, both laughed, and then the first one found the door to the school in the darkness, and said to Hryts:

"Knock on the door! Quickly!"

"What for?" asked Hryts.

"You have to! That's what boys do here, when they come for the first time."

There was a buzz coming from inside the school, as if from a beehive, but when Hryts beat his fists against the door, it grew quiet. The boys opened the door and pushed Hryts inside. At that moment, birch switches struck him on the shoulders. Hryts took fright and screamed.

"Shut up, stupid!" the boys who had caned him yelled.

"Ay-ay-ay-ay!" screamed Hryts. The boys were afraid the teacher might hear him and tried to quieten him down.

"Shut up, stupid, that's what we do here! Anyone who raps on the door gets rapped on the shoulders. Didn't you know that?"

"No, I di-idn't!" sobbed Hryts.

"Why not?"

"'Cause it's my first time in school."

"First time! Ah!" the boys exclaimed, as if they were astonished how one could be at school for the first time.

"Oh, we need to give you a treat then!" said one boy. Rushing over to the blackboard, he fished out a piece of chalk from a box and handed it to Hryts.

"Here, stupid, eat it, but hurry!"

Everyone was silent and expectantly looked at Hryts, who was turning the chalk about in his hands, and then slowly popped it into his mouth.

"Eat it, stupid, but hurry!" the boys encouraged him, barely able to control their laughter.

Hryts began to munch on the chalk and swallowed it with difficulty. There was so much raucous laughter in the school that the windows rattled.

"Why are you all laughing?" asked Hryts in astonishment.

"It's nothing. Do you want some more?"

"No, thanks. What was it?"

"Don't you know? Stupid fool! It was jerusalem, really good stuff."

"Oh, it's not vely nice," said Hryts.

"Because you haven't developed a taste for it yet. It's a nice thing to eat when you come to school for the first time."

At that moment the teacher walked in. Like startled sparrows, the boys scattered to their desks. Only Hryts remained standing, with tears in his eyes and his lips white from the chalk. The teacher approached him sternly.

"What's your name, boy?" he yelled.

"Hlyts."

"Which Hryts? Aha, you're the new boy. Why aren't you sitting at your desk? Why are you crying? What's all that white on your lips? Hah?"

"I had some jelusalem."

"What? What's jerusalem?" the teacher asked.

The boys were almost choking, holding back their laughter.

"The boys gave it to me."

"Which boys?"

Hryts looked about the room but couldn't recognize anyone.

"Well, well! Go sit down and study well, and don't eat the jerusalem anymore, or you'll be punished!"

III

The lesson began. The teacher talked about something, showed the pupils wooden tablets on which were painted various hooks and posts; when the teacher pointed to a new tablet, the boys would yell something, but Hryts couldn't understand a thing of what was going on. He even took no notice of the teacher, for he found the boys around him very funny. One was picking his nose, another kept trying to poke a small stem into Hryts' ear from behind, while a third worked very diligently for a long time, pulling patches, threads, and fringes from his old caftan; a whole pile of these already lay on the seat of the desk in front of him, yet he continued to pluck and pull with all his might.

"Why are you pulling 'em out?" asked Hryts.

"To eat with my beetloot soup," the boy replied, and Hryts thought for a long time if the boy might be pulling his leg.

"Hryts-boy, you're not paying attention there!" yelled the teacher and grabbed Hryts by the ear so painfully that tears welled in his eyes, and he became so badly shaken that for a long time he was unable to regain his senses, let alone pay attention. When he finally recovered, the boys were already reading syllables on movable tablets, which the teacher kept arranging and rearranging. In sing-song voices they tirelessly repeated: '*a-ba-ba-ga-la-ma-ga*'.[5] For some reason Hryts really enjoyed this and he began to shout in his shrill voice, trying to outdo the other boys: '*a baba galamaga!*' The teacher was ready to acknowledge that he was a very attentive and talented boy and to make sure of this, he rearranged the letters, unexpectedly presenting the letters '*baba*' before the pupils. But Hryts, whose eyes were glued to the teacher, cried out in a thin melodic voice: '*galamaga!*' The class burst out laughing, together with the teacher. Hryts was astonished, and turning to the boy next to him said out loud: "Why aren't you saying *galamaga?*" The poor fellow only realised that something was amiss after he felt the sting of the teacher's cane on his shoulder.

"Well, what did they teach you there at school?" asked his father, when Hryts returned home in the afternoon.

"We learnt to lead '*a baba galamaga*'," replied Hryts.

"And did you know how to?" the father asked, without delving into what the strange lesson was about.

"'Course I did," answered Hryts.

"Keep it up, then!" his father offered words of encouragement. "After you finish learning here in the village, I'll send you to a bigger school in town, and then you can study to become a priest. Eh, woman, let's have something to eat."

"Yeah," replied Hryts.

IV

A year had passed since that important day. The father's high hopes for a bright future for Hryts had long since dissipated. The teacher told him that Hryts was simply 'dumb as they come' and that it would be better to take him home and have

....

[5]   *a-ba-ba-ga-la-ma-ga* – Ukrainian phrase to teach children to read; *a baba galamaga* literally means the "old woman is a babbler".

him tend geese once more. Indeed, after a year of schooling, Hryts returned home just as wise as he had been the year before. True, he had thoroughly memorized the miraculous phrase '*a baba galamaga*', and even in his sleep it would escape his lips. It seemed to symbolize the threshold of all knowledge, one which he was destined never to cross. Apart from learning this phrase, Hryts made no other progress in class. The letters of the alphabet seemed a jumble before his eyes, and he could never recognize them by sight, unable to differentiate 'Ш' from 'Т' and 'Л' from 'М'. As for reading – there was no point even discussing the topic. It was unclear whether this was due to his lack of understanding or the teacher's poor methods of instruction. The only certainty was that, apart from Hryts, there were eighteen other 'dumb as they come' fellows in his class of thirty, all of whom nurtured high hopes during the school year of being free of the daily caning, belts behind the ears, shoves, and slaps and being able to appear in all their glory and dignity back on the village common.

Hryts thought about this more often and more intensely than most of the other boys. His cursed primer, which he had torn and practically shredded over the course of his year-long struggle with his studies, that darned '*a baba galamaga*', and the cursed teacher's prompts and encouragements to learn had left him exhausted, so much so that he had grown thin and pale and always went about like a somnambulist. In the end, God had mercy on him and sent along the month of July, and his father took pity and said one morning:

"Hryts!"

"Hah?" said Hryts.

"You won't be attending school anymore."

"Yeah," said Hryts.

"Take off your boots, your hat, and belt, put them away to wear on Sundays, and tie a bast rope round your waist, put on your old sheepskin hat, and go tend to the geese."

"Hah!" said Hryts overjoyed.

V

The geese, who were obviously stupid, had no inkling of the joyful change that was about to take place.

Throughout the year, while Hryts had gone to school, they were looked after by the neighbour's small boy, Luchka, who usually just dug holes, made mud pies, and played in dust on the common. He didn't care one bit about the geese, and they wandered freely. Several times they strayed into cultivated fields, and in exchange for the damage they caused, they endured much cursing and even beatings. Additionally, calamity struck the flock several times that year. Five young ganders and ten geese were sold off by the mistress in town and the others found it hard to part with them. The old ash-coloured goose had been killed with a stick by the neighbour while it was in his field. He then heartlessly tied the lifeless body by the leg to a stick, dragged it across the entire common, and then tossed it into its owner's livestock pen. Moreover, one young, promising gander, the pride and hope of the flock, was killed by a hawk when it strayed away from its kin. Despite all these harsh and irreplaceable losses, this year's flock was larger, now totalling over forty members, thanks to the efforts of the white gander, the grey goose, and her two or three young daughters.

When Hryts once more appeared among them with a switch, the symbol of his viceregal authority, all eyes were immediately peeled to him and only a single muted hiss of surprise could be heard. But neither the white gander nor the grey goose had yet forgotten their former good shepherd and quickly accepted him back. With loud cries of joy and a flapping of wings, they rushed toward him.

"Where-where-where-where?" cackled the grey goose.

"I was in school," Hryts replied proudly.

"Oh! Oh! Oh!" the white gander was amazed.

"You don't believe me, stupid?" Hryts yelled at him and struck him with the switch.

"Wo-wo-wo? Wo-wo-wo?" squawked the other geese, gathering around him.

"You mean, what did I learn there?" Hryts reformulated their question.

"Wo-wo-wo?" the geese squawked.

"*A baba galamaga!*" replied Hryts. Again, there was a hiss of amazement, as if none of these forty goose heads could understand such profound wisdom. Hryts stood there, proud and unassailable. Finally, the white gander regained his composure:

"*A baba galamaga! A baba galamaga!*" he shrieked in his resounding, metallic voice, as he straightened and lifted his head high, while flapping his wings. Then, turning to Hryts, he added, as if to further embarrass him:

"There-see, there-see!"

Hryts was crestfallen and embarrassed! In an instant, the gander had grasped and repeated the wisdom that had cost him a year of schooling! 'Why hadn't they sent the gander to school instead?' Hryts thought to himself as he drove the geese to the common.

1883

THE FOREST NYMPHS

(A Summery Fairy Tale)

"Handzia, dear Handzia! Stay at home, my child, I'm going to the forest to pick mushrooms!"

"Take me with you, mummy!" begged little Handzia, puckering her thin lips. "I'm scared to be on my own at home!"

"Come on there, now! You're practically an old maid and still scared to be alone at home on such a bright day! You should be ashamed! How can I take you with me? Will you know how to walk through the forest?"

"Oh, I'll manage, mummy, don't worry," said Handzia, cheering up.

"No, no, you'd better stay at home! There are forest nymphs there, you know, with green hair! They spirit little girls away."

"Don't worry, I'm not afraid of forest nymphs, mummy! I even dreamt of one, and we played so nicely together! And she kept laughing – really, mummy, do nymphs laugh that loud? And she said to me: 'Handzia, peekaboo!' And I replied: 'Here I am!' And she said: 'Come, Handzia, into the forest, we have such fun swings there, woo-hoo! woo-hoo!' Take me, mummy, take me, maybe we'll see her there! I would so love to go on a swing with her…!"

"Oh, come on, you foolish child! Stop talking nonsense! Stay at home, I'll lock the door and no one will come inside. Don't worry, I'll be back soon!"

The mother left. The iron key clattered in the door, sliding the wooden bolt in place. Handzia burst into tears inside the house.

"Why didn't mummy want to take me? I might have seen the forest nymph there! And it's so lovely in the forest, so quiet, green, and warm…! Oh, that mummy of mine! Locking me up in the house… and going off into the forest on her own, all alone…"

The house in which Handzia lived with her mother was on the very outskirts of the village. On three sides, not too far off, stood a dense, dark, perpetually mournful forest, occasionally rustling and stirring up some mysterious song. Such a strange song it was too. Some of its notes ached in one's heart like a recent, barely healed wound; others dragged one's imagination into a dark, fragrant oblivion, into a boundless, opaque expanse; while others stirred the deepest and strongest strings of the human soul, awakening a desire to live, to be full of energy, with a zeal for tireless work and an expectation of a bright future; while still others filled one's heart with an inexorable deep sorrow.

Handzia was born amid the melody of that song; from the time she could distinguish tones, she heard this song most often, and it was no wonder that the song enchanted her entire nervous being. In dreams and while awake, she listened to it on winter evenings as a storm raged and the forest groaned like thousands of wounded soldiers on a battlefield; she admired it in spring when a warm breeze barely stirred the still damp, leafless branches, already filled with fresh sap; she listened to it in the scorching noonday heat of summer, when no wind could be heard, yet there was a secret whisper among the treetops, resembling sighs or the sleepy babble of drowsy trees in the sunshine. Her childish imagination wandered day and night through the forest, finding echoes of her own tiny joys and sufferings in its voices, which for her were so important and all-encompassing. It was no wonder then that this forest song had bewitched all of Handzia's delicate, tender being. In dreams and while awake, her thoughts were always about the forest and its secrets. The best, most pleasant memories of her short life (she was only five years old) were all inseparably associated with the forest.

Ah, how avidly and with what great delight she listened to tales about forest spirits, those partly-frightening, partly-alluring creations of folk imagination, and she especially liked the ones about the forest nymphs with faces white as birch bark and long green braided hair! She could not understand why other children were afraid of nymphs. After all, they were so beautiful, so kind to good children, happily playing with them among the greenery of the forest, swinging on long, thin birch branches (ah, Handzia loved to swing!) while they laughed so merrily and sang so wonderfully! Their voices were like silver bells, often tinkling in Handzia's dreams, and she rejoiced listening to them from afar… But she had never actually seen a forest nymph. What a pity that her mother hadn't taken her to the forest today! She would have certainly spied a nymph, for sure! After all, it was no coincidence that nymphs had been appearing in her dreams these past few nights, singing, laughing out loud, swinging on branches, and always calling to her to join them in the forest…

"Peekaboo, Handzia! Peekaboo, Handzia!" they called, luring her with their little white hands. "Come join us in the forest! It's so warm here, so joyful, so lovely! Just look at our braids! We'll braid your hair like this too! Oh, look at our swings! You can swing on one too! Woo-hoo! Woo-hoo! Come, come…!" Handzia cried. She looked around the house. How miserable, damp, and gloomy it was in here! In the corners stood scary figures. She remembered the ditty people recited to calm her down when she cried:

Crawls a critter,
From behind the litter!

She trembled and anxiously looked at the dark, rough, oddly carved wooden hook fixed to the ceiling. In her imagination, the hook was 'the critter'. Lying in bed, she had often stared at it for long periods, always nursing a secret fear. She associated all the terrifying stories her grandmother had told her with this hook. And now, in silent anxiety, she began to stare at the critter, and the longer she looked at it, the more it seemed to her that the critter was in fact alive. It was a nasty, wrinkled, very old woman with an enormous sack, into which she shoved small children and whisked them away. There, she saw her straightening up, stamping her wooden legs, crawling ever so closer toward Handzia! Handzia screamed in fright, and jumped from the clay oven niche onto the ground; from there she crawled up onto the bench and reached the window. There was more light here. She looked back into the room – nothing; timidly she glanced up at the critter: it wasn't moving, but it was still dark, hunch-backed, and just as frightening as before. But outside, oh, outside it was so bright and warm! From the window, she could see the forest – oh, surely, the nymphs were swinging there, waiting for her…! No, she couldn't bear to stay in this dreadful house, with that terrifying critter. She decided to climb out the window and run off into the forest to play with the nymphs, just for a short while, until her mother returned. And what if she didn't come back in time? What if her mother returned before her? She would be punished then. No, her mother wouldn't come back before her, because Handzia would be right here at the edge of the forest, watching out for her mother as she was returning from the forest with mushrooms.

Handzia crawled out of the house through the window. A light summer breeze caressed her warmly, scattering her short, flaxen hair, and brought a livelier colour to her pale face, though her eyes continued to burn feverishly. She ran through the yard to the reed fence. She felt so light and strong amid the warmth, in the fresh air scented with the fragrance of flowering fields. The gate to the forest was slightly jammed; Handzia could never have opened it – where would her tiny, weak hands have gotten the strength for such a task! Like a mouse, she squeezed through the narrow gap, which only a kitten might have slipped through comfortably, and with a joyous smile on her lips and trembling all over, she found her-self on the path, facing the field. The wind blew harder in her face. Handzia was dressed only in a long shirt reaching down to her ankles, with a red woollen belt tied around her waist. At first, she seemed to feel cold. But no, it was just her imagi-nation, for look how warm the sun was, how could it be cold?

A narrow path stretched across the field to the forest. Handzia knew this path well – it was her favourite, and she loved to run along it because it offered a clear view of the for-est! There it was, large, gloomy, and noisy! Handzia caught her breath, so overcome with joy at the thought that she had just a little bit more to run, before she would be in the forest, alone!

She was running, but for some reason she couldn't move as quickly as before. Ears of rye swayed solemnly as she ran past them, brushing her hand against the stalks. How she loved that rye, those cornflowers and poppies that sparkled like blue and pink stars here and there among the forest of golden stalks!

"Forest nymphs! Forest nymphs!" Handzia shouted with joy, as she ran down the path. "I'm coming, I'm running fast! We'll be able to play."

The eternal forest song grew louder and clearer. Handzia picked it up with her ear, revelling in it. Amid the rustle and murmur of the leaves, she distinctly heard something akin to fish splashing about in clear, crystalline water: it was the laughter and joyous cries of the nymphs. She could even hear them calling out to her:

"Peekaboo, Handzia! Peekaboo, Handzia!"

They must be close now! Just beyond the ditch there! Those darling forest nymphs, they had probably come here to fetch her! And they weren't scared either! Because if people ever caught them, they would surely stuff them into a sack! And hand them over to that nasty critter! But no, she wouldn't let anyone take the forest nymphs, they were so good, so nice!

"Forest nymphs! Forest nymphs!" Handzia yelled at the top of her voice. "I'm here, I'll join you in a moment, it's just a teeny bit further, wait!"

Ah, at last she was in the forest! How quiet, vast, and solemn it was! The birches basked in the sun, their white bark shining from afar. Their long branches, like green braids, hung down and swayed in the breeze. The nymphs must be here somewhere. Ah, surely, they were hiding from Handzia, but she would call them, and they would soon appear from their hiding spots, laughing loudly…

"Forest nymphs! Forest nymphs! I'm here, here, here! Come out, let's play!"

There! One had let out a laugh, but it was so far away! Ah, there was a second and a third one! Handzia knew they couldn't stay hidden for long. Oh, how wonderfully resounding their laughter was! How sweetly they called Handzia to join them! It was dark here, but it was so bright up ahead, where there were lots of herbs, nice and fragrant ones! And swings that were oh so light. Oh, Handzia would run off after them, because it wasn't that far!

* * *

It was getting dark. Handzia's mother had long since returned with the mushrooms and had spent the rest of the day walking about the village, asking if anyone had seen Handzia. But no one had. As night drew closer, the poor mother became increasingly distraught, frantically running from house to house, but there was no trace of Handzia anywhere.

"Ah, to my misfortune she turned out such a weak and meagre child, and now for the past month, whenever she's spoken, it's as if she had a fever! Those old grannies filled her head with tales of nymphs, and now she can't stop talking about them, even in her dreams! My poor misfortune! God only knows where she's gone now. She's never been one to go off on her own, I always keep watch over her and never let her out of my sight…"

But Handzia was nowhere to be found. In the evening, her mother tearfully convinced several people to go into the forest to search for her. But the night passed, and they found nothing. Another day passed and still Handzia had not appeared. It was impossible to describe the poor mother's suffering and where she raced about that day in the search for her daughter. Then, on the third day, while chopping wood in the forest, some people came across a small girl under a birch tree. She was lying there, tightly hugging the tree's trunk with her small, stiff arms. Her open eyes no longer sparkled, but a blissful smile was fixed on her lips; clearly, Handzia had just stopped playing with a forest nymph.

Lviv, 1883

THE DUEL

(A Winter's Tale)

> *Zwei Seelen leben,*
> *ach, in meiner Brust.*[6]
> J. W. Goethe

The battle was in full swing. Cannons roared like fierce beasts, spewing heavy, lethal spheres from their maws. Rockets exploded high beneath the clouds, scattering a hail of bloody sparks. The entire expansive basin groaned, screamed, thundered, and blazed as if it were hell itself. The sun had set, and the twilight, pressing down on the earth, made the entire image of destruction, slaughter, and death seem even more horrifying.

In that fiery, hellish maelstrom, darkness was interspersed with sharp tongues of fire and death appeared in every possible form. A light mist rose from surging streams of human blood and thousands of strong, healthy, and ruddy-cheeked young men stepped over the corpses of comrades as they pressed forward toward inevitable doom. In this abyss of destruction and horror, the human spirit froze, thoughts were lost like needles in a haystack – a man became a soulless machine, a living tree, which knew nothing and understood nothing, merely moving where it was told to go, doing what

....

[6] German: "Two souls dwell, ah, within my breast." From "Faust".

it was ordered to do, and falling to the ground where it encountered inevitable death.

I too had been in such a mindless state for some half an hour. From the moment that our captain had yelled: "Forward march!" and bullets whistled all around us, grenades crackled, the cries of the wounded filled the air and the field was covered in smoke from explosions, from that moment on I lost the ability to perceive anything, becoming a mere machine. I knew only one thing: our goal was the burning houses of a nearby village, from which a dense hail of enemy bullets rained down upon us.

No, I can't say that I was aware of this! Only the fire, slashing through the thick twilight and even thicker clouds of smoke with thousands of fiery swords, drew me and my comrades toward it, like the flame of a lamp attracting moths at night.

We walked silently, trampled on corpses silently, waded through blood silently. Only occasionally, when someone was struck by a bullet and fell to the ground, did a heart-wrenching scream burst from their chest. But only for a moment! They immediately grew quiet under the feet of advancing ranks of men, which, like an unseeing avalanche, rolled over them.

"Charge at a run! Forward!" the captain's voice thundered behind us.

That voice, hoarse but sharp, seemed to grab us in its mighty claws and threw us forward, like a heavy stone. What happened to me a few minutes later I cannot say. In my mind I could see flashes of fire, the glint of bayonets quenched with hot blood, the rumble of shots, cries, curses, the groans of the dying, and deep, terrible open wounds in the contorted writhing bodies of men, illuminated by explosions of flame. I regained my senses only in the middle of the village, amid a sea of sparks surrounding black pillars of smoke, in an open space, as if in some forest clearing.

I was alone. I stopped and exhaled deeply, looking around me, and exhaled once more. After my horrendous experience, I still could not come to my senses, had no idea where I was or what was happening to me, or how I had come to be here.

After a while, my consciousness began to return. The first sensation to remind me that I was alive was a dull, burning pain in my chest. What was it? Was I wounded? No, but the pain, nevertheless, failed to go away. It took a long time before I realised that it was my heart that was aching. But why was it aching? Was I to blame for this terrible ruination? Could I have stopped it? Could I have resisted the almighty force that pushed me along with thousands of others into this hellish valley to endure this bloodbath? Could I, with some magic spell, have healed all wounds, stopped all blood flowing, extinguished all fires…?

Around me everything thundered, roared and bubbled away as if in a cauldron. The battle continued, but it had rolled along like a fiery avalanche in another direction. Around me, in a wide enclosed circle, pillars of smoke were swirling, the burning wood of houses crackled and a fierce fire was roaring. I stood encircled by flames with nowhere to go. The hot air flowed like molten lead into my chest, taking my breath away, blood pounded in my veins like sledgehammers, a terrible thirst was choking my throat, the scene before my eyes began to sway and spin…

Suddenly, a wave of cold, revitalizing air entered my chest, and as I straightened up, I saw myself standing before me. Mortal anxiety pierced me to the bone, my blood froze in my veins and for a moment my heart seemed to stop beating. As if enchanted, my eyes were peeled to the strange apparition standing silently before me, its face reflecting the flames.

"Who are you?" I barely managed to whisper, struggling to breath.

"I'm Myron," the apparition replied boldly and firmly.

Yes, it was indeed Myron! It was indeed me, just as I once had been, in the best, most sacred days of my youth! Standing proud and tall, my own image stood before me in shining armour, eyeing me with the stern, menacing eye of a judge standing before a hardened and an incorrigible criminal. My chest tightened from that gaze; my whole being trembled like an autumn leaf in the wind. Oh, I felt that I would not get away scot-free from this harsh trial.

But a moment later, when I had managed to organize my troubled thoughts, a strong feeling of love toward myself resonated in my chest and allayed my anxiety.

"How can you say that you are Myron," I said, not taking my eyes off him, "when it is I who am Myron!"

"You?" my double replied curtly, with an expression of undeniable contempt. That one short word from this strange apparition was like a hammer blow to the head. I felt a dull, burning sensation in my chest once more and for a long time could not find enough air to speak.

"If you are Myron," I finally spoke up, "then who am I? Surely both of us can't be the same person."

"Indeed, we cannot!" he confirmed with a disdainful smile.

"Then who am I, if you are Myron?"

"You? Who are you? A ghost formed of wind, a figment of my overheated imagination, nothing more!"

"I… am nothing?" I cried out, summoning the last of my strength. "A mere ghost? An apparition? But I have a body, and bones, and blood. I can move and walk independently of you! I was here before you!"

The strange apparition frowned menacingly.

"You pitiful phantom!" he declared. "You lying apparition, the fruit of twilight and anxiety, do you even dare argue with me? Dare to raise your deceitful hands against me, a creation of true, undeniable reality? Tell me, tell me please, how will you prove that you are Myron?"

I stood as if thunderstruck, my thoughts petrified – I could think of no proof.

"Well, tell me, what are you doing with your life, what are you grappling with? Where are you headed? What do you hope to achieve? What are you fighting for?"

"I am defending law and order, I am creating order, I want there to be order, I am fighting for law and order," I mumbled, but felt my strength ebbing, as if someone had torn half of my heart from my chest and sucked half the life from my body.

"You pitiful apparition!" thundered the grave words of my frightening judge. "And you say that you are Myron? Then remember this – Myron considers that this law and order of yours is the domination of turpitude over virtue, and your deeds are a service to tyranny, your struggle is a bloody crime! Disappear! You are not Myron!"

"But how can you prove that you are Myron?" I whispered.

"When I prove that you are an apparition, a ghost, a nothing."

I formed my lips into a derisive smile.

"You still don't believe me! Let me convince you. Come on, I challenge you to a duel! If you are the real Myron, and I am the ghost, then I will vanish when you shoot me. But if I am the real Myron, you will disappear when I shoot you! After all, a ghost surely cannot destroy reality. Shoot then…!"

I took aim, the shot sounded, and my frightening opponent burst out laughing.

"You pitiful apparition!" he said. "May my bullet make you disappear!"

His rifle flashed and, as if struck by thunder, I tumbled among the corpses.

Lviv, 1883

MY CRIME

No, I can't stand this any longer! I simply can't! I need to publicly confess my sin, even though I already know that it won't ease the pain in my soul. After all, reparation here is impossible, for what reparation can compensate for innocently spilt blood, and make up for a life cut short?

It terrifies me when the whole unfortunate event clearly surfaces in my memory with all its painful details. Many years have passed since then, definitely more than thirty. Back then, I was just a small country boy, running through the forests and fields of my native village, playing games.

Spring had arrived, one of those first nice warm days. After being confined in stuffy, cramped houses throughout the long winter, we village children could run about freely. We rushed out to the meadow, which remained bare and grey after losing its winter cover. Only here and there was fresh greenery poking through the earth: thin sharp needles of reeds, horseradish and burdock leaves still tightly rolled into sharp spears down by the stream. Only in the nearby woods had everything turned white from the wild garlic, which was actually finishing flowering, and the white and pale blue wood anemones.

Above us rose the dark blue vault of the sky, the sun smiled benevolently upon us, and large snowcaps sparkled on the distant peaks of the Carpathian Mountains, looking like dazzling diamond crowns. But their beauty didn't move us too much, for we continually felt the cold winter wind blowing down from them. The river reflected this too; in the morning it had been clear and splashed quietly, as if it were summer, but now it churned angrily within its narrow banks and pushed its yellowish, muddy, turbulent waters downstream – these were those same dazzling diamonds that had been melted by the spring sunshine.

But all that could not spoil our spring cheerfulness. We wandered about, leapt and jumped, dashed about, and revisited all our familiar haunts: the old mighty oak at the edge of the forest, whose strong branches we climbed in the summer, chasing squirrels; the tall leaning birch tree with its plaintively hanging thin branches, which we used far too often as a swing, much to the great annoyance of the forest ranger; the quiet springs in the forest undergrowth, where we hid behind the thick maples and elms, watching foxes, badgers and wild boars come to drink at sunset; and finally the deep, crystal-clear ponds, where every Sunday we waited with hooks to catch pike, and when the sun became too intense, refreshed ourselves with shouts and laughter in the pristine cold water.

Every place around those mill ponds, our favourite playground, we inspected and scrutinized quite thoroughly. It was the remains of a large ancient reservoir. Across the valley, from one side of the forest to the other, there had been an enormous dam wall, which had been levelled and long-since ploughed, and now looked more like a long flat mound, broken in three places: by the stream, which wound beside the forest and angrily gurgled and tore at the high, steep banks, and twice more by the aforementioned mill ponds, solitary remnants of the former noble lake. These mill ponds were not too wide, only six feet or so deep, and were shaded here and there by alders, willows, and a tangle of osier. In the summer, dense fragrant grass and flowers of white clover hung from the banks right over the water's surface. Now, of course, the banks were quite bare and sad looking, and all was quiet in the water, which in summer frequently came alive with the splashes of pike and red-eyed roaches that usually swam about in schools led by one of the larger fish. Yet, at each step we still curiously looked into the water under every log, every wilted burdock leaf, and every stump, to see if any of our familiar pike had suffocated under the ice or whether miss otter had been kind enough to pay our fish a visit.

"Dog! Dog!" suddenly hissed two or three boys who had been walking in front of me. They bent down to the ground and crawled quietly forward, trying to surround a stump.

"What's wrong? What is it?" I asked, involuntarily whispering as well.

"It's a bird! Can't you see it?"

"Where? Where is it?"

"In the undergrowth there. It's run off. We've never seen one like it. It can't fly, probably only runs."

While the boys were still gathering around, I went straight into the middle of the thicket, carefully moved aside the mass of branches, and spied a small bird hiding in last year's dry grass. I don't know if it was weak or frightened, but when it saw me looming overhead, it didn't fly away or run, and in a flash I had it in my hands. All the boys gathered around to see my captive.

"Ah, it's so beautiful!"

"I've never seen a bird like that."

"Just look at its eyes!"

"And its feathers!"

It was a small marsh bird which appeared very rarely here in the foothills. Its feathers were an ashen grey with a slight pearly glint, its beak was thin and dark green and it had similar long thin legs. It sat quietly in my hand, without scratching, wriggling or pecking, as most wild birds usually did when caught by hand.

"What are you going to do with it?" some of the boys asked, looking enviously at the beautiful prey in my hand.

"I'll take it home."

"Will you cook it?"

"Who knows. I'll feed it."

"How will you know what to give it?"

"I'll see. If it won't eat bread, then I'll try flies, and if not that, I'll try giving it worms, and if it won't eat worms, then snails, or seed, or millet. I'll find something that it likes."

I brought the pretty little bird home and instead of placing it in a cage, put it in the middle of a double window, where it had more room to run around and fly, more light, and more air. The little bird did not try to fly or perch, but just ran alongside the glass panes, here and there tapping its thin beak against the glass, and from time to time it seemed to me that it looked longingly at the free world outside. Sometimes it would stop, tilt its head to one side and then raise it in a sudden bird-like motion, or twist it sideways, so that one eye seemed to wander over the branches of a nearby apple tree, and then it would shake its head sadly and in resignation, as if it wanted to say:

'Oh, it's so beautiful and warm outside, but my spring is gone! I'm in captivity!'

My heart missed a beat as I watched this little bird for a few moments. I felt a deep sadness.

'Let it go! Why keep it here?' a voice whispered inside me.

"But it's so beautiful! And I caught it!" I answered myself obstinately. "Maybe it'll get used to it. If only I knew what to feed it!"

I indeed had quite a bit of trouble finding something to feed the bird. I set out a few crumbs of bread, several dozen millet seeds, and a few dozen flies, each type of food separately in a clean shell, and set out a crock filled with water, then left to give it some peace. When I returned home in the evening and checked on my bird, I saw that it had not touched any of the food; it just sat in a corner, stretching its thin neck out and, without blinking, stared outside through the window at the purple blaze of the sun setting behind the snowcapped Ridge Mountain. From time to time, it nodded its head so mournfully and hopelessly, that I could no longer bear to look at it.

'Maybe it's a nocturnal bird,' I thought, 'and will start eating at night.'

The thought calmed me down somewhat, and I slept soundly without even thinking about the bird. Early in the morning, before sunrise, I ran back to the room and looked through the window. The bird was still sitting in the same spot where I had seen it the day before, still with an outstretched neck, and still, without blinking, continued to stare out of the window at the wide, free world beyond the glass panes, from time to time nodding its head. It had not touched the food at all.

'Let it go! Let it go!' yelled a voice inside me. 'Why torment the poor thing? It will die of hunger.'

'No,' replied a different, stubborn voice inside me, 'I need to find what to feed it! I'll bring it snails, and worms, and frog eggs.'

I don't know how I got it into my head that it could eat frog eggs. Enough. I dashed off to the common, collected all sorts of little snails, dug up some worms and fished out a good handful of frog eggs from the water, bringing all this to my little captive. But it didn't even pay any attention when I laid out all these goodies before it, showing neither fear nor the slightest bit of curiosity, nor even any appetite for the treats. It seemed that all it cared about was the sun, the warmth, and spring outside in the wide, free world.

That day I had things to attend to, so I left and returned in the evening. I hastened to look in on the bird. It was running about inside, tapping on the glass from time to time, and still hadn't touched any of the food.

'How strange!' I thought and wanted to set the bird free right away. But it occurred to me that it was probably weakened and unable to fly, and if I released it here in the yard this evening, it would be easy prey for our cat. I decided it would be better for the bird to spend the night with me, and early the next morning I would take it back to where I had found it and let it go.

Rising early the next morning, I ran to my captive. The bird still hadn't touched any food and sat, weakened and tired in a corner, its eyes still peering outside at freedom. It calmly let me pick it up and looked at me with those same indescribably sad eyes with which it had gazed outside at the sun and the apple tree branches. At one point, it even nodded his head, as if to say:

'Yes, yes, I know where you're taking me. I've known for a long time it would end this way.'

I took the bird out into the yard. It remained calmly in my hand and didn't try to break free. I could feel the softness of its feathers and the warmth of its body.

'Its meat must be tasty!' a thought suddenly flashed through my mind. 'What if I were to kill it and hand it over to be roasted?'

'Let it go! Let it go!' an angelic voice whispered inside me. 'Can't you see how small it is. There's nothing there to roast!'

'But it's a shame to let it go! After all, I caught it!' a childish stubbornness rebelled inside me.

'Let it go! Let it go!' a voice implored very-very softly from the deepest depths of my soul.

The bird sat quietly in my hand, resigned to its fate. I opened my palm – it did not fly away. Something loathsome and triumphantly malicious was stirring within me. 'See! It doesn't want to go free! You gave it the chance to escape, and it didn't!'

'But it's weak and hungry,' a voice pleaded very softly from the deepest depths of my soul.

'Ah, nonsense!' exclaimed my childish stubbornness, and in the next moment I twisted the little bird's head.

It twitched once or twice with its slender legs, two or three drops of blood appeared on its tiny neck, and the nice little bird was no more. A cold lifeless corpse lay in the palm of my hand.

Suddenly, all my stubbornness, my obstinacy, my pride became shattered and dispersed. I distinctly felt that I had done something senseless and repulsive, that I had committed a heartless murder, heaping guilt upon myself that I could neither atone for nor pray away. After all, I had pointlessly destroyed such a beautiful innocent life! Here, in God's free world, in full sight of this clear, warm, spring sun, I had executed a cruel, unmotivated death sentence. Now I clearly and distinctly felt that this murder was completely pointless. After all, I couldn't even pluck its feathers or eat its poor little corpse. I didn't have the strength to look at it again. I released the lifeless bird from my hand, and embarrassed, troubled, oppressed, and confused, I ran away from it, far, far away, so that I would never see it again, trying to erase even the memory of it from my soul.

I very much wanted to cry, but could not; something seemed to have constricted my soul, and I could not pour out my pain in tears. The beautiful small bird lay in my soul, and I carried it with me, always feeling as if it was looking at me with those indescribably sad eyes, looking in silent resignation, nodding its head, whispering ever so quietly:

'Ah, my spring is gone, I knew all along that my captivity would also be my end!'

Of course, in the soft, vulnerable heart of a child, such concerns do not last long. After two or three days, I had forgotten all about the bird and its tragic fate. It seemed I had forgotten it forever. The memory of my crime settled into a dark corner of my soul, and gradually it became buried under other feelings and memories.

But it had not perished. Twenty years passed, and when the first great blow of misfortune struck me, when I, a young man with a heart full of longing, a desire to live and love, sat wilted and withered in prison in the midst of a beautiful summer, feeling how all my hopes had been shattered, mercilessly beaten, trampled, senselessly mutilated, and everything that I considered to be the most precious treasure of my soul now destroyed – then in the midst of an anxious, sleepless night, that small, lovely bird appeared before me, and its sad little eyes filled with silent resignation pierced deep into my heart, whispering to me with its slow movements those insanely frightening words:

'Ah, my spring is gone! I am in captivity! I know, I know how this will all end!'

And since that day, I cannot rid myself of this memory. It poisons every moment of happiness, shatters my strength and courage when misfortune strikes. It gnaws at my conscience, and it seems to me that everything bad, aimless, cruel, and evil that I have ever done in my life has crystallized into the concrete image of this small, innocently murdered bird, to torment me even more persistently. On quiet nights, I am awakened by the quiet tapping of the bird's beak against at the windowpane. And in moments of anxiety and despair, when fierce pain clutches at my heart and threatens to break my strength of will at any moment, it seems to me that I am that small, weak, hungry bird. I feel that some stubborn, fierce, and senseless force is holding me in its grip, showing me elusive mirages of freedom and happiness, and that it may at any moment, for no apparent reason or purpose, twist my neck.

1898

IN THE BLACKSMITH'S SHOP

(From my Recollections)

At the very bottom of my memories, somewhere in the deepest depths, there burns a fire. A small, unglamorous, but steady flame which illuminates the first outlines emerging from the darkness of my childhood memory. This is the fire burning in the blacksmith's shop my father ran.

I can still see the iron shovel, with which father scooped charcoal from a wooden box, charcoal that he himself made in a pit in the backyard, still called a charcoal pit, although now there is no trace of any charcoal there. He throws it into the forge onto a small heap of glowing coals brought in a crock from the house, and then in his usual hurried manner, he calls out to the servant:

"Come-come-come, Andrus, blow on it, but gently, gently, until it catches alight."

Andrus, who had brought me here from the house on his shoulders and set me down on the charcoal box close to the fire, now grabbed a handle of the bellows and began to blow air onto the fire. The bellows seemed to be short of breath at first, as they weren't yet completely filled with air and hadn't yet started working properly; they fanned the coals, but the fire did not grow stronger.

"Gently there, Andrus! Whoa there, man, gently!"

"It's that wild woman snorting!" Andrus said jokingly and lifted the handle with all his might to fill the bellows with as much air as possible.

His mention of the wild woman gave me goosebumps.

"Where's this wild woman?" I asked.

Andrus laughed.

"Inside the bellows. Can't you hear her snorting?"

I strained my ears – I really could hear snorting.

"Wait a bit. After I throttle her good and proper," said Andrus, "she'll start groaning."

"No! Don't throttle her!" I exclaimed.

I was ready to start crying. I didn't understand the joke. My imagination was populated with phantoms, ghouls, and witches, about whom I heard stories every evening from our two maidservants, Big Ostyna and Little Ostyna, while they spun wool. They often mentioned the wild old woman who sits on the Dil[7] and smokes; but Andrus was the first person to place her inside the bellows, and since then the bellows have filled me with terror.

"Eh, eh, eh, man! Stop telling the child nonsense. Don't listen to him, Ivas, there's no wild woman inside the bellows."

"So what's snorting inside it then?"

"That's wind, lad. See, the bellows fills with air, and when you squeeze them, the air is blown out. Look, I can blow the same way!"

And father blows several times into the fire.

I settle down. The fire begins to grow in intensity. At first, its blue tongues of flame crawl timidly out from among the hot coals. Then the wild old woman begins to blow harder; the blue tongues at the base of the fire turn red and burst forth from the depths of the pile of coals. Gradually, the black charcoal itself also takes on a red hue, the flames hiss and elongate, becoming like a bundle of shiny knives or arrows. But the wild old woman has already inflated her leather belly almost to the ceiling. Andrus presses with both his hands,

....

[7] A mountain ridge in the Carpathian Mountains.

his chest, and his stomach to push the handle down. The fiery knives at the bottom turn white; the red coals become golden, almost translucent, as if they are melting. I can't take my eyes off the small hearth, which boasts little light and barely dispels the twilight inside the small wooden workshop, yet it spits large healthy sparks up into the trough-shaped, clay-covered and soot-encrusted ceiling, harbouring a great amount of heat and a great amount of energy.

Meanwhile father stands at the anvil, holding his small 'nimble' hammer in his hand and strikes the anvil several dozen times in quick succession, like a rapid drum beat. The sound carries across the whole neighbourhood – a sign that the blacksmith has started work.

Now he pulls out various boxes of damaged ironware from under the bellows. There are jagged axes which need to be tempered; one looks desperate, with a split head – the butt has been broken and needs to be completely 'refilled', as father would say in his colourful language. Over by the door stands a ploughshare that needs to be repaired. Under the smithy's small awning near the grinder is a pair of cartwheels ready to be forged, and beside lie new iron bands waiting to be made into hoops.

Father was a famed blacksmith in all the surrounding villages, his axes were especially prized. Even thirty years after his death, when I met an old man from a nearby village and struck up a conversation with him, he said, upon recalling my father:

"No, there's no smiths like him now. I still have his axe. It's no ordinary axe, it has a soul."

When the sound of my father's hammer ringing on the anvil echoed throughout the village, the neighbours, of course, began to drop by. Work in the shop mostly took place in winter, and in the summer, there were only two short seasons: the plough season and the sickle season – apart from that, father only opened the shop in summer if there was something urgent or more substantial to do.

In winter there was little farm work to attend to. Here and there flails swished in some barn; in entrance halls handsaws cut into wood or spinning wheels hummed as they made rope. The work wasn't rushed. But the blacksmith's shop was a lively place. Those who came with bigger jobs – whether to shod a wagon wheel or to make an axe – didn't forget to bring a bottle of vodka tucked under their arm. Going to the blacksmith was like visiting a friend or a neighbour, it was not like asking a tradesman to do a job for you and then – fare ye well.

Father had no fixed rate for his work. He'd merely say: "What's good for the people, is good for me," and if they had nothing to pay with, he could wait. But he loved it when the workshop was lively and noisy. He worked best with a large group of people present, amidst cheerful conversation and shots of vodka. Often, he needed more helpers too. For instance, when fitting hoops on wheels, three or four fellows would grab robust sticks with iron hooks; two others, together with father, using long tongs, would carry the heated hoop, rest it on the wheel rim, and those with the sticks would use the hooks to grab the hoop, pressing the stick ends against the rim, and begin to forcefully push down. Father would grab a big hammer and hit the iron hoop where needed. Wherever the hot iron touched the wood of the rim, it would occasionally burst into flames, but these became quickly extinguished.

"Come on, come on! Easy there, easy!" you could hear father encouraging the others, interspersed with hammer blows on the iron hoop and wooden rim and the clacking of hooks pulling the hoop in different directions. Then, three or four men grabbed the largest hammers and began to rhythmically drive the tightened hoop onto the rim. Thump-thump-thump! Thump-thump-thump! The noise resounded throughout the whole village until the hoop was perfectly in place. The older farmers inspected the wheel with expert eyes, checking if the hoop had tightened the joints enough, if each spoke was in place, if the hub was secure; one of them might lift the wheel with a strong hand, drop it lightly to the ground, and listen to the sound it made.

"The wheel is like a bell," they repeated one after another. This was the highest possible praise for a blacksmith.

And meanwhile in the blacksmith's shop the wild woman moaned and groaned, turning the fire in the forge completely white, and deep within it, something smouldered and shone bright as gold, casting long, branching sparks known as *zyndry*. This was where the eventual axe was being 'cooked'. Father tossed a good two handfuls of old-fashioned, large, hand-forged iron nails into the fire, stoked the coals, and had another man, besides Andrus, fan the fire. It was a tradition in father's shop that whoever came in would sit down and chat, and wouldn't miss out on a fiery show, but if there was a need for some assistance, father nonchalantly turned to them: "You-you-you, boy!" (if it was someone younger) or "Matey! Come, grab the hammer!" Or it might be to operate the bellows! Or whatever else was needed. And my little self was often the subject of his orders in such instances. Whenever it was necessary to handle a larger piece of intensely-heated iron from which large sparks jumped or white-green *zyndry* flew with a crackle, father would always ask someone present:

"Shield the child there!"

I was really scared of those sparks, but I awfully liked to watch as they flew out from under father's hammer like a swarm of fiery bumblebees, and scattered in all directions. Especially in those instances when he needed to forge weld two separate pieces of iron into one. And so, first father hammered the nails in the fire into a single chunk, then after several firings he forged it into a long, flat bar, one and a half feet long and three fingers wide. Then, on the round part of the anvil, he bent it and riveted the ends together. This led to the most critical part of making an axe: to create a good, sturdy poll and to weld, forge, and temper the blade. The thick bent bar was placed back in the fire, and after it was heated to a white glow, a mandrel – an iron tool used to form the hole in the butt of an axe – had to be driven into the irregularly shaped hole. Father hammered the butt very meticulously on that mandrel; his butts never cracked or fell apart, and for a farmer, the butt often served as a sledgehammer. The axe, along with the mandrel, was returned to the fire, but in what a state! The part where both ends of the bar met and where the blade would be, was completely coated with a thin slurry of clay – this was meant to help the iron weld together. Father carefully heaped hot coals onto the axe and then added fresh charcoal, which he also sprinkled with water mixed with clay – this was to produce a better 'spring' to the axe.

And then the wild woman began to groan at the top of her voice. Until bright white *zyndra* sparks began to burst out from the hearth together with ordinary little ones. No, not until then! Only when those *zyndra* sparks began to 'shoot' from the fire in thick swarms was it a sign that the iron had become properly welded. Father slowly grabbed the heated iron with tongs, cleared it of hot coals and melted clay with the hammer, placed it on the anvil, and gave it several light blows with his hammer. These always held a kind of mystical charm for me: they were very light, yet sparks flashed with each strike and scattered all around the shop. And although at such times I usually sat in my elevated spot, shielded from the anvil by the shoulders of some very sturdy 'uncle', my eyes roamed all over the shop, following each flying spark, and at the same time I kept them peeled to the iron which under the strikes of my father's hammer took on an ever-clearer shape. Having given the soft iron the required shape, father would wink at those present, especially the younger fellows, and would typically say:

"You and you, lad! Hup-two, grab a hammer! Lively there!"

Two men would grab the large hammers and would rhythmically strike the iron. 'Clang-bang-bang! Clang-bang-bang!' echoed the blows of three hammers. Father's small hammer struck it delicately, while the other two hit heavily, zealously, as if they were angry.

The blade was welded, but now began father's detailed work. Again he worked on the butt end, until the mandrel could be removed, and then he worked on the bit, and the heel and toe. Father forged and reforged each part several times, taking care not only to shape the iron, but especially to ensure that it was evenly and tightly worked, without any flaws or burrs, so that the axe looked 'as if it were cast'.

Conversations flowed in the shop. The neighbours shared village news: what they had overheard at the local government offices, what they had seen at the market in Drohobych, what some nomadic old beggar had recounted.

Most of the talk was about Boryslav, about the oil pits and diggings: at that time, the extraction of oil and wax had begun in earnest. Thousands of Jews went to Boryslav, wheedling patches of land from the peasants and starting to dig 'burrows'. In neighbouring villages, the image of the archetypal oil worker began to emerge: typically, a young man, from either a poor or a wealthier family, 'scrambling to get black shirts and white bread', as the peasant proverb characterized the life of the oil workers. This was the first manifestation of the industrial-capitalist order in that hitherto quiet, patriarchal corner.

Only murky rumours of this new phenomenon reached our blacksmith's shop. Five fellows had died in the pits that week, and the day before, three had died in a landslide in another pit, and this fellow or that fellow had fallen out of a bucket and was impaled on fencing spikes, which served in place of a safety rail in those downright primitively-built pits. This was a constant topic of conversation. Another topic was about people from Boryslav who had been forced out of their homes or had taken to heavy drinking. One fellow, it was rumoured, had been plied with alcohol by the Jews and was throw down a pit. And then there were the endless, fragmented stories about the Jews swindling villagers, about the hard-drinking oil workers and the good money they made, and how they squandered their earnings, about the explosions ten, twenty, and more yards underground.

I listened to the stories, as if they were fairytales about some distant, enchanted place. Boryslav, with its horrors, wild lifestyle, and extreme swings of fortune, its strange industry, strange way of working, and strange people fired my imagination. Our village lay far from the main road and no one from here went to Boryslav, but, having listened in the shop all winter long about the place, I resolved that come spring, I would not spare my legs and make my way to the highway, and wait there until I saw some oil workers, who travelled by that road from the more distant, poorer villages to Boryslav, or returned home on Saturdays. But my curiosity was satisfied sooner: later that winter, father took me one Monday to Drohobych, and there I saw whole crowds of oil workers and heaps of Jews, who kept asking every peasant, who by his clothing appeared to be a resident of Boryslav:

"Sir, sir! Are you from Boryslav? Do you have pits for sale?"

Father reluctantly listened to those tales about Boryslav. He had become so accustomed to the old ways of rural life that in the new uproar of Boryslav, he sensed something new and hostile to his way of life. He did not show it outwardly, nor did he judge or express outrage like some of the ardent proponents of tradition, but when the supply of news was exhausted, he gladly turned the conversation to other, usually ethical subjects. Father, a diligent and sensible worker, liked to mock the idlers and gas baggers, the gawkers and blunderers. To support his general observations, he liked to recount short stories and parables, usually set against the backdrop of blacksmithing. It was here in the shop that I first heard such stories, like the one about the boy whose father brought him to the blacksmith to learn the trade, and fearing 'that the child might get burnt or a spark might blind his eye,' asked the blacksmith to place his son in a basket nailed to the wall. "The lad will watch everything you do and learn," the father said. The boy 'learned' this way for seven years, but upon returning home, instead of making a ploughshare, produced nothing but a heap of scrap.

Once the conversation shifted to general topics and stories, it became lively. There were many eager listeners, and among our neighbours, there were some exceptional storytellers. Anecdotes and recollections from years past poured out, about the Kossuth War,[8] the famine years, about the journeys of our villagers to Podillia for work, or to Pokuttia and Bukovyna in search of maize. Personal adventures became intertwined with short and pointed characterizations of peoples such as the Podolians, Hutsuls, and Boykos – and places such as Kolomyja, Horodenka, Sadohora, and Chernivtsi.

But finally, the axe was ready. Father heated it one more time until it was red hot, then quickly plunged the blade two fingers deep into cold water to temper it. Then it was off to the vice and a file was used to smooth it, and finally off to the grindstone to sharpen this indispensable companion of the villager, whether in the forest, by the plough, or on a cart – everywhere where 'a firm hand' was needed. The blacksmith cheerfully examined his handiwork, admiring it for a few moments before passing it into the hands of his neighbours. And the new axe was passed around. Each fellow inspected the butt, tested the sharpness of the blade with his finger,

....

[8] Referring to the bourgeois revolution of 1848–1849 in Hungary, one of the leaders of which was the Hungarian politician Lajos Kossuth.

examined the blade to see if it was well-forged, inspecting it as if it were his own axe.

"Well, this one will last!" said one fellow.

"Those oaks I had would have been easily chopped down with this axe!" sighed another.

The happy owner of the new axe looked at it with pride and affection. He had seen it being made from the first moment, from when it was just a handful of old nails. He had helped pump the bellows and helped hammer it during its making – it was partly his own work too. He cheerfully thanked the blacksmith and pulled out a half-litre bottle of vodka from his bag. Father asked for a glass to be brought from the house, a loaf of bread, and half a round of cheese on a wooden plate – and the feasting began as they 'baptized' the new axe.

Father downed a shot of vodka, had a bite to eat, and then set about another job; the rest of the company enjoyed themselves, chatted, and joked. One fellow dreamily mentioned that if he had two to three ares[9] of land he would do this and that, and show everyone up! Another recounted how much money had passed through his hands in the past year.

"Twelve ares – by God, my friend, twelve ares, down to the kreutzer! If only you had a pair of oxen, eh! But as things stand… It's like a splinter in your finger. There's not enough to eat or drink, or dress smartly, just enough to feed your pride."

"And you, Marko my friend," one fellow turned to face our simple-minded neighbour, "if twelve ares landed in your lap now, what would you do with it?"

"I-I-I," Marko stuttered, "wou-wou-would kno-kno-know where to hide them."

"Yeah, you'd wrap them up in a cloth and stash them under the eaves!" someone remarked. But Marko didn't bother

....

[9] One are equals 100 square metres.

to reply, he merely shook his head as if to say: laugh as much as you want, but I know my business!

Others discussed their household affairs: one fellow's cow had calved, another's child had a cough; another boasted that the day before he had threshed a bushel of wheat from a cartload of sheaves. Gossip and judging those not present were not tolerated by my father, and if anyone's tongue strayed in that direction, he knew how to deflect it with a timely phrase or proverb, and sometimes he simply scolded the younger ones: "Mind your own beeswax, sonny!" Similarly, father disliked anything shameful in conversation: he himself, and everyone in his circle, always remained within the bounds of decency, of course, as much as honest, substantial farmers could allow themselves. They occasionally joked about women, and father liked to recount the well-known parable about the temptress to prove that 'a woman's nature can lead the innocent to sin':

"Once upon a time a father lived with his son in the forest for twenty years. The lad grew up without ever seeing a living soul other than his father. And when he turned twenty, his father said: 'Well, son, let's go out into the wide world and see how people live there.' And the son replied: 'Let's go, dad!' And off they went. They came to a village, and on the outskirts was a blacksmith's shop. They stepped inside and sat down, and the son watched the blacksmith at work: 'Dad, maybe I could try my hand at this?' 'Alright son, give it a go.' The young man approached the fire where the red-hot iron was, but did not take the tongs and simply grabbed the iron with his hand, placed it on the anvil, and began hammering it, meanwhile the iron did not burn him one bit. The blacksmith's eyes nearly popped out of their sockets at the sight of such a prentice, but the father said nothing, merely asking his son: 'Well, son, is the work going well?' 'Yes, dad.' 'If you like, you can stay here. But before that, let's walk a little further, because we haven't seen all that much of the world yet.' 'Alright.'

"They continued on their way through the village and in the street they came across a girl. The son stopped and looked. What could this be? He had never seen such a thing before, and he asked his father: 'Dad, what's this?' 'That, my dear son, is a temptress,' said the old man. The son's eyes lit up. 'Eh, dad, if only we could have a temptress like that in the forest!' The old man realized that the boy's blood was stirring, and said: 'Alright, son, it's time we went back home.' They headed back. They reached the blacksmith's shop once more, and the old man said to his son: 'What about it, son, do you want to work some more iron, perhaps?' 'Alright, dad,' said the son.

"And once more he did it his way: he went over to the fire, and grabbed the red-hot iron with his hand. He screamed loudly in pain as he pulled his hand back! His palm was covered in large blisters. He had burnt it completely. And the old man said: 'See, son, that's because you wanted that temptress.' And the two of them set off and returned to the forest."

Father told this parable in a jocular tone. The asceticism underlying it was quite alien to his nature. On the contrary, he was always sociable and loved being among people. 'With the people and for the people' was his motto in life. And I still remember how deeply impressed I was by that story of his about the saint who asked the Lord to free him from human love.

"A long time ago there lived a renowned doctor. He helped many people, and God granted him such favour that everyone loved him. Crowds of people were attracted to him, like flies to honey. Wherever he turned or stepped, he had friends, and anyone he spoke to even once would have jumped into the fire to help him. One day, as he was walking through the forest, he encountered an old man praying inside a cave. The fellow was completely naked and covered in hair from head to toe. 'What are you doing here, old man?' asked the doctor. 'Serving God,' said the old man. 'How are you serving Him?' 'As you can see, I've rejected all worldly things, I've turned my back on everything and I'm praying and atoning for my sins.' 'Do you think you might have served God better had you remained in society and worked for the good of the people?' 'You cannot serve both God and mammon,' replied the old man. 'People and all their anxieties, worries, and deeds – that's mammon. Whoever serves them should expect their reward from them. I serve God, and God will repay me, but those who serve the people, how will people repay them on Judgement Day?'

"With that, they parted: the old man stayed in the forest, and the doctor went about his business. But from that day on he began to think about the old man's words, and gradually he began to hate people and wanted to isolate himself from everyone. He fled to the forest, but people found him there, and when he refused to return to the city, they wanted to live with him in the forest. He ran away from them again, and once more they found him. He hid in some inaccessible jungle – and they found him there too; he went to sea and asked to be left on a deserted rock in the middle of nowhere – and still people found him and clung to him as before. Then he began to pray to God: 'Lord, give me such an ailment that all people will fear me, that they will stop clinging to me!' And as he began to pray, as he asked the Lord for this, the Lord finally sent upon him such an ailment that he began to throw himself about onto the ground, become covered in sores, foamed at the mouth, roared with a voice that was not his own – and all the people became scared of him and ran away. And with each such attack, he always saw demons tormenting him with red-hot tongs, pulling him toward them with iron hooks, beating him with iron rods, and calling out to him: 'Come join us! Come join us!'

"He suffered like this for twelve whole years, but no longer fled to the forests or secluded valleys. Now his soul was drawn to people, but people ran from him. He walked through towns and villages, seeking shelter, but his ailment made him so terrifying that no one wanted to take him under their roof. Whenever he came to a crowd of people, everyone scattered. He couldn't even enter a church because everyone fled from there when he appeared, and eventually they wouldn't let him in any more. Finally, after twelve years he heard a voice: 'Valentyn! Valentyn!' He replied: 'Who's that calling me?' And the voice said: 'How sweet is it for a man to live without human love?' And he replied: 'Lord, I have sinned. Let me die, please don't let me suffer like this anymore.'

"And the voice said: 'You see! Those who serve the people, they serve me. I created man for people, and only with people and through people can he be truly happy. Had I wanted him to be happy on his own, I would have made him a rock. Had I wanted him to serve me alone, I would have made him an angel. As it is, I gave man the greatest gift of all – love of fellow man, and only following this path can he come to me. But you wanted to be wiser and went straight ahead, but ended up in the thickets where those with pincers and iron rods sit. Well, enough of your penance. Because of the time that you served the people and saved them, I will take you to join me, but your weakness I will leave to people as a reminder: let them overcome their fear and disgust and learn to love and save one another even when they are in dire straits.'

"And so, Doctor Valentyn became a saint," father finished his account, "but his weakness still walks among us. And whosoever shall rescue the sick and tend to them will earn God's grace."

Forty years have passed since the sound of the blacksmith's drumming echoed for the last time in that small wooden shop in our village, played by my father's steady hand on the anvil. So much has changed since then! And not only in the blacksmith's shop. Almost everything that was the foundation stone of that quiet, patriarchal life in our corner of the world has vanished almost without a trace. From that cheerful company that chatted around the blacksmith's bench, pumped the bellows, fitted hoops onto wheels, energetically slammed hammers against heated iron, and shared lively anecdotes while downing shots of vodka, probably none are among the living. Fate had extinguished the cheerfulness and liveliness in many of them long before their deaths. Surely, at that time, none of them imagined that the blacksmith's shop, the people in it, and the friendly, joyful atmosphere pervading it would remain indelibly etched in the memory of a small red-haired boy, who sat barefoot in the corner by the hearth, dressed only in a shirt, and whose caring father occasionally asked them to shield him from flying sparks.

That small yet robust fire continues to burn at the very bottom of my memory. In it, blue, red, and golden-white rays keep flickering, glowing like molten coals, and deep within the fire something flashes that is even whiter and more radiant than the sparks intermittently bursting forth. This is the fire in the blacksmith's shop my father ran. And it seems to me that as a child I absorbed its energy into my soul for the long journey of life ahead of me. And it is still burning.

Kryvorivnia, 24 July 1902

IN THE CARPENTRY WORKSHOP

(From my Recollections)

I

Life is like going on a long journey: what falls off your wagon is lost forever. And memories are like a concerned farmer, walking along that road many years later, seeking out those long-lost things.

There's probably no trace left of that carpentry workshop on Boryslav Highway in Drohobych, where I spent the first three years of my life. It was an old house with a yard, separated from the street by a slightly more presentable but very shabby Jewish house and a huge ramshackle Jewish building, which housed a tavern, and between it and the stream stood a very smelly tannery. To the west and south, it was bordered by a small garden planted with cabbage, beets, and other undemanding vegetables. In the yard in front of the house were piles of wooden planks and swarms of screaming Jewish children; the hubbub could be heard from the tavern and the foul smell drifted over from the tannery. All the buildings were wooden, rotten at the base because of the dampness. This was the environment in which I spent the first three years of my life away from the village.

These were the 'lodgings at Koshytska's' which my relatives had been talking about for weeks before they decided to send me to school 'in town'. This Mrs Koshytska, the mistress of the house with a garden and the carpentry workshop, turned out to be some kind of relative of ours – I don't know whether on my father's or my mother's side – and I was instructed to call her 'auntie'. She was a middle-aged woman, way past thirty, with some vestiges of beauty remaining on her yellowed and wrinkled face. She was unusually talkative, like most Drohobych tradespeople. She was Ukrainian and attended the Orthodox church, although she did not shy away from the Catholic church either, being particularly fond of Polish Christmas carols, many of which she knew by heart and enjoyed singing while she worked.

She was called Koshytska out of habit, a surname she inherited from her first husband, although at that time she had already been married to Huchynsky for several years. He was much younger than she was and had once been an apprentice to her husband, but had fallen in love with her back then. Later, he served in the army, participated in the Italian campaign of 1859, and could recount stories about Venice, although I retained nothing interesting in my memory from his accounts. It was while he was in Italy that he had received news of the death of his old master, and that Koshytska had become a widow. From there, he wrote her passionate love letters, which Koshytska kept hidden in a corner of her dresser in a small box lined with Italian shells, probably brought back by Huchynsky as a memento from Venice. Once, during one of the frequent arguments between the older woman and her younger husband, Koshytska pulled out those letters and ordered me to read them. Barely able to make sense of the semi-literate soldier's sentences, I stammered away, and when I reached the passionate part: *Jeżeli cię nie kocham abym sobie trzy razy nogę złamał*,[10] Koshytska wiped away her tears and shouted at her husband:

....

[10]   Polish: "If I don't love you, then may I break my leg three times."

"You think the good Lord has forgotten those words of yours? Oh no, he hasn't! You'll break your leg yet on a smooth stretch of road, believe you me!"

In general, Huchynsky was a good worker but an unremarkable man. To acquaintances and neighbours, he was 'the Master Carpenter', but behind his back everyone called him 'Koshytska's husband'. People said that she had somehow lured him through trickery, and Huchynsky himself, given his limited intellect, had apparently also settled on that idea over time because, during arguments, paraphrasing that famous pathetic passage from his Venetian letter, he would shout:

"*Wolałem sobie trzy razy w jednem miejscu nogę złamać niż się ze starą babą związać!*"[11]

In the carpentry workshop, the conversation was usually in Ukrainian, although the workers were both Ukrainians and Poles; only Huchynsky and his wife spoke Polish during their intimate arguments. I never knew the reasons for those usually rather loud arguments, which sometimes ended in fights, after which Koshytska would lie in bed for a day or two, her head wrapped in wet towels. Whether Huchynsky, a young and unusually sanguine man, gave Koshytska cause for being jealous, or whether he himself was dissatisfied because they had no children, I cannot say. It seems that he was irritated by being the young husband of an older woman, perhaps feeling that despite his intelligence, experience, and energy, she continued to dominate him. It was said that at the wedding their marriage was predicted to be discordant and that he would die before her. Two wax candles, of exactly the same length and thickness, were fixed to the wall above the heads of the newlyweds and lit during the wedding dinner. One was supposed to signify his fate, and the other hers. They

....

[11] Polish: "I'd rather break my leg three times in the one place than get involved with an old woman!"

say that the flames of both candles repeatedly turned away from each other in opposing directions, and finally, his candle became extinguished, having burned only halfway. I am sure that this divination was the first splash of cold water on Huchynsky's fervent aspirations. He was possibly attracted to Koshytska because of her assets and energy, rather than just the mere calculation of running the carpentry workshop left by Koshytska's late husband. Huchynsky hailed from somewhere in Western Galicia and brought Koshytska nothing but his ruddy face, hot blood, healthy hardworking hands, and the not too pleasant habit of getting drunk every Sunday. Both firmly believed that the prophecy regarding their marriage would come true, and from the very first moment each of their lives began to burn in different directions. Traces of the flames of those wedding candles were still visible on the wooden wall in the workshop; they were neither painted over nor scraped off: two black streaks, burnt into the wooden wall, of unequal length and diverging in direction – a true symbol of this mismatched couple.

II

It was a fine autumn morning, on a Sunday. I stepped out into the narrow backyard behind 'auntie's' little house – not into the spacious, common yard in front of the house, but into the smaller, dirtier one at the back, enclosed by a fence, filled with tannery scraps and the stench of very primitively built toilets. In the distance, the bells rang from the belltower of the Holy Trinity Orthodox church and the Polish *kościół*.[12] The sun shone brightly in the cloudless sky. High above that stinking, dirty nest where I stood there was a sense of joy, a festive mood, which carried through the air. In my soul I felt

....

[12] Polish: Church.

the cheerful rustle of the forest, the splash of a crystal-clear stream, and saw images of villagers in sparkling white shirts and girls in red skirts with kerchiefs on their heads. Something grabbed at my heart, like a black crab with a hefty pincer. I shivered all over; feeling that, having grabbed hold of me, the black crab would never let go.

Looking in one particular direction, I peered through a crack in the fence. Beyond the fence was a garden planted with vegetables: the same broad-leaved beets, thin heads of cabbage, and sparsely scattered corn stalks that I had seen before outside the windows of the carpentry workshop. Two or three sunflowers turned their large yellow round flowers directly toward me, like thin, envious yellowed faces. Green dill rose up from among the creeping cucumbers. A large, speckled pumpkin lay sprawled on a garden bed, warming its striped side in the sun. Among the cabbages stood a dark green hemp plant, tall and robust, almost as tall as a man and the thickness of a scythe handle at its base. I gazed at it for a long time, marvelling; I had never seen such a hemp plant in our village.

Beyond the garden beds lay a small orchard with fruit trees. Red apples glistened and blushed in the sun; pears clung so densely to the branches of a large pear tree that the leaves were barely visible beneath them. The slender branches of plum trees bent under the weight of dark blue plums. A true paradise for a child's imagination! A true paradise, yet alas, fenced off with a high wooden fence, without a gate or a stile, and in all my three years living with 'auntie' I never set foot in there.

I have no idea how long I gazed through the crack into that fantasy paradise. But I probably would not have torn myself away from it for quite some time had I not been startled by an unusual rustling sound behind the other fence, the one separating the yard from the tannery. I tore my eyes away from the crack that looked into the garden with the orchard and peered through another crack. There, the view was entirely different. The tiny yard, bordered on three sides by low, dilapidated tannery buildings, looked more like a disgusting refuse dump than a yard. Clumps of rotting straw, balls of animal fur scraped off hides, piles of tannery lime and rotting bark, shards of pottery and dishes, and a single hollow, knotty willow tree, with most of its branches dead and the remaining ones sparsely covered with prematurely yellowed leaves – this was the uninviting landscape. Yet it was not without a living figure to complete the scene. A short, young Jewish fellow, with long, expertly spiralled side curls, a dirty cap on his closely cropped head, dressed in dirty ragged clothes and, with an idiotic expression on his face, was carrying a beautiful, reddish calf on his shoulders. He appeared from around the corner, having left some unseen entrance that led from the tannery to this yard. After reaching the centre of the dump, he dropped the calf to the ground. Only then did I notice that beside this calf lay another one, white with a black patch above its eyes. Both had their four legs bound together, and both lay quietly, helplessly, not struggling, but simply staring with their blue, melancholy eyes in silent bewilderment at this disgusting pit where this fellow had dropped them for some unknown reason. But when the man pulled out a large, shiny knife from his bootleg and, smiling idiotically, began testing its sharpness with his finger, the calves, by some strange instinct, understood the danger they were in and began to struggle and thrash about. Then both began to bleat plaintively.

The young Jewish man paid no attention to this. Approaching one of the calves, he knelt down on its body with such force that I thought I could hear its ribs crack. The calf immediately fell silent. The young man grabbed its head, lifted it up, and twisted it so that its snout rested on his knee, and its eyes met mine for a brief moment. Then, slowly, he drew the knife across the stretched neck. The sharp blade cut into the flesh, deeper and deeper, until a stream of ruby-red blood gushed out, gleaming like precious crystal in the sunlight. The butcher, with one swift motion, had cut through half the calf's neck, then withdrew the knife from the wound and wiped it on the calf's head, which he then dropped onto the ground. The calf began to thrash about as hot blood spurted from its wound. The young man watched the blood with a sort of demonic delight, and once again, that idiotic smile played across his face. He pressed his foot on the slashed neck of the calf, holding it down until all the blood had drained into the muck and the body was completely still.

He then proceeded to do the same to the second calf, which had been lying silently as if paralysed by some wild fear, its nostrils flaring as it sniffed the unfamiliar scent of blood. When the second calf was also slaughtered and the young man pressed down on its neck with his murderous foot, he turned halfway around, as if dancing, and faced me. His gaze, full of some senseless, idiotic bloodlust that kills with a smile and only expresses impatience when the victim takes too long to die or splatters its executioner with blood, burned into me like the sting of nettles. I recoiled as if scalded and ran back into the house.

"What's wrong?" 'auntie' asked me, as she was preparing to leave for church.

"Nothing," I replied almost in a whisper.

"Then why are you so pale?" she grilled me.

"Me?" I said, and without another word, I buried my face in my wooden chest, as if searching for a book that I needed.

'Auntie' asked no more questions and went off to church. And I wept for a long time after that, burying my face in the open wooden chest, pretending that I was searching for some book. I imagined silver bells tinkling, hanging on red ribbons around the necks of those beautiful calves, and a lush green pasture stretched out before them, where they joyfully frolicked and grazed. I could hear the mournful cries of their mothers, now seeking their children in vain. If only their poor imagination could have grasped the immense filth, the disgusting burrow, that cursed refuse dump where they were forced to spill their blood under the foot of that idiotic butcher!

III

I enjoyed my life in the carpentry workshop. Being a village lad accustomed to constant worries about weather, clouds, wind, frost or heat and the phases of the moon, it was a novelty to experience the steady, cheerful life of a city craftsman, detached from nature and its whims, governed entirely by different criteria, laid out on a totally different time scale. What did frost or heat, sleet or fine weather, sowing or harvesting, ploughing or hay cutting, with their various incidents and adventures, matter here? It all translated into a much simpler lifestyle: there was the weekly market on Monday and the annual fair on Trinity Sunday. That was all. Beyond that, there was the monotonous ebb and flow of private orders: dowry chests for brides before weddings and coffins before funerals. Dowry chests and coffins – these were the mainstay of Huchynsky's carpentry workshop. Only occasionally were there orders for cradles, ordinary cupboards, sideboards, beds, and armchairs. More delicate furniture was almost never made, and although Huchynsky boasted that 'he knew his way around polishing', when he once undertook to make a polished frame for an icon, he failed dismally, having rubbed too hard and 'burned' the polish, leaving a dark, matte stain on the frame.

There were three benches in the workshop; besides the master carpenter, two prentices and one finish carpenter usually worked on them. The prentices changed quite often, and in my time there, only two or three fellows stayed for any length of time. The most memorable fellow in the workshop was Mr Stanislaw, a young man from Drohobych, who had recently completed his apprenticeship. He was a very good-natured, cheerful, and always satisfied young man, musical and humorous, with pleasant, though slightly rough, facial features. He had completed all four elementary classes at the Basilian school and could tell me a funny anecdote about each of the Basilian brothers who taught me.

A former rector, who was quite a miser, had taken to sewing the money he had amassed into the collars of his worn-out cassocks. Upon his death several dozen of these cassocks were found in his wardrobe and they were distributed among the destitute beggars. Some, not knowing what to do with the rags, sold them for a few kreuzers to the local ragman, but one fellow, who knew a little of the tailor's craft, decided to make himself a vest. He came upon the money after taking the cassock apart. Without saying a word to anyone, he quizzed the other mendicants where they had disposed of their cassocks. Learning that the ragman had bought them up, he confided in a policeman, a distant relative of his, and dressed as a Basilian father accompanied the fellow to the ragman's ramshackle shed, ostensibly searching for stolen cassocks. The frightened ragman handed over all the old cassocks and was glad to have evaded punishment. Meanwhile the beggar and the policeman pulled all the banknotes out of the collars, divided the money up, and disappeared God only knows where. Having encountered one of the beggars soon after, the ragman started to reproach him for selling a stolen cassock and almost getting him into trouble. The beggar took offence and dragged the Jewish fellow off to the monastery, where he was assured that the cassocks were not stolen. The Jew fearfully recounted the details of the search that had taken place at his establishment, describing the policeman with the sword and the monk in an old cassock. The case took on a more serious, mysterious aspect. No monk from the monastery had gone to conduct a search, nor was the ragman able to identify any of the local policemen who had ostensibly accompanied him. The matter would have rested there, had one of the brothers not found a scrap of rolled-up paper tucked into the spine of an old prayer book belonging to the rector. There, written in the hand of the deceased, was a list of all the sums of money that this miserly rector was able to collect over the years and which he in turn had sewn into each cassock. It added up to more than twenty thousand rinskys.[13] News of this spread throughout the town. Such a sum in those times in a poor backwater like Drohobych (this had been well before the gold rush in Boryslav), seemed like an awful lot. The ragman, having learnt what a treasure he had held onto for almost two weeks, and how foolishly he had allowed it to be snatched from him, hanged himself out of grief. The police rushed to look for the person who had conducted the search at the ragman's, but without any result. Several years later some beggars came across their former companion, who had become a wealthy farmer, and had a wife and children. Recognizing his one-time companions, he wined and dined them for several days, and bestowed lavish gifts upon them. He made no mention of the cassocks, and when asked how he had managed to become so wealthy, simply replied:

"It was God-given!"

And then, after a while, added:

"I can swear, that I didn't kill anyone, didn't rob or wrong anyone. It was just plain luck!"

Who knows if the beggars believed him about not wronging anyone, but that last phrase convinced them utterly: he was just plain lucky! They didn't snitch on him to the police and anyway, what could they have accused him of doing?

Mr Stanislaw liked to recount similar anecdotes, especially in the evening after work, once the master carpenter had

....

[13]   One rinsky equalled 100 Austrian kreutzers.

left, the senior prentice went home, and the master carpenter's wife was busy in the kitchen. Then the three of us: Mr Stanislaw, the finish carpenter Jasko and myself, sat down on the bench near the forge or on the workbenches and began to shoot the breeze. The two fellows who lived in town quizzed me about rural life, and I in turn was all ears listening to their stories, jokes, tall tales and witticisms. Being an inexperienced schoolboy, I was most impressed by the purely schoolboy games and jokes, of which Mr Stanislaw knew so many. He would give me a Polish sentence that would read the same forwards or backwards: *kobyła ma mały bok.*[14] Or he would write down 12 zeros and then create a sentence by adding strokes and dashes here and there: *pogoda od boga.*[15] Or he would say a sentence that seemed to be completely in Polish, and then showed that it was made up only of German words: *on bieg bez las, a ja za nim*[16] (*on = ohn, bieg = bieg, bez = bös, las = lass, a = auch, ja = ja, za nim = sah'n ihm*). Or he would tell us how in the past Germans used to literally translate the names of Ukrainian towns into their language: Peremyshl = Durchdenken, Mostyska = Brücken-drücken, Drohobych = Zweitepeitsche, Sambir = Selbstwald and so on. Then we played games with language, tongue-twisters such as: '*Nie pieprz Piętrzę wieprza pieprzem, bo przepieprzysz Piętrzę wieprza pieprzem*',[17] or '*Fritz frisst frische Fische, frische Fische frisst Fritz*',[18] or '*Przeleciały trzy pstre przepierzyce przez*

....

[14] Polish: "The mare has a small flank."

[15] Polish: "Weather is God-given."

[16] Polish: "He ran through the forest, and I followed him."

[17] A Polish tongue twister, literally: "Don't pepper the hog with pepper, because you'll over-pepper the hog with pepper." Something akin to "Peter Piper picked a peck of pickled peppers."

[18] German: "Fritz eats fresh fish, fresh fish eats Fritz."

trzy piękne kamienice.[19] I remember spending entire evenings struggling to master these phrases. For my part, I impressed Mr Stanislaw with my ability to say a dozen times in one breath, without any mistakes, the Ukrainian phrase: '*Tseber, tseber, polutseber perepolutsebryvsia*'.[20] No matter how much he and young Jasko struggled to master this phrase, neither of them were ever able to repeat it twelve times in a single breath without a mistake.

I must say that Mr Stanislaw, though he loved jokes, did not have an ounce of cynicism in him. He recounted everything cheerfully and colourfully, but never indecently, and generally behaved like a respectable man. Such a respectable, though cheerful tone prevailed in the carpentry workshop during work hours, especially in the presence of the master carpenter. One of the older prentices, named Chemerynsky from memory, who referred to himself as a 'furniture carpenter', liked to tell old guild stories. One was about a prentice, who had arrived from somewhere and wanted to work as a master carpenter in one place. To prove himself, he was told to create a masterpiece; and over the course of a month, having locked himself up in the workshop, he created an exquisite fan, which was inlaid with all the scenes of the Passion of Christ.

Another story was about a clockmaker who built a sophisticated clock for his town. As each hour was struck, a different group of dolls emerged and played various melodies. The town magistrate, fearing that the fellow might make an even better one for another town, ordered that the man be blinded and fed generously until death. After they had gouged out his eyes, he claimed that his clock had another

....

[19] Polish: "Three spotted quails flew through three beautiful tenement houses."

[20] "Pail, pail, half-pail, overhalfpailed."

secret inside it, one that he had not shown to anyone yet. If he were allowed to access the mechanism inside the clock, he could activate this last, amazing feature. The magistrate agreed, they led the master up to the clock and opened the door to the mechanism. He shoved two fingers inside, tampered with something, and the mechanism stopped moving. After that, no matter how much effort various clockmakers put into trying to fix the mechanism, none could find where it had been damaged or how to set it in motion once more.

Chemerynsky was getting on in years and was very taciturn. He had travelled widely and must have endured a lot, though he never spoke about his adventures. There was an incredible kindness in his character, overlaid with some sternness. Sometimes when I made too much noise while horsing around in the workshop, Chemerynsky, without stopping his work, would turn to me with his eyes shaded by overhanging eyebrows and say:

"Na-hoo-loot!

Not a hoot!"

He occasionally loved communicating with such lapidary poems.

What that 'Na-hoo-loot' meant I never did find out. But I remember, when at the end of the school year, after exams, I returned with a book I had received for being 'best in class' and showed it to him. Chemerynsky patted me on the head, was silent for a long time, and then said with a joyous note in his voice:

"Na-hoo-loot!

Well done, coot!"

I never heard him crack jokes or laugh. However, he loved to listen to Mr Stanislaw's jovial accounts and at times would punctuate them with laconic remarks of a general nature, usually composed in verse. I remember, once, after listening to a long argument between the master carpenter and his wife, in which each accused the other of foolishness while claiming wisdom for themselves, Chemerynsky twitched his black moustache about, turned to Mr Stanislaw and said loudly:

"We're all on the same train:
Living as fools, in that we remain,
As fools, we shall die,
Here's the crux, here's why:
Let our foolishness not be others' disdain."

After these words the master carpenter became terribly red in the face and the quarrel between him and his wife was cut short. Though neither of them said a thing to Chemerynsky, a few weeks later he was sent on his way.

IV

The finishing carpenter, Jasko Romansky, holds a special place in my memories. Being the only other youth in the house besides myself, he naturally became my companion. Lively, resolute, sharp-tongued, yet not too eager to work, cynical and unscrupulous in many matters which for me were 'a red line not to be crossed', he was the epitome of a city boy, the complete antithesis of the timid and fearful country bumpkin that I was. It came as no surprise then, that he was the first to introduce me to many details of urban civilization. He taught me to tell the time on a clock face, to distinguish quarter-hour chimes from hourly ones, to navigate the city, find the necessary shops, streets, workshops, and institutions. Under his guidance, on Sunday afternoons and festive days, I ventured to the distant outskirts of Drohobych, where he had family and friends. At other times, when we had to stay indoors and there was no work, he taught me Polish Christmas carols and other festive songs, and often, sitting in the empty carpentry workshop, bent over an old, worn-out book

of carols, we would loudly sing the famous refrain of the
Christmas carol:

Hej, hej, jedni grali,
Drudzy tańcowali,
Pasterze na lirze![21]

Jasko also taught me the value of money. In the village, I saw
everyone cherish money, fight over it, but as for its practical
use, what it could do for a person, that remained a mystery
to me. Villagers bought very little with money: salt, pepper,
leather for boots – things unappealing to my childish imagination. Most of their money went into some vague abyss they
referred to with some fear as 'the treasury', so I too came to
view it as something dreadful and inhuman. When in the
village I occasionally had a few kreuzers – usually wealthier
guests would give their host's children a kreuzer or two 'for
good luck' – I didn't know what to do with them, and after
playing with them for a while, I either lost them or handed
them to my mother. Here, for the first time, I discovered
the value of money as a source of various pleasures. Jasko
taught me to exchange money for sweets, apples and nuts,
explained the different ways townspeople earned and spent
money, characterized the earnings of beggars, water carriers,
rag pickers, and bone collectors, middlemen, gardeners, and
various categories of small-time earners who inhabited the
industrial quarter of Drohobych, spread along the Boryslav
and Truskavets highways, Solony Stavok, and the salt mines.
There were no spacious gardens or fields planted with onions, cabbage, potatoes and cucumbers, which were the main
source of income for people living in the suburban areas of

....

[21]   Polish: "Hey, hey, some played, / Others danced, / Shepherds
strummed the lyre!"

Lishnia, Zadvirna and Zvarych. The people there, half-peasants, half-townsmen, were mocked by the local tradesmen, who referred to them as 'onion farmers', and ridiculed them for their soft pronunciation:

"Dzentleman, dzentleman, pliyz buy some cabbadz!"

Under Jasko's guidance, I would enter the cramped homes of those craftsmen and wage-earners. I knew a tripe seller named Yakubova who made her living by selling hot tripe every Monday in the arcade at the market. She had a husband, a craftsman of some sort, who was rarely home, but just like with my 'auntie', it was clear that Yakubova ruled the roost, and everyone knew of Yakubova in the neighbourhood, while her husband, if mentioned at all, was always referred to merely as 'Yakubova's husband'. Having lived for eight years among the tradesmen of Drohobych and having intimately observed their lives, I had the impression that in these families, even if the women didn't wear the pants in the family, they were at least on an equal footing with the men. They were distinguished by their intelligence and energy, and above all, a nimble and tireless tongue. Neither before nor after have I heard anyone speak as quickly in Ukrainian as some of those suburban women from Drohobych. This spiritual superiority over their husbands probably stemmed from the fact that the husbands, as tradesmen, were forced to specialize in an often mechanical and sedentary job, which was monotonous, unchanging from day to day, week to week, year to year. This would have diminished their ability to be adaptable, energetic, and agile; whereas the women, who took on the running of the household, the child-rearing, and garden work, often also had to handle negotiations with clients or the sale of finished goods at the market, thus acquiring traits that made them the de facto head in the home.

Jasko also taught me games played by city children, which we rural children knew nothing about: playing tip-cat, spinning tops, flying kites, and catching sparrows with traps. If the truth be told, I wasn't too keen on these games, but I was all the more grateful to him for taking me every Sunday in autumn to the outskirts of Drohobych, to the hills, the river and the fields, where we gathered sloe fruit that had ripened and been made sweet by the first frosts; we then baked these and ate them in the carpentry workshop.

Master Huchynsky had found a coarse, soft sandstone on one of the riverbanks, which he liked to use instead of pumice to smooth boards, and more than once he sent Jasko and me to fetch fresh supplies of the stone. Occasionally, we went into the forest to collect mushrooms; here, I was Jasko's teacher, having learnt from my father at a young age to distinguish between various kinds of edible and 'frantic' mushrooms. We collected seeds of different grasses for the canaries and goldfinches, which the master carpenter loved to keep in cages, or went with a sack to collect large forest ants, which 'auntie' boiled up for a bath for herself, as she was suffering from rheumatism in her legs after living for over twenty years in a damp house on a marshy site. In late autumn Jasko and I found other diversions in the yard. We dug up vegetables in the garden, pickled cabbage and gherkins, made a fire and cooked plum jam, and in another cauldron in the hallway we boiled glue from ox tendons and scraps of animal skins. These were tasks which I had never seen performed in the village, and I found them all very interesting. Besides, Jasko knew how to explain the tasks with stories and humour, making them even more interesting.

Jasko's father lived not far from us. He had his own house and garden, and besides this he earned money in a 'big factory' – an oil and earthwax refinery which had recently been built outside Drohobych on the Boryslav Highway near the river. After an explosion at work, his feet and hands were burnt, and Jasko and I visited him in hospital every Sunday – this was the first time I had been inside that place of pain and carbolic acid. Old man Romansky could read and write and, in that small circle of people who frequented 'auntie' Koshytska's place, he was one of the brightest stars there, considered a wise and experienced man. I still remember his terrible wounds, which I saw in hospital when they were being dressed, and the black plaque above his head with the word *Brandwunden*,[22] and the large prayer book lying beside him. His yellowed, martyred face betrayed no pain, only boundless sorrow...

A short time after this, without waiting for his father to recover, Jasko left Huchynsky's carpentry workshop. The master carpenter was not happy and, although Jasko had completed his four years of apprenticeship, he did not want to release him. Jasko fled the workshop, left home with only a few clothes and two rinskys, and set off for Lviv with these provisions. In my imagination, Lviv lay somewhere far away in some mythically distant place. There was no railway connection then, and it took two to three days by cart to get there, and I have no idea how long it would have taken on foot. I marvelled at Jasko's courage to venture on such a long journey alone, without any money to speak of and without a clear purpose. His first letter to his mother, which after several days of anxious uncertainty and searching, finally gave her certainty about what had happened to her son, caused quite a sensation in the carpentry workshop. The master carpenter read it out loud and recalled from memory the route Jasko must have taken that first day and in which village he had bought some sour milk and bread, and in which inn he had stayed the night. I never found out anything more about Jasko – where he ended up in Lviv or what happened to him. He disappeared from my life without a trace, like something that falls off a cart while it's moving quickly.

....

[22] German: Burns.

V

Every Friday and Saturday was 'auntie' Koshytska's time for artistic expression, the time for painting the wooden chests. She often took this part of the work upon herself; her designs were characterized by an incredibly haphazard selection of colours and astonishing shapes of the flowers. True, both these aspects never deviated from her long-established patterns, but 'auntie' liked to let her hand roam free while painting and would substitute colours. Instead of a beet-coloured border, she might use blue; the straightforward stalk of a plant would turn from white to green, and she would depict a phantasmagorical 'rose' with four circles rather than three: the innermost circle in cinnabar, the next one green, then a yellow or blue one, and finally – white; and there were no leaves at all. In the corners of the design, she might include another 'rose' with leaves containing three circles. While painting, she would walk around the chest, eyeing the entire job like some expert, occasionally grabbing a pot of green paint, then blue, red, yellow, white, adding a touch here, a border there, or drawing a line, until it completely satisfied her undemanding taste. And all the while, a continuous stream of devotional songs flowed from her lips, a mixture of Polish and Ukrainian tunes. Here she would put the finishing touches to a terrifying 'rose', whose design and colours would astonish even the wildest savage, and while she was doing this, she would sing:

Ah, hard justice!
The gates of hell
Will open wide.
And you, the sinful
And the damned,
Will hop into that chasm!

A moment later, armed with a brush and green paint, her hand would be creating swirls on a red background akin to the twists of spiralling Jewish side curls, while from her lips flowed a far more humane stream of words and tones:

> *A ty, pani dworko,*
> *Kluczyki na kołku – hej nam, hej!*
> *Kolęda, kolęda, kolęda!*
> *Kaź wódki dolewać*
> *Będziem dobrze śpiewać – hej nam, hej!*
> *Kolęda, kolęda, kolęda!*[23]

Initially I watched 'auntie's' artistic exercises with great reverence, admiring her skill and taste, and marvelled at the completed works.

I was most delighted by the spots where there were large splashes of pure colour, especially cinnabar and blue paint. I did not like lead white, I detested yellow paint, and I was terribly surprised when Jasko first showed me how a mixture of yellow and blue resulted in green. Jasko had the assigned task of grinding paints on stone slabs, mixing them, and storing them in appropriate pots. Grinding lead white and yellow ochre was the hardest, and here Jasko gladly accepted my help: both of us would take the stone pestle and press down on it as we moved it across the slab until we could no longer feel even a single uncrushed and unground grain of paint under the smooth stone. All the paints were diluted with water and gum; however, there were times we had to pre-

---

[23] Polish: "And you, lady of the manor,
Keys hanging on the hook – hey, oh, hey!
Carol, carol, carol!
Order more vodka to be poured
And we will sing so well – hey, oh, hey!
Carol, carol, carol!"

pare oil paint as well. The more expensive chests, cupboards, and beds were decorated with oil paint – and only in green. This must have been quite an old custom, for the image of a green bed was even immortalised in a song. Jasko loved to sing this song: whether when he was boiling hemp oil in an iron pot to make varnish and stirring it continuously with an iron spatula or grinding a mixture of yellow and blue to make green paint, he would squint and crow like a rooster:

> *A w ty nowy komorze*
> *Stoi zielone łoże:*
> *Ej łoże, łoże śliczne, zielone,*
> *Któż na tobie będzie spał?*[24]

In general, songs could often be heard in the workshop. People's interaction with paints and brushes seemed to naturally evoke singing. Only Huchynsky never sang. Having quickly learnt all the popular songs in the carpentry shop, I sang along with everyone in my shrill voice, and by my third year in the workshop, I had even started assisting auntie with painting chests. The joy I felt as I walked around the chest holding a paintbrush and a pot of paint! How proudly I daubed on 'roses' following 'auntie's' example, causing auntie herself to clutch her head and the prentices to run over from their benches to inspect my paintings. They laughed until they nearly burst their sides! Yet, the chests with my creations were popular: because of their unusual decoration they sold more readily, and I was ready to become famous in the trade of chest painting, but fate destined that I engage in a different kind of dabbling. In hindsight, as a man examines

....

[24] Polish: "In that new chamber
There stands a green bed:
Oh bed, lovely, green bed,
Who will sleep upon you?"

the twisting paths and astonishing turns his life has taken, he begins to gradually lean toward fatalism.

The Huchynskys' business was going well. There was such a great demand for wooden chests, that some weeks almost the entire workshop was filled with completed chests. In such instances my bed was made up in one of these, and since work continued late into the night at times, I would wake in the morning as if in a deep well: on top of my chest they had placed another, and upon it a third, and so on – practically all the way to the ceiling. Only after I had woken and began to make bird-calls from my hiding place, was the pile dismantled and I was able to crawl out. There were also times when I had to sleep in freshly-made coffins, when large numbers of them were being made in the workshop. Because of a lack of space, there was nowhere else to put them, except on the bench where I slept: the coffin was placed on the bench and my bed was made up inside it, and I slept very peacefully, anticipating the eternal sleep of its future occupant. However, when my mother learnt of this, she protested vehemently, and they ceased the practice; from memory 'auntie' even apologized to my mother, saying that she had known nothing of this, and that Jasko had made up my bed a few times in a coffin as a joke.

During my third year living with the Huchynskys, they began building their own wooden house in one of the nearby streets. My curiosity had plenty to feast on as I observed the work of the builders and the numerous scenes of construction in town, starting from the evening when Huchynsky and 'auntie' returned home from town quite tipsy, dragging along a sizeable sack of money. From their conversation, I understood that they had taken a loan from the carpenter's guild of something like 120 rinskys – a significant sum at the time – and the guild's treasury let them have the loan in copper coins, so they had to carry the money in a sack slung on a pole, each end of which was supported on their shoulders. They bore it between them like those Biblical spies of Joshua who carried a giant cluster of grapes. There was quite a celebration in the guild to mark this loan, and our master and his wife stayed out late; it was a dark night, the road was muddy, the sack of coins was heavy, and both were unsteady on their feet – no wonder they arrived home covered in mud, exhausted, and angry with each other, and the festivities ended in an uproar, with the master carpenter's wife wishing that the master carpenter would finally fulfil his promise and break not just one, but both his legs and his head too, while the master carpenter, having no comeback, grabbed a large tin colander and ever so delicately placed it on 'auntie' Koshytska's head so that it looked like an old knight's helmet with the visor down, with the edges of the colander tightly wrapped around her neck. Jasko and I had to exert a lot of effort to bend back the metal enough to remove this improvised and quite inconvenient helmet from 'auntie's' head. After this memorable evening, 'auntie' spent two days in bed, and on the third day, getting up to paint wooden chests, she repeatedly sang a verse from a Polish Christmas carol that mentioned the name of Master Wojciech, and each time she swung a paintbrush menacingly in the master carpenter's direction, singing:

Bieg Wojtek bez portek po śniegu, po grudzie:
Śmieją się, cieszą się: cha-cha-cha-cha, ludzie![25]

Meanwhile the master carpenter worked quietly at his bench and at each such allusion turned red as a beet.

....

[25] "Wojtek ran with no pants, through snow, and over frozen clods, People laughed and cheered, ha-ha-ha-ha, what a sight to behold!"

VI

After finishing elementary school with the Basilians, I moved elsewhere, and 'auntie' Koshytska with her carpentry workshop vanished from my horizon. Only much later, during my university years, did I learn about the tragic conclusion to her domestic drama.

The wedding candles had indeed foretold her the truth, but not quite the whole truth. She had outlived her much younger husband, but it was her third one that led her to the grave; this third one was rheumatism. After he died, Huchynsky left her a legacy: he had been a guarantor for a rather significant bank loan taken out by an acquaintance. The acquaintance had failed to repay the loan, and soon after Huchynsky's death, the bank auctioned off his widow's new home and threw her out onto the street – old, disabled and paralysed. The disease had deprived her of the use of her legs, and she could not even go about begging for bread, but had to crawl along on her hands, dragging her lifeless legs behind her. In this state she spent her days under the Church of the Holy Trinity or by the Polish Catholic church. She sat silently, not asking for alms, reluctantly extending her hand when an old acquaintance offered her a few coins. She was withered, yellowed, covered in wrinkles, her fingers twisted and contorted by rheumatism, and only her eyes still shone with intelligence and energy, but their light was dimmed by a cloud of deep sorrow – that same cloud which I had first seen on the tormented face of Romansky, who had been scalded in the factory accident. How many bright and energetic eyes does such a cloud darken in our small towns today!

1902

THE HUMOROUS REVEREND

I

The Basilian father Sofron Telesnicki was known in Drohobych, especially among the Basilians, as a witty humourist. He was an honest, sincere, and frank soul who brought a breath of ease and unforced freedom, a kind of cheerfulness and merriment to any gathering. When he began to narrate something, even without aiming to be witty, he immediately put everyone in a good mood, evoking laughter and cheer where the subject matter itself might not have seemed inherently funny. Such was the golden soul in this unassuming thin man who, it seemed, should more likely be inclined toward a state of melancholy than cheerfulness.

His reputation had preceded Father Telesnicki even before his arrival in Drohobych, and he managed to maintain it afterward. When we finished the second grade and were about to leave school for the holidays, our beloved teacher and guardian, catechist Father Krasicki, told us:

"Well, next year you will have Father Telesnicki as your class master. A golden soul! You will be well off with him. The only thing I fear is that you rascals might take undue advantage of his kindness and become completely unruly."

"No, no, we won't do that!" we shouted joyously, buoyed by the happy prospect as we left for our homes.

The following year, the third grade at the school was unusually large in number. After the inaugural service, we were led into a large room where the class captain, Zając, assembled us in rows according to height – shorter ones at the front and taller ones at the back; one desk, which stood separately near the iron stove, side-by-side with the others, remained empty. We never even asked the class captain why this was so. We were third graders and knew that this was in accordance with a tradition established long ago by the Jesuits – a so-called 'dunce's bench', essentially the penal colony in class. Who would be populating it? But I doubt any of us were thinking about such things at that moment. The classroom was noisy and lively; the sense of school vacations hadn't yet left our heads, and furthermore, the anticipation of such a kind-hearted class master buoyed our young hearts. We talked, laughed, some walked around, and even Zając himself set aside his usual decorum, especially since he hadn't yet officially been named class captain, for this depended on the new master of our class.

At last, the bell rang with a plaintive tone, signalling the start of classes. The hurried footsteps of some late pupils sounded in the corridor, there were shouts, doors slammed, and the classroom fell silent. One could hear the rumble of market day coming from the nearby square, the shrill cries of Jews: 'Fresh cottage cheese!', the squeal of pigs, and the creak of wooden Boyko carts, famous for not having a single iron nail. The children in the classroom no longer dared to speak loudly or move from desk to desk. Occasional joyful whispers, suppressed giggles, the rustle of pages being turned could still be heard. Only class captain Zając paced steadily through the middle of the classroom, ensuring everyone sat in the places he had designated.

"Books on desks! Hands on desks!" he ordered. "Psst! Quiet! They're coming!"

From the passage came the loud, steady clacking of footsteps – not just one pair of feet, but two. Closer and closer they came to the door of our classroom… Suddenly the door opened. First to enter was the corporeal figure of the rector,

Father Barusewicz, with his round, plump, but dignified face. Following him was a tall, thin, lanky figure with a long, protruding, horse-like face, black bristly hair, a low forehead, a wide mouth, and a carelessly shaved chin with tufts of black stubble. His figure was cloaked in a black cassock, girded with a broad black belt, but it seemed as if it wasn't tailored to his measurements, appearing too wide, so that his thin body swayed inside it like a ripe pea in a swollen, still-green pod. The face of the figure conveyed a pitiful impression, resembling either a hungry or a sick man. We saw no trace of the cheer, which flowed from a kind, benevolent heart and seemed to sparkle from every look, every movement, every word of our catechist, Father Krasicki.

"Well, boys!" said the rector, instructing us to sit down. He spoke, of course, in Polish, because at that time, nota bene,[26] during the so-called Germanization (the events in this story took place in 1864), it was either an official language mandated from above or simply a habit and was the official language in the Basilian school. "May I present your new teacher and class master, Father Telesnicki. He will teach you Polish, Ukrainian and German, arithmetic, and singing. Listen to him, be diligent and polite, so that I have no need to complain about you. I know you are decent boys and will not cause him any distress. Well, then!" And with these words, which were meant to be in place of the German 'also',[27] which Father Barusewicz liked to intermingle with his usual conversation, whether be it in Polish or Ukrainian, he shook hands with the new teacher, and escorted him to the steps of the dais – a raised wooden platform on which stood the teacher's lectern on the side closer to the door, and on the other, closer to the window, was the blackboard. Responding with a nod of his

....

26   Latin: Take note.
27   German: Thus.

head to our greeting, expressed by rising from our seats, he left the classroom.

II

"Well!"

This was the first word we heard from the lips of Father Telesnicki. We looked at him. There he stood on the dais – tall, thin, like a scarecrow in a trench; the tails of his long cassock were flared, and beneath them could be seen dirty black trouser-legs tucked into high boots. Although his voice was somewhat harsh and throaty, and although there was not a trace of cheerfulness in his face, yet having heard about his humorous nature, we all burst into joyful, childish laughter.

Father Telesnicki's face turned red. He examined his clothes, flicked the hem of his cassock, and then, casting a sharp look around the classroom, he said:

"What's this all about? Why are you laughing?"

We grew silent.

"Have I given you permission to laugh? Who has given you permission to laugh?" he inquired, sternly looking about the class.

We remained silent, but felt no fear. After the cheerful lessons spent with Father Krasicki, which were often filled with jokes and laughter, we could not believe that the new teacher would consider our laughter a crime.

"I am the master of this classroom!" he said with a seriousness that some of us might have even found humorous. "Remember that. During my lessons you are to laugh only when I tell you, and to cry when I tell you. Do you understand?"

Some of the boys in the class were grinning.

"Halt! You there! What's your name?" exclaimed Father Telesnicki to one such fellow who had been grinning.

The pupil gave his name and surname.

"Why are you laughing?"

"I'm not laughing, sir."

"Don't give me that! I saw you!"

"That was inadvertent, sir."

"Inadvertent? Alright, sit down! And next time, be mindful of your 'intent', otherwise I might make you cry inadvertently."

The usual order of the first lesson began: organizing the roll call, the teacher familiarising himself with the pupils, and seating arrangements. Father Telesnicki, for now, accepted the seating arranged by Zając, and also confirmed him in his role as class captain.

"Well, and now we'll take out our textbooks. German first."

We took out our texts. The teacher called the names of pupils in turn and had them read a few sentences from the book. Meanwhile, he walked with broad steps around the classroom, gesticulating with his hands, nodding his head, and whenever someone made a mistake in reading, he would derisively pick on the mistake, repeating it in various tones, trying to make fun of it even more.

"Aha! *Der Géssell! Der Gésell!*" he exclaimed. "Or maybe it's *der Gisell, der Gósell, der Gásell*, eh? Take a closer look there!"

"No, sir, there's only *der Gésell* here."

"Only *der Gésell!* Hah-hah-hah! Strange. Maybe there's a *der Geséll*[28] there?"

The boy, who until now failed to understand why the teacher was making a point of this word and what was wanted of him (he apparently had no idea how the German word '*der Gesell*' should be pronounced, and was putting the stress on the first syllable, as was common in Polish). He now looked anxiously at the teacher and said timidly:

"Well... I don't know. Maybe it is *der Geséll.*"

....

[28] German: Companion.

"Ah, see! You've finally worked it out! Well, then: *der Geséll*! Continue reading."

Had we been older and understood psychology better, we would have quickly realised that the main, and perhaps only, element of Father Telesnicki's humour was irony, that biting wit that comes from a caustic disposition, a dissatisfied, somehow offended or slighted temperament, from an ailing body or an infirm soul. We, of course, couldn't put our finger on it at the time, but we quickly realised with our childlike souls that Father Telesnicki's humour was not the right nourishment for us; it contained something spiteful and envious, something reminiscent of a demon that threw itself at a pedestrian's feet at night, tripping them to the ground, or shoved a stick between the spokes of a moving carriage, either to tip it over or break a wheel. This malicious, spiteful humour, which exploded with joy only when one of us made a silly mistake, did not lift our spirits at all, instead making us feel oppressed, restrained, and stifled. But these were only the beginnings, relatively harmless beginnings. What came next was something entirely different.

III

The first days of school were so-so. Father Telesnicki shouted, grew angry at times, mocked and ridiculed where explanations and good-natured patience were needed, but the classes went smoothly. We were used to simple teachers, to the Basilian novices and fathers who, instead of explanations, often dealt out slaps, and caned pupils instead of being more tolerant. Father Telesnicki seemed no worse, and in some ways was better than some of the others.

However, he had yet to live up to his reputation as a humourist, as a fun teacher. On the contrary, he became gloomier and more sullen day by day. He seemed to be ailing, lacking something; his face sometimes even looked sallow. Often in fits of anger, he would bite his thin, bloodless lips and look around as if searching for something or someone to unleash his anger on.

And one more thing. Although this was the third grade of a modern, urban-type elementary school and we had barely covered declensions and conjugations in grammar, those of us who were more observant and alert during lessons often realised that Father Telesnicki was ill-equipped even for this basic level. Arithmetic exercises in our *Rechnungsbuch* proved challenging for him; he even struggled with differentiating word cases in German, and distinguishing parts of speech.

One of Father Telesnicki's mistakes brought me into conflict with him for the first time. In German class the pupil sitting next to me had to translate the sentence: *Im Sommer herrscht grosse Hitze.*[29] He translated this into Polish as: *W lecie panuje wielkie gorąco.*[30] There followed the sentence: *In der Hitze spazieren ist schädlichh.*[31] The student began to stammer:

"*W go… w gora…*"

"Well, come on! What is: *In der Hitze?*"

"*W gorącem!*"[32]

"What-what?"

"*W gorącu.*"

"Hah-hah-hah! What did you say?"

"*W go… go… gorącości,*" babbled the flustered boy.

"Hah-hah-hah!" Father Telesnicki roared with laughter. "How are you declining it there, eh? Come on, decline it in order!"

"*Gorąco, gorąca, gorącemu…*"

Once more the teacher burst out laughing.

....

[29] German: "In summer it is very hot."

[30] Polish: "It is very hot in the summer."

[31] German: "Walking about in the heat is bad for you."

[32] Polish: "In the heat."

"What example do we use to decline *gorąco*?"

The boy did not know what to answer. Father Telesnicki stood before him.

"Well, well! Do we decline it like the word *tato*[33]?"

"No."

"Well, then maybe the word *mama*?"

"No."

"How about *osioł*[34]?"

The boy winced. He remained silent, but with his right hand he began to wipe away his tears.

"I see I can't get it out of you! *Gorąco* is declined in the same way as *zimno*[35], you ass. So, what will be the seventh case of *zimno*?"

"*W zimnie.*"

"And *gorąco*?"

"*W go… gorą…*"

The boy's innate sense of language rebelled against the example. He looked around in desperation and finally declared decisively:

"*W gorączce.*"[36]

By this time Father Telesnicki had no patience left. He grabbed the boy by the ear, and twisted it so hard that the fellow involuntarily let out a high-pitched squeal, and then he yelled at him:

"It's *w gorącie*, you blockhead! *W gorącie! W gorącie!* Remember that."

Some malicious or benevolent demon prompted me to raise my hand.

"And what do you want?" asked Father Telesnicki.

....

[33] Ukrainian: Dad.

[34] Polish: Donkey.

[35] Polish: Cold.

[36] Polish: "In a fever."

"Excuse me, sir, but *gorąco* is not declined," I blurted out.

"What do you mean, it's not declined?"

"*Gorąco* is neither a noun nor an adjective, it's an adverb, and adverbs are not declined."

"Is that so?" drawled Father Telesnicki. "And what is *zimno* then?"

"It's also an adverb, sir."

"So is *zimno* declined or not?"

I stood like a skittish calf that had run headlong into a wall.

"It's declined, sir."

"There, see! And how would you translate *die Hitze?*"

"*Upał.*"[37]

"Hah-hah-hah!" Father Telesnicki guffawed. "*Úpav! Úpav, úpav!*"[38] Continuing to repeat the word, making fun of the Ukrainian pronunciation, he ran around the classroom, almost skipping. "Hah-hah-hah! *Úpav.* Well-well, I'll have you 'fall'! Remember, sonny, from now on you are called *Úpav!* And so you don't forget, you can sit right here! Leave your desk now and move to the desk near the stove!"

And he pointed at the dunce's bench. He ran up to the board, grabbed a stick of chalk, and right in the middle of the desk wrote in large letters: UPAV.

"From now on you are to sit where I've written your new name! Quick march!"

I didn't know whether to cry, to feel ashamed, or to plead with him. To tell the truth, I didn't understand the situation and silently moved to my new spot. There was a slight commotion in the class; some of the pupils laughed; others, it seemed, did not quite understand the teacher's humour. Was it a joke, or a punishment, and if it was a punishment, then for what?

....

[37]   Polish: Heat. Stress is on the first syllable.

[38]   Ukrainian: Fell. In Ukrainian the stress is on the second syllable. The teacher is placing the stress on first syllable on purpose.

IV

About a week or two after school started, Father Telesnicki fully revealed his talent, which was truly uncanny and unusual. Its complete manifestation was aided by a seemingly small and insignificant object. One day, during class and out of nowhere, a small cane appeared in Father Telesnicki's hands. Thin, about half a meter long, it was just an ordinary piece of Spanish cane. We hadn't seen him carrying it into the classroom. It just appeared suddenly during class, possibly hidden until then in his bootleg. We barely noticed its appearance. We were all busy writing as the teacher dictated with his usual flourish, walking about the classroom. Then we heard a soft whistling sound. Only then did the bolder ones among us glance up at the teacher and notice the cane in his hand.

Of course, the sight of this pedagogical tool was nothing new to us. So, we didn't gasp or stop writing; on the contrary, it seemed to spur us on to write with even more eagerness, enthralled by the wisdom being dictated by Father Telesnicki.

However, we noticed a distinct change in Father Telesnicki's posture, voice, mood, and demeanour. He was livelier, more animated; his eyes had regained their sparkle, his movements were more lively, resilient, and flowing. From time to time, he smiled sweetly, clearly delighting in some thought or perhaps recalling a memory stirred by the swish of the cane. After finishing dictating, he approached a pupil in one of the back desks, looked at his open notebook, and without a word, struck him powerfully across his bent shoulders.

"Ouch!" the boy exclaimed, perhaps more from fright than pain.

"Ha-ha-ha!" Father Telesnicki roared with laughter, as he stood over the boy. "How have you written *vergeben*[39]?"

....

[39] German: To give away.

"F-e-r-g-e..." the pupil began spelling the word.

"It's V as in Victor! V as in Victor! Vee!" Father Telesnicki instructed, reinforcing each reminder with a new stroke of the cane upon the shoulders.

"I know now, sir! I know! I know!" the boy exclaimed.

"You know now, but this is a reminder for tomorrow, the day after, and forever and ever, amen!" Father Telesnicki quipped in Ukrainian and continued to thrash the poor boy, while roaring with laughter like a madman.

"Please, sir!" the pupil begged, twisting about in his seat, then ducked and hid under the desk.

"Come out at once!" yelled the teacher.

"No, I won't, because you'll kill me!" the frightened boy spoke from under the desk.

"Don't worry, I won't hit you anymore."

The pupil climbed out, but at that moment Father Telesnicki rushed up to him, grabbed him by the hair, and began to slam his head against the desk.

"This is for hiding! There! There! Three bumps on your forehead! You'll leave them there until tomorrow. Hah-hah-hah! Don't dare wash them off or wipe them away; I want to see them there tomorrow!"

We children became petrified at first, hearing the whistling of the cane and the banging against the desk. We thought that the beating would enrage the teacher, make him angry and furious. But not at all! After completing this disgusting abuse of the boy, our teacher was all cheer and smiles, joking, almost skipping as he walked about the classroom.

"Just so that you know," he spoke in a doctoral tone, as if drawing out the moral sense of what had just happened, "*vergeben, verjagen, verzeihen, verleihen,* and other similar words start with a 'v', not an 'f'. Who else knows any similar words?"

"*Verdrehen! Verderben! Vermindern!*" voices called out from different desks.

"*Fertig!*"[40] said my neighbour on the dunce's desk.

"Hah? What?" snapped Father Telesnicki. "Who said *fertig?*"

"Kozakevych."

"Kozakevych? You? How is *fertig* spelt?"

"It has an 'f' at the start."

"So why did you call it out?"

"I wasn't sure if it was similar to the other words, sir."

"Really? So, you want to make a fool of me?"

And Father Telesnicki's cane once more began its pedagogical work.

From then on, Father Telesnicki no longer appeared bored, sallow, or moody during classes. He had a grand diversion that evidently enhanced his good humour, improved his appetite, and invigorated his health. He entered the classroom like a wild animal tamer stepping into a cage, and he moved among us like the unrestrained lord of our bodies and souls. His thin cane moved even more sensitively among us. And not that first small yellow one that introduced us to Father Telesnicki in his new role. That first cane did not last more than two days of strenuous work. It was replaced by another one, pale-straw in colour, thickly knotted and much sturdier. This one was our tormentor's favourite because its knots caused more pain, its blows elicited louder cries, squeals and laments, and amid those screams and commotion Father Telesnicki would rush about the classroom roaring with laughter, clapping his hands, hopping up and down, spouting witticisms. He especially loved to sharpen his wit by making fun of pupils' surnames.

"Kozakevych! You're descended from the Cossacks. Suffer there, young fellow, and you'll become a Cossack leader yet!"

And the cane was ever busy, whether there was a reason or not. And since Kozakevych was a small feeble lad, and had

....

[40]   German: Ready.

a thin, squeaky voice, Father Telesnicki would guffaw with delight when he cried out:

"Oh, maybe you're not descended from Cossacks, maybe you're descended from a goat.[41] Goatie-goatie-goatie, maa! Goatie-goatie-goatie, maa!"

And he beat him and delighted in the child's unworldly screams. Then he moved on and within a few minutes was targeting Moroz[42] for some minor error in his multiplication table and started joking once more:

"Hey, Jack Frost – how many numbers have you crossed? How are you multiplying them, ha? Nine times nine is nine-ty-nine, right? What a multiplication table you have there! My, oh my! I need to keep teaching you! I'll show you!"

And when his hand tired and he felt the need to rest, he walked about the classroom, smiling sweetly as he gazed at the frightened, tear-stained faces of the children. The more such faces there were in the class, the merrier Father Tele-snicki felt.

"Come hither, you martyrs and righteous ones!" he declared, as if rubbing salt into the painful wounds of his victims. "Come hither, oh great righteous ones, oh most beloved ones. The first is Moroz – unable to sit because! Right, Moroz? The second is Korpak – he's just a big schmuck. Third comes Skrypoon – his bum's like a balloon. The fourth is Matkiwsky – no longer so frisky. The fifth is Ortinsky who was caned very briskly. The sixth is Federmesser – his isn't much better. And the seventh, Alerhand, got his with a strong hand."

After several weeks of such activity, the classroom atmosphere deteriorated to the point where the pupils became genuinely terrified and their academic performance worsened

....

[41] "Goat" in Ukrainian is *koza.*

[42] Literally means "frost" in Ukrainian.

significantly. Despite their best efforts and diligent study to avoid beatings, no amount of attentiveness helped. The more fearful pupils, when called to the blackboard, would lose their voice or forget whatever they had learned. Others, even if they knew the answers, lost faith in themselves upon realising that even the slightest mistake would bring the same punishment as that meted out to those who knew nothing. They resigned themselves to fate, either attending class with hopes of divine mercy – hoping the terrifying Basilian might overlook or not pick them – or they stopped coming to school altogether for several days, preferring to face punishment for unjustified absence after enjoying a few days of freedom by the river or in a nearby grove. This was far better than continuously living in fear and facing daily punishment. Meanwhile, constant anxiety, cries, and lamentation filled the classroom, all overshadowed by the savage, almost idiotic laughter of the so-called humorous reverend.

V

We continually lived as if in some fog. Our usual childish cheerfulness had disappeared. We went about as if stunned, appearing sullen and angry. Friendly play was generally forbidden at the time and even sometimes punished; however, that year if third-grade pupils were ever inclined to play, they only engaged in games that started and ended with fights.

They fought among themselves, fought in the streets with Jewish lads, with truants, with street urchins. I don't know if the other children complained to their parents or guardians about the daily beatings in class; it seems likely, because there were rumours that some of the wealthier Jewish merchants, seeing that their children came home covered in bruises day after day, went to complain to the rector, and when this did not help, they withdrew their children from the school. Some people threatened to take the matter to court, but there was no hope of ever winning such a case. Back then in Drohobych, corporal punishment was considered an integral part of the educational process, especially in elementary school. As for myself, I know that I never complained to anyone, never told anyone what happened in class, but the memory of those repugnant scenes, which dragged on every day for an entire year, became deeply imprinted on my soul.

I recall that, whenever I found a moment of free time, I would grab a stick, hide somewhere in the weeds, and slash, slash at all the leaves, the stems, branches, flowers, anything that could be destroyed, beating and slashing away until everything around me turned into a disgusting ruin. Many times, homeowners and housewives scolded me for this, because in my destructive frenzy I failed to differentiate between harmful plants such as thistles, nettles, and burdocks, and useful plants such as beets, beans, tomatoes, and other vegetables. At night I would scream in my dreams, or recite classwork, and then weep and plead for mercy, to the point that 'auntie' could stand it no longer and often woke me with nudges, asking half sympathetically and half angrily:

"What's wrong with you, lad?"

All the same, I was a good pupil, and Father Telesnicki rarely managed to catch me making a mistake. Father Telesnicki began each lesson by choosing his victims with an eagle eye, typically calling out those who looked most frightened and those who, to use his own words, bore the look of a guilty conscience. He had a habit of calling ten or twelve students to the front of the class at once and then he would question and torment them until each in turn had tasted his cane. The 'dunce's desk', where I sat, was a particularly advantageous spot, for between the teacher's desk and me stood an iron pot-bellied stove with a massive base some half a metre in height, which blocked his view of my desk. Thus we, who inhabited the desk, were seldom in Father Telesnicki's line of sight. Usually, he noticed us only after his initial punishments had improved his mood, and he would run down from the dais, joking and jumping about the classroom, waving his arms. At such times, he was 'kind' and liked it when students approved of his idiotic laughter, and only picked on someone not called to the front in exceptional cases.

So, I was rarely subjected to Father Telesnicki's direct attention. Yet, the impressions from that year remain with me, indelible and painful to this day, and not only do I feel they deformed my character and soured my disposition, but they also caused me considerable emotional distress throughout my life. Certainly, other students fared no better, and many indeed suffered far worse.

I'll give just one example. My neighbour in the dunce's desk was a boy named Voliansky – a quiet, meek young lad with a head so elongated and flattened on the sides like none I've seen since. The boy was not made for schoolwork, at least not the kind offered by the Basilians in Drohobych. I have no idea how he managed to reach the third grade, but in the third grade, he was a real dunce: he couldn't read well, add, or write – and forget about declensions, constructing sentences in German, multiplication, and division. I can't remember what incident led him to join me in the dunce's desk – likely it was the work of Father Telesnicki's cane. However, after seating him next to me, our torturer left him in peace for a while. He 'tested' him occasionally when he was in a good mood, but upon receiving no response, was content with his stock joke: 'Voliansky is a Dardanian[43] donkey. He learns as much as a billygoat provides us with milk,' and he would go on his merry way.

At first, I followed the example set by the other boys and the teacher, and made fun of Voliansky, calling him a

....

[43] Dardania – an ancient kingdom from the 4th century BC in what is now Kosovo and Serbia.

Dardanian donkey and the like. But our relationship soon changed. It started with small acts of mutual assistance: one of us needed a pen, another a pencil, someone forgot ink, another a book – we gradually began to give each other a hand. I came to realize that Voliansky was a good boy. Then, during breaks, as we left school or before classes, we engaged in conversation. Naturally, as children from rural areas, we talked about our villages, our favourite games and pastimes. It turned out that we both loved the forest, green meadows, fast-flowing rivers in the foothills, catching fish, birds, picking mushrooms and berries. These topics gave us endless topics for discussion, during which we instinctively avoided the 'evil of the day', all the nastiness surrounding us in class. I also realized that Voliansky had a remarkable gift for story-telling. He did not stammer, did not falter, did not repeat the same words, unlike when he responded to questions posed by our teacher. His words flowed smoothly and freely, were well-chosen and so melodious that they immediately captured my heart. He spoke like an old man, solemnly, though not at all pretentiously, with a tone of muted melancholy. His sweet, steady soft voice still rings in my soul. It had the feeling of something tender, soft, smooth, and effortless, like a long, very smooth silk thread stretching somewhere into the endless distance – and that was the impression his stories left.

I can't recall what he talked about, but the effect his stories had on me will remain with me until the day I die. When he began talking, he seemed to become a different person, as if another spirit entered him and spoke through his lips. And he never repeated himself, never spoke about the same thing twice or used the same words. He always had something new to tell, or perhaps he simply had a fresh approach to telling the story.

I quickly grew to love his stories, like a bee delighting in the honey from another bee's hive, and became his constant companion, or more accurately, his listener. I started visiting him at home, trying to help him with homework for the next day. Voliansky approached homework like a sheep being led to slaughter. We would sit struggling away for half an hour. Whatever homework there was – arithmetic problems or German exercises – we wrote, or rather Voliansky copied from me, but he couldn't for the life of him grasp any of my explanations.

"No," he would say sadly, "that won't stay in my head. Let me tell you something…"

And we would find a spot to sit – whether in some corner of an empty storeroom or in the garden where no one could hear us, and he would tell me another story. When he ran out of his own experiences, he turned to folk tales. And astonishingly, this young boy, who couldn't remember how to decline *die Biene* or *der Bär*, or how much seven times eight was, knew by heart a seemingly endless number of folk tales and could tell them with such intricacy, so nicely and fluently that I, having grown up listening to good village storytellers of various types – both jovial and sombre – was completely enchanted when he spoke. I still remember this boy as an unexplained psychological phenomenon. If you added up all the time he spent telling stories in my presence, it would have surely amounted to at least a week, if not more. And all that time, Voliansky spoke fluently, smoothly, appropriately, without any superfluous phrases – and what was most amazing – he never repeated a single folk tale. His stories flowed harmoniously, like a small stream in the foothills, gently babbling, never pausing, never forming whirlpools, or quiet eddies, or noisy waterfalls, and never turning back on themselves. I was so enchanted by his folk tales that, although I was a poor writer, I tried to record them at home in the evenings from memory. But to no avail! I couldn't! The charm of his storytelling lay in his words, the tone of his voice – at that time my childish hand was unable to transfer even a trace of that onto paper, and I, discouraged, tossed my notes into the fire.

Perhaps I'm exaggerating a bit, that is, through the prism of past years and the boy's tragic death, his figure may have grown larger than life. But that's beyond my control, for memories are truly a blend of *Dichtung und Wahrheit*.[44] The more sincerely a memoirist strives to truthfully depict, with every colour and shade, the image of past events retained in his soul, the greater the danger that he will add something extraneous, which has been overlaid later by the tide of time. But in attempting to go the other way, by providing only the bare bones of a memory, a silhouette or even just the wooden framework, that is even more damaging to the fidelity of memories, for it presents only a skeleton instead of a living body, an empty shadow rather than concrete reality.

Let my little friend Voliansky appear before you in the enlightened form in which he lives in my soul! What harm will it do, if in reality he was less interesting, had less unique talent than it seemed to me then and still seems to me now? And the crime perpetrated against him will not be any the less because of this.

The reason for his death was none other than that same teacher and tormentor of our class, Father Telesnicki! I don't precisely remember how it happened, but once he 'took to him in his own way'. He called him to the blackboard, started asking questions, and at the first wrong answer, began to deride, tease, and harangue him so much, that the poor boy lost his ability to speak.

"Voliansky, you really have learnt nothing at all!" yelled Father Telesnicki, tugging him now by the arm, now by the ear, and hopping around him like a devil prancing around a sinful soul. "I've caught you out, warned you, reminded you, again and again, and still, you fail to learn a single thing. Oh,

....

44   Poetry and truth (German) – the subtitle of Goethe's autobiography *Aus meinem Leben* [From my Life].

sonny, this can't go on! We must see where your legs sprout from! Come here, class captain, assistants! Stretch him out!"

The class captain and his assistants rushed over promptly. Voliansky stood as if stunned, not crying, not pleading, just looking with dazed eyes at Father Telesnicki, who was becoming increasingly amused.

"Come on, lay him down! Or wait! His poor father spent money on those pants… The pants are not to blame. Pull them off."

As if stung, Voliansky dashed forward. From afar I could see his pale face suddenly flush red. He threw himself at the knees of Father Telesnicki, began to embrace them, pleading for mercy:

"Please, sir! I'll start learning! I won't eat or sleep until I learn everything! Please give me one more chance! Only this last time!"

"No!" Father Telesnicki yelled joyously, clapping his hands. "Come on, grab him!"

The class captain and his assistants grabbed Voliansky by the arms and began to unbutton his pants.

"Please, sir! Not on my bare skin! Only not that! I'll be quiet, I promise! Just not on my bare skin!"

"No! Intentionally no!" yelled Father Telesnicki. "You've been sitting on your backside too long, we need to give you a good hiding, so that you won't be able to sit down at least for a few days!"

And he went over to the window and grabbed a metre-long alder stick, gnarled and covered in rough bark. For several days, Father Telesnicki had complained that he couldn't get enough canes for our class, but that day we saw such sticks out of alder leaning against every window. At first, we didn't know why they were standing there; some guessed that it was to keep the curtains open, others reasoned that they were for staking climbing beans that grew under the windows in the monastery's vegetable garden. No one dared guess the true designation of this equipment, one that was duly felt by the skin of each of us. And yet everyone looked at these mysterious sticks with respect, and, though the teacher was not present in class, no one dared touch them, even less to toss them into the garden or onto the street. Now, when Father Telesnicki grabbed hold of one of those sticks and, waving it about, cheerfully approached his victim, we suddenly understood their purpose. Meanwhile, an unexpected change came over Voliansky. The inevitable and even more shameful fight, the likes of which our class had not yet witnessed and of which he was to become the first victim, drove him over the edge. This seemingly weak and small boy became possessed by the power of desperation. He gave a sudden jerk, punched one assistant with his fist, and kneed the other one, who was unbuttoning his pants, in the chest. Both boys jumped away from him. Class captain Zajac, who was holding him from behind, threw him down onto the dais. Voliansky gritted his teeth and began thrashing his feet about. Holding the alder stick in his hand, Father Telesnicki jumped around him, and then at the moment that the teacher leaned down, Voliansky kicked into the air and his boot struck the teacher in the teeth.

"Oho!" exclaimed Father Telesnicki, pressing his palm to his lips. Blood dribbled from his split lip. Father Telesnicki's pain was probably not that bad, because he took out a handkerchief from his pocket, pressed it to his mouth with his left hand, and with his right waved the stick about and, without losing his sense of humour, continued talking:

"Hey, sonny! So, this is your style? Well, we can't have that! We can't let this go unpunished! Alright, lay him out!"

In the meantime, the assistants, together with the class captain, had overpowered Voliansky, pulled off his pants and underpants, and stretched him out on the dais. Both assistants held his legs tightly, while the class captain sat on his shoulders, holding down both his hands, and Father Telesnicki rushed in to start beating the boy's bare body with his stick. After the first blow, Voliansky screamed something terrible. Father Telesnicki stopped, savouring this cry of pain and could not stop himself from joking:

"Oh, I guess for once we've coaxed a human voice out of you! Let's try one more time!"

The second blow resulted in a fresh unworldly scream.

"Oh, this is even better!" joked Father Telesnicki. "Just like in that song:"

> *Dobył tak pięknego głosu baraniego,*
> *Aż się stary Józef przestraszył od niego.*[45]

And then the blows came thick and fast.

"You drew blood, and now it's my turn to draw blood! Blood for blood! Blood for blood!" Father Telesnicki kept repeating.

And the blows continued to rain down... The screams, screeches, and squeals of the unfortunate boy failed to move the teacher. Blood dripped from under the alder knots onto the dais floorboards, but Father Telesnicki kept swinging away. The alder stick became covered in blood, and as the teacher swung it about, blood began to splatter across the white classroom walls. Voliansky no longer let out a sound, he had obviously fainted.

Father Telesnicki stopped. He was breathing heavily from the exertion. He took the bloodstained handkerchief away from his lips, then stepped out into the passage and returned with a glass of water, which he emptied onto the unconscious boy. Voliansky opened his eyes and groaned.

....

[45] Polish: "He let out such a beautiful ram's voice,
That old Joseph took fright there and then."

"Ha-ha-ha! Mister Voliansky! How was your nap?" Father Telesnicki quipped. "Know how it tastes now? Come on, boys, help him get dressed!"

The class captain and his assistants picked up Voliansky and put his clothes in order, holding him up from time to time.

"So, you don't have the strength to stand on your own two feet? But you had enough strength to kick out my teeth! Ho-ho, sonny boy! See how it looks here now? Take a look!"

And he showed him the bloodstained stick and pointed to the specks of blood on the wall.

"See? Do you know what that's called? Remember, it's called *kutya*[46] with poppyseed! Remember how on Christmas Eve it's thrown up at the ceiling and it sticks in splatters? What do people chant then? You don't know? Well, they say: 'Grow and multiply, rye, wheat, and every grain!' The same applies to us. From such seeds should sprout diligence, skill, obedience, submission, respect for your elders, and every other virtue. And now, back to your desk."

Quietly groaning, Voliansky stood without moving. The Class captain's assistants took him by the arms and led him back to his desk.

As he sat down, he let out a gasp from the pain.

"Ha-ha-ha!" Father Telesnicki guffawed. "Feel some tingling, do you? There, it's not good to sit in one place for too long! Ha-ha-ha! Laugh, boys, laugh!"

And the entire class was forced to laugh.

"That's right! Nice! That's how it should be! Didn't I tell you before, that you should laugh and cry when I tell you to? See, I've brought you to this point. Good, boys! I praise you for this!"

....

[46] *Kutya* is a dish of boiled wheat and honey with ground poppyseed traditionally eaten during the Christmas Eve meal.

While laughter filled the class and all that cruel mockery of children's souls continued, I sat in the dunce's desk next to my punished friend, choking back tears. Something clenched at my throat, and tormented me with pain, shame, and pity, as if I myself were to blame for everything that had happened, as if I had committed a grave crime by watching this torment calmly, without screaming for help or lying down to take the blows myself. I secretly leaned over and kissed Voliansky's cold hand, drenching it with my tears.

He sat next to me, pale as a corpse. There was not a hint of rosiness in his face or on his lips. His eyes and face were wet with tears. He looked at me with a mixture of astonishment and silent gratitude, and whispered:

"Will you walk me home?"

I nodded.

"And tell the landlady everything that happened?"

I nodded once more. We stopped talking. Father Telesnicki was already prancing about the class, waving the bloodied stick about, seeking a fresh victim for his cannibalistic humour.

I walked Voliansky to his lodgings and told his landlady everything that had happened. The poor woman grabbed hold of her head, seeing the battered child. While soaking and peeling off his bloodied pants from his wounds, she wept as if he were her own dead child. She cursed the inhuman monk, threatened to go to the rector, to call a doctor to issue a medical report, but probably did nothing of the sort. All she did was put Voliansky to bed. When I returned that evening, he had a high fever and did not recognize me. Only then did the doctor come and they sent me away. I never saw Voliansky again. He died a week later of brain inflammation. We buried him with pomp, the whole school walked in pairs to the funeral. Everyone was happy because that day there was no school.

VI

But I've run a little ahead of myself in the chronological order of events, having jumped to Voliansky's punishment, which was the culmination of all the dreadful events I had to witness that terrible year. Father Telesnicki did not immediately and without some resistance from our side bring us to the point where we cried and laughed at his command.

Certainly, this struggle was entirely childish. There was no thought of any conscious, united action, any possibility of resistance, any protest on our part. We didn't even quickly come up with the idea of complaining to someone about the conduct of our class master. But who could we complain to? As for Father Barusewicz, the rector, although we loved him and considered him even-handed, we had no access to him. Father Telesnicki pre-empted us, complaining about us to him time and again, saying that we were lazy, disobedient, unruly, and that it was impossible to deal with us without meting out punishment. Obviously, in this way he pre-empted any complaints from us about beatings and cruelty. On the contrary, under the influence of his complaints, Father Barusewicz visited our class several times, scolded us sharply, stayed usually for half an hour during the lesson, and having seen firsthand that the boys indeed answered poorly and knew little, he repeated his reprimands and left, shrugging his shoulders, obviously giving Father Telesnicki a free hand to do with us as he pleased.

We would have most likely complained to our beloved catechist, Father Krasicki, but unfortunately, he fell ill in the fall and Father Telesnicki, our tormentor, took over teaching Religion. Only sometime after Christmas did Father Krasicki recover sufficiently to be able to attend our class.

He entered quietly, as he was wont to do, so that we did not hear his steps, then suddenly flung open the door and, as if ambushing us, gazed into the class and laughed with his cheerful, good-natured laughter:

"Hah-hah-hah!"

Ah, but it was not his usual, old laugh! It was a forced, borrowed cheerfulness. And his face was not the one we knew – round, healthy, joyful, with sparkling, joyous eyes. Now it looked somewhat hollow, a brick-red colour, with dark circles under his extinguished eyes, and yellow patches on his temples. And we did not respond to his laughter as before, with friendly, cheerful laughter, but sat quietly, like mice in a trap, tense, and only a few boys smiled reluctantly. Slowly, with his head protruding forward, Father Krasicki walked to the middle of the class, and stood there for a long time, surveying the students, as if searching for something lost or looking like a traveller trying to figure out where he was.

"Children!" he suddenly exclaimed with a playful fear in his voice. "What's wrong with you? Why are you sitting like lobsters in a bag? Why aren't you laughing? Aren't you happy to see me?"

"We are," we replied.

"But what's wrong? I can see that you've forgotten how children should rejoice. Well, how have you been during the time that we haven't seen each other?"

No one said a thing. Father Krasicki began to question us one by one, started to extract the words out of us, and only after some time managed to get one, then another, and then a third to burst into tears and begin recounting their ordeals. At first, Father Krasicki didn't want to believe these stories and ordered one after another of the boys to undress. He gasped and beat his hands against his cassock, seeing the countless bruises on the children's bodies, along with scabs and scars of healed wounds.

"God in Heaven! What is this?" he asked.

"Don't you study, don't you pay attention in class, are you giving Father Telesnicki trouble?"

But then, without waiting for our answers, he added:

"No, even if you weren't children but a flock of sheep, it would still be a sin to torment you like this. Come, come, quieten down there! I'll have a word about this with Father Telesnicki and with the rector, somehow, we'll sort this out."

Obviously poor Father Krasicki did not realise that his good intentions might exacerbate our situation. The next day, before the first morning class, a monastery sycophant – a student from grade four who lived in the monastery, receiving food and clothing there (primarily thanks to Father Krasicki), studied in the school, and simultaneously sang in the church choir and acted as an altar boy's helper – called several pupils from our class, including me, out into the passage and said with a look of considerable concern:

"May the Lord have mercy, boys, what did you do yesterday?"

"What's the matter?"

"Why did you tell Father Krasicki that Father Telesnicki beats you?"

"So? Isn't it true?"

"And what of it! Now you're in real trouble."

"What kind of trouble?"

"Yesterday in the refectory, Father Krasicki began to scold Father Telesnicki. At first, he spoke in a level voice, but when Father Telesnicki claimed that it was all lies, that the boys were lazy and disobedient, and that they had lied about being beaten, Father Krasicki became very angry. I've never seen him that furious. He turned completely red, like a beet, threw down his spoon, and yelled: 'Father, that you have no heart, I was witness to that yesterday when I examined the bruises and scabs on those children. And now I see you have no honour either. You have made a great mistake in choosing your calling. You should have become a butcher, not a priest and a teacher!' Then Father Telesnicki jumped up from his seat and began to scream as well. The rector tried to calm them down, and I was ordered to leave the refectory at that point. I didn't hear what happened next, and only know that upon returning from the refectory, Father Krasicki immediately got into bed and began to cough up blood. I ran to fetch a doctor. I have no idea what the doctor said, but Father Krasicki is sick in bed."

The arselicker was right. Father Telesnicki appeared in class in an exceptionally jovial mood and set himself a lot of work with us that day: he did not rest until every student in the class, including the class captain, Zajac (four of the strongest boys struggled for several minutes with him until they finally subdued him on the dais with Father Telesnicki's personal help), had tasted the stick. It was a day of joy for him! He delivered many witticisms that day, the most dazzling of which was the last one. He wrote on the board in large letters:

'*Dnia 15 grudnia wielka klęska w III klasie*'.[47]

And under this in Ukrainian:

'On 15 December there was a great *kliaska*[48] in Grade III'.

"Hah-hah-hah!" he roared with laughter. "Come on, Úpav!" he addressed me. "Why is it called *kliaska*?"

"Because when people are being beaten, you can hear the sound of smacking, of slaps," I replied.

"Good. So, each of you must write this one hundred times for tomorrow, so that you remember this day and these words for the rest of your lives, and know what it means to complain about one teacher to another."

We never saw Father Krasicki in class again. After that memorable scene in the monastery's refectory, he never left his bed again, although he did live to see the day that Father Telesnicki was transferred from Drohobych to Dobromyl.

....

[47] Polish: "On 15 December there was a great defeat in grade 3."

[48] In Western Ukrainian, *kliaskaty* means "to slap" or "to smack." A play on words with the Polish *klęska* [defeat] sounding much like the Ukrainian *kliaska*.

That same 'arselicker' told me that when he was leaving Drohobych, Father Telesnicki had wanted to enter Father Krasicki's cell to bid him farewell. But the ailing priest refused to see him.

"I have never wished ill on anyone in my life," he said. "I've never quarrelled with anyone, and have never harboured a grudge against anyone who offended me. And I have no recollection what Father Telesnicki said to me. But what he did to those children, I will never forgive or absolve. God may forgive, if He wishes, but I am not God. If it is a sin, then I am willing to take this sin with me to the grave. However, it seems to me that it would be a far greater sin to shake his hand, to warmly grasp that hand stained with the most heinous crime of systematic child murder."

VII

For now, Father Telesnicki had unlimited authority over our class and maintained it until the end of the year. True, he had to overcome another hurdle, but he dealt with this even more easily and quickly than with Father Krasicki. The hurdle was Mr Bilynsky, an interesting figure of the time, about whom it is appropriate to mention a few words here.

We children did not know exactly who Mr Bilynsky was, although he was a daily visitor to our school. Only later did I learn that he was a former public-school teacher who had gone blind from long years of work, lost his job, and, having no other means of supporting himself, and possibly driven by other, more idealistic motives, settled in Drohobych. He bought or rented a small house somewhere on Tkatska Street near Solony Stavok and opened a kind of pension for poor pupils. He took in the children of wealthier peasants or even priests as boarders – ten, twelve, even fifteen at a time. His wife and a maid cooked for them, washed their clothes, sewed them garments, even made them hats (Mr Bilynsky's boarders could be recognized straight away by those hats, unbecoming and all of the same shape, which we dubbed *hyrkani*), and Mr Bilynsky himself not only provided domestic care but also worked as a tutor, reviewed lectures, tested the pupils, and made sure they did their written homework. Although unfit for public service, he was not entirely blind. I don't know what his specific ailment was, but he could only see very close up, almost needing to press a book to his nose or his nose to the blackboard. When walking or sitting, he constantly moved his head from side to side as if he were quickly scanning the lines of a very large book. However, the most interesting thing about Mr Bilynsky was the unusual privilege he had acquired at the Basilian Fathers school, which was extraordinary for that time: he would come to the school every day along with his boarders, drop them off in their respective classes, and then sit in the school throughout the entire lesson, spending an hour in one class and another in the next. He usually sat in the last row, listened to the lessons attentively, particularly when one of his boarders was being questioned, and sometimes he would pass comments or, pretending to scold the boy, cleverly suggest the correct answer.

Mr Bilynsky didn't interact much with the other boys, but nevertheless, we all liked him. During breaks, he sat quietly, never preventing us from shouting or running around, patiently enduring the cloud of dust stirred up by 60 or 70 pairs of boys' feet. And when, before lessons, the whole class was uncertain about a particular grammatical rule or arithmetic calculation, we would approach Mr Bilynsky, and he never refused to explain it to us. His boarders often laughed at him for his frugality (he was parsimonious, wearing simple, patched clothing, and he accustomed his boarders to similarly modest and simple attire), but they loved him for his patience and kindness. There was a well-known joke in Drohobych that Mr Bilynsky had only one punishment for disobedient and lazy boys in his boarding house: to poke the offender with his own week-old, unshaven beard.

At first Father Telesnicki tolerated Mr Bilynsky in his class. Sometimes, when scientific questions puzzled him, he would turn to him and say:

"Mr Bilynsky, and what do you think?"

Mr Bilynsky would get up from his place, continuously nodding his head, and in a stuttering, muffled voice, he would give his response or, stepping up to the blackboard, he would help solve an arithmetical problem.

Accustomed to the old practices of the Basilian schools, Mr Bilynsky never protested when teachers punished students in class. On the contrary, sometimes, when a punishment was inflicted on one of his boarders who had caused him trouble through disobedience or laziness, and whom he hadn't dared to punish at home, he would express his satisfaction with a muffled grumble:

"Ah, yes, yes, yes! He deserves it."

After hearing such words of approval on several occasions, Father Telesnicki grew even fonder of him and behaved in class as if there were no outsider present at all. How great was his amazement when one day, during an exceptionally 'cheerful' lesson – cheerful for Father Telesnicki but painful for several dozen pupils – in the midst of the general, deathly silence of the frightened children, loud sobbing was heard coming from the corner of the last row. Mr Bilynsky, hunched over and pressing his face against the desktop, was crying bitterly.

"What's the matter back there?" called out Father Telesnicki.

No one answered. The sobbing could still be heard.

"Mr Bilynsky! Is that you? What's wrong?"

Mr Bilynsky got to his feet, his head shaking more rapidly than usual.

"Excuse me, reverend teacher! It just grabbed at my heart."

"What has?" Father Telesnicki asked in a mocking tone, as he approached the desk at the very back.

"Something… something you've never felt yourself. Pity… pity toward these poor children."

"Oho!"

"And one other thing… Insomnia. For two months now, reverend father, I have been unable to fall asleep peacefully one single time."

"And why is that?"

"It's all because of these kids."

"Ah, see! Such rascals! Of course, how could you…"

"No, reverend fa… father," Mr Bilynsky interrupted him. "Not rascals. During the day, I can't complain about them. During the day, they are quiet, diligent, and they study. But at night, they scream in their sleep, cry, and thrash about. You know, reverend fa… father, for two months now I haven't been able to sleep peacefully one single night."

Only now did Father Telesnicki understand. His face flushed red. We all held our breaths. We thought that he would attack the old blind teacher, or at the very least whip him with his stick, which he had in his hand. But no, the humour prevailed.

"Ha-ha-ha!" he burst out laughing. "Really, I had no idea that Mr Bilynsky knew how to joke. But you know, Mr Bilynsky, I would ask one thing of you. Can you see letters printed in a book?"

"If they are ve… very big and close up…"

"Well then, the hole through which one exits out of this classroom is quite big. And if you walk up to the door, it will be quite close and you can feel your way out with your hands. So, I beg you to leave now and never show your face here again."

"Sir… sir…" Mr Bilynsky tried to compete with him. "I've been sitting here for ten years and have never been spoken to like this. The reverend rector himself has allowed me to be here."

"You can go to the reverend rector or the reverend canon himself, but as long as I am master of this class, what I say goes, and not anyone else. I don't want to see you here ever again. I won't take any notice of your age or your blindness, and I'll have you thrown out the door."

"Reve… reverend fa… father!" Mr Bilynsky babbled away, wiping the tears from his blind eyes and, grabbing his hat, which we had dubbed an *ober-hyrkania*, slowly left the class-room, sobbing.

We never saw him again.

VIII

Having gotten rid of this solitary external witness to his exploits in the classroom, Father Telesnicki could now amuse himself with us as he pleased. Now nothing stood in his way. By Easter, out of the original 80 students, only half remained in class. What was most interesting was that our kind-hearted rector seemed to see and know nothing, although who knows, maybe he tried to rein in Father Telesnicki but to no avail? We children heard rumours of hostility that was building up against Father Telesnicki in town, across various social strata. Once, it was said, when Father Telesnicki appeared in a sweet shop with the rector, the wealthy Jewish merchants there, taking no notice of the rector's presence, threw our teacher out the door. There was also a rumour that in the suburb of Zadvirna young men had lain in wait for him, hearing that he was meant to visit a farm owned by the Basilians one Saturday. Unfortunately, instead of Father Telesnicki, another brother went, and he was brought back late that the evening, unconscious and bloodied, with words chalked on his back by some merciful hand: 'Sorry, brother, but how the hell were we to know that you weren't Telesnicki'.

Father Telesnicki taught and played. For the final months of the school year, he hardly taught us anything, merely bullying the children. He was no longer satisfied simply beating the pupils, he devised ways to torment their souls more than their bodies. He no longer punished in any way other than 'on bare skin', extending each punishment by five, ten, or even more minutes. When the poor delinquent, his heavy bottom exposed, was laid on the dais or on a bench and firmly held down, Father Telesnicki would walk up and sharply swing his stick through the air, without striking the lad – then burst into uproarious laughter as the poor victim, not yet feeling any pain, screamed from the mere whistle of the stick.

"Wait there, sonny! Why are you screaming? Nothing's happened yet!" he intoned. "Well, tell me, does it hurt?"

"No," the poor martyr replied.

"There, see. What about now?"

And then a strong blow struck naked skin.

"Now that's something else. Now you can holler."

His favourite pastime was bargaining with a delinquent.

"Come, you didn't know your lesson for today. So, tell me, what should your punishment be?"

"Please, sir, I did my homework!" the pupil assured him through tears.

"Alright then, good, so you did the homework, but you never learnt a thing. What should your punishment be then?"

When the student did not answer, he took it upon himself to estimate the number of blows. When the pupil mentioned a small number, he seemed to agree, but demanded the poor boy receive them in silence, without shouting, as his proper due. When the boy agreed, he would hit him with such force that the boy could not stop himself from crying out, and then Father Telesnicki triumphed:

"Ha-ha, sonny! And what about our agreement? You screamed? Then sorry, for that you get a double dose. I'm not to blame here."

That year finally ended. It was surely the most terrifying, most miserable year of my life. We joyfully parted ways with Father Telesnicki and never saw him again. He was transferred from Drohobych to Dobromyl and was made a monastic preacher. The memory of him lay heavily on my heart for many years and has not faded even now; and it will not fade until the day I die.

Who was he? A deliberate criminal, a peculiar doctrinaire who acted in good faith, or a madman who by some mistake of fate had ended up on the teaching podium in Drohobych instead of being confined to the mental asylum in Kulparkiv. I still do not know. I long hesitated to revive my memories of him. But enough of hesitation. I am casting off at least part of those heavy memories. Let them fall as an indelible stain of disgrace upon his memory, and upon all those who appointed and tolerated him in that position, and upon all those who treat teaching like a cruel toy to satisfy their savage instincts, rather than as a great labour of love, patience and self-denial.

1903

THE MUSTARD SEED

(From my Recollections)

I

During the time I attended the gymnasium[49], Drohobych was a town very rich in negative attributes. To enumerate what it was lacking would make for a very long list. There was not a single decent café, nor a restaurant, nor a public library, nor an educational society, nor indeed any societies, whether of a political or an educational nature. There were practically none of the things that even begin to define a European town. There wasn't even any drinkable water, except for the home-sourced brackish kind, which outsiders were unable to stomach. Most streets lacked pavements and lighting, and the rambling suburbs, especially Zadvirne, Zavizne and Viytivska Hora, were mere villages with thatched roofs and paling fences, completely preserving their rural character. The railway from Drohobych to Stryi was opened only when I was in my seventh year at the gymnasium. Until then, Drohobych was a 'free royal town', which, despite its elementary school and gymnasium, was free of everything that exuded civilization and a more lively intellectual life.

This detachment from intellectual life also left its mark on the gymnasium. The teachers who came here, especial-

....

[49] A secondary school that prepares students for tertiary education.

ly the younger graduates, either single or, even if married, were often of weaker character and quickly forgot about any intellectual pursuits, taking to drink. They became regulars at Bayer's solitary Christian shop, which also sold colonial goods and had a breakfast room. They often came to class drunk, and needless to say, their scholarship suffered. Only a few steered clear of this group, notably the Turczyński brothers – Julij, a well-known historian and writer, and Emeryk, a botanist – along with Dr Antonevich and Iv. Wierchratski, both catechist brothers, the Ukrainian Father Toronsky and the Latin rite Father Dronżek. The leader of the drinking circle was Osmulsky. Nicknamed Dragon by the students, he was a substitute teacher, who taught French and occasionally filled in for other subjects, as well as being a humourist extraordinaire. He was a dangerous role model for the drinking circle because his ability to hold his liquor was as large as his girth. No one ever saw him drunk. After a night of heavy drinking, he would enter the classroom as if nothing had happened, conducting his four hours of classes calmy, with even the sharpest students unable to detect any signs of his insobriety. Drinking with him was ruinous for those who were less resilient; his witty remarks and jests encouraged them to drink ever more to keep up with him, and then he would laugh uproariously with his booming beer-soaked voice when his drinking partners slipped under the table or collapsed like sheaves in the marketplace, or mercilessly zigzagged their way through the streets.

Needless to say, after seeing such examples of behaviour by figures in authority, the gymnasium students also sought similar diversions. In junior school, even before my time, there was an old Jesuit tradition of periodically brawling with the Jews. Such fights usually occurred during the months of June and July, the season for swimming in the river. When people went swimming, which was usually on Fridays and Saturdays, fights broke out that sometimes ended in serious injuries, especially as a result of mutual stone throwing. In the past, the senior school also participated in these battles; this was at a time when senior school was predominantly attended by older youths, who sought an outlet for their youthful energies. By the time I reached senior school, a 'younger' generation had appeared, and fighting with the Jews was no longer in fashion.

For many students in senior school, these years were a time of sexual maturation; small wonder then that, finding neither parental guidance nor sufficiently strong intellectual and academic interests to absorb their attention, the boys became involved in various 'romances' with servant girls and female students from the girls' school; some even found sympathizers among the teachers' wives who, bored in the absence of their husbands who were engaged in the worship of Bacchus at Bayer's, sought diversions wherever they could. In and out of the classroom, there were secret, intermittent whispers, laughter, and jokes full of insinuations, obviously lewd and incomprehensible to those of us not in the know. From the general hubbub during breaks or before class, women's names surfaced here and there, and once, to his great indignation, Catechist-Father Toronsky, upon entering the sixth grade, saw a convoluted theological question written in large letters on the blackboard: 'What does it mean to love a girl in a Christian-Catholic way?' The fellow tried to turn this into practically a criminal case, and reported it to the principal, demanding the convening of a meeting and the initiation of an investigation to find out who had written these words on the blackboard, even threatening punishment, but in his zeal, he had forgotten about the need for material evidence: while he was in the office submitting his report, the incriminating words disappeared from the blackboard. The principal found nothing upon entering the classroom and somehow managed to mollify the moralist reverend father, who nevertheless did not give up, doggedly trying to find the culprit on his own – but, of course, to no avail.

Needless to say, the students also engaged in drinking, but to their credit, it must be said that their parties, while louder and rowdier, were generally less frequent and more decent than those of the teachers. The students chatted, sang songs and went their separate ways by eleven o'clock, having drunk two, some of them three or four glasses; there were no instances, as far as I can recall, of students becoming blind drunk, spending the whole night in a tavern or staggering about the streets inebriated. And yet, it was mostly the sons from wealthier families who participated in such drinking sessions; the poorer students rarely visited taverns and drank very little, because they simply couldn't afford it.

There were almost no social or intellectual pursuits, or any common intellectual interests. The students read very little. The gymnasium library was very poor; of the teachers, from memory, only Julij Turczyński had his own private library and occasionally loaned books to those students in whom he had more trust – these were almost exclusively Polish boys. As far as I can recall, school rules forbade the reading of newspapers, and I went through the entire gymnasium without reading newspapers, with the exception of *Druh*, which began to appear in 1874 and which published my poems. But from year five, having read the dramas of Shakespeare and Schiller in fits and starts, I developed a love for books and began to assemble my own library, which by the end of my time in the gymnasium had come to number some 500 volumes. In addition to various classical authors, I managed to acquire many books that were not in the gymnasium library or impossible to borrow from it, and my library became the centre of a small community of students, which, although having neither the character nor the form of any society or organization, gathered from time to time to read and discuss various topics. We read aloud poetry and plays, debated the ideas that were raised there – of course, this was somewhere in an open space outside the city – and we ended the evening with singing that echoed widely across the lethargic streets of Drohobych. Another similar group was a choir organized by my good friend Karol Bandrovsky. Both circles, with a few exceptions, consisted of the same students.

In 1873 or 1874, a mustard seed fell into our circle, which was meant to grow and further influence the direction of our further thinking. I am referring here to our acquaintance with old Limbach.

II

One Saturday afternoon (there was no school on Saturday afternoons) a friend dropped by and said:

"Old Limbach wants to see you."

"Where is he?"

"Outside, waiting in the street."

I grabbed my hat and stepped outside. On the street in front of my apartment, stood a man of average height, with grey closely cropped hair (he had taken off his cap and was wiping the sweat from his forehead). Dressed in an old grey overcoat and nondescript trousers, he wore patched shoes. He could easily have been mistaken for some travelling tradesman or a vagrant. Only the old man's face – healthy, with energetic features and sparkling eyes, his short-cropped moustache and a long creamy-white beard – showed signs of a greater intellectual life than is usually found among people of that class. He approached me and extended his hand.

"Are you Franko?"

"Yes."

"My son told me that you have a fine library," said Limbach. (His son was my friend and was a year below me. He was considered one of the most talented students at the Drohobych gymnasium.)[50]

....

[50] He now resides in Lviv and is a gymnasium teacher. [Franko]

"It's not all that great," I replied. "I mean what can one acquire here in Drohobych, especially with my limited resources…"

I received books in the main from students in exchange for helping them with their schoolwork, and some I bought with money earned from lectures, or put aside by cutting back on food and clothing.

"Can I see them?"

"Please."

We entered the room which I shared with several other students. Without waiting to be invited, old Limbach sat down on a chair near my bookcase and began to browse. He immediately came across Ukrainian brochures and yearbooks of old magazines from the 1850s and 1860s. There was a full shelf of them.

"And what's this?"

"Ah, these are our Ukrainian publications."

"Oh!" Limbach uttered in surprise. "All these?"

"Yes."

"You have so much of this stuff?"

"I grab whatever I can wherever I can," I said. "In villages, in parsonages, because they either shred and burn it or use it for Easter cakes. People are always ready to give them away."

"Must be rubbish!" Limbach muttered dismissively, setting aside a book whose title he obviously couldn't read.

"Depends," I replied, not without some displeasure. "Well, but I need to read them all. Remember what old Fredro said[51]: *'Obce rzeczy wiedzieć ciekawość jest, a swoje potrzeba.'*[52]"

"Fredro? Fredro? What is this Fredro?"

....

[51] Aleksander Fredro (1793–1876) was a Polish poet, playwright and author.

[52] Polish: "Out of curiosity we learn foreign things, but we must know our own."

It appeared that old Limbach was just as unfamiliar with Polish literature as he was with Ukrainian. When he stumbled upon Polish writers on the second shelf of my cupboard – naturally, there were only *dii minorum gentium*[53] there, such as Dżierżkowski, Zachariasiewicz, *Czarny Matwij* by Lozynski, various pamphlets, God only knows how and from where they had ended up in that crow's nest that was my library – he began to thumb through the books with distaste.

"Hilary Meciszewski's *Słów kilkanaście*[54] – what is this?"

I admitted that I had started reading this pamphlet from 1848 several times, but had not understood a thing.

"*Für die Katz!*[55] Why keep things that you don't understand?"

I gave a concerned smile.

"What can I say, it doesn't ask to be fed, and maybe the time will come when I'll be able to understand it."

He looked at me intently, shook his head, and a moment later said:

"Good."

And after being silent for a minute or so, added:

"If people had always discarded and destroyed everything they didn't understand, today we would not have Homer, or Sophocles, or Tacitus."

The old man livened up when we reached the German shelf. German was the sole language in which he loved to read; he knew the works of other literatures only in German translation. The first book that Limbach came across was the memoirs of Benvenuto Cellini in Goethe's translation.

"Now this is a great thing! Have you read it?"

....

[53] Latin: "Gods of the lesser nations."

[54] Polish: A dozen words. Hilary Walenty Meciszewski (1802–1855) – Polish publicist, politician, theatre director.

[55] German: "For the cat!"

"Yes."

"And did you like it?"

"Very much."

"Very much? That's not enough. You should read it thoroughly, delve deeply into its contents. I've also heard that you write as well."

"Yes," I replied, blushing.

"If that's the case, then you must use him as an example. Few in the world could write prose like this Cellini. Goethe knew what he was translating. He wanted to learn how to write memoirs, but he was no match for Cellini. His *From my Life: Poetry and Truth* is verbose, pretentious, and boring – this is the gravest sin when it comes to memoirs. It is boring! *Für die Katz!*"

Next to Cellini's memoirs stood Schiller's *The History of the Thirty Years' War.*

"And have you read this?"

"Not yet."

"And please don't. A waste of time. Schiller is a great poet, the greatest German poet there was, but he is no historian. He wrote this as a potboiler. *Für die Katz!*"

His eyes sparkled with joy when, reaching further, he pulled out Wieland's *Oberon.*

"This is good! Of all of Wieland's works, this is the only one worth reading. And what's this?"

He was holding Kleist's *Der zerbrochene Krug.*[56]

"Kleist? Kleist? What is this?"

I had actually read this wonderful comedy and, seeing that Limbach obviously didn't know this author, I tried to praise him.

"Kleist... Kleister... something soft, pasty, sentimental... Wait-wait-wait! Yes, I remember. I once read his poem 'Der

....

[56]   Heinrich von Kleist's *The Broken Jug.*

Frühling' – good Lord! *Empfangt mich, heilige Schatten, ihr Wohnungen, süsser Entzückung.*[57] Phew! Makes me nauseous! *Für die Katz*, all of Kleister's works!"

I responded that the Kleist who had written *The Broken Jug* was quite different from this 'Kleister' of his, whose name was Ewald.

"All the same! Paste is paste!"[58] Limbach said energetically. "I don't know this new fellow. *Für die Katz!*"

After systematically going through book after book, and commenting critically on each one, Limbach fixed his gaze on me.

"Is this all?"

"Yes."

"Well, don't you have anything by Dickens?"

"I've never even heard of such a writer."

"Well, pardon my language, but you're a fool. You don't know the best of the writers. Anyone who does not know Dickens, naturally knows nothing about literature, has no taste, no eyes. Come to my place, I'll lend you Pickwick. You must read it, and then we can speak. I simply have no desire to talk about literature with people who have not read Pickwick."

This whole conversation with Limbach had a strange effect on me. I had the sensation of fizzy soda water shooting up my nose. Despite my limited understanding of literature at the time, I could discern that Limbach either lacked knowledge or viewed things unjustly, with preconceived notions. The tone of his conversation surprised me; it seemed to contain only two notes – excessive enthusiasm or categorical dismissal – '*Für die Katz!*' Though the conversation did not offer any substantive intellectual nourishment, it felt refreshing,

....

[57] "Receive me, holy shadows, dwellings of sweet delight."

[58] "Kleister" literally means "paste" in German.

hinting at something new and appealing that I could not yet put my finger on. After the dry tone of the school's scant historical literary facts, after supposedly objective assessments, after the artificially elevated tone required when speaking of literary greats, Limbach's blunt and sometimes biased words were unusually valuable. These were the fresh and unofficial ideas of a man genuinely interested in literature. He was no greedy erudite or specialist, not like some drawer stuffed full of old papers, but a man of real temperament, original, and a conscious or unconscious enemy of any cliché, any well-trodden path. Small wonder that among the senior students Limbach quickly gained immense popularity, and I took it as an honour that he first approached me. He borrowed several books from me, including the a priori condemned Kleist, and I gladly went to his place to borrow *The Pickwick Papers* that he had promised me.

III

Both Limbachs, the father and the son, lived far away in the suburb of Zavizne. Though it was a hot summer and there hadn't been any rain for a while, yet the streets had deep puddles of persistent mud in which peasant carts loaded with wood for the salt works continually became bogged. The small dirty house in which the Limbachs lived was made of wattle and daub, and had a thatched roof. From a tiny dark entry hall, small black doors led to the right and left; the Limbachs lived through the right door in a teeny miserable room with one window; through the door on the left was the kitchen, which was equally small but much neater. The landlady lived there and rented the other half to the Limbachs, and for a small fee she also provided them meals and washed the few rags they owned.

It was dark, dirty and unwelcoming in the den where the Limbachs lived. There were two wretched beds covered with nondescript dirty sacking or blankets, a cold stove that had not been whitewashed for a very long time, and a crooked table covered with the texts and notebooks of the younger Limbach. On the pokey window stood a small lamp, and in a dark corner above a bed, which was far more decrepit and dirty and obviously the father's, there was a shelf attached to the wall, on which books were piled rather haphazardly or placed with their spines facing up.

In my presence, old Limbach didn't try to make excuses for the state of the room, he didn't try to apologize or say something ironical, he simply paid no attention to all this. He climbed onto the bed without taking off his boots, took *The Pickwick Papers* from the shelf – a thick and rather tattered volume of a German translation bound in linen – and, handing it to me, said goodbye. After seeing me to the front door, he popped his head into the landlady's room and called out just as straightforwardly:

"What do you have there for lunch? Get me something to eat, because I'm famished."

It was four in the afternoon and this man hadn't eaten yet! I learned later, that if he got into a conversation with someone about things that interested him, he could completely forget about lunch. His constitution was so strong and robust, probably toughened by countless hardships, that this didn't seem to affect him at all, and he was always in a good frame of mind.

From then on, I often met and debated with Limbach, or rather, in the guise of a debate, we exchanged those scraps of knowledge and ideas that each of us possessed. I quickly realized that Limbach lacked well-rounded knowledge or a clear worldview; his knowledge was one-sided, incidental, and fragmentary. It was akin to something clumsily assembled from the most diverse bits of human knowledge that a curious man could gather in the provincial Galician towns of those times. His main and most valuable attribute was his temperament – lively, incisive, quick to draw conclusions, which were bold, unscientific and illogical, but always characteristic and especially interesting to me because they stimulated my own thinking. Limbach was the first and only older man in Drohobych with whom I could speak freely, from whom I could always expect criticism and stand to be corrected, and who not only offered the criticism in a completely simple, friendly, and no way indoctrinating manner, but also accepted just as naturally any comment and counter-argument from me, a mere fledgling student. For instance, he knew nothing about Ukrainian history or literature, and here I could tell him a thing or two. Similarly, he knew little about Polish literature, and here I often opposed his rather hasty and one-sided judgments and defended Polish poets. On the other hand, he knew much more about German and English literature, and I gladly accepted his advice. He disliked the French and their literature and, unfortunately, instilled the same aversion in me. I neglected to learn French in the gymnasium, and for many years I painfully felt this deficiency until I finally managed, albeit with difficulty, to master the language much later in the 1880s.

Limbach's disdain for the French was so pronounced that he failed to recognize the value of French literature, which he viewed through the lens of Lessing's *Hamburg Dramaturgy* and which he barely knew anything about, except for the novels of Paul de Kock, Alexandre Dumas père, and Eugène Sue. We students were forbidden to read these novels, and precisely for this reason many of us felt it our duty to read as many of them as possible. I only managed to read *The Wandering Jew* and some of Sue's *The Seven Cardinal Sins*, one novel by Paul de Kock, and one by Dumas. Influenced by Limbach, I stopped reading others, instead immersing myself in the historical tales of Spindler and Hoffmann's fantastical romantic tales, and even the heavy humour of Jean Paul Richter. Even back then I was drawn to the East. I read the Holy Scripture in the Church text and in German translation, admired the prophets, and translated the entire Book of Job into verse. Once, catching me at this work, Limbach asked me to read aloud what I had written, which I proceeded to do.

"*Für die Katz!*" he announced curtly. "What are you searching for there? And are you really capable of understanding the feelings of those people and conveying them properly? And even if you were, ask yourself: what use is it? Who needs this? Does anyone care today what interested those people all those thousands of years ago?"

Such words, though rarely espoused by Limbach, did not mean that Limbach was against religion. I generally noticed nothing in his conversations that could hint at any religious views. Religion played no role in his thoughts and feelings; it simply failed to exist for him. I would have found it strange to imagine him inside an Orthodox or Catholic church. From a religious standpoint, he wasn't just indifferent, but a complete agnostic: he had no sense of religion – at least that's the impression I got from my conversations with him.

Just as with the Bible, I could not get him interested in Indian literature. I obtained Bopp's translations of some passages from the *Mahabharata* and gave one of these to Limbach to read. He returned the brochure the next day and indignantly threw it onto the table.

"Do you want to spoil your taste with such filth!" he exclaimed. "This is not poetry, this is not verse, but mere sticks tied together in twos."

I said that one should not consider the verse of the text, for that was the work of a grammarian, not a poet, and one needed to consider the work itself.

"Give me a break with those redskins!" he yelled, confusing Indians with American Indians. "One could go mad trying to follow the wild leaps of their imagination. It's a pity that you like this stuff. Nothing will come of you."

Equally, he was unable to appreciate German poetry from the Middle Ages, or *The Song of the Nibelungs*, or the knightly epics and novels, with the exception, of course, of *Don Quixote*. His temperament was realistic, favouring clarity of colour and simplicity of lines. Homer and Shakespeare, *Don Quixote* and Walter Scott, Goethe and Schiller, and especially Dickens – these were his favourite authors.

"Stick with these!" he repeated on more than one occasion. "Learn from them not just how to write, but – most importantly – how to see the world around you. Perception is most important. The same thing seen with different eyes will leave different impressions. Most people are like blind March flies: they don't see whose blood they are sucking. They wander through life as if through a dark forest. One day they read a description in some book of a sunrise, or a warm evening, or a storm, and the fools ooh and ah, exclaiming: 'Ah, how beautiful!' Obviously, they themselves, with their unseeing eyes, have never witnessed such a sight and their chicken brains can't process what their eyes see. That's what makes a great writer, especially one like Dickens. He is the Columbus of his ilk. Such people discover new worlds, the new Americas all around us, they are able to show us something new, unheard and unexpected in the simplest, most mundane things."

Small wonder that with such passionate speeches, Limbach influenced the formation of my literary views and preferences far more than any school education could, which was almost entirely stereotypical and formalistic. True, Limbach himself did not have a clear and single-minded view; alongside such opinions as the one above, he harboured thoughts that poetry and prose in general should deal with 'higher' concepts and needed to elevate the lowest, most mundane subjects. He valued drama above all genres of poetry, naturally written in iambic pentameter, in the style of Shakespeare or Schiller, preferably something historical or a piece where the poet had managed to place his subject on a higher pedestal, giving it a deeper, symbolic or allegorical foundation. He often spent hours enthusiastically discussing the allegorical interpretations of *Faust, William Tell,* and *Iphigenia in Tauris,* and frequently concluded with thoughts completely contrary to the realistic and rationalist views he had just as passionately expressed only an hour earlier.

"Mister Limbach," one of his young audience might ask, "so you assert that this is true?"

"Of course, it's true."

"But less than an hour ago you asserted so and so, quite contrary to this."

"That is true as well!" Limbach said without batting an eyelid.

"How can that be?"

"Because."

"But one contradicts the other."

"It's only in our chicken brains that our own silly notions clash. In nature, in reality, there are no contradictions; rather, millions of contradictions walk hand in hand and laugh at us."

"Alright, maybe in nature! But in your mind, how do you reconcile one thing with the other?"

"I'm not a *Beschwichtigungshofrat*[59]. I'm not obliged to have everything in agreement," Limbach would snap back. "I'm not wed to any idea or viewpoint. I always speak as it comes out in context. Some things come out one way, other things another way – why should I be to blame for that? I speak what I think based on what I know, and you can think for yourself. *Ich bin kein Buch, ich bin ein Mensch mit seinem Widerspruch.*[60]"

I don't know where Limbach got that phrase of Meyer's which served as the epigraph to his epic poem 'Hutten's Last Days'. He must have read it in some newspaper, because he

....

[59] German: An appeasement counsellor.

[60] German: "I am not a book, I am a man with his contradictions."

definitely wasn't familiar with the poetry of C. F. Meyer, which had been published a few years prior. But he liked to repeat the saying often, and it very well characterized this unusual man.

IV

Who was he, from which class and from which city did he hail, what was his family line? It never occurred to me to ask him such questions. Every conversation with him was a flight into airy realms, into boundless fields of spiritual life, an exploration of aesthetic questions and captivating works of human imagination, where all matters of real, practical life, or rather the misery that surrounded us, vanished, simply ceasing to exist. In such moments, we experienced what Goethe wrote about Schiller:

> *Und hinter ihm im wesen losen Scheine*
> *Lag, was uns alle bändigt, das Gemeine.*[61]

I never did find out what Limbach actually did for a living in Drohobych, how he supported himself and his son despite the extreme poverty he always seemed to find himself in. His surname, his predilection for German literature, and the complete lack of any patriotic tone in his conversations – the latter of these traits being one that made conversing with him attractive to me, for it did not introduce any falseness or forced pathos – suggested that he might have come from a German family that had settled in Galicia, perhaps with a public service background. What his initial circumstances were, what schools he attended, what positions he held, and

....

[61] German: "Far behind him in the insubstantial glow / Lay what binds us all, the commonplace."

what reasons led him to descend into the depths of poverty, to that absolute plane of proletarian life where I found him, I do not know. From hints in conversations – rare and uninteresting – with his son, I could only guess that old Limbach himself had initially been some kind of official, that he had a wife who died of grief because of his conduct, having lived to see her husband dismissed from the public service. It was a kind of quiet, silent, family tragedy, and the shadow of that tragedy lay like a barrier between the son and the father. The son almost never participated in his father's conversations with students, keeping to himself, always busy with tutoring others, which he did to support himself and possibly his father as well. Whether old Limbach also gave any lectures, I do not know, but it seemed not to be the case. I considered there was more truth to the rumour, circulated by some in Drohobych, that in secret he plied the profession of a writer, but without any evidence of my own I can't be certain.

Was he a drinker? I don't know that either. But I never saw him in an intoxicated state, nor did I ever smell alcohol on his breath, nor heard any of the cynical conversations which habitual drunkards of his age revelled in. I can't imagine the reason for his dismissal from the public service – that is if my hunch is correct. His destitution attested to the fact that he hadn't stolen anything; he hadn't squandered his earnings on alcohol or lost them in card games – this was evidenced by the lack of any signs of addiction and the youthful freshness and spiritual naivety that was manifested in his conversations and so attracted our youthful hearts to him. Even if he did have a stained past, he still showed an unusual strength of spirit, shedding all former vestiges of himself, descending with his son to the very bottom of poverty and walking along that bottom utterly carefree and impassive, as he helped his son clamber out of it.

After matriculating, I moved to Lviv to attend university and left both Limbachs in Drohobych. A year later we bumped into one another again in Lviv. Once more they were living in a miserable, bare, destitute hovel. Old Limbach remained unchanged, being poorly dressed and carefree, always busy with something and ready to divert from that activity to launch into endless conversations about literature and aesthetics. The young Limbach was in university, attending very good lectures with one of the university professors, and a path into life stretched before him, although one filled with hard work, but sufficient and regulated, far from the proletarian rabble to which his father had become so accustomed.

"Well, what's news? How's life treating you? What new things are you reading?" The old Limbach greeted me with these questions when we bumped into one another in the street one day. "Drop by, we can talk."

And we had lots to discuss. At that time, I was engrossed in Tolstoy's *Childhood, Boyhood, and Youth* and the early novels of Zola, which had been released in Russian and Polish translations (as of 1876 the Germans were still unfamiliar with this writer and had not translated him). I was already aware of the new literary movements, realism and naturalism, of the social question and socialism, and I tried to interest Limbach in all these topics. Unfortunately, he couldn't read Russian, but he did read the first volume of Zola's *Les Rougon-Macquart* in the Polish translation.

"This Mr Zol… Zol… alright, he writes well, that he does," he said, returning the book to me. "But he's angry! He's furious! Why is he so angry? Every account of his is like a bomb. Every dialogue is like a knife driven into the heart. Why is he so angry at the whole world?"

I told him that I could see no such anger in Zola.

"You can't see it? Eh, you don't understand then. He must have suffered greatly, envy must have thoroughly overwhelmed him."

I smiled at this assumption.

"After all, you and I also suffered…"

"Eh, don't say that!" he grunted, and for the first time, I sensed a sad, angry note in his words. "You can't say: 'you and I'. How can you compare yourself to me? You were poor, but you didn't suffer. Do you understand? There's quite a big difference. You lived in poverty, but life was peaceful, ordinary, you knew nothing better, so there was no envy, or what it was like suddenly one day to not know what you will eat the next day or where you will find shelter. Now that's suffering. You're a lucky man. You lived in poverty, but you didn't suffer. So, you can't truly understand that note of suffering in Mr Zol's works."

"But they praise and admire his objectivity, the unmatched fidelity of his accounts and observations, his complete truthfulness," I observed.

"Nonsense! These are just silly formulas! *Für die Katz!*" grunted Limbach. "Truthfulness! What is truthfulness? The truth, the absolute truth, is inaccessible to us. Each person can only see what his eyes allow him to see, and he sees according to how his eyes are set and tinted. Some people's eyes are tinted green, so they see everything in tones of lush spring greenery; others see things through a red lens, so they see everything in a fiery glow. And Mr Zol's eyes are tinted yellow, so he sees everything in yellow tones, like the salon of his old Madame Rougon. I much prefer Dickens. He amuses and frightens, but this fellow is like a robber, he jumps out of nowhere, grabs you by the throat and throttles you. And why? For what reason? What did I do to deserve this?"

Ever since our days in Drohobych, Limbach took a keen interest in my literary attempts, so it was no wonder that he showed an interest now too.

"What new things are you writing?"

I replied that I was working on a series of short stories, intending to depict that part of Galician society that I had come to know so far.

"*Machen Sie aber mich nicht unsterblich!*"[62] he joked, laughing. And then added:

"Well then, show me some of your work. I want to see what you've picked up from this Mister Zol."

I don't know why, maybe it was because of his innate dislike for the French, but Limbach always called Zola 'Mr Zol' in a somewhat pointed way, probably trying to mask the sympathy that he felt for this writer in the depths of his soul.

Sometime later I visited Limbach and read him my *Lesyshyn's Domestics*. He liked the beginning.

"Nice, nice," he muttered. "It has a certain melody to it, there's also plasticity and a slight sensual undercurrent. Well-well, keep reading!"

But when I read it to the end, he knitted his brows.

"Why did you spoil the ending? The beginning suggested such an idyllic outcome, yet in the end, everything turned sour."

I told him that I had never intended to write something idyllic, that I merely wanted to capture on paper the outlines of several people whom I knew when I was a child.

"*Für die Katz!*" Limbach said angrily. "Who cares, if you knew those people or not? First you entice your readers, warm them with your portrayal of nature, you lead them out in clean shirts to warm themselves in the sunshine, and then you go and throw a bucket of cold water over them. Why? What do you get out of it? It's rude and… and disloyal. An abuse of trust!"

I tried to explain myself, but I couldn't convince the old man.

"No, you don't need to follow in the footsteps of that Mister Zol! It's a waste of time. He won't lead you to any good, you must find your own path!"

....

[62] German: "Just don't make me immortal!"

Halfway through that year I was arrested. Only a year later, in the spring of 1878 was I able to meet Limbach again. He seemed reserved in his conversations with me; I rarely found him at home, and our conversations were no longer as frank and naïve as before. A shadow of some sort had appeared between us.

Once I asked Limbach for permission to receive several letters from abroad in his name, because letters addressed to me went missing. Without a second thought, he agreed, but after receiving a letter from Geneva, he took fright, especially since he was unable to read it, so much so that he was ready to run to the police with it. Fortunately, I arrived just in time and rescued the letter. After I read the letter to him to calm him down, Old Limbach seemed rather ashamed of his panic once he realized that its contents were quite innocent. All the same, I wrote back and requested that no more letters be sent to his address. It pained me deeply when, a few days later, I saw old Limbach hurriedly cross to the other side of the street after spotting me from afar, and walk away in the opposite direction to avoid having to meet me. At that moment, I personally experienced the difference between poverty and misery, and I also sensed the bitter undertones that I could not previously pick up in Zola's writing. From then on, I had no more dealings with Limbach.

A year later he left with his son for Krakow, where his son finished university. Old Limbach died there and I never saw him again.

1–3 May 1903

BORYS HRAB

Dedicated to Dr Iv. Kopach

Borys Hrab was the son of a peasant. His father, a wealthy landowner from the village of D. in the foothills near Dobromyl, initially sent Borys, his eldest son, to school in Lavriv to study with the Basilian Fathers, and then to the gymnasium in Przemyśl. Borys studied very well and soon began earning his living by giving lessons. His father wanted him to attend the seminary after finishing the gymnasium, but Borys was determined to go to Vienna to study medicine.

Even in the gymnasium Borys was prominent among his peers, and the teachers regarded him as the institution's pride and joy. Gifted with extraordinary abilities, an immense memory, a quick and clear mind, he combined these innate gifts with great diligence and hard work, a love for order and precision, and physical health and strength which he developed through gymnastics and manual labour. He managed his time so well that he was able to find time for every endeavour and every field of study.

While in the gymnasium, he learnt several European languages on his own initiative and read the main literary works in each, which he was able to find with difficulty in such an unenlightened city as Przemyśl. Apart from this, having boarded for two years with a carpenter, he also learned carpentry. Later he learned woodturning from a turner, and in grade seven, despite being ridiculed by his peers and some of the teachers, he boarded with a shoemaker and in exchange for tutoring the fellow's son, was able to learn this trade, so much despised by schoolboys. Only one teacher, Mikhonsky, praised Hrab for this, and encouraged others to learn a trade, and not to neglect physical labour alongside intellectual work, although, of course, in vain. The effort of combining learning with physical activity brought Borys closer to Mikhonsky, who invited him to his home, often talked with him, and tried to influence him to be more broadminded, free of the pedantry and rigidity of school.

Mikhonsky was a rather unique and compassionate figure, a rare phenomenon among gymnasium teachers. Extremely nervous and sensitive, he knew how to be patient, slow, and gentle. Everything about him, from his uneven hurried gait and quick but fleeting glance, to his teaching method – accessible, lively, and genuinely focused on the subject (he taught mathematics, logic, and psychology) – was simultaneously draped in pedantic forms and petty formalism – everything about him seemed to be deliberately composed of contradictions. Having a kind heart and a good soul, he could nevertheless drive a laidback, phlegmatic student to despair – even one who was capable. He liked students with a nervous, quick, lively disposition. However, this same man watched with pedantic strictness how a student stood at the blackboard, how he held the chalk, how he used the duster, how he bowed – and considered it his duty to remind students a dozen times every hour to be methodical, to think slowly but clearly, to be precise and economical in their movements, actions, and deeds.

"Do not rush too much, nor dawdle, do not do anything in excess!" were his favourite sayings. A student who answered a question too quickly and smoothly immediately aroused his suspicion.

"Show me the book from which you memorized this so smoothly!" he used to say to such a student after hearing his answer, and when the student insisted that he hadn't memorised the words but was speaking his own mind, Mikhonsky would pose a question not found in the textbook, one that required a thoughtful response. With such questions, he tested the ability of his students to think. Once he saw that the answer was indeed the result of the student's own thoughts, of their own intellectual effort, he then held great respect for that student.

"Your own thoughts! Your own intellectual effort, that is what a gymnasium is attempting to teach you!" he often repeated. "Do you think that Latin, Greek, physics, or mathematics, logic, or psychology, which we cover here together, will be of any use to you later in life? Don't believe it! Unless you become a teacher, and even then, only a small part of it will be useful. In everyday life an educated person, an official, a merchant, a tradesman will find none of this useful to him. You will see for yourselves once you leave this gymnasium; within a year or two, half of you will forget how to read Greek, and you'll never pick up a Latin book again, and you'll look at logarithms as if they were something entirely foreign. And where does this lead us? I know some of you will say: 'Stupid teachers, wasting their time and ours, teaching us useless things.' But that's not true! We, like the biblical Saul, who went searching for lost donkeys but instead found a crown, seem to be leading you on a search for such donkeys as grammatical forms, algebraic formulae, historical dates. But that's not the point! The main thing is to learn to control your mind. Just as a small child first learns to look with their eyes, then to grasp with their hands, finally to walk with their feet and speak, so too does the gymnasium teach you to control your mental faculties, develop your memory, think in an orderly, systematic manner, and finally – to think critically. This is what a gymnasium is all about. A gymnasium is like gymnastics, but with a broader spiritual foundation. By going through it, you should be prepared to tackle any job or endeavour that you encounter in later life. There, beyond the doors of the gymnasium, begins what will be useful to you in life, true science. Everything here is mere gymnastics, developing your abilities, among which the highest and most valuable is the ability to think for yourself."

Back in the third grade of junior school, Borys Hrab had caught Mikhonsky's attention. At that time, he was a wild, burly, and unkempt boy, standing out among the students in his class for not cleaning his boots for weeks at a time, wearing dirty shirts, a torn jacket, having uncombed hair and a brash demeanour.

Studies in the first two years at the gymnasium only required a good memory, no clear thinking; thus, Hrab, endowed with an extraordinary memory which allowed him to instantly re-member all the lessons in school, never studied at home. He would complete written assignments straight after they were set by the teacher, and held two to three hours of private lessons after school (he tutored his classmates, such that one or two of them paid him two guilders a month, and then all the dim-wits in class would attend). He would escape the group and entertain himself in his own way. He lived in a very bad part of town, above a small stream, flanked by handrails on both sides. Hrab would climb onto the railing and walk on it, having removed his boots. The railing was not high, about two and a half feet above street level, but it was located on the very edge of the stream, with a bank that was high and steep, rising up like a wall for about six yards. Nothing was easier than to crash from the railing into the stream, whose bottom was either muddy or lined with sharp rocks. Borys spent hours walking on the edge of this precipice; anyone watching him from the opposite bank felt giddy, but it had no effect on him. Moreover, the police hardly ever ventured into that part of town, so there was little chance they could stop these gymnastic feats of his.

Once Mikhonsky passed this way and spied Borys per-forming his balancing act. He thought that after seeing him the lad would run away, but Borys continued walking calmly and steadily, not taking his eyes off the railing, and seemed oblivious to everything around him. He was completely absorbed in what he was doing, like some lunatic. Mikhonsky came up to him and asked:

"And what are you up to?"

Borys looked around and became disoriented. Mikhonsky could see that Borys was on the verge of losing his balance, so he quickly rushed up and grabbed him by the hand to steady him.

"What are you up to?" the teacher repeated.

"I… I… I…" the boy stammered, as if glued to the spot, standing on the handrail.

"Come down from there and speak properly!" Mikhonsky declared tersely.

Borys jumped down off the handrail, but was unable to answer the teacher coherently.

"Have you prepared for tomorrow's lessons?"

"Yes."

"And have you done your homework?"

"Yes."

"Why are you walking on the handrail?"

"What else is there to do?" Borys asked naively.

"You could break your neck."

"No, I won't."

Mikhonsky had taken an interest in the neglected lad. During algebra lessons, he had a tough time with him: Borys was unable to stand up properly, hold the chalk, write, or even speak properly. However, in his answers the teacher saw sound reasoning and flashes of original thought.

"Where do you live?" Mikhonsky asked Borys.

The boy showed him.

"Come, I want to take a look."

Borys took him to where he was lodging.

"How damp it is in here! How filthy! How crowded! So noisy! And stuffy!" Mikhonsky exclaimed from time to time.

"Small wonder that you would rather mount the handrail than stay here. Staying here is impossible! Why didn't your dad find somewhere else for you to board?"

"Because this man is a friend of his."

"When you have some free time, come to my place," the teacher said. "Do you know where I live?"

"Yes."

"Will you come?"

"Yes."

But Borys did not visit Mikhonsky. The teacher lived in a nice house by the river Sian. Whenever he walked by, Borys could see the aristocratic furnishings inside and felt too ashamed to enter. A week passed. Mikhonsky seemed to have forgotten about Borys, despite having taught three classes in the boy's classroom that week. The fourth time, he called Borys to the blackboard. Borys' heart began to pound, his face flushed a deep red, but he tried his hardest to control his mind and body. He tried to leave his desk deftly, to stand correctly at the blackboard, hold the chalk in his right hand and the sponge in his left – trying to do everything the way the teacher preferred. Mikhonsky watched him in silence from the side of the classroom. He merely smiled under his bushy black beard, though Borys failed to notice this.

"You know, he could turn out to be a fine lad!" the teacher said as if to himself, but so that the entire class could hear; Borys heard him too. His heart pounded away, fluttering with a touch of joy; he felt ashamed, knowing that he had not deserved such kindness from the teacher, for he had not kept his word. Mikhonsky dictated an exercise. Borys wrote it down and after thinking a short while, set about solving it calmly, taking his time. Mikhonsky moved about the classroom on tiptoe and admired his work.

"Good!" he said, after Borys had finished. "Good, very good, in fact. Resume your seat!"

Borys replaced the chalk and the sponge and returned to his desk.

"Eh!" Mikhonsky suddenly exclaimed, as if recalling something. "Borys Hrab! Tell me, son, who is the biggest fool in this class?"

"I am, sir," Borys said without hesitation.

"And why is that?"

"Because I promised to come to your place, sir, and never did."

"And why was that?"

"Bee… bee… because…"

Borys stammered, blushing up to his ears, and burst into tears.

"Aha, see!" Mikhonsky said. "So next time don't be such a fool and come along."

"Yes, sir."

From that time on, Borys began to visit Mikhonsky regularly in his free time. Mikhonsky first had to tame him, winning his complete trust with kindness and affection, and then he undertook to 'civilize' this wild boy. He started by teaching Borys how to walk properly, to stay upright without swaying from side to side, keeping his head raised. He taught him how to bow, to sit properly, instilling in him a precision and economy in all movements, words, and actions, which he said should denote a smart and practical person. Mikhonsky also introduced him to indoor gymnastics (a novelty at that time) to accustom him to speed, precision, and grace in his movements. He was able to find healthier lodgings for Borys with a carpenter, advising Borys to learn carpentry in his spare time. He gave him no books to read for the time being. "The school texts you have are enough," he said. "There will be time later for other books. Spend your time at the workbench for now!"

By the time Borys reached the fifth grade, Mikhonsky, noticing that the boy had physically matured, becoming strong and agile, and that his spirit had grown robust and accustomed to methodical work, began to give him books to read from his own library. He naturally started with the basics of human civilization, giving him *The Odyssey* to read in Polish translation. Borys read the immortal poem in a few breaths over several days and gratefully returned the book to Mikhonsky.

"So, you've read it?"

"Yes."

"Well, tell me what it's about?"

Borys was prepared for the question. He recounted what the epic poem was about, following the childish habit of highlighting the more marvellous and fantastic adventures, while skimming over the everyday scenes.

"That's fine," Mikhonsky said. "But do you realize that what you've told me here is only one half of *The Odyssey*."

"One half!" exclaimed the lad in amazement.

"Yes, one half."

"So, there's another half?"

"There is."

"Where is it? Can you let me have it?"

"It's here. In this same book. Take it and read it one more time, and then tell me about the other half."

Borys was a little disappointed. He took the book, but for a few days he had little desire to start reading again.

"How are you enjoying the second half of *The Odyssey*?" Mikhonsky asked him.

"I can't find it, sir."

"Are you reading the book a second time?"

"I am, sir."

"Don't lie, Borys!" Mikhonsky exclaimed half tenderly, and almost in a pitying tone. "You haven't started reading it a second time, because if you had, you surely would have found the other half. Am I right?"

"Yes, sir," Borys said, embarrassed.

"That's it! Because I know that a smart boy like you, having read such a wise book as *The Odyssey*, would surely have found the other half."

The conversation had a profound impact on Borys. He resolved never to lie again and immediately began to read *The Odyssey* a second time. Now, knowing its content, he read it slowly. Vivid domestic scenes brought to mind equally vivid images of the rural life his father lived, and which he himself had experienced since childhood. As he delved deeper into the poem, the fantastical adventures and mythological spectacles faded, but the scenes of village gatherings, wagon journeys on country roads amid fertile fields, village feasts, girls washing clothes by the river, bountiful orchards, rural games, and the life of a shepherd grew more vivid. He read the epic a second time with far greater interest, and this time he recounted quite a different story to Mikhonsky. The memorable scenes from his own life added even more freshness, clarity, and expression to his narrative.

"See!" Mikhonsky said, trying not to appear too overjoyed. "Is it not true that this half is just as interesting as the one you recounted the first time?"

"It's even more interesting!" Borys said, comforted by his discovery.

"And why is that?"

"Because… Because…" Borys hesitated for a moment, as if searching for words to explain something that was not yet entirely clear to him. "I think… it seems to me that the entire *Odyssey* is like a house. These sketches from life – they're the foundation, the framework, and those marvellous adventures – they are like the beautiful carvings and painted decorations, the porches and galleries…"

"Bravo!" exclaimed Mikhonsky. "Indeed, when someone first looks at a house, they initially notice those peripheral things, the columns and windows, the murals on the walls and the drapes. It takes a discerning person and an attentive observer to notice the layout of the house, its entire plan, the durability of the foundations, the placement of doors and stoves. And for those who live in the house, these things are far more important than the decorations, which sometimes even become an obstruction, needing careful maintenance and respect, yet essentially bringing no real benefit. But now I'll reveal another secret to you. What you have seen so far in *The Odyssey*, those two halves of its contents, that's actually just one side of the coin. Beyond what you've noticed, there lies another, far more interesting story."

Borys looked at the teacher with eyes sparkling with curiosity.

"You see, it's like this," said Mikhonsky. "When you read it for the first time, you skimmed through its content as if you were hurrying along a narrow path through a field. You admired only the twists and turns of the path, paying little attention to the field itself. Right?"

"Yes."

"While reading it a second time, you realized that the path was not the main thing. You paid attention to the whole field, its soil, and what was sown upon it. Right?"

"I guess so."

"See, up to now you've studied *The Odyssey* – how should I put it – planimetrically, as if it were a flat surface on which you yourself are standing. You haven't tried – and were unable – to rise above it, to view it not as a plane, but as a distinct entity, rounded within itself, a separate world endowed with its own motion, its own life. This would be, so to speak, a stereometric view. But you are still too young for that! You have time. Someday, perhaps after your matriculation exams or even later, when you begin living your own practical life, when you try to create your own material and spiritual world, try to read *The Odyssey* once more. Then you'll see this new aspect of it. Promise me you'll do that?"

"Gladly."

Mikhonsky shook the boy's hand.

"You won't forget?"

"No, sir."

"And remember my maxim: when reading any book, progress from seeing it planimetrically to viewing it stereometrically. I know this might not be entirely clear to you yet, but in time, you will understand. And do not think that this is all, that by reaching this level, you will have the key to a complete understanding of works of human genius. No, my son (this was the first time Mikhonsky had called Borys his son, and for the first time Borys felt an unusual emotion in his voice, a strange softness), no, this is only the first step, just the beginning, just as planimetry and stereometry are merely the beginnings, the ABC of mathematics. Later, you'll want to understand the internal structure, so to speak, the mechanics of the work, then the components it is composed of, its chemistry; then the very process of its creation, its connection with the era of its author, what he had taken from his past, and what from his own times; then you'll be able to evaluate the underlying ideas themselves, that is the psychology behind the work, and you'll be able to further expand your horizons and ask: where did the people of that time, and that mysterious self-same Homer, get the idea to compose such works? And in such a form? And using such language? And thousands upon thousands of similar questions will come to you, and then you will see how such a work, a part of the fabric of a great nation, leads us to study that fabric and reveals at every step as many boundless horizons and unsolved mysteries as life itself."

"Can one really ask such questions of oneself?" Borys asked timidly, his head spinning from these unexpectedly revealed distant horizons.

"Not only can one, but one must," said Mikhonsky.

"And is there hope of ever arriving at a true answer?"

"You should say: at some answer!" Mikhonsky said emphatically. "What is a 'true' answer? What we see as being true, for others coming after us, may no longer be quite true. The main thing is to properly pose the question and provide an answer that is in agreement with the known facts. Others will have more facts at their disposal or will understand our facts differently to us, so their answer will therefore be different. But enough of this. You still have time for such things," he smiled benevolently. "You are still viewing things planimetrically. Keep reading! Don't read too much at once, read slowly, and try to achieve a stereometric perspective. Then we can discuss this further."

Since then, under Mikhonsky's guidance, Borys read all the best works of Goethe, Schiller, Lessing, and Wieland. He read Shakespeare in German translation because there was no one in Przemyśl who could teach him English. By the time he was in the fifth grade, Borys had enrolled in French at Mikhonsky's behest and, within two years, had advanced to the point where he could read Molière, Racine, and Corneille in the original. Knowing Latin and French, he easily picked up Italian with Mikhonsky's help and read Manzoni's obligatory *I Promessi Sposi*, but he was drawn most to Dante and Ariosto. Mikhonsky advised him to save these authors until after his matriculation exams, meanwhile deepening his understanding of the authors he had read through discussions about the works of major masters of world literature. Seeing in Borys' responses and essays that he was moving from a planimetric to a stereometric stage of understanding, he had him read detailed biographies of these authors, collections of their letters, and memoirs written by the authors and their contemporaries. This trained Borys, on the one hand, to understand any work of the human spirit against the backdrop of the times it was written in and the vibrant human interactions which gave birth to it, and on the other hand, to comprehend the history of that time analytically, from the testimonies and moods of the people living then, rather than from standardised formulations found in school textbooks.

At that time, the comprehensive *Weltgeschichten*[63] by Rotteck and Schlosser were popular among gymnasium students, but Mikhonsky advised Borys against reading them.

"In general terms," he explained, "you study world history at school. You must learn it, even though nine-tenths of it is nonsense. Why would you want to increase the burden of that stuff in your head, filling it with ready-made constructs which may have had some relevance back in the time for their authors, but have none for us? If you want to delve deeper into the study of any historical epoch, go straight to the sources, to writings by contemporaries of the era, or to major monographs. These so-called cream-skimmers, who have supposedly collected the cream off all the specialized works out there, actually provide only a diluted concoction, prepared for us, but written to suit their own tastes. And especially for young people, they are more harmful than useful."

Mikhonsky similarly cautioned Borys against reading compendiums of literary history.

"These are not for you!" he maintained. "Focus on learning from actual literary works first, and then you may delve into the history of literature. I would order nine-tenths of those compendiums to be burned. They simply demoralize rather than educate. They produce entire generations of so-called wise men, who know everything, albeit superficially, from other people's words, and yet they are ready to discuss everything with such certainty, as if they have seen it all, read it all, and mulled over it in their own minds."

The only time Mikhonsky truly lost his temper was when Borys, having borrowed Lemcke's *Aesthetics*,[64] newly pub-

....

[63] A history of the world, from the creation to the present time, containing a general history of human progress, revolutions, wars, etc.

[64] *Populäre Ästhetik* by Karl von Lemcke (1831–1913), a German aesthetician and art historian.

lished in Polish, from a friend, brought it to his teacher to ask how he should approach reading the book.

"Throw that thing away! Don't even look at it! It's utter rubbish! Nonsense from the first word to the last!" yelled Mikhonsky. "Those first words '*Nauka o pięknie*'[65] – they are utter rubbish and a lie. There is no special science of beauty, and aesthetics is not at all a science relating to beauty, in fact it's not a science at all. Beauty is our own subjective feeling of certain forms, proportions, sounds, and colours, just as subjective as love, anger, and disdain. There is no special science dealing with love or anger, just as there is no special science dealing with the sense of beauty. Beyond our personal feelings, there is no beauty, no matter how much those German gasbags shout and stand on their heads. Don't read this stuff! Learn to view nature and art created by human hands through your own eyes, not through the lens of pseudo-aesthetic formulae. The more you see, the more closely you observe, the better will be your understanding of the techniques being applied and the general laws of psychology, and the more refined your taste will become. Such aesthetes merely create schools for producing talking magpies and parrots, Smorgon academies where bears are taught to dance[66] – all in the same manner and without any real understanding of anything."

Apart from some prominent works of literature, there was no hint of any art in Przemyśl at that time, so Mikhonsky gave Borys some good biographies of leading figures in literature and science to read, along with the memoirs and correspondence of great people, thus teaching him to comprehend every work set in its own time and the human relationships

....

[65] Polish: The science of beauty.

[66] The Belarusian town of Smorgon once had a school for training bears.

that gave birth to it. Thus, Borys read Lewes' biography of Goethe and Eckermann's *Conversations with Goethe*, Pasek's Polish memoirs, the correspondence between Goethe and Schiller, the memoirs of Benvenuto Cellini, and Goethe's *Wahrheit und Dichtung*.[67] A lively foundation – this is what Mikhonsky tried to focus his favourite student's attention on. Gradually, beyond the artistic and poetic discussions, there emerged observations about human life itself, about the modern-day efforts and struggles of the human spirit, and about contemporary science – historical, natural and social. But here, Mikhonsky usually contented himself with merely formulating a question and adding:

"Actually, this is what scientists are working on over there, in places where there is more freedom. Well, you'll learn about this in due course. You still have time. This is part of the stereometric way of looking at things, and for this you are not yet fully prepared."

Borys did not insist. He picked up a hint of sadness in Mikhonsky's voice during such moments, something akin to the painful resignation of a man who had been taught restraint because of past sorrowful experiences. From casual remarks made by Mikhonsky and from the stories of other friends, he knew that Mikhonsky was an emigrant from Russia, that he had received an unusually broad education and had probably been preparing for a far more eminent scholarly career, than being a mere high school teacher in some provincial Galician backwater. Some extraordinary catastrophe must have thrown him off the rails and driven him out into the wide world. Dire circumstances must have brought him to this remote Galician

....

[67] *The Life of Goethe* by George Henry Lewes (1817–1878); *Memoirs of the Polish Baroque: The Writings of Jan Chryzostom Pasek, a Squire of the Commonwealth of Poland and Lithuania* (written 1656–1688, but first publ. in 1836); *The Autobiography of Benvenuto Cellini* (1562); *Truth and Poetry. From my Own Life* (1811) by Johann Wolfgang von Goethe.

town and not being all that happy in his personal life, although he did have an unusually beautiful and cheerful young wife and a cute angelic daughter, he felt the need for at least some kind of spiritual, less restrictive work that was not prescribed by strict school regulations and he was able to satisfy this need by working on the broader, unrestricted development of at least one of his students, whom he saw as being the most capable and most distinctive of them all.

However, Mikhonsky's educational endeavours did not end with the development of the body and the mind; the development of a man's moral fibre was for him perhaps the most important thing. Indeed, he understood morality in a much broader and more humane sense than it is usually understood by gymnasium teachers and school regulations. In all the gymnasium minutes of teachers' meetings, where decisions were made to expel students for gambling, drinking, and relationships with girls, Mikhonsky's name always appeared among those who voted against expulsion, and often he was the sole person to cast such a vote.

"I don't condone such actions," he said, "but at the same time, these are not such grievous mortal sins that they require the moral destruction of the boys. And secondly, we teachers are largely to blame for such behaviour. Engage and interest the boys in their studies, set them an example of a truly spiritual life dedicated to knowledge, and they will cling to you with all their soul and won't even think about getting drunk or gambling. As for girls – well, it's hardly worth mentioning what the sparrows on the rooftops should have been chirping about for quite some time!"

Of course, his words did not remedy the situation, and the teachers, under pressure of regulations and school laws, never hesitated to 'morally destroy' several or even several dozen young lads each year for such misdemeanours.

Borys regarded Mikhonsky as a true spiritual father and never even considered drinking or playing cards. Besides, he simply had no time for such things: his work kept him busy and it was so engaging that no game of cards or round of drinks could lure him away. When he grew tired of school studies and extracurricular reading, he would dash off to his workshop. There, he had a small carpentry bench and his own lathe. He would plane, turn, cut, and assemble until his physically exhausted body demanded rest. Beyond these daily tasks lay broad, bright, and limitless horizons of new, even more captivating interests. For Borys, to lose himself even for an hour in cards or drink seemed not just unappealing, but a sheer waste of time.

We have already witnessed the simple, natural way in which Mikhonsky inspired the resolution to never lie in the boy's soul. True, it required years of systematic, patient work on the teacher's part and diligent effort on the part of the student to cultivate this seed into a robust plant – honest openness and strength of character. Having always undertaken constant, varied, yet never overwhelming work, Borys learned to accurately gauge his capabilities when approaching any task. He was equally careful with his words, never promising what he couldn't deliver, and, having promised something, he did everything in his power to fulfil his commitments. Thus, given his straightforward and uncomplicated lifestyle, he never found himself needing to manipulate or deceive. His peers knew and highly valued his reliability. When anyone asked him something, they could be sure that Borys would either provide a detailed answer or simply admit his ignorance; even then, as a well-read student, he usually knew where to find the answer. Initially, his classmates jokingly nicknamed him 'Epaminondas' after a sentence in Schenkl's Latin extracts about this ancient hero, who 'would not lie even in jest'. But the nickname stuck, and the entire gymnasium began to refer to Borys as Epaminondas.

UNDER THE HAYRICK

I

Little Myron was happy on this day. It was a Sunday. He wasn't asked to tend to the livestock today, nor was he sent to gather sheaves, hay, or to do any of the work he usually did on weekdays; today was a proper holiday. Since returning from school in town, this was only his second such day of rest. And he was happy. The whole week's torment in the hot sun, or in the sleet, doing work that often exceeded his youthful capabilities, weakened further still by ten months spent in school – all that was forgotten. All he saw before him was this wonderful Sunday, this beautiful day of rest, when he would be left in peace – and he was truly happy.

He had sprung out of bed early that morning, washed, grabbed a piece of bread, and ran off into the forest. For him, there was no greater joy than to wander alone in the forest early on a Sunday, when there was not a soul around. This was his church. He listened to the rustle of oak trees, trembled in unison with the aspen leaves hanging on thin branches, savoured the delight of each flower, every blade of grass bowing under the weight of its diamond necklace of dew, then again sensed the mystical tremor of the unknown which passed through him when he peered into the Deep Ravine with its steep banks covered in dense brush and tall trees. And he held his breath when a gloomy darkness yawned at him from the bottom of the ravine, and some mysterious rustle reached his ears from the depth of that darkness – whether it was the rustling of snakes crawling through dry leaves, or the murmur of a tiny stream gurgling along the bottom… All these vague feelings, which gave birth to religion in the human soul, transformed Little Myron during his solitary walks in the forest, and they created that strange allure, that magic, with which the forest ensnared his soul.

Although the forest was big and occupied almost a square mile in area, Little Myron felt no fear: he knew every small ditch here, every clearing, and every path; every Sunday he visited the mightiest oak trees, as if they were old friends, as well as the unusually twisted birch tree that creaked like a weeping child in the wind, and the saltwater spring hidden among the dense spruces. He spent hours watching delicate-legged does with their pretty fawns, and long-horned billygoats, and wide-eyed hares which had come to drink here. After watching to his heart's content, he moved deeper into the spruces, to familiar mushrooming spots and, having gathered a heap of mushrooms and piled them together, he pulled out a small knife, sat down next to them on a stump, and started cleaning them, chatting with them cheerfully:

"Ah, my little lord! How white you are from top to toe! Surely, you must have just sprouted from the earth last night. And such a healthy base! That's great. And you, old grandpa! Were you planning to fly off, lifting one side of your cap so high? Oh, this darned branch! It pressed down on your head and has left such a scar! And here's a lovely little lady – dove-grey and plump as a snuff box! Any snails inside? How could there not be? Yes, there is one! Well, it hasn't harmed you yet, just managed to settle in there. Out with you, Hryts boy! Scram from here, go find yourself some old rotting mushroom!"

The neighbour Riabyna, also a fan of early morning strolls in the forest, once overheard Little Myron's conversations and couldn't stop telling everyone about them in his usual nasal voice, continually interspersing his account with 'phew', as if he was about to spit:

"Phew, phew, the little scoundrel! I was walking along a path when I heard someone mumbling. Phew, phew, I thought to myself, what could it be? Obviously not an animal, nor a bird. I listened more closely: it sounded like a child. Phew, it gave me the jitters! After all, I'm in the forest and it's still early, what would a child be doing there? And it was coming from some dense spruce thickets that barely a fox could squeeze through. Phew, phew, that rascal! I tried to reach the spot, but I couldn't get through; I tried elsewhere, still no luck. And it was coming from right in the middle of the thicket, as if hidden behind a fence, just mumbling and mumbling! I became even more scared! Phew, dammit, maybe it was some forest spirit? I thought to myself: should I run or should I see what it is? But then I looked around, it was broad daylight, the holy sun was shining! I listened again, and I could make out words, like someone was talking to someone else, but I couldn't hear the other voice. Suddenly I heard a branch snap, then another – it was coming straight for me. My soul jumped into my throat. But then I saw that it was that boy, that pupil! Phew, phew, the rascal, may he grow to be healthy!"

And this morning, too, Little Myron was in the forest, returning around eleven, just in time for lunch. After eating, he ran off with some neighbourhood boys to swim down by the mill. Once refreshed, he headed home, crossed the river on the footbridge, climbed over a stile into his yard, and slowly made his way up a small hillock, then on through the slightly sloping vegetable beds, then under the fruit trees, and all the while talking to himself:

"So that's it! We've had our swim. We've been in the forest too. Found twenty-eight mushrooms. And now, if only we could find a ripe pear. But, no luck there! The pears are still green. And while they're green, they'll be too tart. Bite into one, and your tongue feels like wood. And they're not juicy either. You chew and chew and then have to spit it out. Well, what do we do now? Some of the boys ran off to the pasture to race one another. But I don't feel like running. My legs hurt. Yes indeed, I went all the way to the old cutting and into Uniatychi Glade. The raspberries were splendid! Maybe I should go for more raspberries? No, I don't feel like it now, and besides, it's probably crawling with people by now. No, I won't go. My legs hurt. Better we do this: climb up into the hayrick and lie down. It's cool there, the hay is fresh, there are no flies, and you can see for miles around. Let's do that!"

With these words he reached the recently-built hayrick, standing some eighteen feet high at the end of the garden, looking very much like a portly rich man who had donned his enormous hat and was comfortably seated among four hayrick stakes as if in a capacious armchair. Although there was no ladder, Little Myron cared little for that. He gripped one of the stakes with his hands and, pushing his bare, hardened feet into the tightly packed hay, made his way up like a cat crawling up a smooth tree. In a flash he had reached the top, where the 'hat' of the hayrick almost touched the hay (at least that's what it seemed like from below, whereas in fact there was still a space of some two feet), and with a deft movement he slid around the stake, jumped into the middle of the hayrick, and for a moment almost disappeared into the fresh, soft, fragrant hay.

"How nice it is here! How wonderful!" Little Myron almost exclaimed, but stopped himself short. He had gradually learned to hide any expression of his feelings from people, and so now he didn't call out, lest someone heard him, and instead muttered these words in a half-whisper under his breath.

II

He lay there for a while on his back, looking up. Above him were the insides of the hayrick: simple sticks, inserted diagonally into the stakes, ran upwards and converged at the top, while thin crosspieces made from hazel twigs, interwoven here and there with wisps of straw, spanned between them, and were topped with a thick thatch of straw. Myron recalled how his dad had built this hayrick. As he observed the work, he had continually asked his dad all sorts of questions, and from time to time his dad had answered him.

"Why are you putting the ends of the stakes into the fire, daddy? Why are you burning them, when they've been so nicely carved?"

"I'm not burning them, just singeing the tops a bit. They will be poking out, and this will stop them from rotting."

"Won't they rot, if they've been singed?"

"No, rot doesn't attack charcoal."

"And why are you drilling the holes diagonally like that? And they're not even all the same, one is more slanted than the other."

"That's how it needs to be, son. When we drive sticks into those holes, they must all converge at one point from all four directions."

Myron still remembered how impressed he was by his father's wisdom and he smiled.

"From all four directions! That's quite something. What about me, when I grow up, will I be able to do this?"

"Learn, Myron, then you'll be able to."

"And I'll be able to build a hayrick like this one?"

"Even better ones. Once you go to school, you'll learn lots and lots of things that I don't even have an inkling about, you'll learn to do even bigger and better things."

Little Myron closed his eyes and dreamed for a moment of the unknown wonders his dad had promised would come to him, and then once more he ran his eyes over the skeleton of the hayrick and over the sticks running from the four corners of the world; guided by his father's wise will, they rose so skilfully and evenly, and came together at a single point.

'That's not a bad thing, after all!' he thought.

At that moment a strange voice caught his attention. Ordinary sounds around him, like the barking of their dog Lysko, the crowing of a rooster, or the chatter of a magpie on a pear tree – these merely reached his ears but failed to register. But this sound, what was it? He moved across to the southern side of the hayrick and peered out through the gap between the hay and the thatch. Before him stretched a view he knew only too well: the south-facing slope of their yard, below which was a narrow river, hidden from view because of its tall banks. He could only see the handrails of a footbridge nailed to two weeping willows, which leaned over the river on each side with their brooding, tufted tops; further on was a small stretch of riverside garden – hemp and cabbage, cabbage and hemp; beyond that, a freshly-mown meadow with the odd hayrick, but mostly it was just bare stubble; well, not really bare but grey-green, already sprouting soft new growth. And past there – and it seemed much closer from the top of the hayrick – stood the dense, dark green wall of Radychiv Forest.

At its edges, he could make out individual trees: over there a white birch lowered its long, flexible branches, which begged to be woven into a swing; and there a massive oak warmed its boughs in the sun; and here, on marshy ground, dwarf alders settled in dense groups, like washerwomen around a puddle. It was all very familiar, very ordinary, although he couldn't help but smile joyously each time he looked at the scene – it was so beautiful and appealing under the hot, bright rays of the July sun. But that voice, that voice! What was that voice he could hear? No one in the village or in the fields seemed to be shouting or sharpening their scythe (it was Sunday, after all!) or washing clothes, which might require Radychiv Forest to echo a response, yet Radychiv – because it was obviously the forest calling – boomed with its powerful voice, repeating a single word that in Myron's ears sounded like:

"Wounds! Wounds! Wounds!"

Myron's eyes widened, he strained his ears and looked around – no, there was nothing he could see that might be the source of these words. Yet the voice continued to float across from Radychiv Forest, the words sounding distinct, but not spoken by any human lips, rebounding off the oaks, birches, and hornbeams.

"Wounds! Wounds! Wounds!"

Myron felt anxious. He looked about once more, strained his ears, held his breath, trying to understand, giving free reign to his imagination: what in the village could have made the sound which was now echoing through the forest. He was well aware that the forest could create an echo and had tested this many times by standing in their yard and calling out various words in the direction of the forest – but this time he couldn't figure out what was happening. Could it be that the forest itself was calling out in broad daylight under a hot summer sun, during the silence of midday? And which wounds was it talking about? He could clearly hear the words, but they didn't frighten him. These weren't the screams of a wounded person, or someone groaning, he could sense no pain in them, or entreaty – this was not at all the echo of any human or animal. These were monotonous, rhythmic exclamations, like the music of the forest itself, condensed and transformed into human words, devoid of feeling, yet strangely moving because of their apparent indifference and elemental force...

"Wounds! Wounds! Wounds!"

There was little doubt! The forest was calling out these words. Like someone who had dozed off in the scorching sun, it was muttering them in its slumber.

'What wounds is it talking about?' thought Little Myron, his imagination taking a small leap to consider Radychiv Forest a living being. And his imagination painted scenes upon scenes of extreme, age-old suffering amid the powerful flow of forest life. Here, under one oak, they had set a fire and burnt a large hole in its living body, for this oak tree had been ailing and was slowly dying! And the number of birches people had disfigured, drilling holes into them to obtain juice! Or perhaps Radychiv was recalling all the does, billygoats and wild boars which had been shot in the forest the previous year? Or perhaps it was crying for the stand of spruce which had died last year from an infestation of grubs?

Myron felt a sinking feeling, as if he had overheard some dreadful secret, as if he had peered into the Deep Ravine early in the morning – no, into an abyss far deeper, filled with unknown and frightful mysteries. His childish forehead became covered in wrinkles, and his young soul experienced one of those tremors that must have been very frequent and intense in primitive humanity, leading to a religious dread of the unknown forces in nature, which the naive human imagination transformed into something above and beyond nature.

III

At that moment, a new sound caught Myron's attention and drew his gaze westward, towards the ridges of Dil Mountain. The sound of thunder echoed from that direction. Curious, Myron could not stay still. He got up on his knees and crawled across the hay to the western side of the hayrick, lay down on his stomach, and cleared away enough hay to have a clear view of everything.

This time, the view before him was incomparably more majestic. Here too, there were initially orchards and vegetable gardens which dropped steeply all the way to the river, and beyond the river lay a flat, already-mown pasture. Beyond it ploughed fields rose higher and higher in small waves, stretching in multicoloured strips across half the horizon, like giant cuts of material: yellow, green, grey, brown, and pale blue, all piled into an enormous heap, the tip of which seemed to form a foundation, a pedestal for the colossal structure of Dil Mountain, which resembled a huge dark-blue wall, shooting up steeply above this chequerboard of fields. Solid, inaccessible, reaching up to the sky and so long that it spanned from one end of the horizon to the other. Its upper contours, gently undulating, were sharply outlined against the pristine celestial blue of the heavens, even though the mountain itself hung over the landscape like a massive piece of that same blue, only a denser, deeper, darker shade. Only in one spot above the line of this blue, between it and the sky, there hung a grey-green patch, the bare alpine meadow of Ridge Mountain – only there, above that meadow, was the thing that immediately captured Myron's attention.

It was a gigantic head, barely smaller than Ridge Mountain itself, with a long, thick neck that seemed to stretch from behind the mountain and, with either curiosity or a certain savage delight, it was peering at the villages, valleys, and forests below. But suddenly it turned its massive eyes directly toward the hayrick under which Myron lay.

He recognized it straight away. Recognized the eyes, and the nose, which was bigger than the town-hall spire in Drohobych, and the low forehead, looking like it was flattened with a washing paddle, and the thick dark locks that scattered in all directions, and the monstrous thick lips stretched into a broad disgusting smile. It appeared to him that this giant of a thing was winking at him, as if to an old friend, and its face broke into a smile. He didn't feel one bit scared, on the contrary, the thick lips, the enormously long nose, and the giant's tousled locks looked ridiculous.

"Aha, this must be one of those giants who stood up behind Dil Mountain and passed an axe to another one in Radychiv Forest," Myron said under his breath. "Come, come, old fellow, climb out from behind that mountain, show us what you are made of."

Indeed, as if echoing the boy's thoughts, the giant's head began to move. However, it was nothing like the motions of a human head. Something peculiar happened that kept little Myron's eyes peeled to it, and made him burst into uncontrollable laughter. The giant's nose twisted awkwardly, one eye rose while the other drifted sideways, the lips parted, gaping wider and wider, and a red tongue lolled out, hanging lower and lower as if attempting to lick the entire forest off Ridge Mountain.

"Ha, ha, ha! Ha, ha, ha!" guffawed Myron. "So, you've shown yourself! But what are you trying to do, you crazy fellow? Hide that tongue of yours, hide it!"

As if embarrassed by Myron's laughter, the giant stealthily tucked away his red tongue, so subtly that Myron hardly noticed. But Myron's attention was quickly attracted by something else – the giant's ears! Just moments before, they had been barely visible, but now they suddenly began to grow. Up and up they stretched, like two thick hayrick stakes, or two enormous horns, and now they looked like two broad, expansive sails. The giant's tangled hair bristled and grew as well, fluttering as if in a fierce wind and was torn off in chunks, like armfuls of hay. Little Myron watched all this unfold and laughed heartily, delighted by the whimsical sight!

"Well? Why have you gone all coy?" he yelled joyously at the giant. "Why aren't you crawling out? Why are you crouching there and pouting? Come on, out you come! Show yourself! Or are you scared of me?"

These last words burst from Myron's lips unexpectedly, instantly unleashing a torrent of thoughts – or perhaps imagined scenes. Indeed, as if provoked, the giant fixed its enormous eyes on him, and no sooner had Myron uttered these words, than a muffled grumble echoed over Dil Mountain.

"Oh, so you're angry!" exclaimed Myron, still in a cheerful mood. "Why are you so angry? Crawl out from behind the Dil! Show yourself!"

At that moment the gigantic head seemed to come to life. Awkwardly and very comically it tilted to one side, then to the other; its neck began to elongate and below it appeared enormous shoulders, like a colossal wall occupying a quarter of the width of Dil Mountain, and those shoulders began to extend further and further above the ridges, while the head, growing ever larger, seemed to pout and grimace in one direction, and then in another. Myron couldn't take his eyes off this bizarre sight – and began to laugh even harder.

"Hey, uncle!" he called out, clapping his hands. "What's the matter? Have you decided to dance? Or maybe you're drunk? Know who you remind me of? That drunken oil worker, whom I saw walking along the Boryslav Highway in Drohobych. The highway was an ankle-deep mire of mud, black as pitch, and he kept zig-zagging from one side to the other, waving his arms about and grimacing, exactly like you, his slobbering mouth wide open and singing a dance tune at the top of his voice:

> *Play for me: with the rhythm!*
> *And once more: with the rhythm!*
> *Play for me a wild whirl*
> *And once more: with the rhythm!*

"Ha, ha, ha! Uncle! Maybe you could dance like him? Maybe you too could sing 'a wild whirl'? Come on, give it a go!"

"Whirrr!" came a distant rumble from above Dil Mountain, and gently, as if hesitating, Radychiv Forest picked up the echo, spreading it across the valley toward Myron under the hayrick. The boy wasn't scared, but his laughter subsided, and he began to observe the giant's head more intently. The head had grown so large that it was barely recognizable, even despite Myron's lively and overstimulated imagination. It formed a huge towering dark-blue pillar over Dil Mountain, and its locks, now white and straight, covered half the sky, reaching right up to the sun. Only two points still had the semblance of a head: these were the giant's eyes. Now, instead of looming over the mountain, they were ominously close, hovering over the upper outskirts of the village, and whether it was from the sun or some internal fire, they filled with a purplish tinge, spinning in place like two fiery wheels, and Myron felt they were looking at him with savage malevolence. He could no longer laugh, but his jovial spirit had not yet fully left him, and he once again raised his voice:

"What's the matter, uncle, are you angry? Did I offend you? I never said a harsh word to you. And if you don't want to dance, I'm not forcing you. Maybe you can play a tune? Eh?"

As if in response, a strong clap of thunder sounded from the summit of Dil Mountain. The Radychiv Forest, the forest in Panchuzhyna, and more distant woods now resounded with a mighty roar. And that roar awakened a fresh force in the valleys. A strong wind burst forth like a fierce beast from its lair and began to rustle and whistle, howling through the trees, moaning along the steep riverbanks, and swirling across the hayfields, snatching hay from the hayricks. On the road running through the fields, yellow-grey columns of dust rose to the sky. And in an instant, the entire landscape became transformed. Clouds obscured the sun, the giant's purple eyes dimmed, the clear, smiling eastern half of the sky vanished, the giant's apparition disappeared, and the entire sky was shrouded in a dark, heavy cloud. From above the Dil, beneath that cloud, enormous grey horses began to race eastward, all heading east, first singly, then in rows, and finally in whole herds. They crossed the sky in minutes and disappeared somewhere beyond the forest; after one herd came another, and then another. Gusts of wind spread their manes across the sky, hundreds of hooves thundered across the heavenly platform, and from under those hooves sprayed large, cold water droplets – at first sparse, but becoming increasingly heavier. Like arrows fired by the invisible giant several of the drops struck Myron's face, which was protruding from under the hayrick. He became startled. He distinctly felt that the giant was angry with him, threatening him, and with his rumbling, whistling, and groaning, he was calling on terrifying forces for help.

The wind reached under the hayrick and began to wrench the hay from around Myron, even blowing an icy cold stream down his open shirtfront. That breath made him cold to the core and he moved away from the edge of the hayrick, curled into a ball, and buried himself deeper into the hay, but kept his eyes peeled to the west. Neither Ridge Mountain nor the Dil were visible anymore. It appeared that the giant had already clambered over the Dil and was lying face down on the foothills. But on the Dil, there was now a constant dull rumble, as if someone was emptying large pales of crushed rock. The giant was moving over the Dil with his enormous belly filled with destruction and ruin, ready to spill its contents onto the fertile fields and the unharvested crops of the foothills.

Myron was trembling all over. He rubbed his feverish forehead with his palms, as if trying to figure out what was happening and where all this was heading.

IV

Gradually, the scene changed.

Until now, red lightning had been flashing only above the Dil in waves, as if invisible hands were tossing red-hot iron rods back and forth. But then it suddenly grew darker. The sky became covered with thick curtains, and under the hayrick, it became almost completely dark. Yet, in that same moment, an angry hand tore the curtain from one edge of the sky to the other and illuminated the entire earth with terrifying, blinding light. It sounded like hundreds of claps of thunder had struck at the same time, like thousands of cannons had been fired. The earth trembled. Myron thought that the hayrick, with its hay and stakes, had jumped a few feet into the air out of fright and immediately plopped back in its place, ready to keel over on its side. The roar was so terrible that the Radychiv and Panchuzhyna forests seemed to lose their voices, as if they were dumbfounded and unable to respond with their usual echo – perhaps they could not produce such a powerful sound. Only the distant ridges of Popeliv and Boryslav Dil responded, and boomed with a long, menacing rumble.

But after this first strike, a second and a third quickly followed. Lightning bolts raced from different directions to the middle of the sky, to the very spot under which the hayrick stood. Gusts of wind pressed the crops to the ground, broke branches off trees, whistled in the willow switches near the hayrick, and seemed to push with strong shoulders against the hay and the hayrick stakes, trying to overturn the hayrick or at least tear off its thatch. An unprecedented mayhem filled the air with roaring, rustling, crackling, and creaking. Myron lay in the hay, feeling nothing, seeing nothing, only staring wide-eyed, covering his ears with his hands and trying hard to remember something.

He was not afraid of death, and the very thought that a thunderbolt might strike the hayrick and kill him somehow never entered his head. He was equally unafraid of the roar of the storm, the rumble of the thunder, or the sight of the pandemonium around him, for all this was familiar to him, as he had observed it many times. He was also unafraid of being alone amid nature's frenetic dance; he enjoyed solitude and was no stranger to experiencing rain and thunder on his own. Yet something made him feel uneasy, something heavy weighed on his soul, creeping up to his throat, choking him; he felt as if he was holding back tears. His mind worked hard, his imagination struggled to remember something, but to no avail, twisting and exerting itself like a living person pinned under a rock. The terror increasingly seized his chest, the hair on his head stood on end, and cold sweat covered his youthful forehead.

"What was it I was meant to do? What was it?" his lips babbled unconsciously, while his hands desperately pressed against his ears so that he wouldn't be deafened by the furious claps of thunder and the howl of the storm.

His memory was jolted when a fresh lightning bolt tore through the belly of the darkness and with a gigantic zigzag dived into Radychiv Forest, immediately scattering with a deafening crash, as if a hundred carts of scrap metal had been dumped onto a glass floor. Suddenly, he understood why he was frightened, understood what that dull rumble in the clouds meant. It was more ominous and heavier than the crash of the thunder and the roar of the storm, and he realized what that faint tinkling meant, barely audible above the general clamour of the wild storm, tinkling like a golden fly struggling in a spider's web: it was the sound of bells, rung to warn people, and to ward off the hail, which now, compared to nature's overwhelming music, seemed like the tinkle of a triangle in a mighty orchestra. Myron understood everything at once. The lightning revealed the wide expanses of rye, which would soon be ripe, the wheat with its full heads, the oats, clover, meadows covered with grass, all bending to the ground under the wild gusts of wind, bowing, praying, imploring:

"Spare us! Spare us!"

And his imagination could already see the fearsome giant up there contorting his face maliciously, frowning, and bellowing with such colossal laughter, that the ridges of Dil Mountain trembled to their core. The giant roared in his terrifying voice:

"Ha, ha, ha! Just you wait! Just you wait!"

The sound of the consecrated bells faded amid the clatter of those immense piles of crushed ice, suspended inside the

approaching dark-grey cloud – no, the bells would be powerless to stop the giant. Myron sensed that a minute more,
another clap of thunder, and the sluice would open up, al-
lowing a fatal hailstorm to burst forth. And the earth would
groan, and everything living upon it would be cast down, and
all the beauty and joy upon it would slip into the mire like
wounded birds. His childish heart stopped beating, his head
buzzed, sparks flew before his eyes and, unaware of what he
was doing, in some fit of exaltation, hysteria and madness,
Myron stretched out both arms beyond the straw thatch of
the hayrick and screamed with all his might:

"Don't you dare! Don't you dare! There's no place for you
here!"

But instead of the feared tremendous clap of thunder
which would have precluded the ruinous destruction, Myron
heard only a dull rumble and the giant's angry grumbling.

"Don't you dare! I'm warning you, don't you dare! There's
no place for you here!" yelled Little Myron, shaking his fists
threateningly.

Rushing past the river banks the wind whistled, whined
and howled, as if in anger.

"No, I won't let you! Don't you dare drop your load here!
I won't let you!" shouted Myron, as if going insane.

A clatter rose over the Dil. It appeared that the piles of
ruinous ice were straining, pressing down on the giant, and
that he was bending and groaning under the burden.

"Don't you dare! Turn back there! Back to the ridges and
overgrown gorges! I won't let you come here!" Myron continued shouting.

A terrible rumble and clatter came from the cloud that was
practically overhead. Lightning streaked over the Dil ridges.
The cloud grew in size, suspended above the earth, becoming
heavier; it seemed that a dreadful weight was pressing down
on the cloud, while something continued to shore it up with
unimaginable effort from below, but was about to let go,

bringing everything tumbling to the ground, crushing and grinding all living things into dust. Strange voices seemed to squeal, whine, moan, and roar inside the cloud, yet the decisive, fatal strike had still not come.

"I won't let you come here! I won't!" Myron shouted. "Your threats are in vain! I'm not afraid of you! You must listen to me! See, I've been able to hold you back so far. And I'll hold firm! And I'll stop you! Turn back! To the mountains, to the Dil ridges! Don't you dare drop your load here!"

The boy rose onto his knees. His face was burning, his eyes ablaze, blood pounded in his temples like hammers, his breath quickened, and something wheezed in his chest as if he himself were moving a colossal burden or struggling with an invisible force, exerting every last bit of his strength.

The screeching, clacking, and shrieking in the cloud became even more intense. It seemed it was about to burst, about to fulfil the giant's threat. Even the wind paused for a moment. The flashes of lightning over Dil Mountain became extinguished. A moment of terrifying anxious tension approached. All living things down below – trees, crops, grass, animals, and people – all stood trembling, holding their breath; the sound of bells from a distant bell tower could now be heard distinctly, but not as a strong, victorious force, merely as a mournful bell tolling for the dead.

And still Little Myron did not relent. He felt that if he grew weak now, if he dropped his arms and lowered his voice, the next moment would bring devastation to the entire village, and the giant would roar with his enormous mouth and obliterate and destroy everything that was alive. Myron felt his strength waning, his hands and feet felt as if they had turned to ice, something cold was squeezing his chest, and he felt a vice was clenching his throat. But with an immense effort of will, he raised his head again, held out his fists against the cloud, and shouted at the top of his voice:

"To the side! To the side! Into the Radychiv and Panchuzhyna forests! But don't you dare here! Don't drop a single hailstone onto these fields! Do you hear me!"

And at that moment, it seemed as if a mysterious seal was lifted from nature, as if some unknown bolt was slid aside, as if a barrier had been raised! Thunder clapped, blinding flashes of lightning struck simultaneously from every corner of the world into the middle of the hail cloud, and the cloud instantly split in two, and a terrible wind roared and began to drive one half toward Radychiv and the other toward Panchuzhyna – the two forests that bordered the village from the south and the north. A moment more – and a huge, thick grey column stood over Radychiv – hail was falling onto the forest. Another moment, and a dull groan came from the forest, there was a crackle and a crunch of trees, the snap of falling branches, and the wind carried green leaves ripped off the trees above this hellish scene. Little Myron shuddered. A spasmodic sob seized his throat and then let go. His energies were spent. He lay on the hay as if lifeless, tears sprang from his eyes, and from his chest came an unconscious laugh.

"Ha, ha, ha! Ha, ha, ha! See! See! I'm stronger than you! You had to listen to me! You had to obey! You had to go where I commanded! Ha, ha, ha! Ha, ha, ha!"

Above the roar of the wind, the clatter of hail over the forest, and the sound of rain striking the thatch on the hayrick, above the frequent but increasingly distant thunderclaps, there could be heard for quite some time the piercing, insane laughter of an exhausted boy. As the storm passed, he fell into a deep sleep, his head buried in the hay.

V

It was growing dark. The sky had cleared completely, except for a dark strip of cloud still lingering in the east. The river roared, its banks full of dark yellow, muddy water.

It was cold; icy gusts blew from the forest: there, hail had piled up nearly knee-deep. Many of the trees were uprooted, and much of the hail was mixed with shredded leaves and broken branches. People, still pale from the anxiety they had suffered, walked through fields, crossing themselves and thanking the Lord that the hailstorm had spared their crops.

"Myron! Myron!" his mother called, as she walked through the orchard and looked around with eyes red from crying. She had already visited all the houses in the village, looked into every nook and every yard; his father and other members of the household, worried that the boy had not returned before the storm and fearing he might have ventured into the forest and been caught in the hail, had scattered into the woods in search of Myron. Anxiety hung heavy in the house and a silent dread filled its corners. The neighbours were concerned too; some had even joined in the search for the boy, others stood on stiles or gathered on the common, talking or comforting Myron's distressed mother.

"Don't worry, dear," Vasyl's wife tried to placate her. "He wouldn't have gone into the forest."

"He went off to Panchuzhyna Forest in the morning," Myron's mother said. "Came home for lunch, grabbed a bite to eat like some sparrow, and ran off. I asked him where he was headed, and he said: 'I'm going swimming.'"

"Some kids went off to swim in the millstream. My Andrus went with them."

"That's what I'm afraid of, that he might have gone off to Radychiv Forest afterwards."

"No, he didn't! My Andrus said, that he returned home from the millstream."

"But no one saw him at home."

"Did you look for him in the barn or under the hayrick? He might have burrowed into the hay somewhere and fallen asleep."

"The lads searched for him. They looked everywhere in the barn. Not there. As for the hayrick, I don't know. How could he even have gotten up there? There's not even a ladder."

"Come on! The boy's like a squirrel. It doesn't take much to clamber up into the hayrick. Why don't you have a look!"

Myron's mother was still young, healthy and energetic. She didn't have to be told twice, especially where it concerned her darling son. Just like Myron, she quickly made her way up the stake and looked inside the hayrick.

"No, I can't see a thing!" she said half to herself, and half to her neighbour, who was standing on the other side of the fence. She was about to come down, when something seemed to catch her eye and she climbed inside the hayrick to take a closer look. And at that moment she spotted Myron, who was fast asleep in the hay. From afar it was easy not to notice him.

His mother crossed herself, then sat down on the hay beside the sleeping boy, gently pulled the hay away from over his head, and gazed into his flushed, childish face. At that moment Myron opened his eyes and saw his mother.

"Oh, is that you mum?" he asked.

"Yes, it's me."

"Have I been sleeping long?"

"The sun's already setting."

"Boy, what a dream I had!"

"What was it about?"

"That behind Dil Mountain there lurked a giant – dark and terrifying – and then he began to rise up, wanting to smother our whole village in hail. And he was terribly angry."

"There really was a storm which came from there."

"Really? And were the fields covered in hail?"

"No, the Lord was merciful. He pushed the hail cloud away, splitting it in two. One lot fell on Radychiv Forest, the other on Panchuzhyna. It wreaked such havoc in the forests that it's frightening to look at. God forbid, had it fallen on the fields, it would have stripped everything to the roots."

Myron smiled strangely.

"That was my doing, mum," he said.

His mother looked at him with astonished eyes.

"You? What did you do?"

"I stopped the hail from falling on the fields."

His mother smiled somewhat wistfully.

"And how did you do this?"

"I fought the giant."

"Which giant?"

"The one that was dragging the hail cloud from beyond Dil Mountain. I stopped him. I scolded him. He was so angry, but he couldn't get the upper hand."

His mother smiled once more and cheered up.

"It was just a dream."

"I thought it was a dream too, mum. But if there really was a hailstorm and it actually struck the forests, then it wasn't a dream. Look, I'm completely soaked, and so tired. And my hands are completely soaked because I held them out in the rain."

"Why?"

"If I'd have even withdrawn one of them, the giant would have defeated me."

His mother smiled again, but this time tears glistened in her eyes. She pressed her lips against Myron's forehead and sensed that he had a fever. Then she kissed her son and said:

"Alright, fine. But not a word to anyone about this. Not even dad."

"Why?"

"Because dad will become very quarrelsome."

"I don't want dad to be quarrelsome."

"And please, don't ever leave home in such bad weather."

"Why?"

"It's not good for little children to be on their own when things are so frightening."

"But I wasn't scared, mum."

"Good, good. But you could have become scared and died of fright. And then I would have cried a lot."

"There's no need for you to cry."

"And now let's get you back inside the house. Dad must have already returned from the forest."

"Why did dad go into the forest?"

"To search for you."

"Gosh, I didn't even know. And I was sleeping here like a baby in a cradle. But it was good that I was under the hayrick today. If it wasn't for me, the hail would have destroyed all the fields."

His mother gazed at him again. Anxiety flickered in her eyes. She was afraid for her son's health. But at the same time, a superstitious dread swirled at the bottom of her soul. Could it be that her boy indeed had a special gift? What if he could commune with supernatural forces? Time and again in conversations with her, he had said things that left her either amazed or fearful. And now again! Could it be that there was truth in his words, and it wasn't just delirium or the fever speaking. Could he have access to some mysterious, higher truth which was inaccessible to her?

She pressed Myron close, made the sign of the cross over him, and kissing his feverish forehead, said once more:

"Alright, alright. But remember, not a word about this to anyone."

"Why, mum?"

"Because everyone will laugh at you. And then your mother will cry again."

"No, mum! There's no need to cry. I won't mention this to a soul."

In a strange, almost festive mood, both the boy and his mother climbed down from the hayrick and walked back to the house in silence.

Lviv, 18–22 January 1905

MY MEETING WITH OLEKSA

(As Told by Myron Storozh)

I am a cursed man, hated, ostracized by 'honest' people – in short, I am proscribed. 'Proscribed' really is the most fitting term. This doesn't mean, for example, that I am going against my conscience or anything like that; no, it simply means that 'honest' people (if you prefer, you can call them the 'rich', the 'powerful', or the 'practical', but it amounts to the same thing) have eliminated me from 'honest' and 'respectable' society, or simply put, I have been cast out from their ranks. And quite justifiably so! My name, along with the names of a few others like me, was a bugbear to all 'peaceful and constitutionally faithful townspeople', for with my name they associated the ideas of revolution, unrest, the toppling of the government. True, at the time that the 'saviours of the existing order' raised the most frightful uproar, I and my comrades were sitting quietly and humbly behind prison bars, counting the days of a wasted short life lived in vain.

But let's assume, for instance, that events did not follow that path at all, that neither I nor my friends ever dreamed of revolutions or upheavals – so what then? Just because I spent time in prison, is that enough to forever tarnish my name in the eyes of 'honest' people? All the same, the all-knowing and all-powerful court did find me guilty, seeing a revolutionary streak in my character, detecting in my veins a drop of the blood which the French 'saviours of law and order' forgot to completely eradicate in 1872; in my eyes the judge saw a spark of the fire that can ignite the homes of 'law-abiding citizens' just as easily as petroleum. In short, the court found me completely guilty, so that the contempt and curses voiced by 'respectable' people became totally justified.

I'm not complaining, in fact, I almost felt relieved. After leaving prison, I felt as free as a bird (*vogelfrei*, as the Germans say). I felt something akin to a student who, after finishing school, steps outside with a good matriculation certificate in his hands and the enticing pleasures of a vacation swirling about in his head. I, too, had completed a course of studies with 'decent people,' sitting beside them for many years, and at the end of it I too received a certificate – admittedly one that was a bit differently worded – but still freeing me from continuing to sit on that cursed bench. I stepped outside into the fresh air! Fresh thoughts and new impressions swarmed in my head, and among them I heard ever more loudly the sounds of a sad and happy song:

> *Slowly all chains are torn asunder,*
> *That bound us to our former life!*

I knew it was true from the way my heart was beating strongly; the chains had been broken, my former life was gone – and just for now, during my first breaths of freedom, this was enough.

One's true feelings, even though they may be strong and passionate, do not burn for long – they cannot last a lifetime. After that first intoxicated outburst, they quickly subsided, and I began to view the world with a more sober eye. Anyone will soon find tiresome the life of a proscribed man, ostracized by people, despised and shunned by all who until recently had assured them of their friendship. At first, one person turns away from you, and you spit and mutter: "You wretch! To hell with you!" But then you see a second, and a third person – and the reaction is the same! Eventually, you find this tiresome and boring, and despair fills your heart. 'What is this,' you think to yourself, 'am I really so vile and horrible, or has everyone flipped?' 'No,' you answer yourself, 'it's neither one nor the other, it's just that they are 'honest and decent' people, while you are… alright, that's enough!'

There's no easy answer to this. Only two choices remain: you either rub ashes all over your head and tear the last rags you are wearing to shreds, and then tearfully regret the loss of having been 'honest and decent' yourself, and then 'walk the streets and alleys of the city' begging every 'decent' person for forgiveness for your terrible, albeit unfulfilled trespass; or you can irrevocably spit on everything and take up your own 'cross'; that is voluntarily and irreversibly join the ranks of the proscribed and the banished and, without looking back, venture forth to find similar company. Of course, that is exactly the path that I took and, believe me, I lost little by embarking upon it, in fact, on the contrary, I was then able to look at my past with a cheerful, critical eye, which for the 'honest and decent' is not at all easy to do.

Living among the damned and the banished from 'decent' society, you quite naturally recall all the similarly ostracized people that you have encountered. I soon found myself doing just this. Indeed, they had probably visited me sooner than most other people, since the ostracized individuals were not just acquaintances; no, they were my kin! All my relatives, every last Storozh, was like that. Throughout the entire village no 'decent' farmer would mention our surname, without adding: "The bandits, may they die, every last one of them!"

But it didn't end at that. The Storozh clan were the laughing stock and scapegoats of the whole community, especially among the community leaders. If something was damaged in the fields, if someone's livestock had eaten or trampled some oats, and they couldn't find the offender – aha, blame the Storozhes! If someone chopped down a marked tree in the forest, and the forest warden couldn't determine who was to blame – well, he simply headed to the Storozh neighbourhood, and even though he could find no evidence, he still unleashed his anger through a steady stream of curses and unprintable words directed at 'those thieving Storozhes'. The village elder rarely listened to their replies or excuses, because 'the whole world knows that you're a bunch of liars and prattlers, you would sell your own mother!' Wherever there was a fine to be paid, a court ruling to be implemented, or a whipping to be handed out – the Storozhes were always implicated, as if they managed to attract every mishap. In short, they were just as much proscribed in the community as I was!

Need I add, that given such circumstances, life for the Storozhes was not rosy? There were three brothers (my cousins). After the death of their father, my late uncle, they divided his modest land among themselves, married after serving in the military, and began to enjoy a life of dire poverty. From an early age, there was no agreement among them. No, I lie, there were moments when there were no more agreeable or cordial people than them, but then there were other times when they fought, pulling out hair and spilling blood over nothing, as if they had lost their minds. Which is why each of them married separately, even though their houses were close together. Naturally, having divided the already small family estate into three parts, they struggled and could never quite make ends meet. At first, things were more or less so-so, but then their unfortunate natures made enemies of all the 'decent', that is, wealthier farmers.

Even as young lads, all three brothers had fiery natures, and people said the slightest spark would set them off. A harsh word here or a lie there, and they were instantly furious. In the tavern it was rare for a night to pass without a fight if the Storozhes were present. If two farmers quarrelled, the brothers would take the side of the weaker one, the poorer one. There was no wealthy man who hadn't received a memento from them.

But very soon the Storozhes were conscripted into the army and they remained there for twelve years. Their father died, the house fell into disrepair, and my father worked their fields during that time. People gradually completely forgot about the Storozhes. And then they returned. The oldest, Oleksa, came back first (the other two brothers still had a year of service left) and he immediately began searching for a wife. My father helped him find his feet, and Oleksa married Olena Malanchuk. Old man Malanchuk was no rich farmer, and Oleksa had no money to speak of either. That first year he farmed the entire paternal field, so it wasn't too bad. But when his brothers returned from the army the following year, discord began, then quarrels, and then a fight broke out over the inheritance. Throughout the village, people spread terrifying rumours: that the Storozh brothers had locked themselves in the house and were hacking at each other with axes, letting no one inside; only shouts could be heard and blood was seen spattering onto the windows. Another rumour had it that they intended to fight until only one of them remained alive and he would inherit everything. Out of all the exaggerated tales, one thing was certain: the Storozh brothers refused to take the matter to court and decided to divide the inheritance among themselves, which, of course, led to a fight. Nonetheless, divide their inheritance they did, and afterward no one heard them quarrelling over the division of the land ever again.

But in the village, along with rumours of their fights, all the old memories endured. 'Oh, those bandits have come together again, they'll be cracking people's heads open! Couldn't one of them twist the other's head off in some ditch?' Such was the talk among most of the village's wealthy farmers, as they nodded their heads and partook of vodka. Unfortunately, their words, particularly those about cracking heads, soon came true. The Storozhes began to dominate the tavern again, just as in the old times. However, the army had left its mark on them. They now appeared gloomy, responded sharply to any question, as if lashing out with an axe, and looked even more scornfully at the wealthy farmers.

Back then, at least they feared the village elder a little, but now – not at all! Their sharpest words were directed at the village elder and they never held back a word. "Bloodsuckers, thieves, butchers," Oleksa once began to yell at the village elder and his deputies. "You've grown rich on communal wealth, and now you strut around! Oh, you filthy swine-herds," he continued, "I'd have you all…!" Only the deputies stopped the enraged fellow from finishing his tirade, dragging him off to the public 'storehouse', which usually stood empty and at times served as a holding cell.

But such verbal attacks were still reasonable. Oleksa didn't mince his words and these days he would grab a bottle or any other container within reach and throw it straight into someone's face. He once disfigured our previous village elder for life in this manner when he found out that during his term, 500 Rhenish guldens had disappeared from the community coffers. The village elder was a young and handsome fellow who, given the opportunity, liked to chase after married women: Oleksa's bottle took away his appetite for that, leaving his face looking like a freshly ploughed field. Understandably, Oleksa spent a full six months in the 'seminary' for his efforts, but he also gave the village elder what was coming to him.

But it wasn't only the village bigwigs who found no favour with Oleksa, even the 'aristocracy', that is the city officials, were wary of him. He was sharply critical of them, and when words weren't enough, he brought his fists into play as well. When it came to bailiffs, court officials, and various other henchmen who typically played the role of bigwigs in villages, these fellows needed to exercise extreme caution when passing through our village, and most of all, they tried to avoid encounters with the Storozhes.

And justifiably so, for the Storozhes had taught a few of these haughty officials a lesson, to the great joy of all the poor who had to endure their prancing about and nitpicking, and to the great distress of the magistrate, who had to answer for everything to the village elder. Understandably, no mercy was shown when punishing and arresting these 'bandits'.

Even the district elder himself, while passing through our village once, had endured an unpleasant encounter with Oleksa. This had been back in the summer of 1872 during an outbreak of cholera. The elder and the district doctor came to check how many people were sick. Understandably, the elder stood in the middle of the street and only shouted at the 'riff-raff', while the doctor, fearful and trembling, cursed everything under the sun as he walked up to the houses… He didn't look inside any of them, but after listening to what the women and men told him, he yelled at them, asking why they weren't doing this or that, and hurried back into the street.

"*A co?*"[68] the elder asked him.

"*E, niema nadziei!*"[69] was the doctor's constant reply, to which he usually added in Polish: "May bright lightning bolts strike them all!" or: "Damned peasants, it's their own fault that they're dying, drinking all that vodka!"

True, the doctor never mentioned the fact that he hadn't actually seen a single sick person, nor that he would have preferred not to inspect any further and to just travel directly to the neighbouring village, where a hearty dinner and a comfortable overnight stay had been prepared for them by the local priest. But the elder was 'conscientious' and would not have abandoned his 'dutiful work' for anything.

But both the elder and the doctor were in for an unpleasant encounter in the Storozh neighbourhood. The women,

....

[68] Polish: "Well?"

[69] Polish: "Eh, there's no hope!"

who tearfully begged the doctor to come into their homes to check on the sick, to which the doctor only responded with curses and swearing, followed the elder's carriage through the village, though they dared not get too close. More and more people joined them – men, defiant and threatening, along with women and children. This procession entered the Storozh neighbourhood. Oleksa, who was doing something in his yard, noticed the doctor on the common ignoring the women's pleas to step inside for a moment and check on this or that sick person. He saw the doctor yelling and cursing, then returning to the street. The old women raised a lament. Oleksa stepped into the street and began to inquire what it was all about.

"Can't you see," said one woman tearfully, "that wretched quack came supposedly to check on the sick. I asked him to come and look at my husband, but he started ranting and raving something bad, my goodness! 'Go away, old hag!' he kept repeating. 'Why have you come here then?' I asked him. But he refused to listen and ran off down the road."

After hearing such an account, the blood rushed to Oleksa's head.

"What," he said, "this scoundrel takes money but won't even look at a patient! Just you wait! Let me come with you and have a word!"

And Oleksa immediately made his way across the village common. The women followed him, talking loudly among themselves. They arrived just as the doctor was getting into the buggy to continue on his way.

"Mister elder," Oleksa called out from afar, "is this how things are supposed to be done here?"

The elder turned around and ordered the buggy to stop.

"*Nu, co tam takiego?*"[70]

....

[70]   Polish: "Well, what's the problem?"

"What do you mean, what's the problem?" Oleksa said, drawing closer. "The doctor came here to visit the sick, but he hasn't entered a single house, and he's only been cursing and offending people."

"*Kłamiesz, gałganie!*"[71] yelled the frightened doctor at the top of his voice.

"You're the one that's lying here!" Oleksa snapped back angrily, the veins on his forehead filling with blood.

"*Co, co, co?*"[72] gabbled the elder as he hopped down from the buggy.

"Exactly what I said! So, the doctor here takes people's money, and the people die without getting any help from him!"

"Ah, you ruffian, ah, you ragamuffin," the indignant elder cried out in Polish, forever sensitive to criticism of his performance of duties and the taking of payments, "how dare you lie to my face?! *Ta jak ty śmiesz?*"[73]

Fury was choking the village elder's throat and he was foaming at the mouth.

"Sir," Oleksa replied, "don't joke around with the people! We've seen far taller poppies than you here! Keep in mind, times are different now – no one knows what's to come: today you're alive and kicking, and tomorrow you're no more!"

"Are you threatening me? Mister magistrate, you're a witness here, grab this robber, grab him, he wants to kill me!" the village elder squealed in Polish.

Oleksa especially detested such 'gentlemanly jesting'. He was about to explode. He couldn't control himself any longer and showered the elder and the doctor with a barrage of not exactly courteous words. The elder shouted back, and then,

....

[71] Polish: "You're lying, you ragamuffin!"

[72] Polish: "What, what, what?"

[73] Polish: "How dare you?"

seeing that the women were standing up for Oleksa, fell silent, got back onto the buggy and, spitting on the ground, ordered the whip to proceed to the next village.

"May the cholera wipe you all out!" he yelled at the people in Polish.

"And may you be the first to die, you flunky, you bloodsucker!" Oleksa yelled after him.

Ever since then the village elder began to regard our village as a den of thieves.

Remembering this not entirely aesthetic, and even less patriarchal scene, my attention was piqued by another interesting fact. When the people were being pressured and there was a need to take a firm stand, to quarrel, or to insist on something – they pushed Oleksa forward. 'Go on, you go, because what's it to you? You don't owe him any favours, but as for us, you know, it can be different!' Oleksa, the hothead that he was, did not ask what he was getting himself into each time, and kept making more enemies, as he went boldly forward and confronted the oppressor. At such times, the 'wealthy' put aside their anger and spoke kindly with Oleksa, joked with him, glad that they could hide behind his back. But just as soon as the pressure was gone – oho, once more my Oleksa was an ugly fellow, and a robber, and a thief, and who knows what else. And the poor, even though they often see things as they really are, still live at the mercy of the wealthy and must keep quiet, or even follow suit…

I remembered Oleksa Storozh after I found myself in a similar situation to him, among our 'noble and honest' citizens. 'Why not?' I thought to myself. 'I should go and visit him. This will be an interesting meeting of two people proscribed for similar acts. What will he say? How will he greet me?'

This thought did not torment me too long. Having obtained money for the trip, I boarded a train and left.

Of course, my first move was to visit 'my' house, that is my parents' place, where my two brothers now lived, both still young, nineteen and fifteen years old, along with my stepfather and stepmother. My stepfather, a man in his prime, was considered one of the 'most decent and honest' farmers. He received me very sincerely and cheerfully – even, it seemed, much too cheerfully. He quizzed me about current news, about the war, the Treaty of Berlin, the shooting of Emperor Wilhelm and with strange tact avoided the question of my 'misdemeanours' and my 'conviction'. True, while chatting about all sorts of things, we eventually touched on this sensitive issue, but my stepfather did not seem to show much interest. I uttered a few general insignificant phrases, he nodded his head, and we turned to other subjects.

I asked about Oleksa, and mentioned that I wanted to see him.

"Oh, come on, that brigand!" my stepfather blurted out in disdain, but at once corrected himself, his face forcibly taking on a somewhat cold, indifferent expression, and he said: "Well, if you really want to, then maybe, why not, you can go and visit Oleksa tomorrow."

I knew my stepfather's temperament all too well, and from that conversation, I saw that something significant must have come between him and Oleksa in the past two years. I began to gently inquire about the circumstances, approaching from different angles, but apart from news of the usual quarrels and hostilities, I learned nothing more. Indeed, my stepmother even said in her usual flattering tone that 'dad is now in Oleksa's good books, so much so that the whole village is surprised'.

This really threw me and made me all the more eager to see Oleksa the next day.

But that very same evening, having learnt that I had arrived from Lviv, Oleksa came running to me. I had already eaten dinner and was preparing to go to sleep in the barn when I saw Oleksa walking up the riverbank with his usual slow, steady gait. His short, slightly stocky figure, his long soldier's moustache, large grey eyes, and that half-kindly, half-mockingly amused face, which now beamed a benevolent smile at me – all this made me vividly recall the Oleksa I had known in the past: a lively prankster, who used to carry me, a little runt, in his arms across the river to where my late father was fishing with the other Storozh.

"Ah, just once, just…" Oleksa said in a drawl, as he approached.

We exchanged greetings.

"Why are you angry with us, brother, been rubbing shoulders with the nobility for too long?" he said, and a biting smile played on his face for a brief instant.

"Yeah," I replied, "what can I do, brother, when the nobles have taken such a liking to me that they won't even let me step outside for a breath of fresh air?"

"Aha, I see," Oleksa said.

"It seems we Storozhes are not in their good books," I noted.

There was a hint of sorrow in Oleksa's smile. My remark had clearly touched a sore spot.

"Are you off to bed already?" he remarked.

"I was heading out, but I don't feel much like sleeping."

"Well then, maybe you can come along with me, and take a look about the Storozh neighbourhood. Because who knows if we'll come across you again anytime soon." I went off with him, not refusing the invitation. The path took us down through the vegetable gardens, across the river and past pastures, then as the crow flies past the village outskirts and to the Storozh neighbourhood.

We said nothing for a long time. I saw Oleksa's face become sullen, and figured gloomy thoughts must have been beating about in his head.

"Well then, Oleksa," I broke the silence, when we reached the pasture, "tell me what's happening here, how have things been for you all these past years?"

"For us all? It's been the same old story," Oleksa answered reluctantly. "More of the same old stuff. Why don't you tell me, what you've been up to instead."

He looked at me with such a strange expression, that I did not know what to answer.

"Eh, dear brother," he said plaintively, "we didn't expect this of you. We thought: well, at least one of our Storozhes will finally achieve something, and it will improve things for us too, but then came all this shame."

Oleksa broke off and looked away.

These words, coming out of the blue, were like a hammer blow to the head. Blood rushed to my face...

"What do you mean – shame?" I barely managed to utter in a trembling voice.

"Come on, you think it's an honour?" Oleksa seized on the word. "To spend time in prison with criminals, and for what?"

"Alright, for what then, for what?" I asked.

"God only knows what for. Whether you've killed someone, or burgled them, or whatever else, who is your witness? As for us, everyone keeps saying we're criminals, thieves – God only knows – but we never heard such things said about you. And suddenly – wham! There had to be something to it, after all, you couldn't have been thrown into prison for nothing!"

How harsh, distressing, and frightening I found these words. A deep, burning pain filled my heart, pressing heavily on my chest. So, it seemed, I had reached a point where even my near and dear ones were turning away from me – even Oleksa, that unfortunate, forever scorned and persecuted man, who must have once hoped that I would support and rescue him – even he now shunned me! What must my stepfather think of me then! His frosty sweet demeanour suddenly became clear to me. I felt awfully bad. The whole world seemed foreign, cold and inaccessible. I felt detached from everything, feeling that every healthy connection to life was severed, and that if things went on like this for any longer, it would drive me insane, and I would bring about my own end. I decided to tell Oleksa everything, to explain my transgressions to him.

"Well, why are you silent, won't you tell me what happened?" Oleksa asked in a slightly more conciliatory tone, seeing that his words had affected me deeply.

"I'm silent, because I don't know what I should say? I can see that you have believed the lies which have been spread about me. If I start to justify myself, you'll think that I'm lying."

"Come on there," Oleksa replied, "I believed their lies? Who knows what to believe here. People are saying all sorts of things, and how am I supposed to know if it's all lies or not? Why don't you tell me the truth, then I'll know. I mean, someone there spread a rumour that you'd already killed yourself, and others said that you'd been taken to Bern for the term of your natural life! Eh, the things that we heard here, and the tears that we've shed! Lord Almighty! And your brothers too!"

"Alright then," I asked, "didn't they tell you what I was meant to be doing time for? Surely, they must have said something?"

"Do I know? People said all sorts of things, but I couldn't make head or tail of it, and then your stepfather said: 'You know,' he said, 'what our Myron was locked up for?' 'Well, tell me,' I said to him. 'Eh,' he says, 'he got mixed up there with some lowlifes... they wanted to start a rebellion, they renounced God!' 'Well,' he says, 'can't you see the man's out of his mind?' When I heard this, I didn't know what to think."

"So that's what our stepfather told you? And did he mention what the rebellion was all about? Something to do with Poland, maybe?"

"No, he didn't."

"Wait a minute, Oleksa, you've been in the army and seen all sorts of things. Tell me, if a person is guilty of rebellion and murder, and other similar stuff, how do you think they'll punish him? Will they sentence him to a month or two, or will they throw him in the clink for five years or more?"

"Eh, that's a tall story! I told that to your stepfather! I told him that if that was the case, they wouldn't have given you a month behind bars, but more likely ten years! But he kept insisting: 'Eh, what do you know!'"

We walked again in silence for a while, side by side, through fields planted with green oats. Night was falling. In the distance ahead of us loomed the massive black ridges of Dil Mountain, with the last remnants of evening light still glowing above them in the west. Behind us was a fragrant pasture, much like a sparkling green lake, upon which the evening mist began to settle more heavily. The croaking of the frogs carried across from the river over the dew-covered grass. Bats swirled in the air like large, black flashes of lightning, sometimes brushing the surface of the greenery in their silent flight. A cold breeze blew from the north. We walked faster to reach the village in good time. Oleksa seemed to want to ask me something, but couldn't quite muster the courage.

"Come on, Myron," he said at last, "tell me truthfully, do you intend to abolish God there, and the government, and everything else?"

I was expecting the question and smiled.

"And what do you think, do we want to or not?" I asked.

"Who knows! To my mind it can't be! But there's this official in our town – I come across him every so often – and he says to me once over a beer: 'Eh, what do you know, Oleksa! You lot think that everything is just like the priests say it is, and you believe them, and give them money, and meanwhile the nobles and priests laugh at you! They believe in nothing, and say religion is just a fairytale dreamed up for simple folk, to make them obedient.' Is that true?"

"Maybe, maybe not," I replied, "but tell me, was that official tried in court, like me?"

"Tried in court? Yeah, right! He struts about town like some wild animal – not a single hair of his will fall to the ground."

"There, you see, he told you there was no God, and no one took him to court, while you've heard nothing of the kind from me, and they tried me in court. So, it must have been for something else."

"Yeah, that's what it seems like to me," replied Oleksa.

"So, I'll tell you what we were tried for. We were told that we – there were several of us – had formed a secret society in order to promote socialism among the masses."

"Aha, aha," Oleksa interrupted me, "our priest mentioned something about that socialism as well. Tell me, what is it?"

"Socialism," I replied, "is a kind of science, so that, for example, instead of people each working a field in individual parcels, each one for themselves, they work it together, combining all the plots into one communal field, and everyone works on it together. And whatever is produced, goes into a communal storehouse, and then a communal council distributes to each according to their contribution; those who worked more, receive more, those who worked less, receive less."

Oleksa listened in astonishment.

"Well, really," he said, "so this is some kind of science?"

"Yes, it's a science."

"And is this science forbidden?"

"No, it's not."

"So why did they put you on trial, if it's not forbidden?"

"What they said about us was that we had supposedly formed a secret society, and that is against the law."

"And did you form such a society?"

"Hah," I said, "they didn't exactly prove that we did, they just deduced it from the letters they found, which we wrote to one another."

"But tell me," Oleksa began after a short silence. "People here said that you wanted to overthrow the government, but you talk of a community-based government, one which will supposedly distribute everything among the people?"

"Well, yes," I replied, "those who said that about us were clearly lying. We merely want every person to be able to work for the good of the entire community – and then the community can ensure a comfortable life and benefits for every person, which even the wealthiest farmer does not enjoy now."

"How can that be?" asked Oleksa.

"Well, if everyone in the community works together, they will be able to achieve far more than if each person works on their own. Look, a man, working decently, will always produce more than he needs to survive. The grain won't all be consumed within the community, even though no one will go hungry, and when it comes to selling the surplus, they can do so collectively, to someone who offers them the best price. And there'll be profits. For instance, you know that various agricultural machinery has been invented: better ploughs, seed drills, threshers, mowers, choppers, and many others. They perform the work better and faster than a person can with their own two hands. On his own a farmer doesn't have the means to acquire even one such machine, but as a community, working a large farm, the people can easily acquire such machinery: then work which now takes a month to complete, will be finished in two weeks, which means that instead of working all day long, people will be able work half a day. There can also be another benefit here. Now, every farmer works by himself doing the same old work, forever in the fields. But if all the farms in the community merge into one large farm, and they have machines, not as many people will be needed in the fields, and then some people can take up various crafts and trades. Then there will also be enough manpower to drain the swamps, build proper roads, clear the thickets, keep bees and cattle. Children, who now graze cattle in the summer, will be able to attend school, because their relatives won't have to rely on them for every little thing, the community will look after that. For its own good, the community will want them to grow into healthy and intelligent people. It will be possible to help the poor, and this way there will be no poor and no wealthy people – all the people will be equal, working and living well, and not suffering as they do now."

Oleksa remained silent. Despite the gloomy darkness, it was evident that he was trying to make sense of everything he had just heard.

Meanwhile, we reached Oleksa's home. Enclosed by an old, partially collapsed fence and shielded by several half-dead apple trees, it leaned to one side, looming in the twilight with an old, rotting thatched roof and warped walls barely held up with supports.

"Welcome to my luxurious palace!" announced Oleksa with a bitter smile. "Step inside, brother, stay a while, we can talk."

We proceeded inside. I saw Oleksa's wife Kateryna. Still young, but greatly worn out by hardship, she was surrounded by a whole bunch of small children. She was feeding them cherries, while holding a baby against her breast. She greeted me, overjoyed.

"Well, the Lord be praised, we never expected to see you, after people spread the rumour that Myron Storozh was no more! The tears I shed then!"

Kateryna began to wipe her eyes with her sleeve. Meanwhile, Oleksa stood to one side, smiling good-naturedly and looking around the room. The house was extremely wretched, all the utensils were worn, the children were thin and frail (for almost a week now they had been subsisting on almost nothing but cherries, because the bread had run out, and the new season's potatoes, the only staple before the new harvest, were not yet ready!)

"See – so this is my household!" Oleksa piped up. "Well, come on, sit down!"

I sat down. Oleksa drew up a chair and sat opposite me. He began to insist on putting something on the table, but I declined. Kateryna started to tell me about her life and how my stepfather was taking advantage of my brothers. I don't have the heart to repeat the terrible facts, which became indelibly etched into my heart, and they really don't concern you, dear reader.

Although he occasionally interrupted his wife's conversation, Oleksa was obviously thinking about something else. After Kateryna had finished, he addressed me once more:

"You know, it's a strange science, the one you told me about. But I can see that it makes a lot of sense."

"What science is this?" Kateryna asked.

Oleksa began in his own way, and in his own words, to explain to her what he had been referring to. She was astonished. Jumping up from her seat, she kept exclaiming from time to time: "Well, imagine that! People sometimes daydream about such things, and now they even teach this in schools!" As Oleksa spoke, he himself became worked up, his grey eyes began to shine and he could not sit still. Finally, he declared:

"Lordy Lord, why is man so ignorant, why can't he see anything that's happening in the world! Look, woman, if all people began to understand these things, it wouldn't be so hard to make them happen. And no one would dare stop them! But tell me, brother, if this science is not forbidden, then why are they attacking you like that?"

"Ah, there are various reasons," I replied. "First you need to consider who is against this. The ones who scream the loudest are the bad people, the idlers and fleecers, because they can see that if it came to that, their free ride would suddenly end. And then there are the fools who scream, who have no idea what we want: they've been told that we are rebels, that we want to bring down the nobility, the priests and Jews, and so they scream. And as you can see, we don't intend to bring down anyone, not even to drive anyone out, but on the contrary, the more people that come together, the better! More hands make light work! Of course, those who will not work will get nothing and may as well pack their belongings and leave."

"Yes, yes! That's how it should be!" Oleksa exclaimed. "I've said the same to our Jews and even to the nobles: 'You drink human blood in vain! Why does God allow you to exist in this world?' Yes, my dear brother, stick to that, don't give up your struggle, no matter how much they want to slander you! They attack me here in the village just the same!"

I smiled.

"Aren't they already slandering me? Don't worry, there are those who, if they could, would be glad to see me swinging from the gallows! And as you can see, letting go is not that easy. Once a man has seen the truth, he can't renounce it, as long as, of course, he wants to remain an honest man."

"So, what do you think will happen to you?"

"What will happen? I plan to earn enough to buy some land and farm it: maybe, I can be of some use to people."

Oleksa and Kateryna, apparently, did not expect this. They were surprised by my talk.

"After all those years of study, and all for nothing?"

"Why, all for nothing? Do you think that only he who becomes a priest or a gentleman, and can fleece people has not studied in vain? No, brother, now the best knowledge is to know how to live honestly for the benefit of the poor, instead of prolonging their suffering! The science now says that one must toil for the common good. What I have learnt over so many years, is like a debt incurred to all people who sustained me, gave me books, clothing, food, because I certainly didn't earn all that. Therefore, this debt must be repaid as conscientiously as possible!"

During our conversation, Oleksa's face brightened and flushed with blood – he got up from his chair and, after I finished talking, grabbed his forehead with both hands and exclaimed:

"Hear that, hear that, Kateryna! Hear what he's saying! Do you understand everything? Oh, my dear, dear brother! May God grant that one day one of us Storozhes will be of some use in this world, even if it's just a tiny bit! May the good Lord help you to stay on your path, now that you've set foot on it!"

And he began hugging and kissing me. Wiping away her tears with her sleeve, Kateryna also came up to me, while the small Storozh children gathered around me, chirruping and looking on. For the first time in two long years, tears of emotion welled in my eyes. The whole world seemed a finer place to me and I felt revitalized, as if each one of these poor, oppressed, despised people were pouring a part of their life, their hopes, and their strength into me!

But indeed, such moments are experienced only by those who are 'proscribed', just as someone who has stood under the executioner's knife feels the beauty of life ten times more intensely! True, the life of a 'proscribed' person is sometimes sad and difficult, but in the midst of the terrible circumstances we find ourselves in, it is the only thing that can be called life. Inner peace, strength and clarity of conviction, a clear conscience, and that eternal, relentless struggle against ignorance, falsehood, and idleness! And yet, one such moment is worth a lifetime spent in the poisoned, suffocating air of weakmindedness! Ah, for the sake of the struggle itself, for a few such moments in one's life, it is worth spitting on all 'constraints', it is worth becoming 'proscribed'!

Lviv, 1878

DOWN AND OUT IN DROHOBYCH

I

On a sunny Sunday afternoon in spring, two policemen sitting in the 'guardhouse' of the Drohobych commune were very surprised when a young gentleman of medium height, dressed in dusty but fairly decent clothes was brought in.

"And where's this one from?" asked the corporal and measured the young man from head to toe with eyes bleary from drink.

"They sent him from the district administration, he's meant to be transported under guard," the policeman accompanying the young gentleman replied.

"M-m-m," the corporal hummed and fixed his gaze on the remnants of meat and salad on the plate before him, and then slightly raised his eyes to admire the full mug of beer awaiting its turn.

Meanwhile, the policeman pulled out a letter from inside his coat and handed it to the corporal. It was the sentence handed down by the district administration. The corporal took the letter, unfolded it, glanced here and there, and tried to utter the name of the prisoner, but, apparently unable to cope with the task, decided to ask the fellow himself:

"What's your name, sir?"

"Andriy Temera."

"And where you from?"

"Ternopil."

"Ternopil? Hm! And what's brought you here all the way from Ternopil? Hah?"

Temera seemed not to hear the question, standing and looking about the guardhouse. He placed his hat and coat on a chair.

"Why have you come here?" the corporal asked menacingly a second time.

With a calm and steady voice Temera replied:

"It's not about that."

The corporal stared at him, then considering something, said:

"All the same, please answer my question!"

"It's not up to you to question me in regard to this."

The corporal turned red with anger but clenched his teeth.

"Oh, you're a smart alec, that you are! What's your trade?"

"That's my business," Temera replied and began to walk about the guardhouse, peering through the window at the gymnasium garden inundated with the greenery of various trees. Dressed in festive attire, people of all ages were walking along the twisting paths in the garden, all of them cheerful and free. He could hear the ringing laughter of children, the silver tones of women's voices, and the sweet rustle of the lush greenery. A cloud of regret and sadness passed across Andriy's handsome young face, some disturbing thought must have upset him, for his mouth trembled convulsively, while his eyes remained fixed on that lake of greenery, luxuriously absorbing the bright rays of sunshine.

"Oh, young man, I can see that you are very wise, and yet so young," said the corporal in an effort to contain his anger, and emptied half the mug of beer. "It is not good when someone becomes so wise at such an early age, for he does not have long to live in this world then. Well, maybe you can visit our 'hall' now. We have a separate hall for such wise gentlemen as yourself, a magnificent hall, ha, ha, ha!"

Temera swung around. There was an expression of anxiety on his face.

"Will the inspector be here soon?" he asked.

"Oh, yes, soon," the corporal replied derisively.

"Then maybe I could wait here until he arrives?" asked Temera, despite the tone of the corporal's reply.

"Eh, it's all the same, whether you wait here or there," the corporal said, "except that it's safer there, and it's where you belong, young man. Please, exert yourself."

"But I would ask that you allow me to remain here, if possible," Temera requested.

"That's not possible, young sir," sweet-talked the corporal, glad to be able to pay back the defiant fellow.

"Mr Corporal, sir," interjected the policeman, who was sitting silently by the table, "there are eight souls in there already! Maybe we can leave the gentleman here until the inspector arrives."

"What?" barked the corporal. "Eight people! What do I care! There'll always be room for a ninth in there. But if you like, he can stay here, he'll be your responsibility!"

"Mine? Who am I here? Why do I have to assume responsibility for the prisoner?"

"Well, if you won't assume responsibility for him, then don't poke your nose where it's not welcome," the corporal snapped back. Taking a key off a peg, he made his way out of the room. Temera grabbed his coat and hat, and followed him.

The entrance hall was small and led on one side to a long porch paved with stone slabs from Terebovlia, and on the other to a passage. From above, bright sunshine poured down, even reaching the entrance to the passage. The passage was empty. The walls were clean, painted, the floor was laid with stone, the ceiling was not vaulted and had been freshly whitewashed – all of this gave the narrow and not too long passage a rather pleasant appearance. Walking past these walls adorned with green flowers and ornaments, surely no one would have thought that behind them could lurk something terrible, something completely contrary to this appearance, something utterly opposed to any human notion of a dwelling to house people. And so, our Temera walked calmly behind the corporal, lost in his own thoughts; not about his current fate, but rather about some distant, more pleasant moments he had experienced.

A step away from the door to the cell the corporal stopped and jingled a small iron padlock that was dangling on the small beechwood door, washed clean and with practically no iron cladding. He fiddled with it for a long time before inserting the key into the lock. The key creaked with an almost cheerful grinding sound, the latch rattled and the door swung open. The corporal stepped back, grabbed Temera by the shoulder and pushed him forward, adding with a drunken smirk: "Please, step inside!"

II

At first Temera stood stock-still in the doorway. A dark twilight struck his eyes like tar, momentarily blinding him. A thought flickered through his mind that he was standing at the entrance to some secret underground cellar, the likes of which he had read about in ancient fairy tales. Inside the dark cavern he could discern neither people nor objects. It was as if a strong, invisible hand had grasped his chest and held him in the doorway, stopping him from entering. However, the visible hand of the corporal, apparently stronger, shoved him inside, and then closed the door to the dark dungeon behind him.

He stood by the door, looking around and listening for any sign of a human voice, but heard nothing. After some time, his eyes adjusted to the gloom, and he was able to take a closer look at his new surroundings. It was a small cell, no more than six steps long and four wide, with a single small barred window. The window was located high up near the ceiling and opened onto the porch, revealing only the grey, ageing shingles and the eaves above the porch. The sun never peeped in here. The walls of the cell were dirtier than one could imagine, and low down they were practically covered in droplets of condensation. The asphalt floor was wet with spilled water, covered in mud brought in on shoes God only knows when, and saliva. From the inside the door was not as yellow and innocent as from the outside; rather, it was black with mould and reinforced crosswise with two thick iron bars. Even the small square hole cut into it for ventilation was plugged with a wooden board and nailed shut.

In the centre of the cell stood a narrow iron bed with a mattress, damp and dirty like everything else, stuffed with long since rotted and unrecognizable straw. A second such bed stood in the corner against the wall. There were no sheets, no blanket, not even the usual prison pillow filled with straw. The air in the cell was dank and stale because neither the window nor the door could admit the necessary fresh air. In the corner near the door stood the usual prisoner's 'bucket', covered with a chipped, ill-fitting lid, from which emanated a horrid stench that filled the cell, penetrating every corner and seeping into every object in this hellish torture chamber. And beside the bucket stood another one filled with drinking water – it was large, wide at the top, and uncovered!

Temera looked around for a long time, straining his unaccustomed eyes until he made out all these objects, which seemed to mock him with their crudeness and inhumane filth. His heart felt as if it had been seized with icy tongs, the foul air took his breath away, and he coughed until tears formed in his eyes.

No one in the cell had yet said a word, though the strained wheezing of several chests could be heard. Temera began to examine his comrades in misfortune.

On the straw mattress against the wall lay an old man of around fifty, stretched out and sucking on a clay pipe. He had a round, closely cropped black beard, a full, swollen face, and a wooden peg near his right leg. He was, however, a broad-shouldered, robust man. His tattered shirt looked as if it hadn't been washed for several months. He lay propped up on his elbow, his legs covered with a dirty linen coat. His small grey eyes looked calmly and even somewhat humorously at the new prisoner.

At the old man's feet, curled up tightly like a little dog, lay a small dark-haired lad dressed in black city trousers and a dirty shirt made of thin store-bought cloth, mercilessly patched on all sides so that his dark-bronze skin was visible everywhere. Andriy could not see his face, for he was sleeping soundly and was not even woken by the sound of the door banging shut.

On the other bed lay a middle-aged man, stout and short, with a shaven chin and a clipped moustache. His clothes were still decent and not too dirty – it was evident that he had only recently arrived in this place of 'stench and sorrow'. But his sullen face had turned as dark as the earth, his eyes were deeply set, and his bushy, strong hands involuntarily clenched the iron bedrails, as if seeking their usual daily toil. He lay on his back, staring at the ceiling with an angrily indifferent expression and did not once look at the new arrival, until the fellow eventually addressed him.

Beside him, or rather at his feet, lay a young country lad, his head resting on a woollen coat which he used as a pillow. His small swarthy face radiated health and that delicate beauty of features often found in our rural folk, who live in direct contact with Nature – the mother of all beauty. Long soft hair fell in thick waves over his shoulders, and at the front it was trimmed in a circle. His large, shiny black eyes glowed with childish gentleness and curiosity as they surveyed the new occupant. Only his hands and feet, muscular, rough, and well-developed, attested to the fact that this fine boy had not been raised in comfort but had grown up exposed to strenuous work, struggling long and hard to eke out an existence. Andriy was very sensitive to all things beautiful and could not take his eyes off the lad's handsome face, which looked so splendid, shining with natural intelligence, curiosity, and unspoiled sensibility.

The rest of the residents of this 'hall' were forced to occupy the floor. Andriy's eye quickly ran over the unfortunate souls scattered on the wet and muddy asphalt floor, made slippery by the gobs of phlegm. There, against the wall, right by the door, lay an old Jew with a terribly gaunt and wretched face, with tufts of grey in his beard; his arms looked like rakes. His head, with closely cropped hair, rested heavily on the damp tiles, and the veins on his long thin neck bulged like tight ropes. He slept soundly, his toothless mouth agape, wheezing heavily as saliva dribbled onto his beard. Beside him sat a drunken peasant in a tattered coat, his boots tied with rope, wearing a motheaten sheepskin hat. His linen pants were missing a trouser leg and instead of a belt, he had a bast rope around his waist. Sitting on the floor, he quietly emitted sobs from time to time, as if he had recently stopped crying.

On the other side of the bed, against the wall facing the door, lay a young fellow who was no more than 28 or 30 years old, with a fair complexion, blue eyes, and short blond hair. His unruly beard had obviously not seen a comb or scissors for quite some time and looked like a destroyed blackbird's nest. This man had so many rags wrapped around him and draped over him that, lying on the floor, he resembled a heap of old footcloths, breathing deeply and heavily in this overcrowded and stuffy holding cell.

Anxiously, with a pained heart, Andriy Temera ran his eyes for a long time over these bodies, these human faces, not knowing what to say or think. The amount of sorrow and suffering he encountered in this dark, terrible cage left him awestruck! After all, these were human beings, brothers like himself, capable of sensing beauty and filth in life! These people being kept here in this horrid pit were parents of children, people who worked for their daily bread! How could it be that there was suddenly this terrible chasm between two lots of people? What was this? Andriy dropped his head, as if he had received a heavy blow, and lowered his shoulders. At that moment, he felt so bad, his heart filled with coldness and contracted, and he felt as if someone had thrown him from the free, bright world into a deep well, and he now found himself at the bottom, broken and bewildered. 'Yes, I am indeed at rock bottom,' he thought, 'down and out, and this around me is the dregs of society. What are these people but cursed pariahs, branded with the terrible, shameful mark of 'poverty'?'

III

"Where might you be from, sir?" the old man was the first to ask Andriy.

"Ternopil."

"So, what happened to you, that you've ended up in here?"

"What happened! Well, I finished school in Lviv and was making my way here to a village to study with a friend. And, of course, if a man doesn't feel he is doing anything bad, he doesn't expect misfortune. I didn't take any documents with me, nor a passport, nothing. But when we arrived here, some gendarmes chanced upon us in the street and began to question me where I was from and what I was doing. Seeing that I didn't have any papers, they directed me to the district administration. There they questioned me further, and then ordered that I be brought here. They declared that I was to be dispatched under guard to where I was born. So that's why I'm here!"

"Yes, it happens!" the old man said. "You see, I'm in a similar boat, sir. I'm from Voloshcha, if you know the place, it's a village not too far from here. I served in the army… my leg was shot off in Italy, well, and since I was no longer fit for service, they let me go. I came home on crutches, and there was no work whatsoever… you either went begging or died of hunger. And when a man still has strength in his body, it's a crying shame to go begging, but you can't work in the fields without a leg. So, I made my way to Boryslav. The work there's different, you merely stand beside a winch all day. I worked there a dozen years or so… made barely enough to survive… But, if the truth be known, there were times I went hungry – all the same I put away a small nest egg in the event that I became sick or grew old… Well, I put away a penny here and a penny there, bought some clothes… Of course, when you're feeling fine, you live and dream… And then one fine Sunday in spring I fell seriously ill… it struck me all at once, as if someone had cut me down with a scythe. I spent six months in bed in a Jew's storeroom… fortunately, it wasn't winter. I left there just as it began to snow. What was I to do? My money had run out, I had to pawn my clothes… I should have remained in bed, but the Jew threw me out into the street because I couldn't pay anymore… I hadn't the strength to return to work… I was in a terrible way! What could I do? I realized that no matter which way I turned, I had no other option. Swallowing my pride, I sewed a bag and went begging from house to house. Well, thank God, I managed to survive that harsh winter, and just as spring came, I decided to go back to work, but that's when the constables caught me, right near the square here. 'Where you from, old man?' 'I'm from Voloshcha,' I said. 'Don't you know that it's against the law for beggars from other parts to wander through local villages? Every village must support its own beggars, and wandering about from place to place is not allowed.' 'But I'm no beggar,' I protested. 'I just went a few times to ask for a piece of bread, because I was too weak to work…' But they wouldn't let me finish speaking… one of them, God rest his soul, hit me on the back of the head so hard that I saw stars, and then they dragged me off to the district administration. There, the deputy district head – he was acting head, because the actual head had died – didn't even listen to me, but sent me packing to the petty court for vagrancy. They sentenced me to two weeks in jail and to be sent back to my village. I served those two weeks, and then I was transferred here, and here I am, thank God. it will be a month and a half on Friday that I've been stewing in here. And though it appears that I am no longer being punished, but God forbid lest anyone should suffer like this! This is worse than hell! And I don't know how much longer this will drag on, because no one seems to be in any hurry here, and no one seems to know anything!"

"But how do you manage in here?" Andriy asked. "Don't they take you outside for walks?"

"Eh, don't make me laugh!" replied the old man with a smile. "Although they do let us out… each day we go out in the morning to sweep the streets in town."

"Everyone?"

"No, just me and Mytro, this small guy here from the Boyko region, and Stebelsky as well, that fellow over there covered in rags – but that's all."

"But what about the rest? Don't they ever get to go out into the fresh air?"

"They don't at that, except that sometimes the farmer over there goes into the city to buy bread. Earlier today they brought in this old Jew and that weeping Mary Magdalene in one and a half trouser legs and half a coat, so I don't yet know what will happen to them. The Jew here, he's already spent two months in Boryslav before they dispatched him under guard here. He says his papers have already arrived, and that he'll be leaving tomorrow or the day after. I know him pretty well, the poor fellow, he worked a winch with me in Boryslav for many years. But now, everyone without a labour card is being driven from Boryslav under armed guard. They picked him up too."

Andriy looked at the wretched, gaunt face of the Jewish fellow, which seemed as if it were made of sticks and covered with brown, wrinkled leather. The heavy wheezing coming from his chest was a sign that this man didn't have long to live, and his entire figure loudly proclaimed that his past life was one of constant suffering and poverty.

"He's a kind soul," the old man continued, "has a heart of gold. No matter how bad things are, he'll never complain to others about his problems, but will be more than ready to show sympathy toward others and help them as best he can, just like a brother. You won't find many Jews like him, by God, you won't. It's understandable, he grew up among our people, suffered and worked hard from a young age just like our people, so that now, were it not for his beard, side curls, and that bekishe, no one would say by his nature that he was a Jew!"

"How do you manage to live in here?" Andriy asked, examining the cell more closely as his eyes slowly became accustomed to the dim light. He saw the iron stove, half-built into the wall at the head of the bed where the old man lay, and on the stove, he noticed a large loaf of rye bread, which suburban women sold each day at the Drohobych market.

"How do we manage?" the old man replied. "On bread and water alone."

"Bread alone?"

"Yes, on bread alone."

"They don't give you anything hot?"

"Eh, dear sir, the Lord be praised, it's been a month and a half since I've had anything hot in my mouth! And where would we get the stuff? They give you those 14 kreutzers a day, but what can you buy with that? Ten kreutzers worth of bread a day is too little, and then you still need to buy some salt, some onions now and then, and then the money is all gone. Look here, every second day I get a loaf of bread like this, it costs me 20 kreutzers – sometimes there's a bit left over for the third day, and then I can buy some cheese to go with the onions. If I had the money, I could buy some warm tripe in town. For five kreutzers you can get a piece the size of my palm – but that's nowhere near enough. I'd rather buy some onions – then I have a whole bunch of them, and I have something to eat with my bread all day long. But these others, unfortunately, don't even have even that; if one of them gets a ten-kreutzer loaf in the morning, they don't leave a crumb, they eat everything, and then they have to wait until the next morning. Only that Boyko fellow does what I do – he buys a large loaf for two days, so he manages somehow. But he could be better off, except that he can't eat dry bread. And this fellow here," the old man pointed with his foot at the curled-up sleeping boy, "they take his bread from him. They eat their own in the morning, and by noon they're at him, like it's their own pantry: 'Mytro, give us some bread!' And the fool gives away his bread."

"But why should I sit on the bread while they're going hungry?" Mytro responded in a resonant voice, and a wonderful gentle smile spread across his handsome face. A sparkle in his large eyes added even more beauty and charm to his appearance.

"Come, come, you fool, I can just imagine what they would say to you if they had bread and you were starving. The only thing you'd manage to cadge from them would be a blow to the head!"

"That's alright," Mytro said, "then I wouldn't ask them for any."

"And what are you in for?" Andriy asked Mytro, turning toward him. "What did they throw you in here for? Whose head did you smash?"

Mytro laughed.

"No one's," he said, in a typical Boyko drawl. "I was picked up in Boryslav, because I didn't have a labour card."

"Where are you from?"

"From Dzviniachchia. Mum died of cholera, and after that dad hit the bottle, sold the farmland, then mortgaged our house, and last autumn he went and died. So, what was I to do? Our village lads were heading off to Boryslav, so I joined them. Well, there wasn't much I could do there! I couldn't negotiate, I didn't have the strength to pull heavy loads, maybe operate a fan or pick stuff out of a pail – for that I got paid four, at best five shistkas.[74] I somehow managed to survive the winter, and in the spring, I set off to find some work, but they grabbed me."

"And how long have you been in here?"

"It's been a month now," Mytro said calmly in his steady sonorous, almost childish voice. "All of us here are from Boryslav," he continued, "except for Stebelsky."

"Well, if the truth be known, he brought this misery upon yourself," the old man said with a sad smile. "He was an educated man, finished the gymnasium, every class, but, you see, he has a few screws loose here (the old man twisted his hand about in front of his forehead). He worked as a clerk in Sambir in the district administration. Later, he says, he worked for some lawyer, and then things went completely downhill."

"Grandpa, grandpa," Stebelsky's weary, half-asleep voice interrupted him, "why don't you speak the truth! What's this 'things went completely downhill'? How have things gone completely downhill?"

The old man smiled.

"You see," he said to Andriy, "something began gnawing and eating away at him. 'What am I doing here?' he would say. 'Sitting and writing things, and what use is my writing to anyone? It only makes people weep and swear. And they even give me money for this!' Well, and so because of those people's tears he became disgusted with his writing, and de-

....

[74] One shistka equalled ten Austrian kreutzers.

cided to stop doing it. He sold off his fine clothes and began to make everything himself. Just take a look at his uniform! He sewed it himself!"

"A man who can't be self-sufficient in everything," Stebelsky piped up once more, fixing his wandering gaze on a dark corner of the cell, "must borrow from others. And he who borrows is a debtor… and must repay the debt. But what if he has nothing to repay with and doesn't know how to repay? And then the creditors, both men and women… cry and curse! You can't sleep at night… it's frightening… you keep hearing their crying and their curses! And worst of all are the children – so wretched, naked, and swollen… and they don't even curse, they only cry and die. Like flies… After two years, I couldn't get a wink of sleep, always hearing their cries at night. And I had to drop everything. But when I began to be completely self-sufficient, I started to feel better."

"How did you manage to become self-sufficient?" Temera asked him.

"How?" Stebelsky directed his listless eyes at him. "Simple. I do only what is useful: I dig, carry water, tend livestock. I eat only what I have earned. I wear only things that I have made myself. I sleep on the ground. And most importantly, I eat no meat and never take a pen in my hands. Because meat makes people savage, and a pen in human hands becomes more frightening than a lion's claws, a tiger's teeth, and a snake's poison."

"There, see," the old man said after Stebelsky had finished talking, "such thoughts are always running through his head. But he's a healthy lad. And hardworking, no doubt about it, and very sincere! When he does something, he puts his whole heart and soul into it. So, as I told you, he left the life of a gentleman and hired himself out to a farmer. But even there, he couldn't last long."

"Ah, how could I have," Stebelsky said indifferently, "when the farmer was rich, hired servants, did nothing himself, and as soon as a servant did something wrong, wham, punched him right in the face."

"And that's how it was everywhere!" the old man said with a laugh. "Just like they say, a fool gets beaten up even in church. I feel sorry for him! He's an educated fellow, from a family of priests. Still has his books and hasn't given up reading them. He even brought them here with him, but the police confiscated them."

"So where did they bring him from?"

"I told you, from Sambir. He lived there for many years, and no one said a thing to him, until suddenly this spring, he heard somewhere that they were calling up reservists for training. He was born in this district, you see, so he decided to come here, to report for duty. But he already had a discharge notice, ever since he got frostbitten fingers."

"How did they become frostbitten?"

"I told you, he's not quite all there… you know… He told me that he was walking along one winter in a harsh frost from some village back to Sambir, and saw a piece of scrap iron by the side of the road, a bar or something. He figured that someone had lost it and that he needed to take it to the police station, so that the owner could be found. And the fool picked up that hunk of iron with his bare hand and carried it for more than a mile…"

"A mile and a half," Stebelsky corrected him off-handedly from where he was lying on the ground and listening to the conversation. Andriy glanced at him, and the old man continued talking as if it made no difference that Stebelsky was listening in on their conversation. "So, he brings it to the police station, and everyone there bursts out laughing. They try to take the hunk of iron from him, but lo and behold, it's stuck to his hand. They immediately send him off to the hospital, but the doctor there has no choice but to cut off all his fingers."

As if in confirmation of this, Stebelsky raised his right hand, on which the first phalanx of each finger had been removed.

"I feel sorry for him, he's an educated man, he's calm and doesn't do anyone any harm. They're supposed to take him to where he was born, and he's been sitting here for a month. They make him suffer so much in here, and to top it all off, they give him 14 kreutzers each day from his own money. Because when the police picked him up in the square here, they took his discharge papers and the thirty-nine rinskys[75] he had on him, and they're feeding him with that money."

"They also took my school report from grade eight," added Stebelsky, "three books and thirty-nine rinskys," he mumbled, as if he had learnt the sentence by heart. After this, he sat up on the floor and, turning his pale, expressionless face toward Andriy, asked:

"*Et dominus, intelligit latine?*"[76]

"*Intelligo.*"[77]

"*Et germanice?*"[78]

"*Intelligo.*"

"*Und Sie... Sie kennen die allgemeine Geschichte von Gindely – die hat man mir abgenommen – drei Bände: Geschichte des Alterthums, Geschichte des Mittelalters und die, die Geschichte der neuen Zeit.*"[79]

"A learned man... a smart fellow..." the old man babbled to himself, "and it's a pity what's happened to him! It runs in their family... Same thing happened to his dear departed mother..."

....

[75] See footnote 13 on page 110.

[76] Latin: "And the master, does he understand Latin?"

[77] Latin: "I understand."

[78] Latin: "And German?"

[79] German: "And you... do you know Gindely's general history – it was taken from me – all three volumes: History of Antiquity, History of the Middle Ages and History of Modern Times."

"Et quas scholas, dominus absolvit?"[80] Stebelsky continued asking.

"I studied Philosophy in Lviv."

"Ergo, philosophiam majorem!"[81]

"No," said Andriy, "there is only one philosophy, and it's neither major nor minor, except that it might be less false or more false – but even there only the good Lord knows!"

Stebelsky listened to his words with eyes wide open, as if not understanding a single thing, then bowed his head and lay back down on the wet, slippery saliva-covered floor.

<h1 style="text-align:center">IV</h1>

"And this fellow here," the old man said after a moment's silence, pointing with his foot at the dark-haired boy sleeping on his bed, "he's a local. Looks very much like a pickpocket. I don't know why they're keeping him here or for what. But he's been here for about two weeks now. Isn't that right, Mytro?"

"Yes, tomorrow will be exactly two weeks," confirmed Mytro.

"Who knows what will become of him, because they haven't called him out yet to compile an official report."

"Not even once in two weeks?" exclaimed Andriy.

"That's right, not even once. He just sits and sits here, and no one gives a hoot about him. The inspector is in no hurry… Well, and that other fellow over there – that's our 'governor', he's spent all winter here."

"Which other fellow?" Andriy asked, not able to see anyone else.

....

[80] Latin: "And what schools did the master finish?"

[81] Latin: "Major philosophy, then?"

"We have another 'burgher' here. Get up there, you lazy-bones! Move your rotting carcass!"

At the old man's call, something stirred in the dark corner at the end of the bed, and from there, as if rising from the grave, a dreadful, otherworldly figure slowly emerged. He was a young man of about twenty-four, of average height, with a broad face, a flat, receding forehead, a small black moustache and a beard, and long, dishevelled hair, which added an even more terrifying look to his already wild and frightening face. His large, motionless eyes shone with a lifeless, glassy gleam, like a rotting carcass that glowed in the dark. The colour of his face, like that of all the inhabitants of this burrow, was somewhat swarthy, but it was clear that this unfortunate man's face had not been washed for a long time, and dirt had formed a crust on his temples. He was, moreover, almost completely naked, as it was hard to call the shirt he was wearing clothing, with only the collar, sleeves, and a strip hanging down his back to the waist remaining. He wore nothing else.

Andriy shuddered with pity and disgust, seeing this extremely neglected and feral human being. And yet, it was clear that his wildness was not of his own making! Looking more closely at this man, Andriy noticed that his legs were swollen like barrels and gleamed with a bluish sheen, characteristic of water oedema. Likewise, his belly was terrifyingly large and swollen, reminding Andriy of those American savages who ate earth, and whose drawings with similarly bloated bellies he had once seen. Only his strong and healthy arms testified to the fact that he was once a hard-working man, though now separated from labour by some unfortunate twist of fate and cast into this place to perish.

"So, this is our burgher, or rather Bovdur,[82]" said the old man, "we've dubbed him Bovdur. He's the governor of the

....

[82] Literally "boofhead".

cell, because we have a custom here that whoever has been in the cell the longest becomes the governor. And he, bless the Lord, has survived the winter here. Look how well-fed he is now! He's in good shape and quite handsome! We're keeping him as a showpiece, hoping someone might buy him for slaughter. We feed him a lot more now, and he just lies there because, you see, he's so well-fed that he can no longer stand properly on his own two feet. Only what he grabs with his hands is his – oh, his arms are still strong – but that's nothing, he'll outgrow that as well!"

Everyone in the cell roared with laughter at the old man's jokes, apart from Andriy and Bovdur. The latter remained standing in the same place where Andriy had first spied him, swaying back and forth on his thick, swollen legs – standing and hesitating, as if contemplating some bold move. His clenched teeth were visible through his half-open blue lips, as if he was gathering all his courage to undertake a plan of action. His eyes slowly roamed about the cell, though his gaze always settled on the man lying on his back on the bed, dozing amid the quiet murmur in the cell.

"He doesn't go out into town," the old man continued, "nor does he venture out to work; at first he refused, but now, even if he decided to change his mind, they wouldn't let him out."

"That's right, I refuse to go!" Bovdur piped up in a hoarse voice. "The devil take them with their work! What will they pay me for it?"

Having said that, Bovdur stepped over the old Jew sleeping on the floor, then over the sobbing peasant, and with unsteady steps made his way to the bucket. He lifted it as if it were a feather and drank some water, then reached under the head of the dozing farmer, pulled out a small clay pipe and scraped out the remnants of tobacco remaining inside it. He popped these into his mouth and slowly began to chew, occasionally spitting out some black tar, which stuck to the walls or the floor. Having completed this daring act, he sighed with relief and stood in the middle of the cell. Waving his arm with a flourish, he said:

"I refuse to work for them! They can go to hell! I'd rather rot away here than go!" At these words, he spat another black wad onto the wall, right above the head of the slumbering Jew.

"And why are they keeping you here for so long?" Andriy asked in a trembling voice. Bovdur gave him a wild look, as if Andriy's question had struck a very painful and sensitive spot.

"They keep me here because they feel like it!" he grumbled, and then added: "They wanted to take me under guard to the village where I was born, and I kept telling them that I wasn't born in any village, I was born on the road. So, they asked whose land the road was on? And I told them it was on nobody's land, because there was no land there: I was born on the water as my mother was being taken by ferry across the Dniester River. And they asked me where the ferry was, but I told them it must have floated off with the current, because sure as hell I don't have it in my shirtfront. Then they asked where I was baptized. I have no idea, I told them, go and ask the people who held me up to the cross and took away my good fortune. But where did you hide, they asked and I told them: among bad people. But they wanted to know in which village, and I told them that there were bad people in every village! That's how my interrogation went. They didn't ask me nothing more, and only ordered that I be brought here. Thank the Lord, they locked me up here and haven't bothered me since with any of their stupid questions."

Bovdur spat once more, stepped over the sobbing peasant and the sleeping Jew, and dived into his corner, covering his legs with some bedraggled sack.

Andriy was even more horrified after hearing Bovdur's account. What had life given this man? What must his memories be like now, and his hopes? He tried to imagine himself in such a hopeless situation and felt his thoughts getting muddled, knowing he would quickly suffocate in such a dreadful hole. Obviously, Andriy's agitated imagination added a lot of bad light to the already grim reality, painting a picture of an illegitimate orphan, being maltreated by everyone who laid hands on him, being beaten and trampled on from a young age because of people's disdain, having never experienced joy, sincerity or love. And while this was true to some extent, it wasn't entirely so. Bovdur had experienced moments of happiness and love, and he also had loyal friends – desperate souls and orphans like himself – but all of this was now buried under a thick layer of savagery and vacuity. His thoughts, as if cursed, revolved around the tobacco he chewed and the hunks of bread he ate, not reaching further into the past or the future.

Meanwhile the police 'inspectors' were in no hurry to release him, and so Bovdur remained here, forgotten by God and humanity, swelling and rotting alive, forgetting everything that had once been part of his life, and as his strength waned, he grew more and more averse to work.

"So, he lives on bread alone?" Andriy asked the old man.

"On dry bread alone. For six months now he's been paying 14 kreutzers each morning for a loaf, which he places in front of him and gobbles up to the last crumb, and then waits until a new loaf arrives the next day. In the meantime, he begs this dumb Boyko here to lend him a hunk of bread in the evening, of course with no intention of ever repaying him..."

"So, he never leaves the cell?"

"No, as long as I've been here, I haven't seen him go outside once. I don't know what it was like before. Bovdur, did you go outside anywhere before?"

After a fit of dry coughing, Bovdur growled:

"No, I haven't been outside, except for that one time when I was interrogated."

"How he managed to survive the winter in here dressed like Adam, I can't imagine," said the old man. "When they brought me here, we had the last frosts of winter. I walk in here, and it's so cold you can hardly stand it, and there he is all on his own, lying in that same corner where he is now, covered in that same old sacking. He was the colour of lilac, but said nothing. I walked about the cell, rubbed my hands together, and then, seeing that nothing was helping, I started to scream: 'Hey, good people, I'm not the Son of God here, why are you tormenting me like this? Those Pharisees only tormented the Son of God this bad!' They barked at me a bit, but then they went and lit the stove for a change and we felt a little better. And from then on, until the frosts ended, they lit a fire practically every second day."

"And before you came, they didn't heat the place?" asked Andriy, shuddering as if feeling the cold.

"Well, Bovdur here says they did, but only rarely, whenever they felt like it."

"So, why didn't you speak up?" Andriy asked the fellow.

"Yeah, didn't speak up!" Bovdur barked back angrily. "At first I yelled, but they would just beat me, because I was here on my own."

"You were here alone!" Andriy exclaimed in amazement. "How long for?"

"A whole month. They didn't bring anyone in, and if they ever did, they put them in another cell, just to get to me."

"Does a doctor ever visit here?"

"You're pulling my leg! A doctor! Who's going to pay that doctor to come?" said the old man with a bitter tone in his voice.

"Well, I saw there was a regulation that a doctor must inspect all the guardhouses every day, or at least every week, to ensure that it's safe to keep people in them."

"Maybe there is such a regulation elsewhere, but not here in Drohobych! They don't give a damn about regulations here! They are their own lords and masters!"

"So, no one ever comes here to inspect the place?"

"Imagine that they don't."

V

A commotion arose in the cell. Those who were sleeping woke up and got to their feet, and only Stebelsky remained lying. Bovdur merely propped up his head on his elbow, continuing to chew his tobacco. The old Jew began to question Andriy first in Yiddish, and then in Ukrainian, while the peasant sitting next to him on the floor burst into tears once more, grabbed his head in his hands, and began rocking back and forth, continually muttering in a broken voice:

"What ill fate brought me-e to this Drohobych! I should have stayed put i-in Boryslav or bought some flour for my-y children with the meagre five shistkas that I e-earned, and headed home!"

"Now there's a smart one for you!" the old man joked. "Worked for a day in Boryslav, earned five shistkas, and now, on a festive day, he sets off to Drohobych to buy bread. And by God, all dressed up, like a dandy at Easter! Hardly any pants on him, but I guess it's easier to walk when there's not much cloth flapping about. And his coat's also festive – he tried to tuck up the tails, but must have torn them off by mistake. Or maybe he was at a party, and his dear friends didn't want to see him go, and grabbed him by the coat-tails? No, the poor fellow was biting at the bit to get to the city, to check out people in the streets, to disport himself, so he ripped off the tails and escaped from his good friends! No sooner did he arrive in town, than he stopped outside the church in the most visible spot, and here the apostles of God came running, grabbed him by the arms, and said: 'Dearest sir, we invite you to our chambers!'"

The fellow wept the whole time that the old man was speaking, while the others laughed.

"My children," he wailed, "what will become of them? I left them all alone in the house, so small, without a crust of bread! They'll die of hunger there if I don't return tomorrow!"

"Oh, that tomorrow of yours is still far off!" said the black-haired young Jew. "You should have returned home today, instead of heading for Drohobych in search of good fortune!"

"You'd do better to keep quiet and stop cutting me to the quick!" exclaimed the fellow and, dropping his head, began to sob like a child.

"But no," he said decisively a moment later, "they must let me out today. What have I done wrong? Have I stolen something or killed someone? What reason can they have to hold me here?" With these words he picked himself up off the floor and stood near the door, pressing his face against the sealed peephole, where through a small crack, he could see a bit of the hallway and the fleeting shadows of passing policemen.

"Grandpa Panko!" piped up the farmer, who was lying on his back on the bed. "Grandpa Panko, was it you who picked out the remains of the tobacco from my pipe?"

"No, it wasn't me," replied the old man, "you had another visitor there."

"Who?" the farmer asked, menacingly furrowing his thick black eyebrows.

"Our burgher there! See, he's still chewing on it."

The farmer said nothing for a moment, glancing angrily into the corner, where Bovdur was curled up, and then, without uttering a word, came up to him and hit him so hard from above with his clenched fist, that Bovdur's head struck the wall.

"You stinking Bovdur, haven't I told you not to help yourself to my stuff! Keep your sticky fingers to yourself! The fruits of my labour are mine!"

Instead of an answer, Bovdur kicked the farmer full force in the stomach, although this caused him so much pain in his leg, that he let out a squeal. The farmer swayed and rested his shoulders against the wall.

"May thunder strike you down!" he yelled. "So, this is how you repay me for my goods?"

"May you enjoy such weal in the afterlife, you pig!" Bovdur exclaimed, and with effort, got to his feet. "You'd be ready to kill for a few lousy cigarette butts then?"

"And I'd poke your eye out too!" the farmer replied. "You don't touch what's mine! Got it? Roll up your sleeves, and earn it yourself. And I surely won't go grabbing any of your stuff!"

"Really? Yes, you won't touch it while I'm watching! But soon as I turn my back, you'd grab it quick smart! I know your type!"

Instead of answering, the farmer punched Bovdur with his fist.

"Can't let go of that wad of tobacco?" Bovdur said, looking him sullenly in the face. "Here, take it then, if you're so desperate for it!" And he spat out the remaining chewed-up tobacco into the farmer's face.

A putrid black liquid flowed down the farmer's face, onto his beard, then dripped onto his shirt, leaving behind a black trail. Grandpa Panko burst out laughing. Shaking, Mytro rolled into a ball on his coat, fearing a fight.

"What have you done here, you worthless dog?" rasped the farmer, choking with rage, as he approached Bovdur with his fists raised.

"I've given you back what's yours, with a little extra!" Bovdur replied sullenly in a voice thick with anger. Without waiting for further provocation, he kneed the farmer in the stomach so hard that the man yelped, staggered, and collapsed onto the floor. After this, Bovdur calmly returned to his corner, ignoring the enraged screams of the bruised farmer.

"This one's our 'field marshal'," Grandpa Panko joked to Andriy. "He guards his stuff like the apple of his eye, and is always threatening to take out Bovdur's eye, but somehow, he's been merciful to him so far. An eye, indeed, for a wad of chewed tobacco!"

"Where are you from?" Andriy asked the farmer, who was still huffing with anger. Pretending he hadn't heard Andriy's question, the fellow returned to his bed and began puffing on his pipe, his eyes fixed on the ceiling.

"He's from Dorozhiv," Grandpa Panko began again with a chuckle. "Dorozhiv is a big village, and it's home to some big troublemakers, big arsonists, and big thieves who are always quarrelling over what's mine and what's yours. In the end they've become so confused that no one knows what's mine and what's yours anymore."

"Grandpa, you'd do better to close your trap and shut up, instead of talking nonsense!" the man from Dorozhiv grumbled back.

"A pox on you!" Grandpa Panko replied, laughing, "and you still find that offensive, you glutton! It's none of your business what I talk about! The poor sinner," the old man continued speaking to Andriy, "they locked him up over that same 'mine' and 'yours' business: he bought an animal hide from some Jew for 30 kreutzers, but it was worth only half of that. The Jew took the 30 kreutzers and did a runner, and he, the poor hired hand, was grabbed by the Jews and dragged off to Ivan's place!"

The old man began to laugh once more, followed by Mytro and the black-haired young Jew, whom the old man had called a 'pickpocket'. The fellow from Dorozhiv didn't respond anymore, blowing smoke in a huff toward the ceiling. Meanwhile, Andriy stood the entire time by the wall beside the old man's bed, holding his coat over his arm. His legs were aching and trembling, but he could not overcome his disgust to sit down somewhere in that filth and squalor. Unable to remain standing in the one spot, he began to walk about the cell, making his way among the beds and the people lying on the floor, although even so, he was able to take no more than five or six steps. All the vile and sorrowful aspects of prison life, which had suddenly rained down on him like water from a bucket, swirled about like a chaotic, raging blizzard inside his head. All the misery, filth, and depravity surrounding him in this cramped cage – and beyond its walls, throughout the world – made him acutely aware of his place at the very bottom of human society. All this overwhelming human suffering pressed down on him with immense weight, enveloping him in a broad, relentless grip that drowned out his own searing personal misfortune.

There, beyond the walls of this wretched cell, in a yard flooded with sunshine and paved with smooth stone slabs, policemen were laughing loudly and heartily as they played cards. The sounds of a skittles game reached them inside the cell, along with laughter, arguing voices, and the shouts of some Jews, who had been picked up on the road with a herd of oxen and driven into the communal yard. The creak of an iron pump could be heard, as someone drew water from the well. But nothing else reached their ears, and nothing else could be seen; it was the same gloomy twilight, the same cursed and motionless shadows clinging to the dirty walls covered in gobs of saliva, the beds, and the slippery floor.

"Who knows how soon it will be evening," Grandpa Panko said, packing tobacco into his pipe. "And you, sir," he asked Andriy, "do you smoke?"

"No, I don't. I've picked up many habits in my lifetime, but I could never manage to master that one!"

"You're a lucky man then. But I would have kicked the bucket in here, if I wasn't allowed to smoke. I go through two pouches a week, it beats buying cigarettes."

Meanwhile, in an effort to see how close it was until evening, Mytro stood on the iron bed frame, grabbed hold of the bars on the window with his outstretched arms, and lifted himself up a bit so that he could peer outside. But just at that moment, there was a sharp crack, and as if scalded, Mytro let go of the bars and fell to the floor, hitting his ribs against the iron bed.

"You rotten thief, can't you sit still in there? Trying to sneak a peek outside!" came the corporal's voice from outside. He had been passing under the window with his leather whip in hand and had happened to spy Mytro's hands on the bars. He struck them with all his might. Mytro yelped, straightened up, and looked sorrowfully at his hands, where two wide bruises had formed, resembling sausages. With tears in his eyes but a smile on his lips, he informed Grandpa Panko: "The sun will be setting soon!" After which he sat down on his bed, wiped the tears away with his sleeve, and began to blow on his stinging hands.

VI

The key creaked in the lock, the door opened a fraction, and the corporal's head appeared in the opening, without letting in a single ray of light.

"Andriy Temera! To the inspector!" the corporal called out and locked the door again after Andriy.

There was a short silence in the cell.

"What an amiable gentleman, the poor fellow," said Grandpa Panko.

"Ah, he's just an idler and a vagrant," the farmer from Dorozhiv blurted out. "Amiable gentlemen don't travel under police escort!"

"And amiable farmers from Dorozhiv do?" Mytro asked caustically.

"Butt out, frog-face! Keep your trap shut and mind your own business!" the farmer yelled at him angrily.

Everyone grew silent again and only Grandpa Panko could be heard puffing away on his pipe, together with the pitiful sobs of the man in ragged clothing who remained standing next to the door, as if he was expecting the ironclad door to suddenly be flung open and allow him to walk free with his five shistkas, so that he could be with his small hungry children.

The lock rattled again, the door opened a little and allowed Andriy inside, his coat hanging off his arm.

"What did they say?" several voices asked in unison.

"Nothing," Andriy replied in a sad voice. "They questioned me and told me to wait till my papers arrived." He became silent and began pacing about the cell. The other prisoners also said nothing. They all recalled that each of them too was waiting for their papers to arrive, and maybe some of them, despite their own misfortune, felt sorry for this young gentleman, who on the say-so of the district head and the inspector was destined to endure a long wait, just like them, cut off from his work, his friends, from the beautiful free world out there, and kept captive in this horrid cellar!

Bovdur was the first to break the heavy silence. He got up from his corner like some phantom and, stepping up to Mytro, said harshly, with hand outstretched:

"Mytro, give me some bread!"

"Give him some boiling pitch instead," said the farmer from Dorozhiv.

But Bovdur took no notice of the cordial admonition and moving his hand practically under Mytro's nose, repeated:

"Mytro, let me have some bread!"

"I've only got a bit left myself and won't be able to have any for breakfast, until they bring fresh bread. And I need to head off to work."

"Hand over the bread!" Bovdur insisted stubbornly, not caring about any excuses.

"I told you, I've only got a bit left myself."

"But I don't even have a crumb, and I'm hungry!"

"You shouldn't have gobbled it all up in the morning, you should've left some for the evening!" said Grandpa Panko.

"Shut up, you old bag of bones!" Bovdur barked back and once more addressed Mytro: "Come on, give me some bread!"

But this time Grandpa Panko could tolerate Bovdur's disrespectful words no longer. Like a young man, he leapt off his bed and his wooden peg leg struck the floor.

"You rotten scoundrel," he yelled at Bovdur, "who do you think you are, some kind of lord, that no one has the right to speak to you? You're a penniless wretch! Into your corner there and keep rotting until the maggots finish you off completely!"

And with a mighty shove he pushed Bovdur away from Mytro, sending him flying to the floor.

"Just you keep grumbling there, may the fever take you!" Bovdur muttered back through his teeth.

"May you shiver to death yourself!" Grandpa Panko retorted. "Leave the boy in peace! Does he eat your bread? And stop shoving your paws under his nose!"

"Yeah, and what are you going to do about it!" Bovdur persisted.

"It's not for me to do anything, you devil! The one who climbs spruces will deal with you!"

Andriy felt terribly upset listening to the argument. He tried to calm the old man down, and then pulled a good hunk of bread from his pocket and handed it to Bovdur, with the words: "Here, have some for dinner, if you're hungry. This is what I have left from home, but food is the farthest thing from my mind right now!"

"Eh, good sir," said Grandpa Panko, "why are you handing out bread here? If not now, then in an hour or tomorrow morning you'll want to eat, and you'll have a long wait before they bring in fresh supplies."

"No, no, I won't be hungry," replied Andriy, "and even if I was, I can wait until they bring it."

"Do you even have any money to pay for it?"

"Yeah, I do. I've got fifty rinskys with me: it was a deposit from the fellow I was going to teach; I'll have to spend some of that money, though honestly, it's not really mine."

"Well, of course, in such a situation, a man has to look out for himself as best he can," said Grandpa Panko.

Meanwhile Bovdur was eyeing Andriy with a strange, frightful gaze. He was still holding the bread in his hand, without having thanked Andriy for it, having said nothing; but it seemed as if Andriy had given him a piece of red-hot iron rather than a hunk of tasty wheaten bread. Bovdur's entire face became contorted, adopting a wild, indescribable expression. Whether it was pain, desire, or gratitude that was expressed on that face, it was difficult to discern, and the other prisoners paid no attention to him. After looking at Andriy for a moment, as if sizing him up from every angle and gauging his strength, Bovdur gripped the bread with his right hand, bit off a large chunk, and silently crept back into his corner. All that could be heard was the muffled sound of his mouth chewing on the dry bread.

"Good Lord, how different people are in this world!" Grandpa Panko began. "One, like our man from Dorozhiv, would gouge out his brother's eye for a piece of bread, while another, even if he is starving himself, would give away his last crumb to another man. And it's not just individuals who are like this, entire villages can be the same. In some villages, people are constantly at each other's throats, fighting over fence lines, bridges, stretches of grass, a thistle even – it's simply hell. They refuse to help out an old man or welcome a traveller into their homes – they won't help anyone. All they do is chant: 'This is mine! This is mine!' They worry themselves silly over what is 'theirs' and in the end lose their perspective on things, finding the world an ever more crowded place. But in other villages, people live like brothers, in harmony and friendship... No disputes or slander there, they help one another with work, with money, lend livestock in times of need, never turning away the poor and welcoming travellers, feeding them – and somehow, they don't end up any the poorer for it, they have enough for themselves, and leave something for their children. I know what I'm talking about, even though I didn't travel all that much when I was begging for bread. But I can tell you, over there in the foothills, the people are far better than those up on the ridges."

"Maybe because they are poorer?" said Andriy.

"God only knows why," replied the old man. "It's kind of like that, but also not quite. Because up there, the land is better, and the farmers are richer, but there is so much bitterness among the people, such enmity, that God forbid. But here, even the poorest person won't send a person on their way empty-handed; they'll always find something to give them, even if it's just something little, they'll press it into your hand."

Meanwhile, it was starting to grow dark outside. The sun had set and it became quite dark in the cell. Grandpa Panko got to his feet, followed by Mytro, and they dropped to their knees to pray.

"Well, it's time we went to bed," the old man said after finishing his prayers. "Only I don't know, young man, where we can put you. I'd gladly give you my spot, but I'm an old cripple…"

"No, there's no need," Andriy interrupted him. "That would be too much! I don't feel like sleeping anyway, I'm still young and healthy, I'll spend the night on my feet, and then we'll see what the good Lord provides."

"You say that now! It's easy to say, but it doesn't work that way," the old man replied. "Eh, you from Dorozhiv, why don't you give up your spot for our young gentleman here!"

"There's no place here for gentlemen," grumbled the fellow from Dorozhiv. "Let gentlemen rule the world and not crawl into the jail. And if they happen to end up here, they can roll under the bed. It's safer there, there's room to spread out their wings, and they won't fall!"

Andriy was deeply offended by such harsh words, but said nothing and told Grandpa Panko not to worry, that he would manage…

Just then, Mytro tugged at his coat and whispered: "Sir, keep walking there for a while, and I'll fall asleep. Then when you get tired and want to sleep, wake me and I'll let you have my place."

"Thanks, brother, God bless you," Andriy said. "Here, take my coat and cover yourself, because it gets cold at night. Even though it may be light, the coat's starting to weigh on my arm."

Everyone lay down, some undressing, others not. Meanwhile Andriy, his eyes wide open to avoid stumbling over anything in the gloomy darkness, began to pace about the cell slowly, like a restless soul, his boots rhythmically striking the wet asphalt floor.

VII

His thoughts, weighed down by the burden of the day's experiences, at first were scattered and confused. Disconnected fragments of the things he had witnessed and heard that day flashed through his mind, searing his brain with their glaring injustice, freezing his blood with their boundless filth. But ever so slowly, as the darkness more thoroughly sealed his eyes, his mind began to calm down, to gather strength, becoming more ordered. His memory took control of his imagination, and with great determination his spirit seemed to claw its way out of the dark abyss he found himself in toward the bright stars, clear waters and the free joyous world he had left behind that morning – who knew for how long!

That world had never seemed so beautiful, so joyful, or so free as it had in these last few days, especially early this morning! Never had his soul felt so strong and courageous as it had today, just before his deep, dreadful fall. Never had so many bright hopes for the future swarmed in his mind as they had today, just moments before the blow that would nip them all in the bud. Never had the star of love shone so brightly, so wonderfully, so alluringly for him as it had today, before the moment when it was to be extinguished – perhaps forever!

His entire life had been spent in poverty and hardship, in a constant struggle for survival and to obtain an education. By the time he finished school he was a complete orphan, without father or mother, supporting himself through his own labour. From a young age, he had grown accustomed to work, had come to love learning, and the higher he advanced in school, the more fervently he applied himself to his studies. His greatest joy was encountering good teachers who could spark his interest, give him space for independent thought, and encourage him to study on his own. Beyond his studies, beyond reading textbooks and general-interest books, he knew little of the world. He was a child during his years in the gymnasium, an ascetic, and even before his final exams, he began to suffer from chest and eye ailments.

After graduation, he went into the mountains to stay with a friend and improve his health, and there he met his friend's sister, Hania. The previously unknown feeling of love for a woman was awoken within him, it began to stir his young blood and slowly opened his eyes to life, dispelling the bookish mist through which he had previously seen little of the real world. His new university environment also introduced him to fresh ideas, opening his eyes to new perspectives on life, the purpose of education, and the goals of human endeavour. His past appeared to him in a different light, and many of his preconceptions and beliefs from his gymnasium years faded without a trace. This inner struggle was difficult, long, and exhausting, and only love sustained him, giving him strength.

Hania, with whom he corresponded frequently, went through these phases of intellectual growth with him. Their shared journey strengthened them both in their commitment to continue along the path they had stepped onto. They vowed to dedicate their lives to the fight for freedom: freedom from foreign domination, freedom of individuals from fetters imposed by others and unjust societal structures, freedom to work and think, and freedom of heart and mind. They passionately discussed these new lofty ideals, followed their development across the entire modern world, rejoiced in the growing number of supporters and endeavoured to build their own worldview based on these principles. These were precious moments for Andriy and Hania – times when two people bonded over their shared, cherished ideals. In these moments, they offered each other support and solidarity in their most sacred beliefs.

Yet, both felt that something was still missing. After intense discussions on theory and reading the most respected treatises on their favourite subjects, they would find themselves gazing deeply into each other's eyes, searching for something beyond mere intellectual agreement. Their eyes burned with a passion stronger than their convictions, and their lips trembled not with scientific proofs but with unspoken emotions. When they were together, their blood pulsed more vigorously, creating a powerful attraction between them. Often, in the midst of reading or during a heated theoretical debate, their voices would tremble and gradually fade, their hands would instinctively reach for each other, and their eyes would seek the gaze of the one they loved, and...

"Oh!" Andriy let out a muffled shriek, and began to pace more briskly about the dark cell. "Why did those moments pass so quickly? Why couldn't they have lasted longer? Why did I have to lose you forever, Hania, my true love?"

With anxious trepidation he recalled the sombre, difficult times of persecution, the agony he suffered because of his cherished beliefs. He saw himself in prison, before the court – his mind haunted by the scornful, shameless mockery by the press of his thoughts and his love. He shivered from head to toe, as if from the cold, overwhelmed by the memories. And once more he recalled his loss. Hania's family had forbidden him from visiting their home, from seeing Hania or writing to her; they intercepted the letters he sent secretly to her, their only means of exchanging a few words in their time of distress. Soon, even this was impossible…

A few more flashes of his former happiness appeared – for a moment – then came the night, a dark night of grief, doubt, and despair… Hania was pressured to marry someone else… Andriy suffered through this heartbreak, watching it unfold with resigned calm.

'The fellow's a good man,' he thought, 'he's sincere, he won't crush her thoughts, won't stifle her heart, she's happy with him, she loves him… But what about me! What am I without her? She was my soul, my strength, my hope – and what am I now without a soul, without strength, without hope? A mere corpse! A walking corpse! Everything that I loved most in this world has turned to sorrow. If I hadn't loved her with all my heart and soul, I might have been able to find someone else to share my new happiness with! If I hadn't so utterly loved freedom, I wouldn't be suffering in captivity now, or at least captivity wouldn't be so hateful to me, so painful!'

He recalled their last meeting, now that she was married, just the day before, in the morning! Their conversation, their joy mixed with sorrow and pity, had consumed him, tormented him, crushed him. And yet he was happy, oh, so happy! Because in those moments, he felt that his love had not become extinguished, it had not died, but was alive, still glowing, still ruling his thoughts, still holding the reins of his desires and cravings… True, he now felt his loss far more acutely; the wound, which had gradually healed over time, was now reopened, the blood, calmed by grief and illness, was racing again, but so what! With his old love rekindled, he also felt reinvigorated, once more eager to work, to struggle for freedom…

"Hania, my dearest, what have you done to me?" he whispered to her, struck down by the poison of happiness.

"What have I done to you? You yourself said that you wouldn't tie me down… And I've endured so much because of you! For years, whole years!"

Tears streamed from her eyes as he held her close, as if the old, beautiful moments of their free love had not yet passed.

"Hania, my destiny, what have you done? Will you have enough willpower to resist the filth surrounding you, to grow and stand firm for freedom and justice, as we once vowed to do?"

"I haven't forgotten that, my dear, and I never will. And I do have the willpower. My husband will help me!"

"And what will become of me, Hania? Who will help me to survive on the difficult road ahead?"

She embraced him and smiled.

"Don't be afraid, my dear! Don't worry! Everything will be fine, we'll all be happy, all of us!"

Andriy grabbed his head in his hands and began pacing about the cell again.

"We'll all be happy, all of us?! No, that's a mistake, Hania! It's only the future generations who will be happy, our distant descendants who won't even know what their ancestors had to suffer, what their grandfathers and great-grandfathers had to endure so that they could be happy… But what about us? We're just a speck in the ocean! And we want to be happy when millions around us are born with tears in their eyes and die in misery… No, *mein Lieb, wir sollen beide elend sein.*[83] You don't believe that? You'll see…!"

....

[83] German: "My love, we should both be miserable."

He continued walking, his eyes wide open, as if trying to absorb the thick darkness around him. And it seemed to him that the darkness was indeed flowing into him, filling his every pore, seeping into his nerves, filling his muscles, bones, and veins, so that there was no longer any blood, but only congealed darkness, coursing coldly toward his heart. He shuddered, fear gripping him for a moment, but only for a moment. He wanted to shake off this hallucination, but soon realized that it was no hallucination, it was harsh reality. He continued walking, absorbing wave after wave of cold darkness, imbibing it like a sponge, breathing it in, feeling its cold presence in his throat, his lungs, everywhere. And he started to feel better. The pain subsided. Memories grew silent. His imagination settled down, no longer presenting him with visions – neither those covered with the frost of sorrow nor those bathed in the bright light of happiness, warmed by the fire of love. Everything went numb, froze, and stopped.

He felt as light as if he were swimming in summer. Gently splashing about in the clear, soft waves that quietly, lightly caressed his body. And suddenly his veins were cut – painlessly, without any feeling, and the blood flowed from them so gently, so sweetly, and so pleasantly. His restless, revolutionary blood slowly drained away, and was replaced by thick, viscous, cold darkness, which began to circulate in his veins without resistance… As the last drops of blood left his body, hot tears flowed from Andriy's eyes. A distant bell, like a clap of thunder, shattered the silence, striking Andriy's ear like a hammer. He stirred and came to his senses.

"My, it's one o'clock, and I'm so tired, barely alive!" he whispered and began to seek a place on the bed next to Mytro.

"Is that you, sir?" Mytro whispered, having woken. "Lie down, and I'll get up."

"No, no, there's no need," Andriy replied, "there's enough room here for me next to you!" He nestled beside Mytro, wrapping his arm around his neck. No, the hot revolutionary blood had not yet drained out of him, and tears began to flow anew from his eyes. He started to passionately kiss Mytro's face, and his hot tears fell onto the young, childlike face of his unenlightened brother.

"Why are you crying, sir?" Mytro asked softly.

"Because I'm unhappy, Mytro!"

"Don't cry," the lad replied. "Things will work out. Look, I might be even more unfortunate than you, and I'm not crying!"

A heavy darkness settled over the cell, pressing down on every heart with its weight: some beat calmly, others anxiously, some painfully, and others contentedly. And on the edge of the bed, two young heads, one enlightened and the other not, slept side by side in an embrace. They slept peacefully, as if no sorrow had ever touched their dreams.

VIII

The following morning, the prisoners were roused very early by the corporal's yelling and swearing. Stebelsky and the fellow from Dorozhiv were ordered outside to sweep the offices and passages, and to carry water for general 'household' duties. Grandpa Panko, Mytro, and the man who had been weeping the previous day (who hailed from Opaka), and the black-haired young Jewish fellow were sent off with brooms to sweep the town. The only people left in the cell were Andriy, Bovdur, and the old Jew, who still lay with his bald head on the damp floor, wheezing like a wounded animal. Bovdur, too, did not get up, didn't even think of washing, but simply drank some water and, silently dragging his bare, swollen legs, returned to his corner.

Daylight was breaking. The sun was rising gloriously into a clear sky, and people were waking to begin work. Fresh hopes were being rekindled, and heartfelt prayers were offered for daily bread, for health, and for a peaceful, quiet life. But none of that was present in the cell. Here, human consciousness was awakening to new torment; the first words to be heard were curses, and the first sounds to escape from people's lips were blasphemies.

"May thunder strike them down together with their regulations!" grumbled Bovdur in his corner. "They keep people starving until ten o'clock, until some swineherd there decides to get up and hand out those meagre kreuzers! May they be stung as many times during the day as the number of kreutzers they give me!"

The grey twilight of daytime filled the cell, and making use of the slightly more spacious room, Andriy began to pace about the cell. His legs were still trembling from exhaustion and his head was heavy. He felt as if his body had been sprinkled with lye during the night, and he loathed the thought of lying back down on the stinking straw mattress. It seemed that the rot and dampness from it had seeped through to his skin, embedding the filth into his blood. As he walked, thoughts swirled about in his head.

'Why isn't man just a machine, one that can simply be operated by reason alone?' he thought. 'Why is there this other, extraneous force – emotion – that muddles and interferes with the proper functioning of the mental machinery? By logic, should I even be here today? No! I should be living in Lviv, patching up misfortune with misfortune, still living, working, and learning, free and safe... at least for the moment. But something has compelled me to travel to Drohobych, just to see her, even for just a day, even for a moment. And yes, I did see her, I felt a new surge of that feeling in my heart that has brought me so much sorrow in exchange for a drop of sweetness. It's unfortunate how things have turned out. Although I feel revitalised now, ready to launch into work – but what of it when my hands are tied?'

While walking about the cell, Andriy glanced several times at Bovdur and noticed that the fellow was watching him intently with a grim gaze. Andriy started to feel uneasy at the sight of those inhuman eyes, shining with a faint phosphorescent glint. He began to feel even more confined within these narrow walls, his heart anxiously pounding, as if trying to escape to the bright world outside this repulsive hole, inhabited by a vampire slowly sucking the warm blood from his chest. But Andriy did not succumb to the fear; his heart held too much love for people, especially the 'humiliated and denigrated' and he had too much faith in the goodness of the human spirit to immediately suspect this unfortunate fellow of any ill intentions. He attributed his involuntary anxiety to exhaustion and, overcoming his dread, threw himself onto the old man's bed to rest a bit. However, after a moment, he jumped up as if scalded, trembling all over, clutching at his chest, his hands, and his head, and was compelled to keep walking about the cell. But he couldn't keep this up for too long. Exhaustion took its toll and he collapsed onto the bed and quickly fell into a very deep sleep.

He dreamt that a slimy, vile hand, cold and disgusting, was slowly unbuttoning the clothes on his chest; then it parted his ribs and forced its way inside. It seemed to reach for his heart, cautiously manoeuvring through the tangle of veins and arteries like a hunter trying to catch a sparrow in the bushes. Now it was close – he could feel its cold, like the blade of a knife made of ice. But now his heart, too, sensed the approaching enemy, it started thrashing about, flailing in all directions, like a bird in a cage, trying to evade capture. But the mysterious hand, driven by some unknown force, kept pushing further and further, spread its strong fingers wider, and was about to capture his fluttering heart, to grab it and crush it! A sharp, piercing pain, like lightning, shot through Andriy's body – he woke up and jumped to his feet.

"What was that about?" said Andriy, rubbing his sleepy eyes and looking around the cell. It seemed to him as if someone had just lifted a great weight from his chest that had been pressing down on him while he was sleeping. He also thought he saw, in a moment of drowsy half-sleep, Bovdur's dark, terrifying face looming over him. But that must have been a dream, because there was nothing pressing down on his chest, and Bovdur was sitting quietly in his corner, legs wrapped in a sack, not even looking at him, but staring into a corner as if examining the outlines of stains on the wall.

'Eh, it must have been the weight of the blanket,' Andriy thought to himself, pushing the blanket away and lying back down on the bed.

He was awakened by the clanking of keys and the noise of prisoners returning from work. They brought with them a breath of fresh air, a scent of the free world, and the dark, gloomy cell seemed to brighten. The young Jew had found four kreutzers while sweeping, which delighted him greatly, and for which he would have happily bought all sorts of luxuries to celebrate this fortunate day. Stebelsky and the farmer from Dorozhiv brought a handful of cigarette butts; the farmer showed his and then quickly hid them, but Stebelsky shared his with everyone in the cell. The butts were the only payment the prisoners received for sweeping the offices, and even so, it was a significant and tempting payment.

Finally, the sergeant arrived with the money and after allocating 14 kreutzers to each prisoner, dispatched the old man and Mytro in the company of a policeman to town to buy bread and whatever else was needed. Andriy was also given 14 kreutzers, to which he added his own 20 and asked that they buy him the same bread they ate and some sausage. When Andriy was taking the 20 kreutzers out of his pouch, he failed to notice that from his corner Bovdur watched every move he made, assessing the size and contents of the pouch, observing with envy and anger where Andriy placed it, lighting up at the sight of those 20 kreutzers, and reacting as if they had been taken right from under his own heart.

And once more Andriy began to pace about the cell, thinking about Hania, her life as she had described it in her letters; he thought about his own loneliness, about his weakened state after losing his beloved. But then, a brighter thought sprang up: 'No, I'm not alone! I have friends, sincere, warm-hearted friends who passionately share the same ideals as me. They will help in times of need, give advice, provide comfort! But still...' His thoughts broke off once more, then resumed in a sombre, painful tone.

'But no,' a comforting new thought surfaced, 'she is not lost to me. She loves me just as much as before, she doesn't shun me, does not wall herself off from me with her marriage as though it were some barrier. She corresponds with me, gives advice, entertains me just as sincerely as before. And he is a good man, my friend, of the same frame of mind... Oh, but still!' And again, the cheerful thought was interrupted, and Andriy lowered his head, as if weighed down by great pain, and two timid, trembling tears rolled down his cheeks, burning like fire and not easing the pain in his heart in the slightest. He quickly wiped them away and continued pacing about the cell, trying to think of nothing but mundane, immediate things, like food.

"It's interesting," he said to himself. "Until they mentioned food, I didn't feel at all hungry, and my stomach was quiet, even though quite empty. But now that they've reminded me, it's like an old dog beginning to growl and grumble. This would be something to include in a psychological diary – 'the influence of thought on bodily functions'... It would be fascinating to keep such a diary, recording every sensory experience, every impression, day by day, over a long period! It would be a fascinating statistic of spiritual life! We could understand what impressions, what feelings most occupy a person, what the everyday life of that 'divine spark' is like, which in rare, exceptional moments can rise so high…."

The idea of keeping such a diary captivated him, and he explored it in detail, as if he were about to start one right away. 'You would need a dozen or so people, conscientious and dedicated to seek the truth,' he thought, 'They would need to divide among themselves the main manifestations of psychological activity, so that each would concentrate on certain manifestations, and others on more general things. No, that wouldn't work, they wouldn't reach any conclusions because differences in temperament, momentary feelings, and circumstances would confuse everything. If only some mechanical psychometer could be invented, similar to the one Wundt devised to measure the intensity of sensations. That would be an interesting and significant device for science. So far, psychology deals with the quality of impressions, but has little notion of their quantity.'

And yet, it seemed that here lay the key to unravelling more than one psychological knot, for surely those emotions and feelings that were most frequently repeated left the deepest mark on the soul. Statistics would help to delve deeper into the mysteries of human character and disposition, just as they had already helped to some extent in understanding the psychology of communities and social groups!

Slowly, ever so slowly, Andriy was calmed by such thoughts about science, and theories that did not affect the heart or emotions. He remembered his comrades, young, passionate, sincerely devoted to the idea of freedom and human happiness; he remembered their debates, their efforts at expanding their knowledge, their childlike joy at discovering every new truth, and he felt so light and joyous, as if he were once more with them, as if neither he nor anyone else in the world were still oppressed by humanity's age-old serpent – tyranny! His lips, pale but happy, whispered the words of a song:

Not always does the sea roar loud – often it calms down!

Not all boats perish in the storm! – find solace in these words!

And who knows, perhaps in the tempest, you will find your way,

Maybe it's you who'll reach the goal, come what may!

IX

The padlock clanked and the door opened – the prisoners had returned from town with their purchases. A commotion began. Grandpa Panko handed out loaves of bread, salt, tobacco, and onions – whatever each prisoner had given him money for. The prisoners sat down wherever they could and began to eat. Bovdur, who was evidently irritable today, cursed Grandpa Panko in a low voice for giving him such a small loaf while giving the dark-skinned fellow such a large one.

"Come on, man, his cost 19 kreuzers, while yours was only fourteen," the old man explained, disregarding Bovdur's curses.

"May fourteen teeth fall out of your mouth, beggarman!" Bovdur retorted instead of an answer and began to tear into his bread like a wolf, neither cutting nor breaking pieces off.

"Here, grab a knife, Bovdur," Mytro offered.

"What for? To cut your head off?" Bovdur barked back and took a huge bite out of the loaf, leaving only a small crust in his hands.

Andriy set about eating as well. He cut up the sausage, which had been brought, into equal lengths and divided them among everyone in the cell. The farmer from Dorozhiv and Bovdur never said a word of thanks. Bovdur grabbed the proffered piece and, without even taking a second glance at it, tossed it into his mouth, as if into some abyss.

Watching Bovdur eat, one might have thought that he was terribly hungry, for he tore into his bread with such ravenous greed, so quickly did huge chunks disappear into his mouth. Before the others had even properly started on their bread, Bovdur didn't have a single crumb left. For a moment, he gazed sadly at his empty hands, and there was such a look of hungry torment on his face, as if he hadn't eaten for several days. Andriy looked at him and was startled by the insatiable expression on Bovdur's face, that look of voracious hunger. He felt that Bovdur was capable of eating anyone who came near him, that at any moment he might pounce on one of the prisoners and tear off a piece of their flesh with his teeth, just like those chunks of bread that had vanished without a trace in his mouth.

"Is he always this hungry?" Andriy asked the old man, turning away from Bovdur in disgust.

The old man glanced over and quickly turned away as well.

"What's wrong with you, Bovdur?" he asked. "Have you got rabies, do you want to bite people, or what?" Then, turning to Andriy, the old man added. "No, it's just something that's come over him today. Maybe he ate something bad, or who knows what. Usually, he devours an entire loaf, drinks half a bucket of water, and lies back down, just like that."

"Who knows, maybe it is rabies," Bovdur replied sullenly, "but I badly want to eat."

"Maybe the gentleman wouldn't mind waiting a bit, until the servants bring him a roast from the tavern," the old man teased him.

"I'm hungry, I want to eat!" Bovdur repeated with blunt emphasis.

"Well, then eat, who's stopping you?" said the black-haired young Jewish fellow.

"You're not stopping me?" Bovdur said, his eyes fixed on the half-eaten loaf of bread lying before the young Jew. "You're not stopping me, well, that's fine. Let me have it then!" He stretched both hands toward the bread, but the young Jew quickly snatched it away.

"Give it to me!" yelled Bovdur, and his eyes shone with a frightening glint. "Let me have it, otherwise you die or I die!"

"Now there," the young Jew teased Bovdur, "otherwise you die or I die! So, I'm to die? Because of what? I have to waste away, when I want to eat."

"But I want to eat too," Bovdur answered in a gentler tone. "Let me have some bread!"

"Are you out of your mind, or what? Leave me alone!" exclaimed the young Jew. "You've already harassed Mytro there, and now you come crawling to me!"

"Let me have some bread, go on, take pity on me!" Bovdur pleaded in a whining voice, but his eyes filled with an ever more frightening fire.

"If you please, my dear little Bovdur," the Jew replied in a similar gentle tone, "Go with God's grace to the devil!"

Instead of responding to the pitiful plea, Bovdur raised both fists high and, like two hammers, brought them down onto the young Jew's head. The Jew crumpled to the floor, as if felled by an axe, blood gushed from his nose and mouth onto the bread, the floor, and Bovdur's feet. But the young man didn't scream. After regaining his senses, he leapt to his knees and like a madman dug the fingernails of both hands into Bovdur's bare, swollen legs. Bovdur let out a deep roar of pain, thrashing his legs about, unable to shake off the fellow. He grabbed the young Jew by the hair with one hand and began punching him between the shoulder blades with the other, but the young Jew wouldn't let go, continuing to dig his sharp nails ever deeper into Bovdur's flesh until blood oozed from under every nail.

Still clutching the young Jew's hair, Bovdur jerked backward, and the fellow fell face-first onto the floor. Yet even then, he didn't cry out but quickly grabbed the bloodied bread, took a swing with it and struck Bovdur square in the stomach, causing him to gag and groan. Bovdur released his hold on the fellow's hair and clutched his stomach with both hands, as if fearing it might burst apart like a shattered barrel. Meanwhile, the young Jew rose to his feet, still clutching the bread. His face, blue with pain and anger, was almost entirely covered in blood, tears streamed from his eyes, his lips were swollen and split, and his teeth were clenched tightly. He stood upright, and without saying a word, swung the heavy loaf of bread toward Bovdur once more.

"For God's sake, someone break them up!" Andriy shouted, horrified by the dreadful sight, and looked away. He was deeply sensitive to pain, other people's pain more so than his own, and it seemed to him that every blow was landing on him.

"Nothing doing!" replied the old man, continuing to eat calmly. "There's no need. They need to have a bit of exercise, to stretch their legs… It's good for the liver. And if they bleed a little of that bad blood out of themselves, they'll feel a helluva lot better. Just leave them be, they're like two dogs: they'll fight and then lick each other's wounds. But if anyone tried to break them up, I bet my shirt they'd both turn on that person."

Meanwhile, panting and sweaty, the two men stood facing each other, waiting to see who would strike first. But they didn't wait long; as if on command, both lunged at one another. Bovdur struck the young Jew's hand, making him drop the bread, while the Jew landed a blow between Bovdur's eyes with his left hand. They then grappled together, and it was impossible to tell who was hitting whom. There was lots of shoving, punching and scratching, until both of them fell to the floor, still gripping each other tightly, and then together, they roared like wild animals: "Help, someone! Help!"

At the sound of the shouts, the corporal rushed into the cell with a whip in hand. Seeing the blood-spattered prisoners struggling on the ground, shouting and continuing to claw one another, he turned the whip around to use the 'hard end' – that is, he grabbed the leather strap with his hand and began blindly striking them with the wooden handle wherever he could. The handle cracked against their bones and thudded against swollen, bloated bodies as if it were hitting a pillow, but the men continued to grapple with one another, and did not stop screaming, sounding like a pig into whose chest an inexperienced butcher had clumsily driven a knife. The corporal became enraged and, without saying a word, began to kick both of them in the ribs with the tips of his boots. Only then was he able to separate them. They let go of each other and scurried into the corners, but the corporal continued to strike them with the whip handle.

"You scoundrels! You thieves! You bandits!" hissed the breathless corporal. "One misfortune isn't enough, you still want to fight? Wait, you vipers, I'll teach you!"

"He was the one who attacked me!" roared the young Jew through his tears. "He tried to take my bread from me! Why should I let him have it?"

"Why, you filthy rat!" snarled the corporal, and once again, the blows rained down on Bovdur's back like hailstones. Bent double, Bovdur remained silent, until the corporal grew tired and stopped beating him.

"Just you wait, I'll teach you to steal bread from others! Don't you have enough of your own, you insatiable wretch?" yelled the corporal as he made his way to the door.

"It's not enough!" replied Bovdur sullenly in a muffled voice.

"Still opening that trap of yours?" the corporal raged, lashing him with the whip from afar. "Can't keep quiet, you stinking pile of shit? Just wait, if you think that's not enough, then I'll make sure you don't see any for a while! I'll make sure you starve a bit. Then maybe you won't be so quick to fight. I'll make sure to ask the sergeant to give you nothing tomorrow! I'll teach you to talk back to me! And you all here," the corporal turned toward the other prisoners, "make sure he doesn't get a sniff of anything! Let this scum learn the consequences of fighting! And if he starts anything, call me immediately, I'll show him!"

A gloomy, heavy silence settled in the cell after the corporal left. Everyone felt as if they were being choked, and no one could get any bread down their throat. Everyone felt that what had just happened before their eyes was far too cruel and inhuman.

Only Stebelsky, sitting in his usual spot on the floor, calmly continued munching away, helping the bread down with small pieces of sausage. When the cell fell into dead silence, he turned to Andriy and, gesturing around the cell, said:

"*Homo homini lupus!*"[84]

Deathly pale, Andriy stood up and turned toward Bovdur, who was trembling, curled up in a corner, covered in blood and bruises, and as blue as a bush of flowering lilac. The sight drained Andriy of his strength once more – he was unable to utter a single word and stood there looking at Bovdur with an expression of deep suffering on his face.

"Was that really necessary?" Grandpa Panko piped up, returning to his meal.

Bovdur said nothing.

"Bovdur," Andriy finally spoke, "if you're that hungry, man, you should have told me. I can't eat all of my bread anyway. Why start a fight? I'll give you as much bread as you want..."

And he took his bread, cut a small piece off for himself, and handed the rest to Bovdur.

"I don't need your bread! Chew on it yourself! Choke on it!" Bovdur roared without raising his eyes and threw the proffered bread under the bed. Andriy froze in fear and surprise, and took a step back without saying a word. Mytro

....

[84] Latin: "Man is a wolf to man!"

crawled under the bed, retrieved the bread, wiped it, kissed it, and placed it in front of Andriy.

"And you, you fool, what do you think you're doing?" Grandpa Panko said sternly to Bovdur. "Why are you throwing holy bread about? You, miserable wretch, you deserve to be struck down!"

"May you all be struck down," Bovdur barked back, "all of you! And me as well, for all I care!"

After saying this, he slammed his fist against the floor with a loud crack, then curled up into a ball and lay down on his bed.

X

Andriy walked about the cell for a long time, unable to settle down. When he regained his spiritual wellbeing, he tried to escape in his thoughts far, far away from this cursed place of weeping, misery, and complete lack of human dignity. He transported himself to other, better places where young, pure hearts proudly raised the banner of humanity, where powerful armed ranks were being forged, which would one day soon rise to fight for humanity, for its sacred rights, for its eternal natural struggles. He also thought of the place where a lonely woman's heart, perhaps at that very moment, was bleeding with sorrow because of his misfortune. In his thoughts, he comforted Hania, urged his comrades to boldly keep the flag raised high, not to lower it even for a moment, for millions upon millions of people were suffering – humiliated, oppressed, downtrodden!

He thought about his cause, his love, his misfortune. But he gave no thought to Bovdur, with his pain and angry determination.

Oh, you young, passionate, self-centred mind! In your holy fervour, you can't even see how self-absorbed your thoughts and efforts are! Your cause, though it aims for universal brotherhood and the happiness of all humanity, is it not precious to you right now only because it is yours? All your thoughts, desires, convictions, and goals focus on it, and the work and suffering you endure to achieve it bring you pleasure. And although you don't try to possess the person you love, and you truly wish happiness for her with someone else – don't you hold her dear only because your happiest moments were spent together? Because her kisses still burn your cheeks, and the touch of her gentle hand still makes you tremble?

Oh, young and self-centred mind! You would do well to stop thinking about yourself for a moment, to stop comforting yourself! You should look around you carefully, attentively, with a brotherly, loving eye! Maybe then you would see those around you who are less fortunate than you! Maybe you would then see those who have brought nothing at all with them into these depths of social oppression: neither clear thoughts, nor happy memories, nor even bright, though deceptive, hopes. Maybe just one sincere, kind word from you might sweeten their destiny, calm the struggle in their hearts – a struggle more terrible than anything you can imagine – and break the thick crust of ice around their hearts, built up through endless, relentless misfortune!

A great misfortune indeed has taken possession of them, closing up their hearts just as the evening cold closes flowers into a tight ball. And with closed hearts and lips pressed tightly together, these unfortunates walk past each other in silence, when a few kind words could have rid them of half their sorrows, even a single warm brotherly handshake… Oh, you people! You are not murderers, criminals and transgressors, the rulers and the ruled, the torturers and the tortured, the judges and the judged – you are simply poor, crushed, deceived people!

Meanwhile, Bovdur lay in his fetid corner with a painful, decaying body, a shattered soul, without a spark of hope, comfort, or consolation, and his head spun with thoughts, his memories flashed before him in unclear images.

Misery from early childhood… Scorn and beatings… Mocked by children who shunned him, wouldn't let him play with them… Because he was an illegitimate child! A foundling! A Bovdur![85] He endured hard labour at the hands of cruel strangers… Sleet, frost, thirst, fatigue – these ills troubled the master, but never the servant! A servant was made of iron, a servant endured… he had to… for that was what he was paid for! Weak, frail, worn out, poorly paid, poorly clothed… Without a friend, without a companion… No, there was a friend, there was a bosom buddy – found while working on the winch in Boryslav. A sincere friend, a faithful companion, he was a kind fellow. Ha, ha, ha! But he had envied Bovdur the only happiness he had, stole the girl he loved, took her and married her! If only the wind hadn't always blown in the poor man's face, maybe the poor man wouldn't have been poor!

Bovdur's early years flashed before him in such fragmented images, interspersed with words half-whispered. There was nothing comforting in them, nothing that the soul could find solace in or feel joy in recalling. His thoughts flew on and on, flipping through each memory like a man who had slipped money into a book and was hastily seeking to find the banknotes between the pages.

What had driven Bovdur to come to Boryslav? That he did not even want to recall. It was a thought that chilled him to the bone. But soon, it seemed, he would have to confront that memory. Enough – he had fled and, while fleeing, had looked back one more time from the hill at the burning houses… or was it just the glow of the setting sun? And he cursed the place. He never admitted to anyone from which village he

....

[85]   Literally "moron, fool, dummy."

had fled, although five years had passed. Who knows, maybe even he had forgotten the name of the village!

In Boryslav, he had revived a little. Although the work was tough, it was well paid at first, and there was plenty to eat, not like when he was employed as a servant. Like a hungry wolf, he pounced on the food, and ate and ate mindlessly – he spent every last kreutzer that he earned on food, going about practically naked, but he ate to feel sated for at least once in his life. At first, he didn't drink, but that came when the money ran out. Then he took to drinking heavily…!

In Boryslav, while working at the winch, for the first time in his life Bovdur befriended someone – another orphan like himself. The fellow was sincere, and Bovdur lived with him for four years as if they were brothers. They worked together, lived together, and hardly ever parted ways. In times of need, they helped each other out without a second thought. Though, to be honest, Bovdur took more than he gave. Even now, although he considered Simon a traitor and a fraud, he still fondly remembered those times of their friendship. They were good times, but the devil took them. It was a pity they hadn't lasted longer!

The comrades parted ways over a girl. Both fell in love with a poor, destitute worker, a complete orphan like themselves, who had grown up in scorn and oppression, accustomed to silent obedience, to boundless submission, and to renunciation of her own will and opinions. A strange thing had happened to Bovdur then. His harsh, self-centred, wild, difficult nature became even harsher and wilder in the presence of that quiet, gentle, obedient, and kind woman. He loved her, but his love oppressed her more than she had ever been oppressed. The arguments, the beatings she had to endure from him! The countless tears she shed! But Bovdur never heard a single word of complaint from her. And this enraged him even more. He pushed her to the brink, trying to awaken some resistance in her, but her strength was that of a pliant, silent, and obedient love... For she, quiet lamb that she was, loved this beast! And that love gave her the strength to endure all his seemingly insane but naturally driven whims, to respond to beatings with affection, to repay his curses and insults with tenderness... And the names he called her! A bitch, a frog – and she said nothing.

In the end, her boundless submission and pliability disgusted him, and although he didn't stop loving her, he beat her up one day in a fit of anger and threw her out. She went off to his bosom buddy; they soon married and now had a child...

"And she, the bitch, is happy with him!" grumbled Bovdur. "Both of them are so indecisive... so weak-willed! To hell with them! I don't even want to think about them!"

The number of times he had promised himself to stop thinking about them, and yet they kept creeping into his thoughts. Because, by force of contrast, they were kindred spirits, they complimented each other! Because deep in his heart, beneath its thick layer of ice, there still smouldered an unextinguished spark of love for those two weak-willed people.

And so, the good times had ended. Everything went topsy turvy. He began to drink. Damn it! He drank heavily! He would come back from work in the morning – he worked the night shift in the pit – and head straight to the tavern. "Innkeeper, give me something to eat!" Great. "Innkeeper, give me something to drink!" And he would drink until the money in his pocket ran out, until he couldn't stand on his feet anymore. And when his legs gave out, he would collapse under a bench and sleep there until evening, until they woke him and he headed off to work. It was great; there was no need to rent any accommodation. The innkeeper wouldn't throw him out during the day, knowing that he would come back next time – and the innkeeper's dogs even licked his mouth clean...

This was the only time that Bovdur recalled with a kind of drunken fondness. That time of eternal stupor, eternal hangovers, and eternal incoherent voices seemed to him the only truly happy time in his life. He lacked nothing then. And yet, who knows, maybe something was missing, but he, by God, wasn't aware of it. No thoughts, no memories, just endless vacuous chatter, like the grinding of a mill wheel in his head… Trrrrrrrr! And that was that: people, houses, the sun, the sky, the whole world kept turning and turning! Trrrrrrrr! And there was nothing else, neither on earth, nor in heaven, nowhere!

"God, if only I could experience that once more, just for a day, just for a moment!" sighed Bovdur. "A man could forget then, but otherwise everything comes alive again, thoughts start to stir! Or better yet, if I could wake up in the morning, and the spinning would be there in my head: trrrrrr!

"Everything merging together before my eyes, turning round and round! I can see, but I can't recognize, I can hear, but I can't understand, I am living, but I don't even know it – and so it would drag on forever, for all of eternity! No need to ever drink and yet be forever drunk! To be completely, utterly drunk out of my mind!

"But if that's not possible, then what? Let the memories come, as long as they keep coming. We'll drive one evil out with another – something even worse! There's no other way out… And why look for another way? Just once more before it all ends, but… with a bang!… Spend five-ten shistkas, just not the last two – by God, it would be well worth it!

"And my early years? To hell with them! They were just thorns and nettles! Damned be those times!

"And those two? To hell with them! They left me, betrayed me… No, I don't even want to think about them!

"But maybe, just maybe, things might be better someday? No, don't even hope. That's false hope! Damned be my hope!

"But what about him? Maybe he has a father or a mother? Well, let him! I don't have anyone and never did!

"But maybe… some woman… Damn it, should I even care about that? What difference does it make? Let her find someone else!

"And just maybe? Well, what else was there? Nothing! Nothing at all! Round and round it's all turning! Oh, how it hurts, how it burns, how it stings! Here, and here, and here, everywhere on my body!"

It was the dead of night, after midnight. All the prisoners were asleep, as if knocked to the ground by logs. Andriy was asleep as well and did not hear these fragmented conversations, whispered in a hushed voice. He did not hear them and did not know of the terrible torment this man was suffering, made savage through misfortune and driven to the brink of despair. And yet, who knows – if Andriy had heard these words, if he had understood the fellow's torment, perhaps one kind word from him might have prevented the dreadful consequences. But Andriy slept peacefully next to Mytro, and in his dreams, he was in his Hania's embrace, who was equally not his.

<h1 style="text-align:center">XI</h1>

The day began once more with the usual noises, cursing and taunts, the clanking of chains, shouts, and work. Andriy walked about the prison cell again, pale and weakened by the lack of fresh air, deep in thought. A dry cough started to rack his weak chest, and his thoughts became confused. He felt a terrible fatigue in his body, as if it were made of lead. How much he longed to rest, to lie comfortably and quietly under a clear sky, in the fresh cool air! His dreams of love had faded, and in vain he tried to summon them in their former clarity. Even Hania's face refused to appear before him, and instead wild, grotesque faces with dishevelled hair, unwashed and threatening, flashed before his closed eyes. He lay on his back on the bed, eyes wide open, and stared at the ceiling, trying not to think, not to remember. But then the ceiling came to life, contracting, expanding, swaying about, and slowly those same menacing ugly faces emerged from the twilight against the yellowy-brown background. He jumped to his feet and began pacing the cell again.

'What's happened to me?' he thought to himself. 'I've never been prone to hallucinations! Where do they keep coming from? Has my distress increased that much? But it seems I'm not suffering that much! Bah, this is not good!'

Meanwhile, Bovdur lay in his corner, mulling over his plans. Once he had the money, he'd need to hide it so that no one could find it and take it from him. But how could anyone take the money, if they didn't know about it? 'I might need to play mad, or something of the sort – but what do I care!' he thought. 'When the time comes, I'll work out what to do. But first, I need to hide it well. Then, maybe I can afford to enjoy one more good time, a really good one, to make up for everything!'

First, he'd buy some bread, good white bread, or even better, some buns – lots and lots of them, so that he could eat his fill. And a whole stack of sausages and all sorts of meat! And then something to drink – beer and wine by the bottle! He would down a bottle at a time, so his head would always be buzzing and spinning, so that nothing, absolutely nothing, could bother him, and no thoughts or memories would surface! Just keep everything spinning until the very end. And as for the end – it was momentary! And not frightening at all, as long as his head was spinning and buzzing… 'We'll see then, if it's scary or not – after all, you only live once, dammit!'

'But he's so young, so kind!' a timid thought hesitantly whispered from the depths of Bovdur's heart.

'To hell with it! And am I not young?' replied another thought. 'Until now he has been happy, experiencing only happiness every day, more than I managed to experience in my whole lifetime! That's not fair, I need to balance things out!'

A quiet, deep thought tentatively surfaced in Bovdur's mind, suggesting softly: 'But maybe it doesn't have to be this way?' Yet it was swiftly countered by a louder, dominating thought: 'Why play games? It'll be better for both of us if it all ends quickly!'

'Maybe he has a father, and a mother?'

'To hell with them! Let them suffer some hardship! I have no parents and never had any, but am I not a man?'

Strangely, despite the louder dominant thought calming Bovdur and fortifying his resolve, he was still trembling, glancing fearfully at Andriy and clutching something in his hand that even he feared. And yet he guarded it as if it were the apple of his eye.

"I want to eat," he murmured, "I so badly want to eat! It's that damned bread of his that has made me hungry! And he acts so kind and gentle! No, young fellow, your kindness won't save you, you can't fool me!"

The door opened and an old policeman with a kind face appeared in the doorway.

"Mister Temera!" he announced warmly.

Andriy stirred. He imagined that it was his father's voice, a voice he had heard long, long ago, when he had been a child. He came up to the door and looked into the policeman's face, but was unable to recognize him.

"Don't recognize me, eh? Well, naturally, you were still a small boy when I left Ternopil. Your departed dear father and I were neighbours and such great friends, God bless him! May the Lord rest his soul! But what has happened to you? I couldn't believe my ears when they said that Temera from Ternopil was being held here! What, I thought to myself, which Temera? There was only one Temera there. Must be his son, or something of the sort! Poor lad! And they've put you among such riff-raff! I've already had a word with the inspector, and he promised me that from tomorrow you'll be moved to the guardhouse. I'll vouch for you."

Andriy thanked the old man with heartfelt words, but at these words something akin to alarm flashed across Bovdur's face, as if something he had already considered his was about to slip through his fingers.

"Maybe I can get you something? Something to eat or drink perhaps?" the old fellow asked. "The corporal is away today, and I have the keys, so I can fetch it for you. Decide what you want, and I'll be back shortly. I first need to visit the office."

The old fellow closed the door and shuffled off to the office. Andriy felt instantly brighter, a heavy weight seemed to have lifted from his chest when he heard these friendly, sincere words, when he realized that this kind soul was doing what he could for him. Ah, how relieved he was by the news that tomorrow he would be moved from this den to the guardhouse! It seemed to him as if he would be completely free tomorrow. Light, air, greenery, and nature – those daily, ordinary gifts from God, whose value is usually unrecognized until they are lost – how precious and desirable they were now to Andriy!

"Sir!" Bovdur interrupted his thoughts with his terse voice. "Ask him to bring some vodka, a whole quart, that'll be enough for a few shots all round."

"Is it even allowed here?" Andriy asked.

"Why not! The old man will get it for you!"

Though Andriy did not drink vodka, he knew that for the other prisoners this would be a great celebration, to be able to have a shot each. So, he asked the old man to bring some vodka, sausages, and a few other food items. The old man initially hesitated to bring a whole quart, but Andriy assured him that he would ensure it was consumed gradually, and after all, a quart of vodka between nine men really wasn't that much. Convinced, the old man agreed to fulfil his request.

It was midday. Chatting merrily, the prisoners gathered around the vodka and food. Their eyes delighted in the feast, the likes of which they hadn't even imagined for a long time. Everyone thanked Andriy for his kindness. Only Bovdur sat like a log in his corner, occasionally eyeing the bottle of vodka. Suddenly, he sprang up, grabbed the bottle, clutched it with both hands, put it to his mouth, and began to guzzle. Stunned, the others merely looked on, but soon they tried to intervene. It wasn't easy. By the time they had gotten to him, nearly half the bottle had disappeared down Bovdur's throat.

"May you be beaten with a dry fir stick, you wretch!" Grandpa Panko cursed. "Can't you wait your turn, guzzling ahead of everyone, like a pig?"

"A-ah!" Bovdur roared, catching his breath. "The Lord be praised! That's in memory of the old way, the Boryslav way! It went through my veins like a hand running across my body, and now my head is buzzing, roaring, and spinning!"

He grabbed a chunk of sausage, popped it into his mouth and unsteadily slumped back into his corner.

The prisoners chatted for a long time, sharing the vodka, condemning Bovdur's deplorable actions, but the man lay there as if deaf to their talk. He only blinked, staring blankly ahead.

"Oh, I had a knife here somewhere," Andriy suddenly exclaimed, fumbling about in his pockets, "and now it seems to have fallen out! I have nothing to cut the bread with. It wasn't a fancy knife, but it's more an inconvenience to lose it, than a pity."

"Look for it well," said Grandpa Panko, "a knife isn't a needle, it can't just disappear in a cell."

But the knife was nowhere to be found.

"Then use my knife to cut it, and we can look for yours later," offered Mytro. "Maybe it slipped through a hole into the straw mattress while you were asleep. Such things can happen here, you know, given all the holes in these mattresses!"

"That's true too," Grandpa Panko agreed. "We'll have to search for it later."

But the prisoners got so caught up in their eating and chatting that they eventually fell asleep without giving the missing knife another thought. Bovdur fell asleep too. Only Andriy, who had not drunk any vodka, kept pacing about the cell, seeming to feel much better because of the good news of his impending release from this dismal place.

"Ah, if only I could be completely free soon!" he whispered, filled with longing. "Then I could embark on new work, face new challenges, and perhaps something good will come of it. But we must organize ourselves properly, unite everyone, and avoid wasting time and resources! We need to learn – not the useless information they stuff into our heads in school. Few have experienced true science, but how it revives the spirit! How the soul clings to it! Why do people resist it? Why do they look down on it with disdain? Is it because it doesn't present its findings as the final, unquestionable truth? Unfortunately, people still cling to authority that dictates from above: this is how it must be! They still seek a scripture that defines where wisdom begins and ends, beyond which everything else is deemed false or unnecessary. But no, the reign of such authority will not last long! Thinking minds are rising from all sides, toppling the walls that have blinded people for thousands of years. If only the final blow could come sooner! If only freedom – clear as day and vast as this world, recognizing only nature and brotherly love – would hurry and come!

"What is our miniscule effort compared to such a grand goal? What are our tiny sufferings and indeed our entire lives in comparison? They are like a speck of dust compared to a mountain. Yet it is comforting to be able to contribute even a dust particle to bring the goal closer!

"And maybe all our thoughts, our struggles, our battles – perhaps all of this is merely one big mistake, one among thousands that have already rushed past humanity like strong gales. Maybe our work will amount to nothing? Maybe we are building a road heading away from the true path, setting up a city on a deserted island! Maybe the next generation will set off in a completely different direction, leaving us by the wayside as a monument to the fruitless struggles of humanity to achieve an unnecessary goal? Ah, such thoughts pierce the heart, gnaw at the brain! But yes, this is possible! And we must be ready for such an eventuality. If our path becomes incongruent with the natural laws of general development, with the eternal human struggle for virtue and universal happiness, then we must turn back immediately!

"But for now, we must keep going forward. All our energies must be directed toward achieving freedom! Whatever must be done, will be done. As long as it is done conscientiously, sincerely and wisely – the rest does not matter!

XII

Night had fallen. The prisoners were asleep, breathing heavily in the thick, stale air. Occasionally, one would cough with a long, dry cough, turn over to the other side, sigh deeply, or call out in his dreams. The cell was shrouded in deep darkness because it was cloudy and stifling outside, and from afar, from beyond the ridges of Dil Mountain, claps of distant thunder could be heard.

Only Bovdur could not sleep. His soul was even darker than the cell, but, wearied by long suffering and dulled by vodka, his thoughts no longer flowed, his memories no longer stirred. He sat on his bunk holding Andriy's knife with its long blade. From time to time, his fingers caressed the blade, as if testing whether it was sharp enough. His whole body trembled with a nervous jitter and he was drenched in cold sweat. He waited for complete silence outside and in the cell, waiting for the dead of night.

"I can hear thunder," grumbled Bovdur. "Sleep is always deeper when there's thunder. I could have fallen asleep… Ah, to be able to sleep for ages, forever! Tonight, someone here will sleep like that!"

The sentence struck him with its unexpected intensity; he shuddered and fell silent.

"My," he started again after a while, "what a devilish thing words are! Say something stupid, and you can make a man freeze in his tracks. But think without words, and it's nothing, there's no problem. Eyes get used to the most terrifying things, but the ear, that's a problem – it rebels straight away…"

"But what the heck, it was all nonsense, he needed that money! And to think, what fools people were. Like this fellow here… He had money, but did he know how to use it for his own benefit? He bought food and didn't even eat it all himself! I would never do that! Eh, I would kick up my heels, at least for a few days! And I will, damn it, I will! Maybe it's time?"

He sat up and listened. At first, he heard nothing, but then the duty policemen on the porch started talking in gruff voices.

"Well, and," one of them said, "was the poor soul no longer alive when you found him?"

"No, when we reached him, he was still slightly warm. But what good did that do? His throat was slit clear to the bone!"

"Lord Almighty," babbled the other fellow, "the end of the world must be coming! How wicked people have become, everyone's turning against one another, not letting each other breathe! How could someone have the heart to kill such a young fellow…"

There was a loud clap of thunder and Bovdur didn't hear the rest of the policeman's words. But he was seized with anxiety. He curled up in the corner and his teeth began to chatter, as if the policemen had guessed his intentions and were about to come and put him in chains. His hands dropped limply by his side. The knife fell to the ground. Its metallic clink shook him more than the clap of thunder. He sat curled up in the corner, eyes closed, and covered his ears, so as not to see or hear anything. Unaware of how it had happened, he dozed off for a while.

Suddenly, he woke and almost screamed. He had dreamt he was wading through a river of blood; but then he stumbled into a deep part and plunged into it. The blood, bubbling, warm, alive, splashed malevolently around him, overwhelming him, covering his whole body, mouth, and eyes. He wanted to escape, but he felt the blood entangle his body like viscous tar, binding his hands and feet.

"Hah, what a terrible dream! It's made me break out in a sweat! But it's just a dream, empty wind! Well, maybe now it's time?"

He got up again and listened intently. Nothing could be heard except the breathing of the sleeping prisoners. He bent over and began to feel around on the floor for the knife. But suddenly, as if scalded, he jerked his hands upwards. He had grabbed the old Jew by the throat and felt the throbbing blood in his veins and the voice box moving, as if disturbed by his touch.

"May Christ strike you down, you damned Jew!" snapped Bovdur. "You scared the living daylights out of me! I thought I'd grabbed a snake. A curse on you!"

He bent down again, searched, and found the knife. Then quietly, on tiptoe, he began to make his way to the bed where Andriy was sleeping. He ran his hands over Andriy's body to make sure he was not hugging Mytro in his sleep, and realizing that he wasn't, he boldly picked up Andriy by the torso, lifted him up like a child, and quietly placed him on the ground.

"Yes, it will be better here," he muttered. "If he thrashes about, it won't wake the others."

Andriy slept soundly. But as his head touched the damp floor, he became startled and called out in his dream:

"Hania, help...!"

Thinking Andriy had woken up, Bovdur quickly pressed his knee into Andriy's chest, grabbed his throat with his left hand, and slashed fiercely with his right. Andriy shuddered and cried out, but his voice was muffled, as his throat was constricted. Blood gushed onto Bovdur's hands. He raised the knife a second time, feeling that Andriy was struggling fiercely.

"Where's the money? Hand it over!" he whispered, bending over Andriy.

"Oh!" Andriy groaned. "The head... took..."

He didn't finish. The knife's blade severed his windpipe at that instant, cutting through the tendons to the bone. Blood gushed out more forcefully, his body's movements grew weaker, until they ceased altogether. Andriy Temera was no more... But what of his thoughts, his hopes – did they perish with him too? No! For his thoughts represented humanity, and by cherishing them, he was but a small part of humanity. Humanity survived because while certain parts continually perished, they were always replaced by new ones...

Bovdur knelt over him, as if thunderstruck. The district administration head had taken the money away – this meant that it had been pointless to kill Andriy! It was as if a veil had lifted from his eyes... What had he done? Why had he taken the life of this young man? What cursed evil had possessed him? He stood over Andriy's body for a long time, his mind blank, motionless, as if he himself were a corpse. His right hand still gripped the knife, while his left, bathed in Andriy's blood, clutched the young man's cooling throat...

Suddenly someone's cold hand touched his shoulder and a deep sleepy voice said:

"What are you doing here, Bovdur?"

It was Stebelsky's voice. He had been awakened by Andriy's moaning.

Bovdur said nothing; he neither trembled nor felt fear – he loomed like a stone edifice over Andriy's body.

"What are you doing here?" Stebelsky asked, shaking Bovdur's bare shoulder. "Why aren't you asleep?"

Stebelsky's words and the touch of his cold hand seemed to slowly rouse Bovdur from his stupor. He stirred, lifted his head, sighed heavily, and then announced in a gentle, almost joyful tone, with no trace of the savage cruelty that had possessed him just moments before:

"Wait here, and you'll witness something funny."

"What?" Stebelsky asked in a hushed voice.

"Be patient, you'll see in a moment."

He got to his feet, stepped over the body, and approached the door. Using both hands like hammers, he pounded the door with all his might. The sudden, piercing noise drowned out the howling of the storm outside. The prisoners jumped to their feet, startled by the deafening racket.

"What's up? What's up?" they all asked, alarmed.

"Where's the young gentleman? Where's Mister Temera?" asked Mytro, not able to feel Andriy by his side.

But Bovdur took no notice of their chatter, he stood by the door and kept pounding it with all his might.

"Have you gone mad, or what?" yelled Grandpa Panko. "Why are you hammering at the door? What's this about?"

"It's some kind of comedy," replied Stebelsky, "I'm just not sure what kind."

Screams and curses reached them from the guardhouse. The corporal had woken up, grabbed a lantern and came running to the door, dressed only in pants and a shirt.

"Who the devil is pounding on the door?" he yelled. "May the devil pound away on your stomach! What do you want?"

"Open the door!" yelled Bovdur, continuing to hammer at the door.

"Quiet there, you cursed lump of lard! See if you don't regret it, when I open this door!"

"Open the door! Do you hear?" Bovdur would not relent and struck his fist so hard against the block of wood nailed into the bean-slot, that it flew out and struck the wall opposite.

"Ah, you scoundrel!" railed the corporal. He placed the lantern on the ground and set about unlocking the padlock, foaming at the mouth, for Bovdur did not relent with his hammering. No sooner had the corporal opened the door a fraction and bent down to grab the lantern, than Bovdur flung it wide open and struck the corporal between the eyes with his clenched fist so hard, that the fellow fell backwards onto the floor and the lantern flew from his hand, shattering and becoming extinguished.

"I told you to open the door, you dog! But you were in no hurry! So, there!" Bovdur admonished him, holding the door open.

"Help! I'm being attacked! Save me!" the corporal yelled.

Policemen came running with lanterns.

"Damn you, Bovdur, what are you up to?" they shouted, rushing toward him.

"I'm lighting a match for this swine!" Bovdur replied calmly. "Maybe next time he'll shake a leg!"

Like wild animals the policemen lunged at Bovdur, but with a single leap, he retreated into the cell. The group rushed in after him, lanterns in hand. However, as soon as their light cast its yellow beam across the cell, the policemen froze in their tracks and gasped involuntarily. Andriy's body was lying in a pool of blood in the middle of the cell, and Bovdur was kneeling beside it, bathing his hands in the blood.

"God, what's happened here?" everyone exclaimed.

"It was me, I did this," Bovdur said quietly. "Don't believe me? Here's the knife. See, I used his own knife!"

"Why have you taken his life, you brute?" asked Grandpa Panko. But Bovdur didn't respond, as if he couldn't hear or understand the question. He knelt over the body, staring at Andriy's pale face, still handsome even in death. A strange transformation began to take place in Bovdur. His own features visibly softened, and he became gentler... The eerie gleam in his eyes faded... The grim, angry furrows on his forehead became smooth... It was as if a human spirit was returning to his body, which until then had been the dwelling place of some demon, some wild, beastly soul. Suddenly, tears gushed from Bovdur's eyes... He pressed his face against Andriy's blood-stained face and wept heavy, heart-wrenching sobs.

"Oh, my dear brother! What have I done to you! Why have I killed you? Forgive me, holy, pure soul! What have I done, what have I done! Lord Almighty, what have I done!" Bovdur cried out, his voice filled with anguish.

For a moment, the prisoners and policemen stood as if enchanted, listening to Bovdur's lament. But soon they snapped out of it.

"Gather your things, sir!" one of the policemen said to him. "This is no longer the place for you. It's time to move you to new lodgings. Now is not the time to cry!"

Bovdur raised his eyes and looked at them with a mixture of anger and pain.

"Cursed be you all, you jailers!" he said. "Look!" He placed his hands over Andriy's gaping wound, dividing it in half with his palms. "See, this is my half, and this is your half! This is mine, and this is yours! Don't worry, I will atone for both halves here, but there is also a God who is just, and He'll be able to tell which half is mine and which is yours!"

The iron shackles clanked, and Bovdur allowed himself to be chained, offering no resistance. Meanwhile, the prisoners crossed themselves and recited prayers over the body, while Mytro wept quietly in a corner. Stebelsky remained silent for a long time, and then, as if speaking with a voice that wasn't his own, he finally said:

"*Quidnam, domine? Diem supremum obiisti?*"[86]

Hearing no reply to his question, he turned around to face Bovdur, and pointing at him, said:

"*Pereat homo, crescat humanitas!*"[87]

But, unable to see either praise or reproach for his wisdom on the faces of those around him, he turned to the wall and went back to sleep.

Kolomyja, 17–20 June 1880

....

[86] Latin: "What is this, sir? Have you finished your last day?"

[87] Latin: "Let the man perish, let humanity grow!"

THE PEASANT COMMISSION

I

Ah, what are you young crooks talking about! Walking on city sidewalks and picking pockets is no big deal! Big deal, if the cops catch you? They'll take you to the guardhouse, maybe rough you up, maybe not, and that's that. You should give it a try… Eh, but you're not up to it! Just hearing about it makes your skin crawl. Or do you already know what a peasant commission is! It would be something for a lightweight like you to fall into their hands! You'd learn the price of pepper very quickly.

I'm not talking about myself. There were those who had it worse than me. But I've had my fair share too. Well, such is the road a man is given to travel, whether because of fate or evil people – who knows? Enough said – that's life for you! Here I am, twenty years in prison, and you think it's as easy as wagging a finger? And soon, after my release, I'll have to return to my old ways – rummaging through other people's barns. I must, because what else can I do, how else will I survive? I have no trade, no land, no one will hire me, so that only leaves the company of thieves. And that too is a fast horse – you're riding high one day, and the next moment you fall, and you're back inside. And even that's not the worst of it. I've had my share of hard and bitter times, especially when I've fallen into the hands of peasants. Then, beg or cry as much as you like, nothing helps.

One time in a village – you've no need to know which one or where – suffice to say, I targeted a rich farmer. It was quite a job. The barn, you see, was crammed full of all kinds of goods. We didn't expect to find so much stuff and so turned up without anything to carry away the loot in. A fellow from that same village showed us the way. There were three of us in on it: we grabbed what we could, carried out the lighter stuff, split the goods up – and made tracks! But the peasants rallied, and were soon onto us – how they managed that is none of your business either – the long and the short of it was that I was the one they went after! They grabbed me three miles from the village.

Autumn was just beginning. They were still harvesting oats and only starting to dig potatoes. There were few people in the fields. The weather was balmy, the sun still warmed the earth. My hands were tied behind my back, three of them were driving me along the main road.

We caught up with some salt miners on carts loaded with salt.

"God bless!"

"God bless!"

"Where you taking your companion?" they pointed at me.

"A fine fellow," said my overseers, "a barn thief."

"Aha! Well, it wouldn't hurt to leave him a little memento," said one of the salt miners.

"Sure wouldn't, and he'll get one."

"Maybe, you'd allow us to add a pinch of something as well?"

"If it pleases you," replied my overseers with a laugh. The salt miner from the last cart came up to me.

"C'mon, young sir, on your feet!"

I stood up. He rolled up my trouser legs to above the knees and tied them in place with string.

"Off you go now!" he said and let me go ahead of him past the cart. I had hardly taken a few steps when suddenly I felt as if a snake had struck both my calves. The salt miner had whipped me so hard that I jumped from the pain.

"Hoppity-hop, young fellow!" the salt miner exclaimed and burst out laughing, and everyone else joined in. The rope of the whip was braided with wire and was knotted, so it felt like a knife wherever it touched my bare skin, and the knots were like leeches, burrowing into the flesh… I quickly made my way past the second cart, and the second salt miner did the same. I dashed past the third cart – the same thing happened. There were six of them, and by the time I passed all the carts, my legs were slashed, as if with knives, and blood trailed behind me. Eh, I remembered those salt miners well, and later when I learned which village those refined gentlemen were from, I made sure they remembered me too! Meanwhile my overseers were roaring with laughter and praised the salt miners for their novel approach.

"Oh, we know how to deal with such gentlemen!" one of them bragged. "You see, no mishap will befall him, and he'll be left with a nice souvenir. Ha, ha, ha, ha!"

II

It was still well before evening when we arrived in the village. They took me to the village magistrate's house. When we got there, he wasn't at home; he'd gone into the fields. Only his wife was bustling around the entrance to the house. She glanced at me and said nothing.

"Any idea, where we might put him, dear?" my escorts asked her.

"How do I know? Put him wherever you like, as long as it's not here. I don't need the worry!"

And there I stood, my eyes pleading for her to have mercy… Because I already knew that if I didn't stay at the magistrate's house, I would be spending the night at the home of the person I had burgled. And there, surely, no good would come to me.

Meanwhile the news had spread throughout the village that the thief had been brought here! Everyone who was at home came running. They gathered around, watching; some cursed me, others threatened me, while still others just stood there. And then the farmer whose place I had burgled, squeezed through the crowd and approached me. A tall, solid fellow, with the ruddy face of an executioner. He drew close and glanced at me…

"Ah, it's you? Well, let's get to know one another then."

I said nothing.

"Friend," he says to one of the fellows who brought me, "take him to my place, he'll be safe there. I'll keep an eye on him."

"Definitely, take him there, that's the best place for him," said the village magistrate's wife, standing in the doorway. "My old man will be back soon and I'll let him know to drop by."

They led me away. And my farmer walked ahead, gritting his teeth in fury. He went over to a fence and ripped out a pole.

"Bring him here!" he called out, turning into his yard and letting me go ahead. As I was walking past him, he took a swing at me. It certainly would have been the end of me, if others hadn't restrained him.

"No, my friend," said one fellow, "that's not the way! If you kill him, you'll end up in jail yourself."

"What, me?" the farmer exclaimed. "For killing this low-life? It's no sin to kill people like him."

"No, my friend, give it a rest. You can scare him so he won't burgle anyone next time, just make sure you don't kill him. He's your responsibility."

"I'll frighten him so badly, that he'll keep shaking until Judgement Day!" the farmer explained and, drawing up to me, punched me between the eyes. I fell to the ground like a sheaf of wheat, the world turned black and I lost consciousness…

III

When I came to, the sun was setting. I was propped up on a bench, my shirt all wet; they had obviously doused me with water. My face was swollen, but I felt no pain, as if my entire body was numb. Loud voices came from the house. Several men were sitting under the eaves, others stood on the stile, chatting and occasionally glancing at me.

"The chief's here!" I heard a commotion.

One of the men rushed to open the gate.

The village magistrate arrived – a short, chubby man with a good-natured appearance. He walked quickly, holding a thick cherry branch like a cudgel in his hands. Coming up to me, he said:

"So, sonny, they caught you, did they? See! Did you really need to go and do that? Now you've created trouble for the community, someone has to keep an eye on you until they can hand you over to the court. And it's a busy time now, sonny, no one has time to spare."

"Sir," I became emboldened, "allow me to stay at your place in the meantime."

"Oh, oh, oh," exclaimed the magistrate, "no, sonny, that's impossible! But don't worry, Matiy here won't harm you, he'll watch over you well. Stay here, sonny, for a day or two, until Sunday, and then Matiy can take you to town with my deputy."

It was Thursday. 'That means two more days,' I thought to myself. 'Oh, well, what can I do, I'll just have to suffer.'

"Well, and now get to your feet, sonny, when I'm talking to you," said the magistrate.

"Come here."

I stepped into the middle of the yard.

"Lie down, sonny!"

I stared at him in disbelief.

"Well now, sonny, can't you hear me? Lie down! I'm the head man in this community, I vouch for you, but I also have the right to give you five strokes of the stick, no more."

I had not heard of such a right, but what could I do…

"My dear deputy, here, take this cherry stick and give him what is rightfully his according to the law!" said the magistrate and, after counting to five, prepared to leave. "And you, Matiy, watch him closely and make sure nothing happens to him. The community needs to deliver him to court alive… Remember, he must be alive!" he said, smiling, emphasizing the word 'alive'. "I'll drop by here tomorrow morning. Farewell!"

IV

By the time the magistrate's deputy had finished putting me in chains, it had grown completely dark. Matiy stood to one side like an executioner towering over his victim, waiting patiently for the deputy to leave, which he finally did.

"Well, young master, now it's just the two of us, right?" he hissed through his teeth, holding the chain that bound my hand and foot. Suddenly he yanked the chain, and I fell forward, hitting my head on the ground.

"Oh, I see you're drunk!" he burst out laughing. "And I was about to ask you inside to dinner. Alright, get up there and come along!"

I got up and he dragged me into the house.

A fire was burning in the oven. His wife was bustling about the house, preparing dinner. In the corner sat an old woman, the fellow's mother. Both women were pale and began to tremble once they caught sight of me. They only rarely dared to glance my way, and when one did, there was so much pity in their eyes…

Matiy sat me down on a bench and made himself comfortable at the head of the table, snorting like a blacksmith's bellows. Suddenly, he rose, slammed his hand on the table, and shouted:

"No, I won't let him leave here alive! No matter what, I won't let the brigand leave this house alive."

At these words, the women began to sob loudly.

"Matiy! My dear son! Have mercy! We've recovered everything he took. And would you want to take such a sin upon your soul? Fear God!"

"And did he fear God when he snuck into our barn?"

"Really… Let him settle his accounts with God himself!"

"No, I'll give him a helping hand. First, I'll break every bone in his body. Come here, young master!"

Once more, he grabbed the chain, lifting me off the bench, and slammed me to the ground. Then, placing his boot on my chest, he tightened the chain so much that I curled up in agony, my ribs cracking. Darkness clouded my vision. The last thing I saw was his boot swinging toward my face. I felt pain in my chest, my ribs, my side, and after that there was nothing…

V

I came to once more. The fire in the oven was dying down, and it was dark and quiet in the house. I was under the bench, curled up like a snail. I moved, and felt agonizing pain. Every little bone, every part of my body ached… My throat was parched, burning. I let out a groan. A dark shadow flitted across the room, murmuring indistinctly. I saw a yellow, wrinkled face leaning over me; a trembling, cold hand moved across my face.

"Are you still alive there, sonny?"

"Yes…! Water…!" I moaned.

The old woman gave me some water.

"Drink up quickly, because he's about to return, and I'll be in big trouble! He's such a brute!" the old woman whispered. "You poor, poor boy, but what can I say?"

"May God pay you back!" I whispered.

The door creaked. The old woman disappeared like a shadow, and when the man of the house entered, she was already pretending to be asleep on the oven.

"Has the thief come to?" he asked.

"No, my son."

"Dammit! Just my luck to suffer such misfortune."

I felt a little relieved. 'Perhaps,' I thought to myself, 'he'll take pity on me and loosen the chain.' But no such luck! He grumbled and grumbled, put out the flame in the oven, and went to bed.

"Either way," I heard him mutter, "if he's alive now, he'll be alive in the morning, and if not, may the devil take him!"

I didn't close my eyes all night long. The suffering I endured in those few hours would have lasted me ten years. I thought maybe I would bleed to death and I begged the Lord to let me die. But no! Perhaps someone luckier might have had their prayers answered, but I was not so fortunate. One way or another, that night was perhaps the hardest and longest of my life. Maybe if the old woman hadn't given me that drink of water, I mightn't have survived. But it seems this was how it was meant to be!

VI

It grew light. Everyone got up in the house. The first thing the farmer did was come up to me. He stooped and listened – I was breathing. I heard a sigh of relief.

"Ah, you're still alive?" he exclaimed. "Well, pray to God that he keeps you in my hands a bit longer! But you won't be able to pray away what still awaits you. I only need to deliver you alive, and then you can perish there!"

Fool! He had his plans, and I had mine, and in the end, I came out on top!

He pulled me out from under the bench, loosened the chain – ah, thank God, I felt better straight away. But I had no strength to stand. So, he kicked me outside into the yard, and told his wife to wash away the blood in the house.

I sat on the porch once more. The morning was cold. My whole body was numb, so I couldn't feel any pain. There was a ringing in my ears and a sharp pain in my chest when I breathed in. They lit the fire in the house, and the smoke went billowing under the thatched roof and into my eyes. Tears streamed down my face, I coughed hard, but said nothing. The farmer meanwhile went to tend to his cattle, to feed the oxen and to water them. As the farmer walked past me, he couldn't resist hitting me over the head with a whip handle. I heard him preparing to go into the fields with his plough, to get it ready for sowing rye. I was a little relieved. 'At least my executioner will be away for the day,' I figured.

But then I heard a commotion. I looked and saw the village magistrate and his deputy on the stile. He came up to me, looked me over and smiled:

"They take good care of you here, sonny?"

I could barely breathe and was covered in blood.

"Why are you silent, sonny? Pipe up! Don't worry, I won't tell anyone."

"Mister… magistrate," I groaned, "I won't be able to survive… another night… like this one."

"You won't be able to, sonny?" the village elder smiled. "No, don't worry, you'll pull through. Your type knows how to survive. Well, and now, sonny, you know what's my right."

I stared at him.

"Oh, what a bad memory you have, sonny! Come on, up you get and stretch out! I have the right to cane you five times for breakfast, no more. Mister deputy, here, take this cherry rod and do him good!"

"And you, my friend," the village elder said to the farmer, who happened to walk up, "you'll have to set out with him to the city tomorrow afternoon. You'll go with my deputy here, myself, and of course the prisoner."

So, it would be tomorrow! The farmer looked at me savagely and fiercely, as if some deadly enemy was escaping his hands, and he wouldn't have time to strangle him. And a shiver went down my spine when I imagined that I would have to endure another night with this heartless man. And why all this torment? Honestly, maybe we took stuff worth a hundred rinskys, but he got most of it back. And he was rich! If you had strong hands, you could have taken far more from his barn!

VII

"Meanwhile, my deputy will stay here for the day to guard the prisoner," the village magistrate said as he left.

The deputy inspected my chain and lock, and then sat down on the porch, chatting with the farmer, his wife, and the old grandmother. The farmer pulled out a plough from the shed, carried out a yoke, and then went to check on the oxen. Meanwhile his wife had already prepared lunch and called him inside the house.

And there I was, so weak, aching all over, and so hungry, my Lord! It was cold in the shade, even though the sun was already very high in the heavens. I crawled out into the sun, sat myself down on a stone slab, and looked toward the porch. I heard the clattering of spoons coming from inside the house, conversations, they called out to the deputy to join them.

"May the good Lord bless your meal!" the deputy replied, sitting in the doorway with his back to me. "I've had breakfast," he said, "and my wife will be bringing me lunch."

And not a thought about me. And then I smelt that fragrant borsch so strongly, oh God! Lord Almighty, I was ready to give away a year of my life for a small bowl of that borsch!

They finished eating. The farmer went off to fetch his oxen. And then I saw the old woman skulking toward me, bringing me a bowl of borsch.

"And what about you?" she said. "Poor thing, has everyone forgotten about you? Here, my orphan, have a slurp, but hurry and eat up, before that devil sees you!"

"May the Lord reward you a hundredfold, granny," I muttered and took the bowl from her. My hands were shaking, and the old woman's knees were trembling with fear. But no sooner had I started to drink the soup, than the 'devil' approached. When he saw what was happening, he exploded.

"What," he screamed, "you're feeding this thief with the fruits of my labour? All he deserves is hot tar!"

With those words, he snatched the bowl from me and threw it at the old woman; thankfully, he missed her. The bowl shattered into small pieces against a rock. The old woman ran away, and he rushed up to me.

"Even if you were to die of hunger, I certainly wouldn't give you a bite of anything. My hand would wither, and God would not bless me!"

"Careful there, friend!" announced the deputy.

"What? The magistrate only told me to watch over him, but no one will force me to feed this darned thief. There's no law about that."

And he went off to his oxen. But as he passed by, he gave me a mighty kick to the ribs. Sitting there on the slab, I fell back and lost consciousness. I just remember feeling as if someone had suddenly tightened a rope around my throat. When I regained consciousness, I was somewhere else, drenched in water, the old woman and the deputy were fussing around me. After each breath I felt a sharp pain in my chest. He had broken one of my ribs, and it still troubles me to this day.

VIII

It was midday and the sun was scorching hot. The deputy sat down under the shed and, having finished the lunch his wife had brought him, sat on a log and dozed off from time to time. The lady of the house was busy somewhere inside, and the old woman rummaged about the yard like some chicken. The old woman took pity on me, but she was also afraid.

"Eh, granny," I said to her, "the good Lord will grant you health, if you could just bring me a little something to eat!"

"But I'm afraid, sonny."

"Don't be! The deputy here won't stop you, and *he* has gone off into the fields."

The old woman thought it over, then went inside, bargained a little with the farmer's wife, and finally brought me out a second bowl of borsch, a slice of bread, and some porridge with milk, so that I, thank God, regained a little of my strength. 'Lord,' I thought to myself, 'if only I can find enough strength now to escape.'

The old woman set up her spinning wheel on the porch, sat down, and began to spin. The deputy started talking to her, but lazily. It was scorching hot outside.

"Eh, mister deputy!" I groaned. "Take pity on me, I'm so beaten up and in pain! Look how hot the sun is! Allow me to rest a bit here in the barn. After all, when the master comes home, I won't be able to sleep a wink tonight."

"Oh, yes, yes!" the old woman added. "How that fellow tormented him last night, may the Lord have mercy! I don't know how the poor orphan managed to survive."

The deputy hesitated.

"You're not going to run away on me, young man?"

"God Almighty, how can I escape? I can't even take a step! I'll be lucky if I can reach town and make it to a hospital. And then there's this heavy chain on me. If only I could rest a bit on the straw on the barn floor."

"Let him go, please, mister deputy," said the old woman. "There's still some straw there from the day before yesterday, and blankets and a sheepskin coat that the head of the house covered himself with when he slept in the barn. And if you open the door, you'll be able to see him easily from here. And where would he escape, anyway?"

"Alright, go and lie down, for all I care," said the deputy and rolled his log closer to the shed so that he could keep an eye on me.

'The Lord be praised!' I thought to myself and crawled on all fours toward the barn. I lay down on the straw, covered myself with the sheepskin coat – ah, how much better I felt! I sensed a new lease of life inside me, became filled with fearless courage. I lay face up, looking around. The rails were full of sheaves, stacked right up to the rafters. And above the rafters, there was nothing, so one could crawl through there. 'If I can make it up there,' I thought to myself, 'it will be easy. I can make a hole in the thatch, come down the roof and drop into the garden behind the barn, and then…' I didn't even want to think what would happen then. 'If only I can get from here to there.'

I looked back at the house. The deputy was nodding off, the old woman was spinning on the porch. If I could manage quietly – they wouldn't even hear, and by the time they realized what had happened, quite a bit of time would have elapsed. But alas, I had the iron chain linking my right hand and left foot! What could I do about it? 'Well,' I thought to myself, 'maybe try slipping the manacle off my hand.' I tried once – no use. I tried again – it barely budged. 'Eh,' I thought to myself, 'even if I have to skin my hand, it'll be worth it!' But for now, I was still afraid the deputy might come to check on me! I thought: 'Let's wait a bit more! Meanwhile, I need to make some thin ties from the hay to wrap around the chain so that it doesn't clink.' The hay was lying in the corner; I grabbed a good handful and, keeping my hands under the coat, twisted the dry stalks, keeping an eye out in all directions. Suddenly, I saw the deputy getting up, looking around, and heading toward me.

"What are you up to there, you thief? Sleeping?"

"Napping."

He came up to me, looked at me and returned to his log.

IX

'It's time!' I thought to myself and spat on my bound hand to make the iron slip off more easily. As I pushed hard, I felt it slip off, although my bones crunched loudly. Well, thank God, my hand was free! Quickly, I wrapped the chain with the twine I had made and tied it to my leg, pulling my trouser leg over it. And now up into the rafters! I looked around: the deputy was dozing in the shade of the shed, the old woman was spinning wool. Good! Gently-gently I crawled out from under the sheepskin coat, making sure it lay the same way so that from afar it would seem as if I was still there. I quickly dashed to a corner where I couldn't be seen by the deputy, and from there clambered up the wall to the rafters. It was tough going, but fear lent me strength – I reached the top! Once on the rafters, I crawled up to the ridge. There, I climbed onto the rye, slipped into a gap, and reached the thatched roof. Quick smart I tore several tufts from the thatch, untying the ties, and squeezed through an opening onto the roof. God, how sweet the world seemed when I poked my head through that thatched roof! Battered, exhausted, and trembling, I felt like a rat emerging from a sack of flour. Onward, onward! I clambered down the thatch and dropped into the garden, hurried to the bottom of the orchard, and on to the river! It wasn't a wide river, but it was deep and calm. There was no time to think – I dived into the water! On the far side was a pasture, followed by thickets of willow and alder, and beyond that the vast expanses of hayfields, thickly dotted with haystacks, like stars in the sky.

I plunged into the river without a second thought, and the water refreshed me so much that I reached the far bank in a single breath. I ran across the meadow and disappeared into the osier thickets. Here I was king! No one would be able to find me here!

At this point I paused for a moment to rest and strained my ears. Oho, there was uproar and a commotion in the village! People were dashing about the orchard, looking, asking each other for advice. 'Eh,' I thought, 'you might as well look for a needle in a haystack now!'

I slipped through the tangles of osier and into the hayfields. Where people were working the hay, I kept my distance, hiding behind haystacks. In those parts the hayfields stretched quite some distance along the river. They belonged to several nobles. In some places the hay was loosely piled up, in others there were already hayricks or haystacks – these areas were completely bare.

Night began to fall. I was terribly tired, very thirsty, my whole body was aching. I badly needed to rest. I found a large haystack on a hillock right by the river. The stack had long ago been completed, topped with sheaves of straw, and girded with crisscrossed willow rods. I clambered up the rods to the very top, chose a spot in the hay right under the very top to make a burrow, so that I would be completely covered, and then stuffed the hay I had removed under the rods. Then I went down to the water! I stripped completely, washed the blood out of my rags, and washed myself. If you could have seen my body – it was the colour of lilac flowers, and there were so many red scars, like a tangle of crosses...

I washed well in the water, waited until my rags had dried on the riverbank, and then crawled into my burrow. It was positioned high up, so that no one could reach me from the ground. At the same time my head was completely covered by a sheaf of straw, but I could still see everything far and wide, as if it was all on the palm of my hand. But I didn't look around for long. It was deserted, there wasn't a soul in sight. After these adventures, I tell you, I never crawled out of that burrow for two whole days. At times I felt so weak that I felt I couldn't move my hand or foot, and I simply waited for death to come and get me – but then fresh strength would surge through my body, and I began to plan once more what I should do next.

<h1 style="text-align:center">X</h1>

What next? I lay there for two whole days without moving, and I couldn't stay any longer. I was too hungry and thirsty. I figured out what to do, waited until it grew dark, crawled out of my hiding place, and, of course, returned to that same village! I had a friend there, and I went to his place. I ate, regained my strength, and that very same night we gave that same farmer's barn a visit. Well, we cleaned him out so thoroughly, he surely had no reason to complain! I was so angry with him that, unable to take two of the sheepskin coats with me, I cut them into shreds.

Since then, I've asked strangers what my farmer was up to? They laughed. They said that initially he set on the old woman, almost killed her, accusing her of letting me escape. But after he was cleaned out completely, he grew quiet as a mouse. People said he was afraid his farmhouse might be set alight.

"What an old fool!" I told them. "Let him know that there's no need to be scared in that respect. I'm not as stupid as him, to steal stuff and leave a trail behind me. The punishment for arson is heavy, and I get nothing out of it. Tell him to fill his barn again with all kinds of goodies and I'll remember to pay him a visit one day for old time's sake!"

Lviv, February 1881

ABOUT THE AUTHOR

Ivan Franko (1856–1916) was a prominent Ukrainian poet, writer, journalist, and social activist. Born in a small village in Galicia, then part of the Austro-Hungarian Empire and now Ukraine, Franko emerged as a leading figure in Ukrainian literature and cultural revival during the late nineteenth and early twentieth centuries.

Franko's literary career began with poetry, where he expressed his deep love for his homeland and its people. His works often touched on themes of social justice and the plight of the Ukrainian peasantry. He also contributed significantly to the development of modern Ukrainian literature, introducing innovative literary forms and styles.

Beyond his literary pursuits, Franko actively engaged in political and social activism, fighting for the recognition of the Ukrainian language, culture, and education. He co-founded and edited several Ukrainian newspapers and journals, using them as platforms to promote his ideas.

Franko's contributions extended beyond literature and politics. He was an accomplished translator, bringing the works of many Western European authors to Ukrainian readers. Additionally, his plays and novels, such as *Zakhar Berkut* and 'Stolen Happiness' remain staples of Ukrainian literature.

ABOUT THE TRANSLATOR

Born in a working-class suburb of Melbourne, Australia in 1954, Yuri Tkacz grew up speaking no English until he entered school. A warm love for Ukraine and its literature led him to abandon his profession as an engineer, and in 1979 he began to translate Ukrainian authors into English full-time. His published translations include works by a diverse group of authors, such as Igor Kaczurowskyj, Oles Honchar, Anatoly Dimarov, Valeriy Shevchuk, Sergij Kariuk, Volodymyr Vynnychenko, Yuri Yanovsky and Borys Antonenko-Davydovych. He lived and worked in Canada in the early 1980s and in Ukraine in the early 1990s, but has now returned to Melbourne. His translations of *Hardly Ever Otherwise* by Maria Matios, *Hard Times* by Ostap Vyshnia, *The Lawyer from Lychakiv Street* by Andriy Kokotiukha, *Precursor* by Vasyl Shevchuk and *Boryslav in Flames* by Ivan Franko have all been published by Glagoslav Publications.

- *A History of Belarus* by Lubov Bazan
- *Children's Fashion of the Russian Empire* by Alexander Vasiliev
- *Empire of Corruption: The Russian National Pastime*
  by Vladimir Soloviev
- *Heroes of the 90s: People and Money. The Modern History
  of Russian Capitalism* by Alexander Solovev, Vladislav Dorofeev
  and Valeria Bashkirova
- *Fifty Highlights from the Russian Literature* (Dutch Edition)
  by Maarten Tengbergen
- *Bajesvolk* (Dutch Edition) by Michail Chodorkovsky
- *Dagboek van Keizerin Alexandra* (Dutch Edition)
- *Myths about Russia* by Vladimir Medinskiy
- *Boris Yeltsin: The Decade that Shook the World* by Boris Minaev
- *A Man Of Change: A study of the political life of Boris Yeltsin*
- *Sberbank: The Rebirth of Russia's Financial Giant* by Evgeny Karasyuk
- *To Get Ukraine* by Oleksandr Shyshko
- *Asystole* by Oleg Pavlov
- *Gnedich* by Maria Rybakova
- *Marina Tsvetaeva: The Essential Poetry*
- *Multiple Personalities* by Talyana Shcherbina
- *The Investigator* by Margarita Khemlin
- *The Exile* by Zinaida Tulub
- *Leo Tolstoy: Flight from Paradise* by Pavel Basinsky
- *Moscow in the 1930* by Natalia Gromova
- *Laurus* (Dutch edition) by Evgenij Vodolazkin
- *Prisoner* by Anna Nemzer
- *The Crime of Chernobyl: The Nuclear Goulag* by Wladimir Tchertkoff
- *Alpine Ballad* by Vasil Bykau
- *The Complete Correspondence of Hryhory Skovoroda*
- *The Tale of Aypi* by Ak Welsapar
- *Selected Poems* by Lydia Grigorieva
- *The Fantastic Worlds of Yuri Vynnychuk*
- *The Garden of Divine Songs and Collected Poetry of Hryhory Skovoroda*
- *Adventures in the Slavic Kitchen: A Book of Essays with Recipes*
  by Igor Klekh
- *Seven Signs of the Lion* by Michael M. Naydan

- *Forefathers' Eve* by Adam Mickiewicz
- *One-Two* by Igor Eliseev
- *Girls, be Good* by Bojan Babić
- *Time of the Octopus* by Anatoly Kucherena
- *The Grand Harmony* by Bohdan Ihor Antonych
- *The Selected Lyric Poetry Of Maksym Rylsky*
- *The Shining Light* by Galymkair Mutanov
- *The Frontier: 28 Contemporary Ukrainian Poets - An Anthology*
- *Acropolis: The Wawel Plays* by Stanisław Wyspiański
- *Contours of the City* by Attyla Mohylny
- *Conversations Before Silence: The Selected Poetry of Oles Ilchenko*
- *The Secret History of my Sojourn in Russia* by Jaroslav Hašek
- *Mirror Sand: An Anthology of Russian Short Poems*
- *Maybe We're Leaving* by Jan Balaban
- *Death of the Snake Catcher* by Ak Welsapar
- *A Brown Man in Russia* by Vijay Menon
- *Hard Times* by Ostap Vyshnia
- *The Flying Dutchman* by Anatoly Kudryavitsky
- *Nikolai Gumilev's Africa* by Nikolai Gumilev
- *Combustions* by Srđan Srdić
- *The Sonnets* by Adam Mickiewicz
- *Dramatic Works* by Zygmunt Krasiński
- *Four Plays* by Juliusz Słowacki
- *Little Zinnobers* by Elena Chizhova
- *We Are Building Capitalism! Moscow in Transition 1992-1997* by Robert Stephenson
- *The Nuremberg Trials* by Alexander Zvyagintsev
- *The Hemingway Game* by Evgeni Grishkovets
- *A Flame Out at Sea* by Dmitry Novikov
- *Jesus' Cat* by Grig
- *Want a Baby and Other Plays* by Sergei Tretyakov
- *Mikhail Bulgakov: The Life and Times* by Marietta Chudakova
- *Leonardo's Handwriting* by Dina Rubina
- *A Burglar of the Better Sort* by Tytus Czyżewski
- *The Mouseiad and other Mock Epics* by Ignacy Krasicki

- *Ravens before Noah* by Susanna Harutyunyan
- *An English Queen and Stalingrad* by Natalia Kulishenko
- *Point Zero* by Narek Malian
- *Absolute Zero* by Artem Chekh
- *Olanda* by Rafał Wojasiński
- *Robinsons* by Aram Pachyan
- *The Monastery* by Zakhar Prilepin
- *The Selected Poetry of Bohdan Rubchak: Songs of Love, Songs of Death, Songs of the Moon*
- *Mebet* by Alexander Grigorenko
- *The Orchestra* by Vladimir Gonik
- *Everyday Stories* by Mima Mihajlović
- *Slavdom* by Ľudovít Štúr
- *The Code of Civilization* by Vyacheslav Nikonov
- *Where Was the Angel Going?* by Jan Balaban
- *De Zwarte Kip* (Dutch Edition) by Antoni Pogorelski
- *Głosy / Voices* by Jan Polkowski
- *Sergei Tretyakov: A Revolutionary Writer in Stalin's Russia* by Robert Leach
- *Opstand* (Dutch Edition) by Władysław Reymont
- *Dramatic Works* by Cyprian Kamil Norwid
- *Children's First Book of Chess* by Natalie Shevando and Matthew McMillion
- *Precursor* by Vasyl Shevchuk
- *The Vow: A Requiem for the Fifties* by Jiří Kratochvil
- *De Bibliothecaris* (Dutch edition) by Mikhail Jelizarov
- *Subterranean Fire* by Natalka Bilotserkivets
- *Vladimir Vysotsky: Selected Works*
- *Behind the Silk Curtain* by Gulistan Khamzayeva
- *The Village Teacher and Other Stories* by Theodore Odrach
- *Duel* by Borys Antonenko-Davydovych
- *War Poems* by Alexander Korotko
- *Ballads and Romances* by Adam Mickiewicz
- *The Revolt of the Animals* by Wladyslaw Reymont
- *Poems about my Psychiatrist* by Andrzej Kotański
- *Someone Else's Life* by Elena Dolgopyat
- *Selected Works: Poetry, Drama, Prose* by Jan Kochanowski

- *The Riven Heart of Moscow (Sivtsev Vrazhek)* by Mikhail Osorgin
- *Bera and Cucumber* by Alexander Korotko
- *The Big Fellow* by Anastasiia Marsiz
- *Boryslav in Flames* by Ivan Franko
- *The Witch of Konotop* by Hryhoriy Kvitka-Osnovyanenko
- *De afdeling* (Dutch edition) by Aleksej Salnikov
- *The Food Block* by Alexey Ivanov
- *Ilget* by Alexander Grigorenko
- *Tefil* by Rafał Wojasiński
- *A Dream of Annapurna* by Igor Zavilinsky
- *Down and Out in Drohobych* by Ivan Franko
- The World of Koliada
- *Letter Z* by Oleksandr Sambrus
- *Liza's Waterfall: The Hidden Story of a Russian Feminist* by Pavel Basinsky
- *Biography of Sergei Prokofiev* by Igor Vishnevetsky
- *The Food Block* by Alexey Ivanov
- *A City Drawn from Memory* by Elena Chizhova
- *Guide to M. Bulgakov's The Master and Margarita* by Ksenia Atarova and Georgy Lesskis

And more forthcoming . . .